A self-confessed bookworm, Vera Morris studied Zoology at university and then went on to become a science teacher and, later, headteacher of a secondary school in Oxfordshire. After retiring, she turned to crime writing and hasn't looked back since. *The Ship of Death* is the fourth book in her much-loved Anglian Detective Agency series, set on the ever-changing Suffolk coast, an area Vera loves and knows well.

By Vera Morris and available from Headline Accent

The Anglian Detective Agency series

THE SHIP OF DEATH

VERA MORRIS

ACCENT

First published in 2020 by Headline Accent
An imprint of HEADLINE PUBLISHING GROUP

1

Cataloguing in Publication Data is available from the British Library

ISBN 978 1 7861 5993 9

Typeset in 10.5/13pt Bembo Std by Jouve (UK), Milton Keynes

Printed and bound in Great Britain by Clays Ltd, Elcograf S.p.A.

HEADLINE PUBLISHING GROUP
An Hachette UK Company
Carmelite House
50 Victoria Embankment
London EC4Y 0DZ

www.headline.co.uk
www.hachette.co.uk

For two dear friends, Jill and Margaret.

For all the people, past and present,
who have made Minsmere a magical and special place.

'Have you built your ship of death, O have you?
O build your ship of death, for you will need it.'

'The Ship of Death', D. H. Lawrence

Chapter One

Wednesday, February 23, 1972

The raucous cries of the squabbling rooks penetrated and briefly lessened Daniel Breen's grief. He knew if he looked from the window of his parents' bedroom, he'd see, in the dying light of the day, birds fighting over nest-sticks in the leafless oaks at the back of the farm house. Mum loved them, saying their early nesting heralded spring.

He looked down at her. Four flickering candles, one at each corner of the coffin, played light and shade over her waxen face. Death had smoothed her skin, making her look younger than her sixty-seven years. He glanced from her to the photographs of his parents, taken shortly after they married. They were placed on small tables on either side of the bed his parents had shared all their married lives; the bed where forty-three years ago, he and Caleb had been born within minutes of each other. He knew the story: he was born first, crying lustily and a good weight, followed by Caleb: tiny, blue, and silent. The doctor revived him, but told Mum and Dad he didn't think he'd survive the night. Dad fetched the vicar to baptise both of them.

As he bent down to kiss her, the candles guttered from a gust of air from the half-open window and smells of molten wax and death met him. The undertaker had been offended when he said her body was to return to Rooks Wood Farm until the funeral; he wasn't having her stay in some Chapel of Rest. She would remain in her beloved home until she joined Dad.

He stroked her cheek and kissed her – skin as cold as the ice on the dew pond. She'd never changed her hairstyle, it was the same as in the photograph, framing her delicate and beautiful face; now it was grey, not fair. His pain deepened, gripping his heart, and he slumped over the coffin. What would he do without her? How could he cope without her love and support? How would he be able to run Rooks Wood Farm and look after Caleb? She'd spent so much time with him, calming him down when he was upset, reminding him to feed the chickens, helping him collect eggs, nursing him when he got the winter coughs. Dear God, please give me strength, he prayed. He bit his lip and gripped the side of the coffin. Anger swelled inside him, almost swamping his grief. Anger with Caleb, with his mother, and with his father for carelessly killing himself in a stupid accident, but most of all with himself. He shouldn't have let his love and loyalty to Mum and Caleb stop him from making a life of his own.

He went to the half-open window. In the fading light he saw rooks flying in from the Suffolk fields and hedgerows, the slow deep beat of their wings mirroring his fluctuating grief. Their harsh kaah-kaah-kaahs filling the air, as they roosted for the night, huddling together against the cold. A strengthening breeze, bitter from the North Sea, brought with it smells of brine and marsh mud. He shivered and realised how cold he was. He looked at his watch; five thirty, the light was fading fast; he closed the window and drew the curtains.

The door opened and Caleb came in. No one, meeting them for the first time, would believe they were twins, or even belonged to the same family. He looked at the photograph of Noah, his father; it could have been himself when he was thirty-two: tall, blond, strong. Caleb, who did he resemble? Certainly not their parents, and there was no one like him in all the photos in the Breens' family album. Some of the older Dunwich folk said he looked like Mum's elder brother, but there were no photos of him, and he'd never seen him; he lived abroad and Mum wouldn't talk about him. People stared at Caleb's strange appearance: his widely spaced eyes and dark hair, with its defined widow's peak, like that of a pantomime villain. And when they saw his hands . . .

'Come and see Mum, she looks beautiful,' he said.

Caleb moved to his side. He'd several days' growth of beard, and rank smells of earth, chicken shit and sweat attacked Daniel's nose and made his throat contract. That would be another problem: getting Caleb to take regular baths and shave. Mum was good at that.

Caleb gripped the side of the coffin. 'Why did she have to die?'

'She didn't want to. I've told you, it was her heart, that's what Dr Smythe said.'

Caleb touched her cheek, his fingers splayed apart like a child greedily reaching for a sweet, the webbing of skin between his fingers almost translucent against the candle light, except for the areas scarred by cuts and bruises. He bent and kissed her. 'Mum, I love you. Who'll love me now?'

The childish words said in his gruff, deep voice, pushed away the last of Daniel's anger and he gently moved Caleb's hand away. '*I* love you, Caleb. I'll look after you. Mum's at peace. We need to do one last thing for her. We must get ready for the funeral on Friday, and look our best, so she'll be proud of us. We have to help each other.'

'I don't want her to go to earth. Daniel, you mustn't let them take her.'

'No, Caleb, on Friday she must be buried in the churchyard with our father. They will be together at last, at peace.'

Caleb looked up at him, anger and grief playing over his face. 'I don't want to go to the funeral. They'll stare at me. I can't stand it.'

Daniel sighed. All he wanted to do was grieve. To grieve and to make sure the funeral went well. 'We mustn't think of ourselves, only of Mum. When the funeral is over, we'll sit down together and work out how we'll manage. You mustn't worry, we'll be all right.' It was a life sentence, the thought of looking after Caleb, with no one to help. No, he mustn't exaggerate, there were some old friends of his mother's, people they'd known since childhood, they were helping with the funeral.

They'd talked together, he and Mum, about Caleb's future when she eventually died, but it had seemed like a distant prospect: she was fit, active and only had the occasional cold. He'd never faced the problem square on. He'd reassured her he'd never desert Caleb, but now reality was staring him in the face, and although he loved his brother, the responsibility was mind-numbing.

Caleb looked at him, his brown protuberant eyes filmed with tears. 'Oh, Daniel, you can't do all the work and look after me. What about when I'm ill, and the cough is bad? And who'll cook the meals?'

At least he'd stopped thinking about the funeral. 'You do your bit, the poultry's doing well, also Mrs Gorst might be willing to do more work. She's not a bad cook.'

Caleb violently shook his head. 'She's all right, but that Jonas, he's evil when no one's around.'

Daniel tried to move him away from the coffin. 'He's only a boy, half your age. Don't let him upset you. I'll have a word with his father.' The Gorsts worked for them and lived in a farm cottage.

'Fred's all right; he's always polite.'

Fred Gorst knew his job and home depended on good relationships with the Breens, Daniel thought. He wasn't too keen on Jonas himself, a surly young man, but strong and a good worker.

'Come downstairs, Caleb. I'll make us some supper.' He blew out one of the candles.

Caleb gripped his arm. 'Don't leave her in the dark.'

'We haven't got many candles left; Leiston shops have run out of them. I'll put the electric light on, it's too dangerous to leave an unguarded flame.'

'Supposing we have another power cut? She'll be in the dark all by herself.'

'The miners' strike's over, Caleb. They'll be going back to work soon, and all the picketing will stop. The lights will stay on.' That was a lie; they were due for another cut this evening, but he had to get him away from this room.

He looked round; the coffin, on its bier, stood beside the large bed, its size matching the room, with oak beams running the length of the ceiling, and also set into the white, plastered walls. As a child he'd loved to creep in here when Dad left early for work on the farm, and Mum had returned to bed with a cup of tea after cooking Dad his breakfast. He would climb in next to her and she would tuck the sheet and blankets round both of them. 'Where's Caleb?' she'd ask.

'He's still asleep.'

She'd put an arm round him, kiss him on the forehead, and tell him a story. A favourite was about the rooks: how they were magical birds, and it was said if they ever left their home in the oaks, it would mean bad luck for the family. She'd smile and brush back his hair. 'They've never deserted the Breens, not in hundreds of years, and they never will,' she'd say, kissing and hugging him. She'd tell him stories about seabirds, or seals, or people who lived under the waves. Dad would raise his eyebrows when he told him about the stories. 'You read too many books, Rosalind,' he'd say, but Daniel could tell he was proud of her, with her gentle manners, her education and the way she was held in high esteem by all the people around, for she was a De Lacy before she married Dad.

He remembered how Dad smiled at her and she would give him a loving look. They'd known true, deep love. An older pain, one he knew well, gripped him. The slim chance he might find someone who was prepared to share life on the farm and responsibility for Caleb had disappeared for ever with the death of his mother. It would be too much for any woman. A few weeks ago, Mum told him Theresa had come back to live in Dunwich. 'Why don't you look her up?' she'd said. 'She asked after you. I think she still cares.' Lovely Theresa, his childhood sweetheart, who wanted more from life than being a farmer's wife; she'd left Suffolk for travel, adventure and eventually marriage to a Canadian. Widowed and childless she was back with her parents and working in Ipswich.

'She didn't care enough before.' But despite his rough answer, a flicker of hope started to burn, and he wondered if she still felt as he did? Now, he'd never be able to find a woman to love, marry and have children with. After he and Caleb died there would be no more Breens at Rooks Wood Farm. When his mother's coffin was lowered into the grave, his hopes and dreams would be buried with her. He blew out the three remaining flames and moved towards the door. Caleb turned on the light.

As they came down the narrow stairs, the telephone in the entrance hall shrilled out.

'Rooks Wood Farm, Daniel Breen speaking.'

'Daniel, it's Aunty Dot. How are you coping? Everything all right at your end for Friday?' Her brisk, no nonsense voice made Daniel smile. He watched Caleb go into the kitchen. 'I may have some trouble getting Caleb to take a bath,' he whispered, grinning as he imagined the look on Aunty Dot's face.

There was a brief silence. 'Would you like me to come over tomorrow? Everything is arranged at this end. I've checked with The Ship and they've catered for thirty, that should be enough, and the ladies will do the church flowers tomorrow.'

'Thank you, Aunty Dot. You've been a great help.'

'The least I could do for dear Rosalind and you two boys. And tomorrow?'

Daniel sighed. 'I'll give you a ring about twelve; if I need the fire brigade can you come in the afternoon?'

'I won't be hosing him down!'

'You might have to,' he said.

'The sight of me waving a flannel and a bar of soap will soon get Caleb into the bathroom.'

Daniel went into the kitchen, glad of the warmth from the Aga. Caleb had made a pot of tea and was rinsing out two mugs. He stopped himself from inspecting them and sat down at the table. 'That was Aunty Dot. She says all the arrangements for the church and the wake are fine.'

Caleb brought the mugs of tea to the table and sat down opposite him. 'That's kind of her. I wish Aunty Emily was still alive, I liked her best; Aunty Dot can be bossy.'

'They were both good friends to Mum, and they looked after us when we were little, even though they weren't much older than we were.'

Caleb slurped his tea. 'I looked forward to them biking over from Dunwich in the school holidays; Aunty Dot was more fun then.'

'That was before the war; it changed everything.' It was a good cuppa. He took another mouthful and gave Caleb the thumbs up.

He grinned. 'Is Aunt Dot really a detective? Isn't it dangerous? I don't want to lose anyone else.'

Daniel drained his mug. 'Mum said she went undercover last summer at the holiday camp near Orford. Nearly got herself killed.'

'I know she told me, too. What's it called, the something agency or other, where she works with all the other detectives?' Caleb asked.

'It's the Anglian Detective Agency, and Miss Dorothy Piff is the chief administrator, so mind you do what she says. She might come and visit us tomorrow, if she sees you looking like that,' he scratched his own chin, 'she might put you in handcuffs!'

Caleb's eyes seemed to move even farther apart. 'I better have a shave before she gets here – she's a real fuss pot,' he said.

Daniel smiled. 'I think you'd better; if you haven't shaved, she'll throw you in the horse trough.' He went into the larder. 'Sausages OK?' he asked.

'With mash?' Caleb asked.

'You can peel the spuds, and we'll have cabbage as well.'

Caleb pulled a face.

'You've got to have your greens, Caleb. Remember what Mum used to say.' Daniel opened the packet of sausages. If Mary Gorst wouldn't take on some cooking, he'd better buy a few cookery books; he should have paid more attention when Mum was busy in the kitchen. Thinking of her – her graceful way of performing the most menial task – brought back his grief and sorrow. If only Dad were here, life would have been so different. How could he have been so careless? Whenever he'd been out shooting with him Dad always checked the safety catch was on, always asked him if his was. After the accident Mum was convinced someone had shot him, she wouldn't let it go, but at the inquest the verdict was accidental death. Questions were asked about his state of mind, or if there were money troubles, but suicide was ruled out as well. He hadn't thought about that for years, but Mum's death brought it all back into focus. If someone did kill him, who? And why?

7

Chapter Two

Laurel Bowman was lying on a rug in front of the fire in the sitting room at Greyfriars House, admiring her six-month-old Labrador, Bumper, asleep in his basket. Stuart Elderkin, his pipe clamped between teeth, was reading the *Daily Express* and Frank Diamond, looking cool in a cream polo-neck sweater and black flares, was engrossed in a book.

Stuart tapped the paper with the stem of his pipe. 'They don't like this Treaty of Accession; it goes against the grain bringing British law into line with Common Market regulations. They'll have a devil of a job getting it through Parliament.'

Frank looked up. 'My dad thinks they should concentrate on getting unemployment down. He's in dreamland at the moment. Soon he'll be running the country, with all his other trade-unions buddies.'

Laurel ran her hand over Bumper's side, his fur was fine and soft; he twitched, no doubt dreaming of plunging into the North Sea, then he settled down, snuffling into the plaid blanket lining his basket. Smells of approaching dinner drifted in from the kitchen. She ought to go and see if Mabel needed a hand, but the peaceful atmosphere made her want to remain here. Dorothy was talking to someone on the telephone in the dining room, which also served as their office, but she couldn't hear what she was saying. For once, the members of the Anglian Detective Agency were relaxing, their latest case recently completed, and only one new case in prospect.

Dorothy's voice got louder. 'I won't be hosing him down!'

Frank looked up and raised his eyebrows. 'That's a shame.'

Laurel smiled at him. 'Good book?'

He held up it up.

'*Shroud for a Nightingale*; P. D. James. Really, Frank, haven't you had enough of murder? We've got enough real carnage as it is.' She shuddered as she thought of the bombing at Aldershot Barracks yesterday; six people killed, five of them women.

'Yes, it makes our cases small beer, but I've got withdrawal symptoms, it's over six months since mayhem at Orford Ness.'

Stuart tapped the newspaper again. 'It was bound to happen; after Bloody Sunday the IRA wanted revenge, but *we've* had a relatively peaceful time, nice quiet cases with old-fashioned, non-violent villains; let's keep it that way.'

Dorothy walked in and went over to stroke Bumper. 'Fast asleep, the little tyke, and the rest of you look as though you're about to join him. Come on, Frank, get cracking with the drinks, or Mabel will have that casserole on the table.'

Frank looked at Dorothy and pulled a face. 'Haven't you some shorthand notes you should be typing up, Dorothy? As administrator, can't you go and administrate and leave us in peace?'

Dorothy plonked herself next to him on the sofa. 'Gin and tonic, please.' Frank sighed, but got up. 'Stuart!' She waited until he'd lowered his newspaper. 'That was Daniel Breen on the phone. The funeral, as you know, is on Friday, two o clock. I assume you and Mabel are going?'

Frank turned from the sideboard, a bottle of Gordon's Gin in his hand. 'Stuart won't be able to make it. We've got an appointment at the bird reserve at two thirty, business comes before pleasure, Dorothy.'

She lowered her blue-framed glasses and glared at him. 'Rosalind Breen was a dear friend, and I've known the boys most of my life. Both Stuart and Mabel knew Rosalind. You want to go, don't you, Stuart?'

Stuart shrugged and waved his pipe about. 'We need to find out what the Warden wants us to do. We haven't got another case at the moment. I'm a reserve member, Dorothy. I'd like to be there, I know the place well, Frank's still a novice twitcher.'

Dorothy bristled. 'I'll see what Mabel has to say about that!' She bustled off to the kitchen.

'I think you ought to go to the funeral, Stuart,' Laurel said. 'I can go with Frank to the bird reserve.'

Stuart's face dropped and he stuck out a lower lip, making his resemblance to a basset hound even stronger.

Dorothy came back with Mabel, whose face was flushed. Laurel hoped it was from the heat of the kitchen and not anger with Stuart. The peace of the evening was waning.

Stuart looked at Mabel's face. 'I'll go, of course I'll go. Laurel can go with Frank.'

Mabel put her hands on her hips. 'I should think so!'

'Like a Babycham, dear?'

She went to him and kissed his cheek.

Frank passed round drinks. 'Peace restored. There's no need for you to come, Laurel. I can't see what the Warden might want us for, Stuart was only coming to boast of his avian knowledge.'

Dorothy turned to her. 'Why don't you come with us? I know you don't know the family, but I'd like a good turn-out for Rosalind.'

Stuart pointed the stem of his pipe towards her. 'You can cast your eyes over Daniel Breen, Laurel. He's a good-looking chap and tall enough for you. A bachelor, and he runs a productive farm.'

Frank stopped pouring a bottle of beer into a pint glass. 'Do you want this beer in the glass, or over your head, Stuart?'

Laurel laughed. 'I've got my man, thank you.' She tickled Bumper's stomach.

'Stuart's right, Laurel, Daniel's a well-built chap, but a tad too old for you, I think.' Mabel turned to Dorothy. 'Mid-forties?' Dorothy nodded. 'And you'd have to take on his brother as well.' She shivered. 'Wouldn't fancy that!'

Frank passed a brimming glass to Stuart. 'What do you mean,

take on his brother? Laurel would have to bed both of them? Talk about Seven Brides for Seven Brothers!'

Dorothy tutted and told them about Caleb.

'Webbed fingers,' Frank mused. 'Sounds like a genetic defect to me. Interesting. Wouldn't mind a butchers.'

'He's not a specimen in a peep-show,' Dorothy said. 'He's a strange boy, but Daniel will look after him.'

'Has he got Down syndrome?' asked Laurel.

Dorothy shook her head. 'No. He's reasonably intelligent, but he's never been able to mix socially, he's very conscious of his strange looks. I'm afraid his father, Noah, was unable to hide his disappointment in him; all his affection went to Daniel. Rosalind tried to make up for it, but I'm sure Noah's lack of love for Caleb shaped him into the recluse he is today.'

Laurel sipped the Tio Pepe Frank had given her, its dryness making the inside of her mouth pucker. She took another sip. Poor man, she thought. 'I'd like to go with you on Friday, Dorothy, if Frank doesn't mind.' She looked at him, dark curly hair grazing his shoulders, green eyes looking at her over the rim of his glass.

He wiped a trace of foam from his lips with a finger. 'You're hooked, aren't you? Good-looking farmer – not interested. A lost lamb and Miss Bowman to the rescue.'

She felt her face flush. At times he was too perceptive, but his remark about throwing beer over Stuart for suggesting Daniel Breen as a likely prospect was heartening. She turned to Dorothy. 'Is the Breen's farm near here?'

Dorothy took a deep draw on her cigarette. 'Rooks Wood Farm is a few miles west, as the crow, or should I say, rook flies. By the way, I believe it *should* be as the rook flies, their flight is more direct than crows. Rosalind told me that. Is she, or should I say, was she right, Stuart?'

Stuart nodded. 'She was right. Can't stand any of the corvids myself, nasty black birds, best thing you could do with them is bake them in a pie.'

11

Laurel wrinkled her nose. 'Ugh! Disgusting.'

'I've had rook pie,' Mabel said, 'you make it from the breasts of young rooks, tastes better than pigeon pie. There's a recipe in Mrs Beaton.'

Stuart looked at her with horror. 'Don't make me one, please.' He paused. 'You could try it out on Inspector Revie, the next time he comes to dinner.' They all laughed. Because of the agency's co-operation in a former highly secretive case, involving many important men, they had a special relationship with the Suffolk constabulary, with Inspector Nicholas Revie as their contact.

'We haven't seen him for a bit, or that nice Mr Ansell. Besides, we'd have to wait until rook-shooting day, May the twelfth; they shoot the young 'uns when they're still in the nest as they're only tasty for a few months.'

Laurel quickly took another mouthful of Tio Pepe.

Dorothy blew a stream of smoke toward the ceiling. 'Mabel, when are you and Stuart moving in? The rooms are ready.'

When Stuart and Mabel married, the idea was to let Stuart's bun-galow in Leiston and to move into one of the many unoccupied rooms in Greyfriars House. Mabel preferred to live at Leiston; Lau-rel knew she was embarrassed at the thought of her and Stuart making love in Dorothy's house.

'Can't prise her away from that new kitchen, although she does most of her cooking here. I'm ready for the move; a bit more money from letting it out would be useful,' Stuart said.

Mabel didn't say anything, continuing to sip her Babycham.

'What's the Breen's farm like?' Laurel asked Dorothy. Mabel shot her a grateful look.

'Changing your mind about Daniel? Checking his bank balance?' Frank said, raising his half-empty glass to her.

'Just interested. Well, Dorothy, are they good farmers?'

'Daniel is, he went to agricultural college, had to leave before he'd finished his full three years. His father died in a shooting acci-dent. Rosalind and he ran the farm, Caleb is in charge of the poultry, he doesn't do a bad job and they employ two men. Father and son, the Gorsts. Daniel's just told me he's hoping to get Mary Gorst, the mother, to do some cooking for him and Caleb.'

'Was anyone else involved in the shooting accident?' Frank asked.

'No,' Dorothy replied. 'Noah was out shooting pigeons. When he didn't come back for his evening meal Rosalind went out to look for him with Caleb. Daniel was in college. They found him in the oak wood; the rooks had already started pecking at him.'

Laurel shivered. 'That's awful. She must have hated those birds after that.'

Dorothy stubbed out her cigarette in an ashtray. 'No, she loved the rooks. She was convinced someone had shot Noah. She couldn't accept he could have been so careless. She made a terrible fuss, wouldn't let it go, she kept bothering the police. Daniel finally persuaded her to accept the coroner's verdict of accidental death. She'd sometimes talk to me about it, and say she still couldn't believe he'd be so stupid. She adored him, she never looked at another man, not in that way, although there were a few who'd have been more than willing. She was a beautiful woman, even in old age, and the De Lacy name still carries weight round here.'

'De Lacy?' Frank asked. 'Who are they?'

'An old family, pots of money; they own an estate a few miles from the farm. The only one left is Bryce, Rosalind's elder brother. He lives abroad, never married, so I'm not sure who'll inherit the estate. It's a pity relationships between the Breens and him aren't better, as Daniel and Caleb are his only blood relatives. I don't know why Rosalind wouldn't have anything to do with him, I tried to squeeze it out of her, but she refused to tell me, and asked me not to ask again. So, I didn't.'

'What's he like, Bryce?' Laurel asked.

Dorothy shook her head. 'I've never seen him, a manager runs the estate, no one lives at Shrike Hall, apart from some old nanny, if she's still alive. Rosalind used to see her sometimes; she must be pushing a hundred if she's above ground. I've heard Bryce sometimes visits her.'

Mabel got up. 'I'll be dishing up soon. Stuart, would you help me?'

Laurel started to get up, but sat down again as Frank shook his head. The look on Mabel's face said it all. She wanted to get Stuart to herself and talk about moving, or not moving, into Greyfriars House.

Stuart groaned and followed Mabel out of the room.

Dorothy blew out her cheeks. 'I wish I hadn't mentioned it, but the work is all done, their new bathroom looks lovely, better than ours.' She nodded to Laurel. 'They've got spacious rooms on the ground floor, with their bathroom next door, so we won't hear their shenanigans, it's quite private. They were keen to move as soon as they knew you,' she nodded to Laurel again, 'were not leaving the agency, but now I think it's Mabel who's got cold feet; Stuart would move in tomorrow. Laurel, could you have a word with Mabel? See if you can find out what the problem is?'

Her stomach sank. Why did she always get lumbered with having conversations she didn't want to have? She supposed she should be flattered for having a reputation for knowing how to handle people, but she didn't want to spoil her relationship with Mabel, who was certainly prickly at the moment. 'I'll try.'

'Good girl. I'll give Stuart a hand.' Dorothy marched off to the kitchen.

Frank raised an eyebrow. 'You have all the luck, don't you? Tomorrow a funeral of someone you've never met, and then the dubious pleasure of a tête-à-tête with the out-of-sorts Mabel.'

'I wish I was going with you to the reserve, I'm not a fan of funerals.' She stroked the tufts of hair growing between Bumpers pads, and burrowed her nose into his fur.

Frank put the empty glasses onto a tray. 'I can't imagine what the Warden wants us to investigate; have the little terns taken a turn for the worse and are trying to have their wicked way with the avocets? Or has someone raided the till at the shop and stolen all of two pounds and thirty pence? I can't see there's going to be much mileage for us there.'

She smiled at him. 'A walk round the reserve is better than the inside of a church.'

'Remember, you'll get some funeral meats afterwards.'

'I'm not staying for that. I'll say I've got to get back for Bumper.'

'I think you'll have a more interesting time than me, you'll see the Breens. I wonder which one will turn you on – Daniel or the peculiar Caleb?'

She gave Bumper a final pat and got up. 'If one of them has green eyes, he'll do,' she said, giving him a side-long glance. She smiled as she saw the startled look on his face.

Chapter Three

Friday, February 25th, 1972

Frank decided he'd walk to the bird reserve from his cottage on the Minsmere cliffs; it was a short walk along the beach to a reserve entrance which led directly to the centre and shop. He could have driven, but he'd recently kitted himself out for country life, buying suitable gear from a shop in Ipswich, and he thought this would be a good day to put it to the test.

He laced up the expensive Swiss hiking boots and tucked his flared jeans into woollen socks. The canvas duffle coat with its woollen lining and corduroy cuffs wasn't quite up to his leather jacket, but it was a damn sight more with it than some of the others he'd tried on. He laughed at himself. Was he turning into a country bumpkin? Did he care? Not really. Those bitter winds straight off the North Sea made you forget style, what was needed was protection. He didn't expect to see the Warden, Ian Hebditch, in a three-piece suit and kipper tie. He picked up the binoculars Stuart persuaded him to buy when he'd joined the reserve and become a novice twitcher.

The day was raw but dry, the breeze ruffling hair and scouring his scalp – he'd drawn the line at a woolly hat, or a tweed cap. There was no one in sight as he strode from the fifty-foot high, crumbling cliffs down the stony lane which led to Minsmere beach. He headed for the path between a grass-covered seawall, with reed beds to his right, and sand dunes knitted together with tufts of marram grass to his left. That was better, there was shelter from the wind.

He passed through a gate onto the reserve and followed a path, with reed beds on both sides, which would lead him towards the reserve's centre. There were two stretches of open water to his left and he stopped and looked through his binoculars at two shoveler ducks dipping for food, the male gaudy with his shiny dark green head and bright yellow eye. He'd hoped he'd see something a bit rarer so he could impress the Warden; why he wanted to do that he wasn't sure. The teacher's pet syndrome? He didn't think he'd ever fitted that description.

Stuart had told him the Warden's office was on top of a specially dug Sand Martin cliff, above the car park; no signs of them whizzing about at this time of year. The wooden hut at the eastern end of the car park was the shop. He ran up the steps and knocked on the door and went in. Two men were leaning over a table studying a map. They both looked up.

Frank held out his hand. 'Mr Hebditch? Frank Diamond.'

The older man shook his hand. 'Good afternoon, Mr Diamond, I'm Ian Hebditch, welcome to Minsmere, although you're no stranger to the reserve, I believe.'

He was about five nine, in his mid-fifties, with a pleasant, open face, dark, slightly wavy hair receding at the temples, and a soft, well-educated voice. He waved a hand toward the other man. 'Mr Diamond meet Henry Rudder, my deputy, Henry, Mr Diamond.'

Frank shook his beefy hand, which matched the rest of him.

'Call me Hal,' he said.

Hebditch frowned. 'Shall we go through to my office?' Rudder made to follow them. 'Henry,' he said, giving emphasis to his name, 'I need to speak to Mr Diamond in private. I'll discuss any developments with you later. Could you check on the men working on the reed beds in the North Levels? Thank you.'

Relationships between the Warden and his deputy didn't seem so hot. Certainly, Rudder's looks weren't prepossessing. He was well-named, with his bristly ginger hair and beard, covering a round head with well-furnished eyebrows of the same colour. Big chap, probably about six two and weighing a good fifteen stone. But if he loved wildlife he couldn't be that bad. Or could he?

Not waiting for a reply, Hebditch opened the door to an inner room with walls covered in maps, charts and photographs of birds. He moved behind a battered wooden desk and pointed to the solitary armchair covered in brown fur in front of it. 'That is my coypu chair,' he said, smiling proudly.

'Coypu? They're South American rodents, aren't they?'

'Correct, dreadful pests – I cured the pelts and had the chair covered with them. Heaviest was nearly nineteen pounds.'

Frank lowered himself carefully onto the chair. Gruesome, but comfortable.

'How do you control them?'

'Trap, sack them and dispatch by a hefty blow on the head.'

Hebditch had a dark side; he was moving uncomfortably in his chair, tapping a biro against a sheet of paper.

'Mr Hebditch, how can the Anglian Detective Agency help you? Now you've dealt with the coypu, I hope you don't want us to chase escaped mink who are eating your young birds?' he said, hoping to lighten the atmosphere and relax the prospective client.

Hebditch stared at him as though regretting the meeting already. The phrase lead balloon seemed appropriate.

Hebditch sighed. 'I'm not sure if you're the correct firm to help us.'

Then why the fuck did you contact us? Frank thought. He'd have been better off going to the funeral. 'Why not tell me what the problem is, Mr Hebditch, then we can assess whether we are the appropriate people to help you.' He hated himself.

Hebditch relaxed, slightly. 'I must ask you not to repeat what I'm going to tell you.' He paused, staring at him, obviously waiting for Frank to solemnly nod.

'Everything is discussed with the Anglian team before we decide to take on a case. I assure you, my partners and I, will treat all you say with discretion.'

Hebditch puffed out a long deep breath.

My God, what was the man waiting for? What could be so disturbing, so warranting such a fuss? Had a volunteer started nicking avocets eggs? Or had the Deputy Warden turned into a taxidermist and was killing and stuffing birds?

'Very well. But I must emphasise the society does not want any whisper getting into the press. This would only encourage copy-cat behaviour.'

Frank tried to lower his rising shoulders; he nodded in what he hoped was an encouraging manner.

'I presume you have visited the two public hides?'

He had. Both were accessible to people walking along the beach; anyone could enter them and view the bird activity on The Scrape; a man-made shallow lake with controlled brackish conditions. He'd thought it was a great idea to get people, and especially kids on holiday, interested in bird life. He nodded.

Hebditch nodded back. They could have been two great-crested grebes, performing a courtship ceremony, but he didn't fancy Hebditch.

'We've had problems in these hides, and . . . in hides in the reserve.'

Interesting, well, a bit more interesting. 'Yes?'

'It started five weeks ago. A night-fisherman, who been casting for school bass, decided to eat his breakfast in a hide on a Sunday morning, about five. Still pitch black, of course. He said the door of the hide was gaping open and the light from his torch showed the inside was a wreck: empty beer cans and spirit bottles, fish and chip paper scattered round, a viewing bench broken; it looked as though they'd been dancing on it, and it stank of urine and vomit.' His facial expressions, and shaking head, showed the level of his disgust.

'Did you inform the police?'

'Of course, at once.'

'And?'

'They came the same morning, well, it was nearly afternoon before they arrived. They took some of the bottles, said they'd fingerprint them, but I'm not sure if they did. My impression was they

19

didn't think much of it, said it was probably some stupid youngsters letting off steam and no one had been hurt, had they?'

'Is that it?'

'It certainly isn't,' bristled Hebditch. 'The same thing happened the next weekend, the same kind of mess, but this time I noticed tyre tracks in the sand outside the hide, several different tracks, God knows how many idiots were in the hide.'

'They must have come via the path from Minsmere cliffs, there isn't another way of getting to the hides by car, is there?'

Hebditch jabbed a finger at him. 'Correct! The police were again informed, but I was told they couldn't keep a watch on the hides at weekends as they were having problems in Leiston and Aldeburgh, and they hadn't the man-power to cover both. If things calmed down in those two towns, they'd be pleased to help.'

He hadn't heard of any such problems from his main source of local gossip: Mabel. 'Did they specify what was going on?'

'No, they were reluctant to discuss it further.'

The man was deeply disturbed by the illegal use of the hides, but why? OK, there was some damage, but the teenagers, they had to be teenagers, weren't doing any harm, apart from a bit of vomit and littering the hide with bottles and cans. Yes, they damaged a bench, and yes, they shouldn't do it, but what the hell, you were only young once and if the Warden knew what he'd got up to when he was their age, he wouldn't be asking the agency for help.

'Obviously something else happened?'

'Hebditch's brow creased until it resembled corrugated iron. 'Last weekend they trespassed, they penetrated the reserve and used the Tree Hide for their orgy!' His voice was full of rage and disgust. 'They smashed it up, and then set it on fire!'

Frank started to be on his side. 'That's awful. Did they disturb many of the birds?'

'They must have done.'

'Fire's a dangerous thing; it can easily get out of control. I'm afraid we're going to see more tragedies as people have to use candles during the power cuts,' he said.

'Indeed,' Hebditch replied. 'That poor woman, who was burnt to death yesterday when a lit candle rolled under her bed. Where was that?'

'Streatham,' he replied. 'The hide fire isn't generally known, is it? I certainly haven't heard about it, and neither has Stuart Elderkin, who I think you know.'

The Warden slumped in his chair, and shook his head. 'We decided to try and keep it quiet, hoping the police would finally become involved, and hopefully catch them if they came back. I was hoping Mr Elderkin would be with you today, he's been a keen supporter of the reserve since its beginnings, he and his first wife helped to make The Scrape.'

'Why ask us to help?'

'An Inspector Revie phoned me, he apologised for not having the manpower to keep a vigil at the reserve, but he suggested I contact your agency to see if you would be willing to help us catch these criminals. The breeding season will start soon and if these vandals persist, and if, God forbid, it escalates, thousands of birds, especially those who come here to breed, will be disturbed and will not stay. It takes very little to make birds wary of a certain area and to leave to try and find a safe place to build their nests and lay eggs. For these birds there are few safe refuges, and a whole season will be lost. For some of our rarer species this could be devastating.'

Frank could see why he was incensed. Stuart had told him how Minsmere reserve had been slowly built up over many years: this stretch of coastal land was flooded as a defence during World War Two, and after the war it was leased by the reserve to form a wetland area providing a rich feeding and breeding ground for many threatened species. Dedicated people, including Stuart, had worked hard to bring about its present-day success. But how could the Anglian Detective Agency help? They didn't have enough manpower to stake out all the hides every weekend, and it was too dangerous for any of them to go solo. At first, he'd thought they were kids having a good time, but arson was a serious crime, and if they were Brahms and Liszt, they, whoever they were, might get nasty if they were discovered. There was only Laurel, Stuart and himself capable of keeping watch at night, and if they were lucky and found the vandals, what could they do? They couldn't arrest them. Possibly take photos? They might need some different equipment. He wasn't au fait with infra-red film, but they could probably use the same cameras; it would be interesting to find out what was needed. He'd ask Laurel to look into that; she was the best photographer. Wasn't Jimi Hendrix's last album cover made with infrared photography? Band of Gypsys? He'd gone off funk rock. It was probably all the faces Stuart pulled whenever he was a passenger in his car.

'I'd like to see the hide that's been set on fire, is that possible?'

'Will that help?'

Frank felt like saying: not really, but I fancy a walk. Instead he gritted his teeth. 'It's always advisable to visit the scene of the crime.'

Hebditch stared at his wrist watch. 'Very well, but we'll have to step out, I need to be back to see some of my volunteers at four-thirty.'

Volunteers? Would any of them be able, or capable, of helping? They would need to be fit, strong and not have short fuses. 'Perhaps I could also meet them. They might have noticed something. Do they know about the hide being set on fire?'

Hebditch shook his head. 'No. Only Rudder, myself and the police know. I've told the volunteers the Tree Hide is out of bounds for the moment as work needs doing to make it safe.'

'Are you going to tell the volunteers you're seeing this afternoon the truth?'

Hebditch gnawed at his bottom lip. 'I wasn't, but perhaps . . . do you think I should?'

That was better, he was being consulted. 'It depends. How many are you seeing and who are they? Are they people you know well? Can they be trusted to be discreet?'

Hebditch got up and took a jacket from a hook on the wall. 'Let's make for the hide, I'll tell you about them as we walk.'

They went southwards from the centre through woodland. 'This is the South Belt,' Hebditch said, as he pointed to his right. 'A very productive wood.'

There were English and Turkey oaks, mixed with sweet chestnuts, Scotch pines and sycamores. 'A good mixture of species,' Frank said.

Hebditch gave him a side-long look. 'You have a biological background?

He puffed out his cheeks. He might as well admit it. 'I took an honours degree in Botany before I joined the police, also Zoology to general degree standard; sometimes I wish I'd chosen Zoology, especially when I visit somewhere like this.'

For the first time Hebditch smiled at him. 'That's good to hear.'

'Does this road have a name?' he asked. 'And what killed those trees?' He pointed to his left, over marshland where dead oaks raised bare arms to the sky.

Hebditch smiled at him again. 'This is West Walk and the oaks were killed by wartime flooding; we haven't cut them down, birds nest in the holes and insects feeding on the dead wood are food for some of the birds.'

He was warming to Hebditch, the man was super enthusiastic and obviously deeply cared for the reserve and its inhabitants.

'You were going to tell me about the volunteers you're meeting this afternoon.'

Hebditch turned to him. 'Yes, but first look over there.' He pointed to his right, into the woodland. 'Flock of long-tailed tits.'

Frank raised his binoculars; nine balls of fluff with ridiculous tails were swooping from branch to branch, chattering as they searched for early insects. He decided he wouldn't mind spending a few weeks here investigating a minor crime.

Hebditch smiled like a proud parent watching his children perform a complicated acrobatic feat. 'Not an uncommon species, but one of my favourite birds.' He started walking again. 'Yes, the two volunteers I'm meeting today are very committed to the reserve. They both give an inordinate amount of their time helping us.'

'Really! Are they retired? I can't imagine an employer would let their staff out very often.'

'Edith Chell is, Edith is . . . very keen.'

His tone of voice suggested he wasn't that keen on Edith, despite her commitment to the reserve.

'And?'

'You'll see for yourself. Edith was a biology teacher at Leiston Secondary Modern, hence her interest in nature. From what I've heard she wasn't a very good teacher, she may have known her subject, but I believe she had difficulties with the pupils. Edith is better dealing with wildlife than wild children.' He snorted at his own joke.

They came to a barrier across the road: TREE HIDE CLOSED UNTIL FURTHER NOTICE. Hebditch led him round the side. Frank decided he would not invite Edith to share a stake out with him in one of the hides. 'And the other volunteer?'

'Ah, Samuel Myres, a different kettle of fish!' Hebditch's voice was full of approval. 'Mr Myres is a wealthy man, self-employed, so he's able to give a considerable amount of his time to the reserve. He lives in Westleton, and is a very capable person. You can give him a job and you know he'll complete it. Completely reliable.' He halted and pointed. 'Look, there's the Tree Hide.' His tone had changed to one of rage.

Frank had been inside the hide on his visit with Stuart. Set on stilts, it looked over meres to the south of the reserve. Once a spacious box, with deep observation slits, it was now a gutted heap of timber, and as they approached it the smell of charred wood still lingered in the air.

Frank's nostrils widened, and a spark of anger ignited his determination to take on the case and to discover the yobs who'd done this and see they were punished.

Chapter Four

The wind was sharp against Laurel's cheeks as she waited outside St James church in Dunwich for the arrival of the hearse; with her were Dorothy, Stuart and Mabel. They, together with small knots of mourners, huddled against the flint walls.

'I won't be a minute,' Dorothy said, as she left them to flit from one group to another, chatting briefly, nodding and passing on to the next.

'You forget how many people Dorothy knows,' Stuart said.

'She's lived here all her life, and she'd helped more than a few,' Mabel replied, adjusting her hat and pulling her woollen scarf higher to protect her face.

'Look, she's talking to Jim McFall; she told me she's thinking of asking him if he'd do some gardening for her,' Laurel said.

Jim had been the groundsman at the now closed Blackfriars School, then, he was a possible murder suspect in the police enquiry into the death of Susan Nicholson, the headmaster's wife. It emerged he'd served time for murdering his own adulterous wife, but he was a reformed character, and all the team liked and trusted him.

'Did Jim know Rosalind?' Mabel asked.

'Only briefly, he's helped out at Rooks Wood Farm a few times, when they hit a busy period,' Stuart said, 'but he thought she was lovely woman; had a bit of a crush on her, I think.'

Laurel stamped her feet, and wished she'd worn boots and not court shoes; her legs were also frozen, they weren't used to being exposed to the Suffolk winter air. 'I'm going for a quick stroll round the churchyard,' she said.

Mabel nodded, shivered and moved closer to Stuart.

Laurel rubbed her hands together. What a dreary day for a funeral, clouds were scudding from the east, and the fitful sun was unable to warm the air. At least it wasn't raining. She looked at a large urn, on an even larger pedestal, both made of cast iron; she remembered Dorothy telling her it must have been made at the now defunct Leiston iron works, probably at the beginning of the century. What a cold and heavy monument, she thought. Fancy being buried under that; no chance of escape.

The sound of approaching cars sent her, as well as Dorothy, back to join the others. The black hearse, with its dark coffin, on which lay a wreath of white roses, with sheaves of flowers clustered around it drew up and stopped in the road in front of the church. In the following car two men sat in the back. She was interested to see the Breen brothers, especially Caleb.

The men got out of the car, one tall and strong, the other of a much shorter and lighter build. Daniel and Caleb Breen. Daniel put his arm round Caleb and they joined the other pall-bearers. The coffin was manoeuvred out, and Daniel and Caleb lifted the front end of the coffin, Daniel stooping to accommodate Caleb's lack of height, four other men lined up behind them to support the rest of the coffin. They slowly walked towards the church, the mourners shuffling behind.

Laurel had been into St James several times with Dorothy, and although the inside was plain, it had a neat appearance, and always felt welcoming. Dorothy led the way down a central aisle with wooden pews on either side, light flooding in from deep-set windows. About twenty other people followed, the sounds of their footsteps masked by solemn organ music. Rosalind's coffin was placed on a bier in front of the altar, vases of white roses on either side matching the wreath on her coffin. The brothers sat down in the front pew and they sat down on the pew behind them.

Caleb's head was bowed, his brother looking at him, a worried expression on his face. Daniel turned, and on seeing Dorothy smiled.

'Aunty Dot, the flowers are lovely. Please thank the ladies when you see them.'

She placed a hand on his shoulder. 'You'll see some of them at The Ship later, you can thank them yourself.' She turned towards Laurel. 'Laurel, this is Daniel, Daniel, my partner in crime, Laurel Bowman.' He shook her hand. Stuart was right, he was an attractive man, but his face showed the strain he was under: blue shadows beneath those deep blue eyes.

'Caleb,' Dorothy said, 'this is Laurel Bowman, my friend and colleague.'

Daniel shot her a worried look.

Caleb slowly turned round, his shoulders hunched, wary as though expecting to be attacked. He was a strange creature with his pronounced widow's peak and wide-spaced eyes, like a being from another world.

'Hello, Caleb,' she said, holding out her hand and smiling. 'I'm truly sorry about your mum.' She looked at both of them as she said this. Daniel smiled back, the flash of his white teeth lighting up his face. Caleb looked at her outstretched hand and slowly raised his, his fingers tight together. She enclosed it in both of hers. 'It's truly awful to lose someone you love. My sister died a few years ago, so I think I know how you feel.'

Caleb's eyes filmed with tears. 'Thank you,' he whispered.

She released his hand and he turned back to look at the coffin.

'Thank you,' Daniel Breen mouthed silently, looking at her more intently, then his gaze moved from her face to somewhere behind her, his eyes widening with shock.

She leant against the back of the pew. Stuart, who was on her left, whispered in her ear. 'Well done, but now you've two more admirers to deal with.'

She shook her head at him.

Dorothy, to her right, was craning her head, looking at the rest of the mourners. She pulled on Laurel's sleeve. 'Don't turn now, but three rows back, you'll see Theresa Poppy; she and Daniel were childhood sweethearts. She's second from the end. I'm glad she's come today. I don't think Daniel's seen her since she came back. Wait a few minutes before you look, you can't miss her. Good-looking woman, dark hair,' she whispered.

Laurel obeyed orders, and when a reasonable length of time had passed, she casually turned and looked behind her. She easily picked Theresa out: a handsome rather than pretty woman, with a wide, generous mouth and high cheek bones, and perched on her dark curly hair was a black pill box hat. Her brown eyes seemed filled with sadness. Was she the reason for Daniel's changed expression a few minutes ago? It would make sense.

The service followed with the usual prayers, readings and a short sermon. Daniel read *Remember Me* by Christina Rossetti, his voice choking over the last lines; Caleb was holding a handkerchief to his face, probably to muffle the sounds of his grief as well as to soak up his tears. Dorothy gave the eulogy and spoke movingly of Rosalind, both as a friend, wife, mother and good neighbour; she kept her emotions in check and the only sign of nerves were her hands tightly gripping the edge of the lectern.

Laurel wished the service would end; she hated to see people suffering and not to be able to truly sympathise with them as she hadn't known Rosalind. She could almost taste the grief of the brothers, it seemed to wash over their pew and surround her in waves of sadness and recrimination. Her thoughts slipped to the death of her sister, Angela; the funeral service bringing it back into focus. Angela, cruelly murdered and dumped under Felixstowe pier. If only she'd picked up clues from Angela's behaviour. Shouldn't she have guessed she was pregnant? Finding her killer gave her some satisfaction, but he'd escaped legal justice.

Dorothy's hand touched her arm. 'Are you all right?'

She looked at her and gave a weak smile. 'I'll be glad when it's over.'

Dorothy squeezed her arm. 'I know, it doesn't get any easier, does it?'

She shook her head and placed a hand over Dorothy's. They'd

both lost a sister in the cruellest way, both murdered, taken too soon, with the lingering horrors when you thought of their fear, suffering and horrible deaths.

Dorothy squeezed her hand. 'Thank goodness I persuaded the vicar not to use the new Prayer Book, it's ghastly. Everything new isn't necessarily better.'

Laurel tried to think of something new that was an improvement on the old. She decided the Pill was a great step up from a condom. When she'd been engaged to Simon she'd decided to go on the Pill, but when they'd quarrelled and parted, she abandoned the idea. She hoped she might make another move in that direction before she was past it. She glanced furtively at Dorothy and hoped she wasn't a mind reader. These were not appropriate thoughts for a funeral.

The mourners rose as Daniel, Caleb and the other pall-bearers positioned themselves round the coffin and lifted it onto their shoulders. Rosalind Breen was making her final journey, the minister leading them out of the church.

Stuart, Mabel, Dorothy and Laurel followed the coffin. She longed to get into the fresh air, even if it was cold. As they approached the door the coffin came to a juddering halt, and there were gasps from those behind as the coffin looked in danger of sliding forward out of the pallbearers' grasps.

Laurel stepped sideways into an unoccupied pew so she could see what the problem was. A man was standing close to the coffin, head bowed, shoulders slumped. His hand touched the coffin, then he placed it on Caleb's shoulder. 'Caleb,' he said, 'I am Bryce De Lacy, Rosalind's brother. I am you uncle.' He was a few inches taller than Caleb, with dark hair in a deep widow's peak, far-apart eyes, and the hand on Caleb's shoulder was webbed.

Chapter Five

Frank and Ian Hebditch arrived back at the reserve centre at four-twenty.

'Those are the volunteers' quarters,' Hebditch said, pointing to a couple of sheds at the western end of the car park. 'However, I've asked Miss Chell and Mr Myres to meet us in my office.'

Frank nodded. Stuart had pointed the quarters out on one of their joint visits; he'd declined Stuart's invitation to help him empty the volunteers' chemical toilet into the marsh; it was Stuart's turn on the rota.

'They're both here,' Hebditch said, pointing to two cars that hadn't been there when they'd left to view the vandalised hide.

One vehicle was a new, green Land Rover, the other a blue Austin Mini 1000. Frank decided he wouldn't take bets as to which car belonged to which volunteer. He couldn't see action man Myres in a Mini or Edith Chell behind the wheel of the Land Rover.

Frank was feeling in a good mood; he hoped the rest of the team would agree to them taking the case; Stuart would be biased towards it because of his long association with the reserve, and he couldn't see anyone else objecting, especially as they were going through a fallow period at the moment. Was crime going out of fashion? Some hopes.

Hebditch opened the office door.

'Well, Sam, I must say this isn't like Mr Hebditch, he's usually very good with his timekeeping.' The voice was loud, female, with a strong Yorkshire accent.

'It isn't four-thirty, Edith.' The voice was masculine, crisp and accent-less. 'Ah, here he is.'

The man stood by the table and Edith, he presumed she was Edith, was sitting on a chair near it. Her small, brown eyes widened as she saw him, as well as the Warden.

'Who have we got here, then? A new volunteer?' She didn't wait for an answer. 'We were worried when you weren't here, Ian. What have you been up to?'

Hebditch coloured and he tugged at his collar. 'Edith, allow me to introduce Mr Diamond, a partner in the Anglian Detective Agency. Mr Diamond, Miss Edith Chell, a volunteer.'

Edith bounced up and grabbed his hand. She looked about sixty, and although well endowed, seemed fit. She'd a round face with hamster cheeks and tightly permed grey hair. Thick brown eyebrows framed those inquisitive button-like eyes, which were staring at him.

'A detective? What are you doing here?' She turned to Hebditch. 'What's happened?'

'I'll come to that in a moment, Edith. Mr Diamond meet Mr Myres, another volunteer.' He sounded frazzled.

Frank shook Myres' hand. It was a firm, dry handshake from a tall, well-built man, who looked extremely fit. Deep-set, pale-blue eyes below fine eyebrows, looked at him quizzically. He was taller by about four inches than Frank's five eleven, with short dark-blond hair, and a military moustache above thin, straight lips.

'Pleased to meet you, Mr Diamond. I'm sure Mr Hebditch will reveal all.'

'Shall we have a cup of tea before we start? Edith, would you like to make it? You know where everything is.' He pointed to his office.

Edith beamed. 'We know how to make a good cup of tea where I come from.'

'Where's that?' Frank asked.

Myres coughed.

'Why God's country, of course. Yorkshire! Where do you come from?'

'Liverpool.'

Edith snorted and went into the office.

Hebditch shuddered.

Frank grinned and Myres gave a wry smile.

As they waited, to the accompaniment of clashing crockery and sighs and grunts from the office, Hebditch took three folding chairs leaning against the wall and arranged them round the table.

'Mr Myres–'

'Please call me Sam,' he said to Frank.

Hebditch wriggled in his chair. 'I think we need to keep this meeting on a professional level. Mr Diamond may be working for us in the future.'

Myres frowned. 'Really?'

'Yes, I'll explain when Edith is here.'

'Are you talking about me behind me back,' she said as she came in with a loaded tray, which she plonked onto the table, liquid shooting out of the tea-pot's spout. 'Whoops! Clumsy me!' She didn't sound worried. She placed a plate of chocolate digestives in front of Hebditch. 'Your favourite biscuits, Ian, from your favourite volunteer! I bought them half-price in Leiston Co-op. Don't say I don't spoil you.'

Hebditch gave a weak smile.

'Now sup up and help yourself to biscuits,' Edith commanded. 'Although at the rate inflation keeps rising, you'll be lucky to get rich tea next time.'

Frank definitely wouldn't ask Edith to share a night vigil in a hide. Perhaps Stuart would like to take her on. She might bring him a packet of custard creams. He'd known some lovely Yorkshire people, some witty Yorkshire people and, remembering one girlfriend, some sexy Yorkshire people, but Edith gave that county a bad name. Perhaps he was being unfair, she must love the birds if she was such a rabid volunteer, or was it old Hebditch she yearned after?

Hebditch nibbled at a biscuit, then placed it half-eaten on his saucer. 'Sam, Edith, I want to explain why Mr Diamond is here today.

I must ask you not to repeat what I have to say to anyone.' He straightened his back. 'I hope you can reassure me on this point.'

He looked first at Myres.

'Yes, of course, though I can't imagine what you are going to say.'

'Edith?'

'You know I'd do anything for you, Ian. Are you in trouble? Has Mr Diamond come to arrest you?'

Hebditch puffed out his cheeks. 'Mr Diamond is not a policeman. He is a private detective. Have I your word you will not repeat what I have to say?'

'Of course, I can be the soul of discretion when I want to be,' she said.

Frank found that hard to believe.

Hebditch told them of the parties in the shore-line hides and the burning of a reserve hide.

Myres lips tightened. 'Which hide was set on fire?'

'The Tree Hide. Not your hide, Mr Myres, I'm glad to say.' He turned to Frank. 'Mr Myres has donated a large, new hide to the reserve, and has personally supervised its building.'

'Where about is it?' Frank asked.

'North of the East Hide, overlooking the north part of The Scrape,' Hebditch replied.

'Can you enter it from the beach?' Frank asked.

Myres shook his head. 'No, I'm pleased to say, after what you've told me.' He nodded to Hebditch.

'Sam's funded a new road to the hide as well, so you can drive to it,' Edith said, a meaty hand grabbing the last chocolate digestive.

Hebditch slowly nodded. 'Yes, we're very grateful for Sam's commitment to the reserve, of course visitors will walk to the hide, only the reserve's vehicles will use it; the road will make future maintenance easy, not that I can see any will be necessary for several years, it's been built to the highest standards.'

'I think we should discuss how the Anglian Detective Agency, if we decide to take the case, could operate. I believe from our discussions, Mr Hebditch, you wish investigations to be carried out discretely. Also, is the reserve aware of the fees we charge? If the investigation was prolonged this could add up to a considerable amount,' Frank said.

Hebditch pulled a face. 'Our organization, as you know, runs on voluntary contributions, and the small amount we raise through sales of bird-related goods. I was hoping . . . I thought as Stuart Elderkin was such an involved member . . . you might be prepared, perhaps to lower your fees?' He smiled hopefully, obviously uncomfortable discussing money.

Frank was expecting something along these lines, but he wasn't giving anything away until he'd talked to his partners. 'I think we need to decide if we want to take the case, then we'll talk about fees.'

Hebditch's mouth drooped. 'Of course.'

During these conversations Frank was aware of Edith drinking in every word, her button-bright eyes watching each speaker in turn, her expression changing from soppy when Hebditch was speaking, to glowering when he refused to discuss the fees

She jabbed a finger at Frank. 'Is that all you're interested in: money? This is a local problem, a serious problem. I'll have a word with that Mabel Grill, she's one of you, isn't she? I know her, and the fancy man she married. They'll want to support us.'

Hebditch looked horrified. 'Edith, please!'

Frank placed a hand over his mouth. Fancy man Stuart! 'Mrs Grill is now Mrs Elderkin, Miss Chell. I can understand your concern, but I must ask you to be patient.' Laurel would be proud of his diplomacy.

'Perhaps I can help,' Myres said.

'Really, Mr Myres, you've done too much already,' Hebditch said.

'When we know if you're prepared to take on the case, and we see the breakdown of the expenses, I'm willing to bridge any gap in what the reserve can afford and the fees charged. Also, I presume, if you're to catch these vandals you'll need extra manpower, I and some of my employees might be able to help, if you think we'd be suitable.'

This guy had a good grasp of the situation and probably a good business head on him, as well. 'I'll tell my partners of your offer, and if we take the case, we can talk about this again, that is if Mr Hebditch is agreeable.' Perhaps he'd apply for a job in the United Nations.

Hebditch beamed. 'Thank you, Sam.'

'What about me? How can I help?' Edith asked.

Hebditch blinked. 'Er, I'm not sure at the moment, Edith, let's wait until we hear from Mr Diamond.'

She stared at Frank. 'You'd better get a move on then, we want these little monsters caught before they do more damage.'

Frank gave her his best smile. 'Where do you live, Miss Chell?'

She folded back her face, creating several chins. 'Leiston. Why?'

'I believe you taught at Leiston Secondary School?'

Her eyes narrowed. 'Yes, I did, for my sins. Why? What have you heard?'

'Nothing, should I have?' He must stop playing these games.

She didn't reply.

'As you live and have taught in Leiston, you must know many of the families. Is that correct?'

'Ay, and the things I could tell you would make you hair curl.' She glanced at him. 'Or in your case make it stand straight on end. Did you say you came from Liverpool? That Kevin Keegan plays for them. He's got long, curly hair, too. Is yours permed like his? I don't think it looks right on a man. I like my men natural.' She shot a glance at Hebditch, who looked mortified.

Myres coughed, probably to hide a snort.

'My hair is natural, Miss Chell, and some women find it irresistible. However, if we do take the case, you might be able to pick up some pointers in the town. We all presume the vandals are teenagers, or in their early twenties. There's bound to be talk once details get out, and no doubt they will. You could help us by listening out. I can't see the criminals coming from Ipswich, although we must keep an open mind. They're more likely to be residents of Leiston, or Aldeburgh, or the farming or fishing communities.'

Edith looked perplexed. 'Think you're a right card, don't you?' She looked at Hebditch. 'Do you want me to do that, Ian?'

'We must wait until Mr Diamond, hopefully, gives us a positive answer. Try to be patient,' he said, looking as though his was running out.

'You sound as though you've decided to take the case, Mr Diamond,' Myres said.

'Just throwing out a few ideas,' Frank said. 'I must get back to Dunwich, my partners are going to Rosalind Breen's funeral, that's why Stuart Elderkin couldn't be here today,' he said to the two volunteers.

Hebditch gravely nodded. 'Indeed, I would have attended if we hadn't been meeting. Daniel Breen, although he can't spare much time, is a supporter of the reserve, as is his brother. Not all the local farmers are.'

'Caleb?' Frank asked.

'Yes, do you know him?'

'No, but Miss Piff, our administrator, is an old friend of the family; she's told me about him.'

'Yes, a sad case. We allow Caleb to come to the reserve after all the visitors have gone home. He doesn't mix well. He's very careful not to disturb the birds, and he makes notes of any rarities.'

Edith snorted. 'He's enough to frighten the skin off a rice pudding.'

'Edith!' Hebditch reprimanded.

'I'm only saying what everyone thinks but hasn't the gumption to say.'

'I think you ought to ask Caleb not to come to the reserve after hours, especially at weekends. There's the chance he might run into some of the trespassers,' Frank said.

'Good idea,' Myres said. 'We don't want a human casualty.'

'I'll see to it,' Hebditch said. 'I'll have a word with Daniel Breen.'

Frank got up. 'I'll get back to you as soon as I can,' he said.

'When?' Edith asked.

'We've a meeting scheduled for Monday morning, I'll come

over in the afternoon and talk with you then,' he said, looking at Hebditch.

'Why can't you meet at the weekend?' she persisted.

'Some of us have family commitments; I'm driving to Liverpool tonight – my mother has just had an operation.'

'I'm sorry, not serious, I hope,' Hebditch said.

'Thank you, not life threatening, but fairly major. As I said, I'll contact you on Monday.'

'Make sure you do,' Edith said, glowering at him.

As he opened the door Rudder marched in and Frank had to nimbly step aside to avoid being barged into.

Rudder ignored him and stood before the others, arms akimbo, giving a good impression of Henry VIII. 'Is any one going to tell me what's going on?' He glared at Hebditch. 'What's been decided? I *am* Deputy Warden, and these two,' he pointed at Edith and Myres, 'are unpaid volunteers. Some of men clearing the reed bed seem to know more than me.'

Frank decided it was time to go.

Chapter Six

Laurel pulled up the collar of her navy coat as she walked with Dorothy, Mabel and Stuart from the church yard, up St James Street, to The Ship Inn. She'd planned to go back to Greyfriars House after the burial, hoping Frank would be back and she could find out what the Warden had to say. But the appearance of Bryce De Lacy and his close resemblance to Caleb was interesting, and made her change her mind. Also, the different reactions of the brothers to De Lacy was intriguing; Daniel didn't look pleased to see his uncle, but Caleb was the opposite; even in the brief time she's seen them together in the church, there seemed to be an immediate bond, probably fuelled by their close resemblance to each other.

'This dratted wind,' Mabel grumbled, clamping a hand on her hat, which despite a hatpin, promised to soar away towards Westleton. Her other arm was linked through Stuart's. She'd have to talk to Mabel soon and try and find out why she didn't want to move into Greyfriars, perhaps there might be a chance this evening. She was going to see her parents in Felixstowe tomorrow, it was her mum's birthday, so, if she didn't talk to Mabel today, it would have to be Monday.

The straggle of mourners, leaning into the east wind, slowly made their way towards the inn. St James Street was all that remained of the mediaeval city of Dunwich, the rest washed away by storms as the North Sea ate into the land. The red-brick houses, with extravagant bargeboards, lined each side of the wide road, and at the end, on the corner, was The Ship Inn. Although she and Frank usually ended up at The Eel's Foot, at Eastbridge, they sometimes went to The Ship. It was a spacious red-brick building, an Elizabethan smuggler's inn, with six tall chimneys, grouped in pairs; the banners of grey smoke issuing from two of them were blown westwards by the cutting wind. It was a relief to get inside and soon a gaggle of people jostled for space in front of a blazing log fire.

'Shall I take your coat, Laurel?' Stuart asked, Dorothy's and Mabel's coats over his arm. Having changed her mind about coming for the funeral meats, she was glad she'd taken the trouble to wear her grey suit, instead of the jumper and skirt she'd originally planned to wear.

'I'll check the food,' Dorothy said, 'make sure it's up to scratch.' She bustled off.

Stuart raised his eyebrows. 'There she goes, in her element.'

Mabel shook her head. 'It's a good job someone's in charge. The Breens look upset, well Daniel does. Fancy his uncle turning up like that. This day was difficult enough for them without the shock of Mr De Lacy showing up. They look alike, don't they? It's queer seeing two of them, one was bad enough.'

'Mabel,' Stuart reprimanded, 'no need for that.' He struggled through the crowd and hung up the coats on a rack near the door.

Laurel didn't say anything, although she wanted to. Mabel's remarks were not like her, she was usually tolerant and kind-hearted. She'd have to have that talk soon.

The Breens were standing with Bryce De Lacy near the buffet table, the rest of the mourners giving them a wide berth. She decided she was hungry and moved closer to them. The white-clothed table was decorated with several vases of daffodils and branches of pussy willow. She leant down and sniffed the flowers: she loved the fresh smell of narcissi; she stroked one of the grey willow buds, the silky coat reminding her of childhood walks with Angela, her murdered younger sister, taking pussy willow home to put in jam jars on the kitchen windowsill, watching, fascinated, as balls of yellow stamens emerged. She helped herself to some food, slowly edging closer to the Breens.

'I'm so pleased to meet both of you at last,' Bryce De Lacy said. 'I'm afraid your mother, as you know, didn't want to see me after she was married. I found it very painful.' His voice was soft, his accent BBC fifties.

Daniel coughed. 'I don't think we should discuss this here.'

'No, of course not. Did she ever tell you why she wouldn't see me?' he asked, ignoring Daniel's words.

'No. Please don't say anything more.'

'I'd like to come and see both of you again.' He smiled at Caleb and put a hand on his arm. 'Especially you, Caleb. I was amazed when I saw you. We look alike, don't we?'

Caleb nodded, gazing up at Bryce as though he couldn't believe what he was seeing.

'May I come tomorrow, say two o' clock?'

'No. Sorry, we've too much to do this weekend.'

Laurel had overladen her plate with sausage rolls, ham, and egg-and-cress sandwiches. Daniel gave her a suspicious look. She moved away from the table and moved back to Mabel. The sausage roll was tasty, the pastry light and crisp. 'This is nice,' she said to Mabel, waving what was left of it in front of her face.

Mabel sniffed. 'I've had one; not bad.'

Dorothy came over. 'Is the food all right? The table looks lovely. Nothing exciting to eat, standard fare, but everyone seems to be tucking in.'

Stuart joined them. 'Death always gives me an appetite. Those sausage rolls look good.' He devoured one in two bites, smacking his lips in appreciation.

'Good. You won't want any dinner tonight,' Mabel said, pursing her lips.

Dorothy looked at Laurel. 'Come over and meet the Gorsts.'

'Who?'

'Fred, Mary and Jonas, they work for the Breens, I told you. They're looking a bit lost; you can chat them up, do a bit more snooping. I saw you lingering over your choice of food near the Breens. Ever the detective.'

Dorothy was right, it was a permanent mindset. The three Gorsts were standing away from the rest of the crowd, Mary talking ten to the dozen to the older man, presumably her husband, Fred. The younger man, Jonas, their son, was staring into space.

Fred was a stocky man, about five ten, with a small beer gut. He looked strong and well-muscled, the material of his black suit tight against his body. His bald head was fringed with brown hair which matched his mutton-chop whiskers.

Mary looked a good ten years younger than her husband – early forties? She was slim, with a lively, attractive face; she chattered away, oblivious to the sullen look on her husband's face.

'Mr and Mrs Gorst, let me introduce you to one of my partners, Miss Laurel Bowman.'

Mary Gorst eagerly shook her hand, her face creased in a smile, hazel eyes full of interest. 'Miss Bowman! I've heard so much about you. My, I couldn't do your job, I'd be scared to death, wouldn't I, Fred?'

Fred shook her hand. 'Pleased to meet you.' He didn't look it.

'Lovely to meet both of you, and is this your son, Jonas?' Laurel directed her voice toward him. He turned. He was the same height as his father with broad sloping shoulders, a round face with all the features neatly arranged in the centre, a high forehead, straight dark brown hair and large blue eyes below faint eyebrows.

'Hello,' he said. His father nudged him. He shot out a hand, touched her fingers and pulled it back as though he'd received an electric shock. 'I'm off,' he said, to his parents. 'Got to meet some friends.'

'Where you going, Jonas?' his mother asked, worry lines appearing on her forehead.

'Don't know. Might go to the cinema in Leiston.'

'How are going to get there?' Mary asked, panic in her voice.

'Getting a lift.'

'Don't you come home drunk, or I'll take my belt to you,' Fred Gorst snarled.

Jonas puffed himself up. 'You and who else?' he sneered, and walked away before his father could reply.

'Oh, Fred, you shouldn't have said that to him, you know it'll only make him stay out all night.' She turned to Laurel. 'He's not a bad boy, and he works hard on the farm; you've got to give him that, Fred. He's a good worker, Miss Bowman, you can ask Mr Breen, he'll tell you how good Jonas is,' she prattled.

Fred snorted. 'If Mr Breen thinks we're so good, perhaps he ought to give us a pay rise – every other bugger is getting one, except us agricultural workers; see our pay scheme's been rejected. I wouldn't say no to one like the miners have got.'

'Fred, mind your language!'

'And you're too soft on Jonas. I'm going to get a cuppa.' He didn't offer to get Mary one.

She shook her head. 'Men! Drive you mad, they do. Still, what would we do without them? You're not married, are you, dear?' She looked pityingly at Laurel. 'Never mind, no doubt Mr Right will come along one day.' She smiled, flashing a mouth full of uneven teeth.

Laurel decided Mary was one of those people who tried to be happy and positive, it was in her nature. She liked her, but as for Fred and Jonas . . . 'I think I'll get some tea. Would you like a cup?'

Mary's face lit up. 'That's kind of you, dear, but I think I'll have another sandwich first. It'll save me cooking when we get home. Hope Fred eats enough, or I'll have to get the frying pan out.' She laughed as she went to the buffet table.

Laurel moved to the urn, turned the lever and a brown liquid sputtered from the spout into her cup. She helped herself to milk. Daniel Breen was talking to Theresa Poppy at the end of the table. There was a plate of fruit cake near them, she edged towards it. It looked dry, not a patch on Mabel's; she put down her cup and saucer, took a plate and helped herself to a slice, eating it, between sips of tea, her back to them.

'Theresa, thank you for coming to Mum's funeral. Before she died, she said she'd seen you in the village.'

'I couldn't not come, Daniel. I always liked your mother. She was kind to me when I was younger, when . . .'

'When we were sweethearts?'

'Yes.'

His voice was despairing, her voice low, with a trace of a transatlantic accent. How many years had she lived in Canada?

'I'm sorry to hear about your marriage . . . I mean, about your loss.'

'Do you mean you were sorry when you heard I was married, or sorry to hear I was a widow?' she teased, laughing.

Daniel sighed. 'You haven't changed, you were always quicker than me. I was too slow for you, too steady, not exciting enough. That's how it was, wasn't it?'

There was a pause. Laurel helped herself to another slice of cake.

'The marriage had been over for several years; we'd been living separate lives. I've changed, I was young and immature for my age. Now, I think I've learnt what *is* important.'

Laurel decided she couldn't stay there any longer, she couldn't eat another slice of that dry cake. She liked the sound of Theresa's voice and Daniel sounded as though he still cared for her.

She looked round for the rest of the team; she wanted to go back and talk to Frank. Dorothy was talking to Mary Gorst.

'Sorry to but in, Dorothy, but I think I'll go back to Greyfriars.'

'I'll stay on for a bit, I want to make sure everything is all right.' She took Laurel's arm and they moved away from Mary. 'I'm worried about Daniel, I think it's all been too much for him. First his mother's death, then Theresa Poppy coming back, and now De Lacy turning up unannounced. He should have asked them permission to come to the funeral. Rosalind hated him. I don't like the way he's monopolising Caleb, who seems to be taken with him.'

Laurel nodded. 'I wonder if they'll find out why their mother hated De Lacy?'

Dorothy sniffed. 'She took that secret to the grave, and I'm not sure Bryce De Lacy will tell the boys the truth.'

Laurel squeezed her hand. 'I'll have a word with Stuart and Mabel, see if they're coming home.'

Dorothy beamed. 'Lovely to know you think of Greyfriars as your home. I wish Mabel felt the same way.'

Stuart and Mabel were sitting at a table, not talking. She explained she was leaving. Mabel looked mutinous, Stuart depressed. 'You go ahead, Laurel, we'll follow shortly,' he said.

She found her coat; it was a relief to get outside, even if the wind, sharp and charged with wood smoke, made her gasp. It was early to be thinking about a beer, but that cake had left her mouth sticky and dry. She hoped Frank would be back and they could have some time together before The Glums arrived. She'd have to talk to Mabel as soon as possible

Chapter Seven

Monday, 28th February, 1972

Laurel threw the blue ball on a strip of sand, close to the edge of the tideline, not too close to the sea; she didn't want Bumper to get sodden with salt water and needing a hose down. It was a chilly morning, dry, but cloudy, a few fog patches lingering over the slight sea. The Anglian Detective Agency meeting was due to start in an hour, at nine, and Dorothy had asked her to be back in time to get everything ready for the coffee break, as Mabel had telephoned to say she might be late. She's been with her son and daughter-in-law in Aldeburgh all weekend; it seemed there was something of a family crisis.

Bumper, his black fur shining in the morning sunlight, skidded to a halt as he mouthed the ball, skittering back to Laurel, his tail lashing the air. She laughed at him – a tonic on four legs. She pulled the slimy ball from his jaws, and rubbed it onto pebbles, before pocketing it. She looked at her watch and hooked the lead onto his collar. He looked at her reproachfully. 'Time for breakfast!' He wagged his tail and turned towards Greyfriars House, pulling at the lead. His vocabulary was limited but breakfast was one word he'd quickly learnt. She looked back at the sea; it was much calmer today. She might get a chance to have a quick swim. After going under-cover as a swimming coach at Salter's holiday camp last summer, she'd decided to buy a wet suit and when weather permitted, she'd continued swimming through the winter. She flexed her shoulders, and smiled. Johnny Weissmuller you've met your match. On second thoughts she didn't want a physique like Tarzan.

She'd come back to Greyfriars on Sunday night after celebrating her mother's birthday in Felixstowe on Saturday. Celebrating – not a good choice of word. She felt guilty at the relief she felt when she got back to Greyfriars. They went out for dinner on Saturday night, just the three of them. It hadn't been a successful evening: Dad was quiet, she was sure something was bothering him – probably her mother. *She* spent the evening going on about the past: how happy they'd all been when she and Angela, her younger sister, were children; the wonderful holidays they'd had at Thorpeness; how she'd been so happy when Laurel got engaged and how she'd looked forward to the wedding and the prospect of grandchildren. Then, she went on to moan about the world changing, the strikes, the power cuts, the unrest. What was the world coming to? Would she ever be happy again?

Laurel tried to steer her mother onto other subjects, but it was her father, in the end, who'd lost his rag.

'For Christ's sake, Anne, be quiet and eat your dinner. I've paid enough for it. You're upsetting the girl. You'll put her off coming home if you keep on like this.'

Her mother's knife and fork clattered onto the plate and white-faced, she got up and ran to the ladies.

Her father looked at her and puffed out his cheeks. 'That's torn it, but I've had a belly full, Laurel. She won't leave it alone. She goes on and on, it's always the same, like a record with the needle stuck. It's her fault Angela died, it's my fault Angela died, it's your fault Angela died. Then it's she's sure she's got cancer, or I'm going to have a heart attack and she'll be all alone, then you'll be murdered, just like Angela, and there'll be no one left in the whole world to care about her.'

Laurel's spirits plummeted. 'She didn't used to be like this, she was always positive. She did have her moments, but she'd usually realise she was being silly and selfish and get herself back on track.' She held his hand. 'I think I ought to see how she is. Perhaps when we get home it might be a good idea for us to have a family talk.'

46

'You can try.' He wasn't enthusiastic.

'I'm sorry you've been made so miserable, I didn't realise it was that bad. Do you think she'll see a doctor?'

He shrugged.

When she got to the ladies, her mother was sitting in front of a mirror repairing the damage to her make-up.

'Mum?'

She turned on the revolving stool. 'Not much of a birthday girl, am I?'

'Come back and finish your dinner. You can have a pudding if you don't like the steak. Dad's really upset, I don't think he can take much more.'

Her mother sniffed. 'I can't seem to stop doing it. I know I'm not helping anyone, least of all myself, but it's like a vicious circle, I keep playing the same old tune.'

Laurel's spirits lifted. Mum knew what the matter was, knew she wasn't helping herself; she didn't have to be told. 'Angela wouldn't want you to be like this: living in a morass of guilt, she'd want us all to be happy and to get on with our lives.' She took her mother's hand and pulled her up. 'Go and give Dad a kiss and thank him for the meal. He loves you and you're hurting him.'

Her mother squeezed her hand. 'Yes, Miss.'

When they got back to Greyfriars she gave Bumper a towelling then breakfast. Dorothy was in the office/dining room laying out the table for the meeting. Greyfriars was Dorothy's home, the base for the agency; it was a large Tudor house with numerous rooms and enough space for all of them to both live and work in. Frank, however, had chosen to keep his independence, staying in his cottage above Minsmere cliffs.

'Good walk?' Dorothy asked.

'Yes, chilly but the wind has calmed down. Did Jim McFall come on Saturday?'

Dorothy precisely lined up five sheets of blotting paper and placed a pencil parallel to the right of each. 'He did and he started work straight away. Mabel will be pleased; he's promised to resurrect the vegetable garden so hopefully we'll have our own new potatoes and veg this year.'

'It would be good if something pleased her. I'm sorry, I haven't had the chance to talk to her yet. I'll try today.' She went to the kitchen and arranged the coffee things, looking in tins to see if there was any cake left. There was the sound of a door opening.

'Hello, Dorothy. Are you as glad to see me, as I'm to see you?' It was Frank sounding pleased to be back.

'It depends. How do I rate on your scale of gladness – five out of ten?'

'Eight and a half, perhaps even nine.'

'I'm flattered. How was the journey?'

'The journey was OK, but every time I drive to Liverpool the landscape changes: more motorways, and Liverpool is all high-rise flats and shopping precincts. All the lovely Georgian buildings are being knocked down to make way for God's know what; mostly rubble-strewn car parks. I was glad to leave.'

'How was your mother? On the mend?'

There was a hollow laugh. 'When I got to the hospital, she'd organised everyone on the ward and the matron was in fear of her. They should have upped the anaesthetic.'

Dorothy sniggered. 'Really! She is you mother!'

'And don't I know it. Seriously, she's doing well. A hysterectomy is no joke, but she's a tough lady. Dad's complaining he'll have to do the cleaning and ironing until she's back to her old self.'

'And did she give you the third degree?'

'I'll say, wanted to know when I was going to marry that nice Miss Bowman I'd told her so much about, and make an honest woman of her.'

Laurel inwardly laughed and dashed to the door. 'And what did you say?'

Frank shot back. 'Christ, Laurel, you sneaky bastard. Eavesdropping again. You'll hear no good.'

Laurel laughed. 'I must meet your mother, she sounds like a sensible woman.'

'Laurel, don't forget, it's your chance tomorrow,' Dorothy said.

'Tomorrow?'

'It's February 29th. Leap Year. You needn't wait for Frank to pop the question, you can ask him!'

'God's strewth, Dorothy, you've plummeted to nought out of ten on the pleased-to-see-you scale.'

Before either she or Dorothy could reply the door opened and Stuart walked in. 'Hello, everyone. Mabel back yet?' Stuart had spent the weekend at his bungalow, tidying it up in the hope Mabel would relent and they could advertise for tenants.

'Not yet, she phoned this morning, said she might be late,' Dorothy said.

'She didn't phone me. Last I heard from her was Saturday morning.' Stuart looked worried and sounded displeased.

'Do you know what the problem is?' Laurel asked. 'Can we help?'

He sat down at the dining room table. 'Family problems; I think her son and his wife are going through a sticky patch.'

'Serious?' she asked.

He nodded and took his pipe from a pocket and started filling it with tobacco.

Dorothy sat down beside him. 'No wonder Mabel's been out of sorts, she adores Matt. We know whose side she'll be on.'

'Where's Bumper?' Frank asked. 'I'll go and say good morning to him.'

'Not interested in family matters, Frank?' Laurel asked.

He shook his head and sighed.

'Bumper's in the garden, in his kennel. He's had his walk and breakfast, but he's always partial to a cuddle.'

He looked at his watch. 'We'll start the meeting in ten minutes, whether Mabel is back or not.'

'I felt a bit left out when you were all heading off in different directions,' Dorothy said. 'But from the sound of it I had the best weekend.'

★

49

Frank looked up as Mabel walked into the meeting, which was well underway. She looked exhausted, and at the sight of her Stuart's mutinous expression turned to one of concern. 'All right, love?'

She sat down next to him. 'Tell you about it later. Sorry I'm late.'

'That's OK, Mabel, glad to see you. You've not missed much, we're just coming to the interesting bit.'

She shot Frank a grateful look. 'It's good to be back . . . I'm sorry I didn't ring you, Stuart. I've been so upset.' Her voice was breaking.

Dorothy reached across the table and patted her hand. 'You don't have to stay, you can go home, can't she, Fra–'

'No. I feel better now I'm here with all of you. Go on with the meeting, Frank.'

'Sure?' he asked.

She took a deep breath and nodded.

Frank told them of his visit to the bird reserve and what he thought they'd have to do if they accepted the case. 'I'd like us to take this one on. We haven't got anything else at the moment, and I personally want to catch these yobs before they do any more damage.'

Stuart waved his pipe in the air. 'Totally agree.'

'Anyone against?' Frank asked. No one raised their hand.

'How would we tackle this? There aren't many of us, as you said, to keep watch in the hides, and I think you're right, no one should keep watch alone,' Laurel said.

'If we involved the Warden and his Deputy, two of us could pair up with them, and I think we could use one of the volunteers, Sam Myres to make the third pair. The other volunteer I met, Edith Chell, in my opinion would not be suitable for night duty. Myres looks a steady, fit chap and he's very concerned about the hide he's built and donated. It's not far from the edge of the reserve, so it's a likely target. Laurel would you be prepared to do a shift with Myres? I could double with the Warden, Ian Hebditch, and Stuart could partner the Deputy, Hal Rudder. I haven't put this to them, and they may not be willing, but I'd be surprised if they said no.'

'What's Sam Myres like?' Laurel asked.

Stuart nudged Mabel. 'Here we go again. I've met him, he's tall enough,' he chortled.

Mabel gave him a sharp elbow. 'Stuart Elderkin, we don't want her falling in love and marrying anyone at the moment. You don't want another romance, do you, dear?'

Laurel pursed her lips. 'Only if he has a Labrador bitch to keep Bumper happy.'

Frank thumped the table. 'Order, order. Mr Myres is too old for you, but he looks like he'd be useful in a tight situation. You can meet him before you make up your mind.'

'No, I'll be his companion. As you know, I'm not fussy.' She smiled at him.

Frank did not smile back. 'I'd be happier if there was some police involvement. I know Revie has told Hebditch they can't spare anybody at the moment, but perhaps if we invited him over . . .' He looked at Mabel and rubbed his belly.

She laughed. 'I bet he's not too busy for a good meal.'

'I'll give him a ring this morning,' Frank said.

'Stuart, do you know what's happening in Leiston? What the police are doing there? Did you hear anything at the weekend?' Laurel asked.

Stuart puffed out a stream of smoke. 'Could be they're looking for Ronnie Biggs; they've called off the search at Dungeness. He obviously thinks serving seven years in gaol is enough, doesn't fancy twenty-three more.'

'You're wandering away from the subject, Stuart. We're not interested in The Great Train robbery,' he said.

Stuart glowered at him. 'I went for a wander round the town on Saturday afternoon, I was bored.' He looked at Mabel. 'I missed you.'

Frank looked at the ceiling. 'For God' sake cut out the hearts and flowers. Did you hear anything, or did you merely buy a Chelsea bun to remind you of Mabel?'

Stuart glared at him. 'No, I didn't, but I can see you had a good weekend.'

★

The meeting finished early; Frank and Stuart decided to go to the reserve and see the Warden personally to tell him the agency would take on the case. They also planned to walk round the reserve, looking at it from a different perspective, deciding which of the hides to cover the following weekend. Frank had phoned Revie and he was coming to dinner on Wednesday evening, warning them he might be late, and wanting to know what they were trying to get out of him this time. Frank seduced him with talk of Dover soles and rhubarb crumble. Mabel said she'd have a session in the kitchen, promising better Chelsea buns than you could buy in Leiston and planning the meal for Revie. 'You'd better get to Aldeburgh early on Wednesday if you hope to buy six Dover soles,' she said to Frank as he was leaving. She stomped into the kitchen.

Laurel whispered to Dorothy, who was tidying up in the office, 'I'll have a word with Mabel now about why she doesn't want to move in here, shall I?'

'Do you think it's something to do with her family?'

'Don't know, I'll go carefully. She was upset this morning; I don't want to make things worse.'

Mabel, aproned, with her hands in a bowl of dough, looked calmer. 'Hello, Laurel, come to give me a hand?'

'I'm willing, but you know cooking is not my forte, but I'm great at peeling spuds, or any other job only needing a low level of skill.'

'I'll just put these to rise, it'll only take fifteen minutes, then we could get lunch ready. I expect the boys will be hungry after walking round the reserve.'

Later, with the Chelsea buns in the oven and a pot of vegetable soup bubbling on the stove, the kitchen was filled with mouthwatering smells. Mabel said, 'Shall we have some coffee, we missed out on our break this morning.'

'Good idea. I'll take Dorothy's through, she said she wanted to tidy up the invoices and get the tax up to date.' She came back and sat down next to Mabel. 'Dorothy's going to the Breen's tonight. Bryce De Lacy is paying them a visit. He wanted to come the day after the funeral, then this afternoon, but Daniel gave him short shrift and told him farmers work in the day. He's asked Dorothy to be there, to give him some moral support.'

Mabel stretched out her legs and uttered a long sigh. 'There are problems everywhere, aren't there?'

'Tough weekend?'

Mabel sipped her coffee, then slowly nodded. 'Yes. It's hard not to take sides, but Sarah needs to be more understanding.'

'Sarah? Sorry, is that your daughter-in-law? I should have remembered her name.'

'Yes, it is, but I think I'd better not say anything until I've talked it over with Stuart.'

'I understand. Is this why you don't want to move into Greyfriars?'

Mabel stared at her. 'Who says I don't want to move here?'

Laurel felt she was beginning to lose her way. 'I'm sorry, Mabel, I must have got the wrong impression. You do want to move?'

Mabel's shoulders sagged. 'I do and I don't.'

Laurel decided to remain silent and wait.

'Oh, Laurel, you're a good friend, you got me out of that . . . you know what . . . when I couldn't . . .'

Laurel had helped Mabel to overcome her fears of not being able to have a physical relationship with Stuart, and so not being able to marry him.

'If I can help, you know I will, but as I don't know what the problem is yet . . .' She paused, hoping Mabel would take up the thread.

'When my husband died, it was hard running the chip shop by myself, Matt was still bringing in the fish, but it wasn't the same without Bill. I wanted to get away, I imagined everyone was pitying me, and I started to get grumpy and short with the customers.

'Then Matt married Sarah and she asked if she could help in the chippy. It seemed sensible for them to move into the house with me, it's above the chippy, but soon I felt it wasn't my house or my chippy. When the job came up at Blackfriars School, with the cottage in the grounds, it was a Godsend. I was happy there for many years, especially with the old headmaster. But when the school closed, I lost my cottage, as well as poor Muffin. I often think of that little dog, he was a real character.'

'Especially when he'd caught and eaten a rabbit, and been well and truly ill,' Laurel said.

They both laughed.

'You liked living at Greyfriars when you were getting over the attack and operation,' Laurel said. Mabel had ended up with a fractured skull, and nearly died when she was the cook at Blackfriars School.

'I did, but when I married Stuart and I moved into his bungalow, it was lovely to have a home again, especially with my new kitchen.'

'You don't want to move here? You'd rather be in Leiston?'

Mabel scrunched her face. 'I know it makes sense to move, and Dorothy has gone to all that expense of altering the rooms for us, and the new bathroom is beautiful. I love being with everyone and cooking for you, it's given me a purpose, made me feel useful again.' She shook her head furiously, curls jiggling about her head. 'I'm all out of sorts.'

Laurel hugged her shoulder. 'Take your time. What does Stuart think?'

'That's the trouble, he can't understand why I'm dragging my heels.' She gave Laurel a wry smile. 'Men are not very good at understanding us at times, are they?'

Laurel wasn't too sure, she sometimes thought Frank understood her too well. 'Vive la différence!'

There was the sound of the front door opening. 'They're back,' Mabel said. 'Don't say anything to anyone, will you?'

'No, of course not, but I have to say, Mabel, it would be lovely to have you and Stuart here all the time, and I know Dorothy feels the same. You're my second family.' She didn't say what she was thinking – at the moment, they were preferable to her true family.

Chapter Eight

Dorothy steered her Morris Traveller down the drive that led to
Rooks Wood Farm, the car's lights picking out the dense branches
of the leafless hedgerows. She'd always loved the house, and thought
it was the second most attractive in the district, Greyfriars being
the best, of course. She'd a weakness for rural Tudor buildings and
the Breen's sixteenth-century house, with lots of lovely beams
inside, was charming. It wasn't as large as Greyfriars, only four
bedrooms, but it nestled in a shallow valley and, with the wood
behind, protecting it from winds, she thought it the perfect Suffolk
farmhouse.

Good Lord. Parked beside the farm's Land Rover was a large car;
with the distinctive vertical bars of the radiator and the winged mas-
cot on the bonnet, it could only be a Rolls Royce, possibly a Silver
Shadow; Stuart would know. It must be Bryce De Lacy's. He'd arrived
before he was due. Not a good beginning. She'd hoped to be able to
talk with Daniel and Caleb before he appeared. She felt like giving it
a bump, but her old Morris would have come off worse. She must try
to keep an open mind about Bryce, but she couldn't forget how
Rosalind hated him, and refused to talk about him and what had happened between them before she was married. It didn't seem right – if
she'd been alive, he wouldn't have got over the threshold. However,
it was up to the boys if they wanted to get to know him, not her. She
parked a distance from the Rolls, leaving De Lacy enough room to
manoeuvre and depart; she wasn't going to leave first. She needed to
talk to Daniel and Caleb without him being there.

She raised the brass knocker and gave several raps on the front door. The door opened.

'Miss Piff,' Mary Gorst said, wiping her hands on her apron. 'Please come in. Mr Breen told me you were coming.'

'Mary, good to see you. Have you been helping out?'

'Yes, cooked the dinner, just finished washing up. I'll be away in a minute.'

Dorothy walked into the spacious hall, her footsteps echoing on the stone floor. She pointed to it. 'What's happened to Mrs Breen's Persian rug?'

'Mr Breen moved it. Mr Caleb kept coming in with his boots on and messing it up.'

Dorothy shook her head. 'Where are they? In the sitting room?'

'Yes, I've just taken some coffee in and Mr Breen's pouring out drinks.' She came closer. 'What do you think about Mr De Lacy? He looks as queer as Caleb, well perhaps not quite as strange. What does he want after all these years?'

Dorothy frowned. 'Isn't it time you went home, Mary? I expect Fred and Jonas are waiting for their supper, or have you trained them to fend for themselves?'

Mary put a hand to her mouth and snorted with laughter. 'I don't expect either will be home: Fred'll have gone to the pub and Jonas,' her face fell, 'I don't know what I'm going to do about him.'

Dorothy didn't wait for this topic to get off the ground. 'Goodnight, Mary.' She turned left past the exposed beams of the hall, through an oak door into the room that was both dining and sitting room. It was also heavily beamed, with an inglenook fireplace, around which were two leather armchairs and a sofa. Velvet curtains were drawn against the night. It was a welcoming, if shabby, room, unchanged since Noah's death all those years ago. She sniffed. The boys had probably not used the room since Rosalind died. Next time she came she'd get the windows open and blow away the stale air.

Daniel was at a sideboard pouring drinks, Caleb was sitting near the fire on the sofa and Bryce De Lacy was standing in front of him, passing him a glass of something.

56

'Hello, everyone. I see I've arrived at the perfect time,' she said.

'Aunty Dot. Look who's here! It's our uncle, our uncle Bryce,' Caleb said, putting his glass on a table, next to a cup of coffee. He got up and hugged her.

She hugged him back. This show of emotion was unlike his usual behaviour, and the note of happiness as he spoke of Bryce was unusual too. She turned, and faced Bryce De Lacy. 'Mr De Lacy, pleased to meet you.'

His resemblance to Caleb was extraordinary, but there were differences, apart from the age gap of about thirty years, this was a confident, well-dressed man, seemingly unbothered by his strange appearance.

He shook her hand, his fingers closed tight together. 'Miss Piff, Caleb and Daniel have told me about you, and what a help you've been to them. Please call me Bryce. May I call you Dorothy?'

Not if she could help it. 'I was glad to do what I could for the boys, *I've* known them since they were babies and Rosalind was a dear friend. I miss her.' She deliberately ignored his suggestion. She moved towards Daniel. 'Daniel, how are you?'

He gave her a relieved smile, then hugged her. 'All the better now you're here.' He passed her a cup of coffee. 'Would you like a whisky as well?'

She shook her head; she wanted to keep her wits about her.

They sat round the fire, she and Daniel in armchairs and Caleb and Bryce on the sofa. Caleb, between sips of coffee, kept glancing at Bryce, who, every time he caught Caleb's gaze, smiled at him and nodded as though encouraging him in some way.

'It's wonderful to discover family members after all this time,' Bryce said.

'They haven't been hiding,' she said. 'You knew where they were. Sorry to be blunt, but why haven't you contacted them before?' She knew the answer, but she wanted to hear his version.

Bryce, ignoring her question, put his coffee cup on the table and took out a cigarette case from his jacket pocket. It glinted in the firelight. Silver, or possibly platinum. He turned to Daniel. 'May I smoke?'

Daniel nodded and fetched a glass ashtray.

Bryce opened the case and offered it to Dorothy. 'No, thank you. I'll have one of my own later.' She was dying for a fag, and the case was stuffed with what looked like expensive cigarettes, but he wasn't going to win her over that easily.

Daniel refused, but Caleb tentatively reached out; he looked at Daniel who was shaking his head. 'I've got a bad chest, Uncle Bryce, I'm not allowed to smoke.'

Bryce laughed. 'These cigarettes won't harm you. They might ease your chest.'

'I believe you are incorrect, Mr De Lacy. Our two senior partners in the agency don't smoke, and Mr Diamond told me there is definite proof smoking can cause lung cancer. I'm trying to give it up. I don't think you should encourage Caleb.'

Caleb glared at her. 'I'm not a child, Aunty Dot. I'll make up my own mind.'

Bryce gave a satisfied smile. She was glad Laurel wasn't here, listening to her make another faux pas.

It was a cosy scene, the flaming fire, the smell of burning applewood, the cold night closed off, but the air crackled with tension. Daniel looked on edge, uncomfortable, Caleb looked enchanted and Bryce, his widely spaced eyes looking from one face to another, was the evil-looking cat who'd got the cream, or the killer cat waiting to pounce on a . . . mouse, or nephew. And, what, she wondered did Bryce make of her? Possibly the disapproving aunt. She should have hidden her feelings, found out what Bryce was plotting, because she was sure something was up.

'I've shown Uncle Bryce my collection of old farming machines and tools, Auntie Dot,' Caleb said.

'Really? I hope you were impressed, Mr De Lacy.'

De Lacy nodded. 'I was.' He turned to Caleb. 'I must see if I can help you to add to it.'

Silence fell as they drank coffee, and sipped their drinks. 'How are things on the farm, Daniel?' she asked.

'We've got a tad behind, what with one thing and another, but

58

we'll be drilling the sugar beet and barley in the next few weeks, and Caleb and young Gorst have cleaned out the poultry houses.'

'What barley do you sow?' Bryce asked, before she could make a reply.

'Ruby and Proctor.'

'Ah,' said Bryce. 'Do you sell for seed or malting?'

'We sell about a third for seed, the rest for malting,' Daniel said, sounding resentful.

'Uncle Bryce, I didn't know you were a farmer,' Caleb said, his voice full of wonder.

Bryce smiled at him. 'I don't do any of the hard work, my manager and the labourers do that, but I pride myself in knowing the most up-to-date methods and the best seed varieties.' He turned back to Daniel. 'I presume you drill winter wheat?'

Daniel's nostrils flared. 'I do and before you ask, I sow Capelle, and it's sold for flour. What's your interest, Mr De Lacy, in us and our farm? Our mother didn't want you here, and I'm not sure I do.'

This wasn't like Daniel, but she was glad he'd brought up the subject of Rosalind's hatred of her brother, and it hadn't been left to her.

Caleb's face contorted. 'Daniel, don't be like that. I know Mum didn't like Uncle Bryce, but I do. We look like each other. It's good to have someone else like me, someone who's family. It makes me feel, I don't know, as though I'm not alone.'

Daniel looked stunned. 'But you've never been alone, we've always been together.'

Caleb shook his head. 'You don't understand. People look at you and then look at me. No one would know we were brothers, never mind twins. But you'd know I was related to Uncle Bryce. You don't mind me saying that, do you, Uncle?'

Bryce moved closer to him and put an arm round his shoulder. 'My boy, you've made me proud.' There seemed to be genuine love in his voice, and those strange eyes filmed over with unshed tears.

Daniel would have to tread carefully, she thought. If he banned Bryce from the house, or from seeing Caleb, he could alienate his

59

brother. She decided she had better change tack and hope Daniel followed her lead.

'I'm sure we're all feeling a bit emotional, after all Rosalind, your mum, has only been buried a few days.' She went over to Caleb, and held out her arms. Caleb got up and she hugged him to her. 'Let's sit down together and talk about her; it's good to remember those who've left us. *I* like talking about my own twin sister, Emily.' She guided Caleb to the chair she'd vacated and sat on the sofa next to Bryce. 'You must have some lovely childhood memories of Rosalind,' she said to him. 'I'm sure the boys would like to hear them, I certainly would.' She waited as he shifted nervously on the settee.

'Do you want to hear about your mother as a child?' Bryce asked Caleb, ignoring his brother.

Daniel reddened. She shook her head at him, hoping he'd get the message.

'Please, Uncle Bryce. Mum didn't talk much about when she was a girl, except to tell us about her nanny. What was she called?'

'Ah, old Ada, Ada Spooner. She was nanny to both of us. She stayed on after we were too old for such a person. Yes, Rosalind was very fond of Ada, as I still am.'

'What? She's still alive?' Dorothy asked. 'Gosh, she must be a good age.'

'She's ninety-seven, she still lives at Shrike Hall; she's rather frail now, but her mind is sharp. Still calls me Master Bryce and makes sure I have a clean handkerchief.'

Caleb laughed.

'Is she capable of looking after herself?' she asked.

Bryce smiled at her. The long groove from his nose to upper lip curled up and revealed yellowing teeth. 'There are permanent staff, she is taken good care of, even when I'm not there.'

Daniel coughed. 'If you've finished your drink . . . Bryce, I'd like to know why my mother refused to see you. You were going to tell us when we were in The Ship; now seems a more appropriate time.'

Bryce glanced at Dorothy; he probably didn't want her to be

present when he discussed this topic with his nephews. He made a questioning look to Daniel.

'Miss Piff and her sister, Emily, looked after us when we were children. She may not be a blood relation, but to us,' he looked at Caleb, who nodded his head vigorously, 'she's a dear aunt. One who's been here for us all our lives, I want her to hear what you say.'

Well put, she thought.

'Are you agreeable to that, Caleb?' Bryce asked.

Caleb nodded.

She could almost taste Daniel's anger. He wasn't used to Caleb being consulted, perhaps he, and indeed she herself, shouldn't have continued to treat Caleb as a juvenile. He was a forty-year-old man. If he'd been given more responsibility, perhaps he'd be a more confident and possibly happier man today.

'Very well,' Bryce said. 'I must confess I was responsible for the breakdown between Rosalind and myself. I'm truly sorry for my attitude when she said she wanted to marry your father. I refused to see him. As our parents were dead, and I was the elder brother, I assumed a parental role towards Rosalind.' He breathed out deeply, and took another cigarette from his case. 'Do you mind? I'm finding this difficult.'

Caleb got up and went to him, his face creased with anxiety. 'Please don't worry, Uncle Bryce, it was a long time ago.'

Bryce clasped a hand over his arm. 'Thank you, Caleb.' He made room for him on the sofa. 'Sit by me and give me courage.'

Dorothy had to shift to the far end of the sofa. The man knew how to play Caleb, but the love and concern in his voice seemed genuine. Did he see himself as a young man when he looked at Caleb? She glanced at Daniel who looked both angry and shocked, as though unable to comprehend what was happening.

Bryce took a long draw on his cigarette. 'I'm sorry to say I told Rosalind she couldn't marry your father. My reasons for making that decision were I thought she was marrying beneath her, and I didn't want her to take on the role of a farmer's wife, with all the hard work and uncertainty that life would bring.' He paused.

Glancing first at Caleb and then at Daniel. Neither spoke, but Daniel's eyes narrowed and Caleb looked sad.

'Rosalind was of age and so I couldn't stop the wedding. I know now what I should have done: I should have accepted her choice of husband and tried to make peace with both of them. I believe your father, Noah, would have come round, but Rosalind swore she'd never speak to me again, and I think she made Noah follow suit.' He bowed his head, and placed a hand on his brow. The picture of dejection.

'The impression I got from Rosalind, and please remember I knew her when she first came to Rook Wood Farm, was there was something more serious than you forbidding the marriage. Pardon me for being frank, but she hated you,' Dorothy said.

Bryce shot her a hard look. He hadn't liked hearing that. 'Did she tell you why she hated me?'

Dorothy was tempted to lie and see what the reaction was. This detective business was rubbing off on her. 'No, she didn't.'

Bryce lowered his head again. Caleb patted his hand.

Bryce straightened up and looked at Daniel. 'Did your mother speak to you about this?'

'No, but she said you were not welcome here.'

'Did she forbid you to see me, even after she was dead?' Bryce asked.

Daniel took a deep breath. 'No. Her death was unexpected, it wasn't something we'd talked about.' Dorothy bet he wished they had done.

Bryce's shoulders relaxed. 'Please, I know this must be difficult, but I would really like to get to know both of you better. You're my nearest relatives and I'd like to help you in any way I can. I'm truly sorry for what I did all those years ago.'

His voice faltered over the last sentence, as though he was reliving what must have been hurtful scenes between him and Rosalind. Whatever he said then must have hurt Rosalind to the core to make her hate him so much. Perhaps he said terrible things about Noah, or perhaps maligned her character.

62

Daniel got up. 'I think it would be better if you left now. I want to talk with Caleb and Aunt Dot.'

'Can I see you again?' He was looking at Caleb, not Daniel.

'I'll see you, Uncle Bryce, even if Daniel won't. He can't stop me.'

Bryce hugged him and the two men were locked together in a tight embrace. She didn't like it; it was over the top.

Daniel strode towards them, his eyes blazing with anger, but Dorothy put up her hand to him and vigorously shook her head.

Bryce reluctantly released Caleb. 'We'll find a way.' He turned to Daniel. 'I hope you'll follow the example of your brother and forgive me for what I did so many years ago. I don't want to bring about a schism in your relationships. A brother and sister were torn apart all those years ago. I don't want two brothers to follow the same route.'

Was this sage advice or a threat?

'I'll see you out,' Dorothy said. 'Stay with Daniel,' she ordered Caleb. 'He needs you.'

As she opened the front door, Bryce turned to her. 'I can see you're very important to them. I hope you'll support me so I can help both of them.'

'I love the boys and I lost a dear and beloved friend when Rosalind died, but this is a decision they must make. I would be very upset if you caused a breach between them; Daniel has sacrificed a great deal to care for Caleb.'

His eyes narrowed. 'Then perhaps it is time for him to relinquish that burden and let me shoulder it.'

She swallowed her anger. 'Why now? Why didn't you keep trying to make Rosalind come round? Why didn't you offer help when Noah died? Is this change in your attitude because Rosalind can no longer speak?'

He stared at her. 'I can see you are biased against me. Please, think of the good I can do both of them. I assure you, I only want to get to know them better in the hope they'll come to perhaps like, or even love, me.'

She shouldn't have spoken out so freely, now he knew her true feelings. She hadn't been professional. But this wasn't a detective case, it was the lives of two men she was fond of.

'Goodnight, Mr De Lacy.'

'Good night, Miss Piff.'

She closed the door on him and leant against it. A shiver passed through her body. Something wasn't right. She'd had a similar feeling that evening in Belinda Tweedie's house, when her sixth sense made her leave in a hurry. If she hadn't followed her instincts she wouldn't be here today. She needed a whisky. A large one.

Chapter Nine

Wednesday, March 1st, 1972

Frank looked at Inspector Nicholas Revie, who was slumped on the sofa next to Laurel in the sitting room of Greyfriars House; he looked replete from the large meal he'd recently eaten, but also tired and worried.

'See those two Scotland Yard detectives have gone to trial,' Revie said.

'You think they're guilty?' Frank asked.

'As hell. Can't stand crooked coppers; give us all a bad name.'

Frank remembered his first sight of Revie as he barrelled into the Harrop's house when he was waiting, with two dead bodies, for the police to arrive. After the conclusion of that case, and because of the possible repercussions to the government if the true facts were told, the agency was offered a special relationship with the Suffolk police as a sop for keeping their mouths shut. Inspector Revie, who they'd all come to like and respect, was their contact.

Laurel got up and threw a few pine cones onto the smouldering fire. 'We picked them up on our walk on the heath, didn't we, Bumper?' She bent down to stroke his nose; he opened an eye, gave a solitary wag and returned to dreaming of whatever dogs dream about. The cones crackled and popped, sending out blue sparks and the scent of pine.

She looked attractive; her hair was lit by the flames, turning it to red-gold, the green velvet flared trousers, and matching waistcoat, with a long-sleeved white blouse, emphasised her athletic figure, but also her femininity. Was it Revie she'd made an effort for?

Dorothy poured out coffee and passed it round. 'Anyone like something to go with it?' She gestured to a line of bottles on the sideboard.

Revie put his cup and saucer on a table. 'Small Scotch, please, Dorothy, and I do mean small, I've got to drive back to Ipswich.' He'd arrived late for dinner and announced he didn't want to talk shop while they were eating; he needed a break from work for an hour or two.

Drinks were dispensed and Frank waited until Mabel joined them before he turned to Revie. 'How's work?' was his opening gambit.

'Getting dirtier by the minute, even in sleepy Suffolk. We've a growing problem with pornography; they should never have relaxed the obscenity laws, it's given the crooks another way of making money, and I do mean money – big money!'

'Really?' Frank said. 'I thought it was just dirty old men in white macs lifting stuff off the top shelf.'

'It's rife in Soho, some perverts will pay anything to get their hands on mags, photos and even film. One of my contacts told me you can even get films of people having an enema. Who'd want to watch that?'

Laurel snorted and put a hand over her mouth.

'Sorry, Laurel. Still, at least I'm not in the Royal Ulster Constabulary, those poor buggers are getting shot in the head.' He turned to face Mabel. 'Once again, Miss Mabel, I must congratulate you on the dinner, and as for that syrup tart, I think you got the recipe from heaven.'

Mabel simpered.

Frank had found it far too sweet; he'd been seduced by its appearance: a golden vision in crispy pastry, but the black coffee was washing the gooey taste from his mouth. 'Nick, can we talk about our problem?'

'The vandalism of the hide?'

'Yes.'

66

'I've been thinking about that. You know I can't spare any men?'

'Yes, Hebditch told me.'

'I may have a solution that'd help you,' Revie said.

Frank was surprised; he wasn't usually so forthcoming. 'Really? Thank you.'

Revie leant across Laurel to light Dorothy's cigarette, who'd joined them on the settee; he seemed to linger a tad too long. She didn't look as though she minded. He frowned. Laurel and Revie? Don't be ridiculous, he told himself.

'You know Johnnie Cottam? Well of course you do,' Revie said.

Cottam was a uniformed PC when Frank was a detective inspector in the Suffolk CID. He'd been promoted to a detective constable and showed every sign of making the grade.

'And?'

'Cottam's due for some leave. I mentioned your case to him and he's volunteered to help you, if you'd like him to. In his own time, of course.'

'Excellent. Thanks,' Frank said.

Stuart stopped puffing on his pipe. 'He's a good lad. It means if we catch them, he'll be able to make arrests.'

'Have you decided how you're going to organise this?' Revie asked.

'We talked it over before you came, but we can modify our plan if we've got Cottam on board. Please thank him for me; I'll give him a ring tomorrow.'

'Here's his home number.' Revie passed Frank a piece of paper. 'You probably won't catch him at the station tomorrow, we'll all be out and about, bullying the public.' He gave a hollow laugh.

'What's happening in Leiston?' Stuart asked. 'I don't get into the town much now, we're mostly here, both of us. In fact, we'll be letting out the bungalow and moving in with Dorothy and Laurel soon, won't we, love?' He looked at Mabel, smiling.

Mabel took a sip of her coffee and didn't reply.

'Can you tell us, or is it hush-hush?' Frank asked Revie.

Revie took a pull on his cigarette. 'We're trying to play it down, but I don't see why you shouldn't know. If *you* hear anything,' he looked at Dorothy, 'as you always seem to have your finger on the pulse locally, give me a bell.'

'I'll ask around, when I know what I'm asking around about,' she replied, looking pleased at the witticism.

Revie humphed. 'In Leiston, and Aldeburgh, there's been a spate of vandalism, and as each week goes by, it grows worse. It's mostly happening at the weekend, usually Friday or Saturday nights, after everything's closed and the town folk have gone to bed.'

'Checked on the pubs?' Stuart asked. 'The landlords will know if they've got a group who are tanked up, and look like they'll be trouble after closing time.'

'We have. No leads so far.' He frowned. 'I think there's a new element involved.'

Frank leant towards him, intrigued by the tone of Revie's voice: hard and worried.

'Drugs?' he guessed.

'No! We don't have things like that in Suffolk,' Mabel interrupted, her eyebrows raised in shocked disbelief.

Stuart smiled at her, shaking his head. 'My innocent wife,' he said proudly. 'They're everywhere, Mabel. I bet there isn't a town or village in this country who hasn't got one user, even if it's only smoking a bit of pot on their birthday.'

Mabel shook her head. 'No. I don't believe it. You're telling me we've got drug-users in Dunwich?' She laughed. 'I've never been propositioned by a drug-dealer in all of my life. I wouldn't know cannabis if it hit me in the face.'

'Ah, Miss Mabel, it does my heart good to hear you. However, I'm going to shock you now. We had to give a stern warning last summer to a pair of holiday makers who were smoking weed behind the Lifeboat Station one night.'

'Where were they from?' Mabel asked.

'London.'

She sniffed. 'Well, what do you expect? I dare say they're all drugged to the eyes every Friday night there.'

68

'Let Nick tell us what's happening, Mabel,' Stuart pleaded.

She wriggled in her seat and turned her head away from him. He sighed and took a pull on his pipe.

Revie tipped his glass; the last drop of whisky fell into his mouth. 'If it was a case of a few spliffs being smoked I wouldn't be too worried, but we've found needles, and also other stuff that suggests we've got a problem with hard drugs. I just haven't got enough bodies to make our presence felt around here. Ipswich and other towns can't spare the manpower to cover the coastal areas at the weekends. We need to find the users, and then, more importantly we need to find out who's bringing hard drugs into this region and where they're coming from.'

'Did you have the needles tested?' Laurel asked.

Revie's lower lip curled. 'Yes, heroin.'

Mabel gasped. 'No! That's awful. I saw that film with Frank Sinatra, *Man with the Golden Arm,* or something. He kept on sticking needles in himself. It was terrible. He went cold turkey, he was a real addict, couldn't live without it. You don't think it's happening to people here, do you, Nick?' she said.

'There, don't worry, Mabel, it may not be as bad as I think it is.'

She sighed. 'I hope you're right.'

'What are you plans for catching the vandals on the bird reserve?' Revie asked Frank.

'We're hoping to be on the reserve this Friday and Saturday nights; I'm seeing Hebditch, the Warden, tomorrow. I was going to partner him in the East Hide, Stuart will partner Rudder, the Deputy Warden, and Laurel will be with Myer, a volunteer. But if we can have Cottam, I think we'll get rid of Rudder, I'm not sure if he's the right man for a crisis. Myres looks a cool customer who can handle himself.'

'Won't Rudder be put out if he's not involved? From what you told us he wasn't too happy with the way Hebditch was handling things, leaving him out when he was involving us in the case,' Laurel said.

Frank pulled a face. 'I'll get round it somehow. Perhaps I can find him another job, an important one–'

'Like making the tea at the centre when we come back for breaks during the night?' Stuart chortled. 'I never liked him, he's not good at mixing with the twitchers. He should realise which side his bread's buttered. If it wasn't for the members, he wouldn't have a job.'

Revie started to get up. 'Right, I need to make a move.' He turned to Frank. 'How are you going to communicate between the different hides?'

'With great difficulty. I thought of sending up a flare if the vandals were sighted, but thought better of it. We could do with investing in some up-to-date gadgets, but we haven't got the expertise or the money at the moment. I can see some kind of interconnecting radios would be useful.' He turned to Dorothy. 'Do you think you could do some research on that, please?'

She nodded her head, got up and scribbled on a pad.

'I might be able to help you there,' Revie said. 'I'll get Cottam to see if we've got any spare walkie-talkies. If you could link up, then Cottam could rush over to the hot spot and collar the villains.'

'That's excellent,' Frank said. 'Thanks, if you could help us in that way that would be great.'

Laurel was beaming. 'It's getting exciting, isn't it? Can't wait for Friday.'

'I'll be off.'

A telephone rang out from the office. He halted. 'Might be for me, I left your number in case anything major happened.' Dorothy led him to the office.

A few minutes later he came back. 'There's been a suspicious death in Leiston.' He looked at Frank. 'Want to drive me there? You've not drunk much tonight.'

Frank shot up. 'Can I be your temporary sergeant for the night?'

'As long as you don't say anything, don't touch anything and call me sir, you're on.'

'Can I come too?' Laurel asked.

'You've had your fair share of dead bodies, Miss Bowman. Try and be a good girl and have an early night.'

Frank laughed. She looked ready to give Nick a thick ear.

'When you come back you can bed down here, Nick,' Dorothy

said. 'Although there may not be much left of the night by the time you return.'

'Thanks, Dorothy. Come on, Diamond, rev up your old Avenger and let's leave rubber.' He'd come to life, his tiredness had disappeared.

Frank grabbed a coat and his car keys. Action!

Laurel peeled herself off the settee, unwrapping the blanket she'd used to keep warm as she waited for Frank and Revie to come back from Leiston. Stuart and Mabel had gone home and Dorothy went upstairs at eleven, after making up a bed for Revie. 'Tell him not to snore, he's next door to me,' she said.

Laurel knelt before the fire and riddled the ashes before placing some kindling on them; she watched as the fire sputtered into life. Then she built it up with some beech logs. The yellow and orange flames licked at the wood, warming her face and filling the room with the smell of wood smoke. They'll be glad of that when they got back, she thought, determined to be up when they returned, wanting to hear what had happened.

Why did it have to be Frank who went with Revie? Why not her? To be fair, Frank was an ex-policeman, and Revie was of the old school in his attitude to women, despite knowing everything she'd had to deal with over the past few years. She'd been a match for several villains, both physically and intellectually; she was as strong as most men, and a damned sight stronger than some; her sea-swimming had certainly added to her fitness and strength. She hadn't fainted or been sick when faced with some terrible sights: strangled victims, hanged bodies, a man with a cut throat and most sickening of all, poor Bert Wiles with his body ripped to shreds. What did she, and all the other women who wanted and were capable of dealing with dangerous, unpleasant situations and murderers, have to do to prove they were as good as men, if not better?

With the fire blazing she decided coffee was needed to help her focus when they got back. Bumper was curled up in his basket, his breath so soft she could hardly hear it. She lightly stroked him, not wanting to wake him up. She looked at her watch – ten to one; she made her way to the kitchen.

The coffee percolator had nearly finished bubbling when she heard the muted roar of Frank's Avenger. She got out three mugs and put some milk in a pan to warm.

'Laurel. Couldn't sleep? Were you worrying about me?' Frank came into the kitchen followed by Revie.

Revie groaned. 'That smells good.' He plonked himself onto a chair near the table. 'No milk, but I'll have two sugars, please.' He looked drained, his face grey with fatigue and worry. Frank looked as though he'd been for a short stroll and was ready for breakfast. How did he do it? Did he have a painting up in the attic of his cottage with a portrait of a tired old man, with more wrinkles every time it was viewed?

'Coffee, Frank?'

'Black, please.'

She poured out three coffees, added hot milk to hers, sat down and looked at them expectantly. 'Well? Aren't you going to tell me?'

Frank cocked his head. 'Miffed cos old Nick didn't take you along for the ride?' He turned to Revie. 'Am I allowed to reveal all?'

Revie slurped his drink. 'You better, she deserves it after staying up and making bloody good coffee.'

Frank drained his mug and pushed it towards her. 'More, please.'

She held the percolator above the mug, but didn't pour.

Frank looked at her, his green eyes shining. 'I'll spill the beans, honest.'

She poured coffee into his mug.

'We were called to a terraced house in Haylings Road, a PC was already there, as the police station isn't far away. A teenager was found in his bedroom by his mother when she came home from work. It looks as though the lad had been dead for about eighteen hours; he was probably dead when she left for work this morning.'

'You mean yesterday morning, it's nearly two now,' interrupted Revie.

'Nit-picker,' Frank replied. 'The mother thought he'd gone to work in the morning, and didn't look in his room, until she came home in the evening. She decided she'd change his bed sheets before he came home. She found him half out of bed, vomit all over the floor and he was stone cold.'

Laurel shuddered. 'Was it alcohol, and he'd choked on his own vomit? A teacher at Ipswich Grammar School lost her fiancé that way. It was his stag night and the best man and other friends got him blind drunk, helped him up to his bedroom, and left him. He was found dead the next morning, on the day he should have been married. It was so sad because he wasn't a heavy drinker, he wasn't used to it. If only someone had stayed with him and made sure he was in the recovery position. It was extremely distressing.' She was conscious of the looks on their faces. 'It wasn't drink?'

Revie shook his head. 'I'd be happier if it was, if you can feel happier about one mode of death being better than another. Tell her, Frank.'

'It's not what you'd expect in this part of the world; he died of a drug overdose, probably heroin, from what we saw in his room.'

Her diaphragm contracted. 'Heroin? Why do you think it was that?'

Revie sighed. 'We can't be sure until forensic tests have been carried out, but Ansell turned up just as we arrived and he seemed pretty certain it was heroin. He's had experience of the drug scene when he was studying in the States, seems to know a great deal about hard drugs and their effects on the body.'

'How did the boy administer it? Needles?'

Frank frowned. 'It looked as though the fatal dose had been injected, but we found apparatus in his bedroom that showed he'd also smoked it.'

'Apparatus? What did you find?'

'You don't really smoke it, you vaporise it. He'd been heating it up and then inhaling the smoke through rolled-up aluminium foil. Ansell said it's called "Chasing the Dragon". When he looked at the poor sod's body, he said he wasn't a regular injector, there was only a single injection mark. He thinks that killed him.'

They sat in silence. She looked at their faces. Revie looked shattered and his furrowed brow showed how concerned he was. Frank looked as though he'd like to murder someone.

'Have you any ideas where the boy got it from?'

Revie shook his head. 'That's what we'll be working on from tomorrow. We've got to find the person who sold or gave it to him. It's urgent. We don't want another young life lost.'

'What Ansell said is even more worrying,' Frank said.

Laurel felt the muscles of her face freeze. 'What's that?'

'There was some heroin left, he'll need to do tests, but he says from its appearance, and taste, he thinks it's in a pure form, one that an experienced drug-pusher wouldn't sell. It would be far too expensive; they make more profit by cutting it with something like baking powder. The purer the drug the more lethal it is, especially to a novice user.'

Revie got up. 'I'm off home.'

'Dorothy made up a bed for you, Nick. You're welcome to stay here,' Laurel said.

He shook his head. 'Thank her for me, but I need my own bed. It'll be difficult enough getting a few hours' sleep, without trying to get off in a strange bed.'

'In that case, I'll take up the offer, if that's all right?' Frank said, looking at her. 'We can have a whisky before we climb the wooden hill, as my granny would say.'

Revie chortled. 'Make sure that's all you do climb, Mr Diamond.' He turned to her. 'Are you safe with him?'

Laurel felt her face colour. 'I sincerely hope not, Inspector Revie.' She got up and walked with him to the front door, and opened it. 'Safe journey.'

He went out laughing. 'I feel better than when I came in. Night, Laurel. Let me know what happens.'

'Like a Scotch?' Frank asked her when she returned.

She nodded.

'Small one?'

She shook her head. 'Two fingers. Please.'

He smiled. 'And the same to you.'

Chapter Ten

Saturday, March 4, 1972

Laurel sighed; it was the second night of the agency's vigil in the bird reserve. On Friday night they'd only been able to cover two of the hides; Laurel had been paired with Johnny Cottam in the South Hide, which was situated towards the southern boundary of the reserve, and Frank was with Stuart in the East Hide, which was close to the beach. The Warden, his Deputy, and Myres were unavailable. Nothing happened, apart from learning how to operate a walkie-talkie, and to have a few chats across the ether with Frank.

Tonight, she was paired with Sam Myres in the new hide he'd sponsored, Frank was with Cottam in the East Hide and Stuart was getting cosy with Hebditch in the South Hide. She switched on her torch, making sure its beam didn't wander out of the narrow observation window and looked at her watch. Half-past midnight. Time was dragging. She sighed again. This was almost as bad as when she'd kept watch in her car outside the Harrop's house in Aldeburgh; she didn't enjoy waiting for something to happen. She wished she was with Frank or Stuart, at least there'd have been some craic. Myres was taciturn and gave monosyllabic replies to any questions she asked him.

She tried: 'That soldier who was shot on sentry duty yesterday in Belfast was only eighteen. Hardly more than a child. The troubles seem to be escalating, don't they?'

'Poor bugger,' was the reply. There was no elaboration.

After a few more attempts she'd given up. At least they'd agreed to pack it up at two if nothing had happened.

She looked out of the slit-like observation window, putting her elbows on the ledge below and resting her chin in her cupped hands. The moon was up; in its last quarter, and the sky was pierced by pinpoints of starlight, clouds discernible as slightly lighter patches as they moved westwards, blown by a wind from the North Sea, bringing with it smells of the Scrape: briny water, mud and the promise of spring. All was quiet except for the occasional squawk of a duck, as something disturbed it.

'Are you bored, Miss Bowman?'

She jumped; she'd forgotten he was there.

She turned to look at him, her eyes now accustomed to the lack of light; he sat on the bench a few feet away from her, a blacker bulk than the surrounding air. 'Extremely.'

There was a faint laugh. 'Aren't you used to doing this sort of thing? Staking out joints, or sitting in a car waiting to catch the straying husband,' he paused, 'or wife.'

The last two words were bitter. Should she read anything into his tone? 'This is one part of the job I don't like; I prefer to be active, or to talk to clients. But it's got to be done. Sorry, have I been sighing like a grampus, whatever one of those is?'

His teeth flashed white when he laughed. 'What did you do before this job? I presume you didn't become a detective when you left school.' He slid along the bench towards her.

He smelt expensive: a mixture of leather and tones of ambergris from his aftershave. 'I was a teacher, head of PE at a girls' school.'

'Ah, yes, I remember. You ended up at Blackfriars School, didn't you?'

'Yes.' She didn't want to go into details about that.

He moved a little closer, she wanted to edge away from him, but she didn't want him to think she was concerned by his closeness. He might see it as a sign of weakness; somehow, she didn't see him as a believer in equal opportunities.

'Mr Diamond was the detective inspector on that case, the murdered headmaster's wife, wasn't he?'

He seemed to know a great deal about them; why had he asked the question about her first career? 'Yes, he was and Mr Elderkin was his sergeant.' She decided she'd do some interrogating. 'Where do you live, Mr Myres?'

The dark bulk straightened. 'In Westleton.'

'That's a pretty village. Do you get on with the locals?'

'I don't see much of them, but they seem a pleasant bunch. I help the village where I can: money for the church roof, supplying labour to tidy up the graveyard, that kind of thing. My business takes up most of my time, any spare is spent on the reserve.'

'What is your business exactly? It must be successful if you can help so many people, rather like a Victorian philanthropist.'

He shuffled away from her. 'I'm in logistics, moving goods for firms all over the world.' He turned his body away from her and looked out of the observation window. 'Perhaps we should be quiet now and listen out for any unusual noises.'

Logistics? New word to her. He wanted to know more about her and the agency, but wasn't keen on revealing anything about himself.

Stuart Elderkin was enjoying himself. He liked Ian Hebditch, he also liked the idea he was on a stake out, and there might be some physical action. He'd always relished a bit of a punch-up in his days with the police, when his bulk could be put to good use. It was satisfying collaring a suspect, handcuffing him and then cautioning him. When the arrest ended in a good result, that is a decent sentence, he'd always felt a glow of satisfaction. His first wife, Doreen, knew when he'd had a satisfactory day by the look on his face when he came home. 'He got the right sentence?' she'd ask. He'd pull her to him and give her a quick kiss. 'Judge got it right for once.' Then he'd settle down to a good meal, a pipe and an evening of telly.

He was smoking his pipe now, puffing the smoke out of the observation window.

'Careful, Stuart,' Hebditch said, 'they might see the glow of the pipe's bowl.'

He grunted. There was nothing out there but ducks, geese, and all the other animals that had a right to be there. No sign of any two-legged beasts. It was another dud night. However, although he felt guilty admitting it, he was glad to have a rest from Mabel. If only she'd open up to him about her feelings. She was upset about Matt and Sarah not getting on. He knew he should show he cared about them, but he didn't know them that well. He and Mabel sometimes had a meal with them at Aldeburgh, but they'd never paid a return visit to them at Leiston. Everyone was busy, Matt with his fishing trips, Sarah with the shop, and the agency had kept him and Mabel in a whirl, with one big case after another. He hadn't seen much of Sarah, but he wasn't too keen on her. She was a hard worker, and the chip shop was doing well, but there was something about her. A bit too calculating? He hadn't liked the way he'd sometimes caught her looking at him. Couldn't quite put his finger on it, but she made him feel uncomfortable.

Mabel. He did love her, but my, she could be contrary at times. He wished he'd Laurel's skills; she'd a gift for being able to ask people awkward questions without them going berserk. He'd have to get Mabel to make a decision about moving into Greyfriars soon. It wasn't fair to Dorothy to keep her in the dark any longer.

He sucked the last of the hot tobacco from his pipe and then laid it on the shelf below the window to cool off. 'I don't think we're in luck tonight, Ian. What's the time?'

Hebditch shone the beam of a torch onto his wristwatch. 'Ten past one.' He sighed. 'This is a waste of time. I think you and Mr Diamond ought to think up a different strategy to find the vandals.'

'Don't be impatient; this is only the second night.' A thought struck him. 'You don't think news of our surveillance has leaked out, do you? That would explain them not turning up.'

The bench creaked as Hebditch moved his weight. 'I gave strict instructions to Rudder, Myres and Edith Chell, that they were to say nothing to anyone, even their nearest and dearest.' He sniffed. 'I'm not sure if Edith has got any of those.'

Stuart laughed. 'She is a bit of a blabbermouth; however, being as the instructions came from you, I'm sure she wouldn't let you down.'

Hebditch shuffled on the bench. 'I assure you, I don't give her any encouragement.'

'I don't think she needs any.' Stuart decided to change the subject. 'It's probably one of those things. As soon as we stop guarding the reserve, they'll turn up again for another night of mayhem.'

Hebditch groaned. 'At least we'll have a break until next weekend.'

Frank cursed himself for not remembering to bring a cushion with him; the night before he'd decided the wooden benches were too hard for several hours of continual observation. Somehow, when you were there bird watching, your elbows on the shelf, binoculars trained on the birds, you didn't notice the wood beneath your rear, but hours of boredom, waiting for something to happen, seemed a torture; the hardness penetrating through to the very bones of his hips.

He wished he could change places with Rudder, who was at the reserve's centre, ready to receive any messages from the hides, via the walkie-talkies, and phone Leiston police station if they needed back up. Although, from what Revie said, there might not be much of that. At least Rudder could listen to the radio or read a book by torch light. Anything was preferable to these hours of boredom. He didn't have enough information or any idea who these people were; if he had, then he could have used the time to let his mind concentrate on solving the problem. If they didn't have any joy by the end of next weekend, the agency would have to try and think of another way of catching the vandals.

'Do you miss the police?' Cottam asked. 'We certainly miss you, sir.'

'Please call me Frank, I'm not your boss any more, Johnny. As to missing the police . . . yes, I do at times. It's frustrating when a case is taken out of our hands by you lot, I still want to take charge.

However, I like being my own boss and the people I work with, especially Laurel, give me a dimension I never had as a detective inspector. We're a good team – I not only like the people I work with, I respect them.'

'I can't say I respect everyone in the police. I was glad when those crooked detectives were found guilty and given good sentences.'

'They got seven and six years, didn't they?'

'That's right. They still talk about you at the station, ask me if I've seen Danger Man lately.'

Frank groaned. 'That's something I don't miss. Still, I think I prefer that one to the other nickname: Donovan. He's a right wanker.'

'You should have cut your hair, then you wouldn't have got those nicknames.'

'I was compared to Kevin Keegan the other day, and asked if I'd had a perm!'

Cottam sniggered. 'He was a brave man.'

'It was a woman, by the name of Edith Chell, a volunteer at the reserve. I think she's got a crush on the Warden.'

'She didn't fancy you?'

'No, and the feeling was mutual.'

The walkie-talkie bleeped. Cottam picked it up. 'Cottam here.' There were garbled sounds. 'OK, Rudder, I'll be with you in a few minutes.' He switched the machine off. 'A hysterical woman has turned up at the centre saying she knows there's a policeman on the reserve and she needs to speak to him. Rudder can't make out what she's on about. She's in a bad way. Says she's tried to get hold of the police at Leiston, but there's only one duty officer and they can't send any one out to help her.'

'I'll pack up as well; it's nearly two. You go ahead, I'll let the other two hides know what's happening. I think we can call it off for tonight. No one is going to start an orgy at this time of night.'

The lights were blazing from the centre's windows when Frank arrived. A raised voice could be heard from outside. He puffed out his cheeks. He wasn't keen on female hysterics at any time, and certainly not at two in the morning. He pushed open the door. Rudder, his face matching his name, was leaning over the table, his hands splayed out as he stared open-mouthed at the woman facing him. Cottam was trying to get her to sit down, but she shook his hand off her arm.

'What are you going to do? You've got to find him. I know something's happened to him.'

He didn't recognise her.

Cottam turned towards him. 'Here's Mr Diamond, Mrs Gorst. Why don't you sit down and tell us, from the beginning, what you're worried about?'

So, it was Mary Gorst, the wife of the man who worked for the Breens. Laurel had told him about them, how she liked Mary but didn't think much of her husband or son.

'What good if he? He's not the police. Something's happened. I know it has. He's never been missing for two nights on the trot. One maybe, but when he didn't come back tonight, I had to do something.'

Frank pulled out a chair. 'Mary? It is Mary?'

She nodded, her eyes as wild as her hair.

'Do you remember Laurel Bowman, you met her at Rosalind Breen's funeral? She told me about you and how much she liked you.' Bit of an exaggeration, but it might get through to her.

'Laurel Bowman? I remember her. She wanted to get me a cup of tea.' Her voice was a tad calmer.

'Here, Mary, sit down.' She collapsed on to the chair. 'Mr Rudder, talking about tea, how about making us all a cup?' He smiled at her and she weakly returned the smile.

'Not lost your touch, sir,' Cottam whispered, looking relieved. He sat down behind Mrs Gorst.

Frank nodded to him, and sat down next to her. 'First of all, Mary, who is missing?'

'It's Jonas.'

'Your son?'

'Yes.'

'When did you last see him?'

'Friday night. He had his tea then he said he had to meet someone.'

'Someone? He didn't say who?'

'No. I thought he was going to meet his friends. He usually goes out on a Friday night. Well, all young people do, don't they? It's the end of the week, they want to enjoy themselves after working hard.' Her voice was defensive.

'Do you live on the Breen's estate?'

'Yes, we've got a nice cottage, Mr Breen's a good landlord and employer; if you want a repair doing, he soon puts it right.'

'Did Jonas drive to meet this person?'

'No. Fred won't let him use his car. I thought he must be getting a lift to Leiston, he usually does.' She was shifting uncomfortably in her seat, her voice rising, as she started to lose control again.

Rudder came in from the office and clumsily placed a mug in front of her, the tea slopping over the rim, spreading out over the table, threatening to soak some papers.

'Oh, dear,' she said, getting a hanky from her pocket and dabbing at the brown liquid. 'I am sorry. What a mess.'

Rudder returned with two more mugs of tea.

Frank gave him a hard look. 'Careful with those, Rudder.'

Rudder glared back, but carefully placed the mugs on the table. Frank indicated with his thumb for him to get back in the office. His glowering presence was not helpful.

Frank picked up Mary's mug and pressed it into her hands. 'Don't worry about that, it wasn't your fault. Take a few sips, then tell me what's the matter.'

She closed her eyes as she obeyed him, then put down the mug. 'Jonas didn't come home Friday night. I tried to keep awake to hear him come in. I always feel better when I hear the door open and shut. I can go to sleep then. But Friday night I'm not sure what time I dozed off, but when I looked in his room the next morning, his bed hadn't been slept in.'

Frank nudged her hand and pointed to the tea. She raised the mug to her lips.

'Was this the first time he'd stayed out all-night?'

She shook her head, then took a few more mouthfuls of tea. 'No. He's been doing it quite a lot lately. He stayed out the previous Friday night, the day of the funeral. His dad was furious with him, they nearly came to blows when he turned up the next day, but Jonas is getting too big for Fred, I think he's getting a bit wary of what he might do.' She sounded as though she quite liked the idea of Jonas giving his dad a touch of his own medicine.

'He's never stayed out more than one night before?'

'No, never. He's always turned up for his Saturday dinner. He might go out again, he usually does, and sometimes he might not come back on a Saturday night, but he's always come home in between.'

'Mary, you must try not to worry. There's a first time for everything. He's probably staying with a friend. Has he got a girlfriend?'

Her eyes widened, as though this was a shocking idea. 'No, not that I know of. Do you think that's it?' Her face softened. 'If only he'd fall in love and marry. That would calm him down.'

Frank wasn't so sure. 'What about Mr Gorst? Is he worried?'

She sniffed. 'Fred? He went to the pub as usual, came back, ate his supper, watched *Match of the Day*, and went to bed. Said I was a mad mare. He'll go hopping mad when he finds out I've been here.'

'How did you get here?'

'I drove here in our car. They said at Leiston police station there was a policeman on the reserve. I had to do something.' She looked at him, her eyes pleading. 'I feel a bit silly now.'

'Are you up to driving home? I'll follow you in my car, make sure you're OK.'

'That's kind. I'm sorry, I don't even know who you are. You're not a policeman, are you?'

'I'm Frank Diamond, one of the detectives from the Anglian Detective Agency.'

Her eyes lit up. 'Oh, that's how you know Miss Bowman. You think that's what I should do, go home?'

'Yes, Mary. And if Jonas doesn't turn up tomorrow, give me a ring.' He wrote the Greyfriars' number on a sheet of paper and handed it to her. 'I'll get in touch with the police for you and see if someone can come and see you.'

She looked puzzled, and pointed to Cottam. 'He's police. Why do you have to do that?'

Rudder came into the room, folded his arms and leant against a wall.

Cottam coughed, and pulled at his anorak. 'I'm not here officially, Mrs Gorst. I'm helping Mr Diamond while I'm on leave. Mr Diamond used to be my boss.'

She didn't look any the wiser.

Cottam turned to Frank. 'I'll follow Mrs Gorst home, then you can wait for Miss Bowman and Myres.'

'Miss Bowman? What's she doing here at this time of night?' Mary asked.

Frank inwardly sighed. He wasn't sure they'd managed to keep their vigils secret, but this news would be all over Leiston and the surrounding district by the end of next week. Cottam mouthed 'Sorry'. He'd realised he'd made a mistake mentioning Laurel being on the reserve.

Rudder leant towards Mary. 'We're checking on the arrival of migratory birds at night, Mrs Gorst. These gentlemen and Miss Bowman are helping us. They're all keen bird-watchers.'

Frank decided Rudder did have a brain after all. 'We'd be grateful if you didn't mention this to anyone else. We don't want twitchers descending on the reserve, thinking there was a rare specimen present. Too many people can disturb their nesting.'

She still didn't look as though she'd totally grasped the tale. 'Of course, I won't mention it, if you don't want me to.' She turned to Cottam. 'I think I'll go now; perhaps Jonas will be back home in his bed. I'm sorry for the bother I've caused you.'

Frank helped her from the chair. She was still a bit wobbly. 'Give me a ring if he isn't back by tomorrow morning, and I'll contact Inspector Revie.' He *would* be grateful for more work. 'Are you sure you're OK to drive?'

She nodded and grasped his hand. 'Thank you, Mr Diamond.' She followed Cottam out of the office.

Laurel was right, she was a nice lady. He turned to Rudder. 'Thank you for the quick thinking.'

Rudder looked pleased. 'Another cup while we wait for Miss Bowman and Mr Myres?'

'Why not, thank you.' What he really needed and wanted was some malt whisky with no water, followed by a long sleep in a civilised bed. Next time, if there was a next time, it was a feather cushion, or perhaps one of those rubber rings for people suffering from piles. Laurel would like that one.

Laurel pushed herself up from the bench, wincing at the stiffness of her legs and back. She'd need a long run, or better a swim, tomorrow morning, to get all her joints working properly. But not an early one; she glanced at her watch By the time she got back to Greyfriars it would soon be time for breakfast. She hoped Dorothy would give her some leeway and allow a lie in. It was Sunday, after all.

'Muscles seized up?' Myres asked, although he didn't sound sympathetic.

'A little. And you?'

'I'm fine. Can you walk to the office or would you like me to fetch my car?'

Cheek of the man, he was treating her like an aged aunt. She shook her head. Or he was being kind, and treating her like a lady? She wasn't used to that. 'A walk will do me good. I'll have a swim tomorrow morning, that will get rid of any stiffness.'

He switched on his torch, its wide beam reaching into the farthest corners of the hide, and she was able for the first time to appreciate the quality of the build.

'Ready?'

She zipped her anorak higher and followed him out. He held the door open for her, and it swung shut under its own weight. He locked it and also secured a padlock through a large hasp.

'No one's going to get in there easily,' she said.

'Only bird lovers.'

'Does the Warden have a key?'

He turned, the torch's light blinding her. She put a hand in front of her eyes.

'Sorry.' He focussed the beam on to the ground. 'Yes, of course. I'm too busy to open up every day.' He started to walk away from the hide.

'I believe you also funded this road,' she said. 'The Warden and all members of the society must be very grateful. I'm appreciating it tonight, it's a much better quality than the other paths on the reserve, at least the ones I've seen.'

He was walking ahead at a brisk pace, the beam playing on the path and the reed beds surrounding them. 'Thank you, it certainly makes it easier for maintenance; also we've been able to bring some of our disabled members here by car. They've appreciated being able to watch the birds.'

The reed beds on either side of the road seemed endless; their spiky silhouettes picked out by the powerful beam. Did he need such a strong light? Wouldn't it disturb the birds? A breeze from the sea played on the dead stems, clicks rippling like a pianist running a finger along a keyboard. She shivered. There were no signs of life; it was hard to imagine birds and animals sheltering there, the reed beds seemed cold and sterile. She couldn't wait to be back to Frank in the Warden's office, away from this boring man and the sinister noises of the marsh.

'Monotonous, isn't it?'

It was as though he'd read her mind. 'Are reeds invasive?'

'They're one of the most successful colonisers of marshy conditions. If they're not managed, they soak up so much water during the growing season, conditions become too dry for them and they eventually self-destruct. Other plants move in like sallow and alder and the marsh disappears.'

'So, no more water birds?'

'Exactly.'

'How do you stop that happening? Do you cut them down?'

'We use a herbicide, the reserve's been using it for about ten years with great success.'

'Is that safe? Won't it kill the fish?'

He laughed, presumably at her ignorance. 'It's selective, only acts on grasses. If it wasn't used you wouldn't have stretches of water like this mere.' He played the beam onto a small lake. 'There's a score of these small meres in the reed beds. They –'

Laurel grabbed his arm. 'What's that?' She hoped she was mistaken.

He peeled off her hand. 'What's the matter?'

He sounded cross, probably thought she was spooked by the blackness and the whispering reeds. 'Give me the torch,' she commanded.

He moved away from her, grunting in surprise.

'Please give me the torch, Mr Myres.'

'Very well, but I don't think this is a good time for flights of imagination.' He passed it to her, and impatiently walked a few paces away.

He didn't like taking orders from a woman. Tough. She directed the beam to the area she thought she'd seen something suspicious, something that shouldn't be there. Damn. She couldn't find it. Perhaps she'd imagined it. Had the ghostly sounds of the night played tricks with her mind? Ah, there. No, it was just a heap of mud.

'I think we should move on, Miss Bowman.' His voice was cold, dismissive.

She put up her hand to silence him, then moved the beam back over the far edge of the mere, starting further left this time. There it was, half-in, half-out of the water. 'Hold the torch,' she commanded. 'Keep it on that spot.'

He obeyed. 'Good God!'

She got out her binoculars from their case and focussed on it. It was a man's body, face down, his arms and legs splayed out, his feet and the lower part of his legs submerged in the black water of the mere. She took a deep breath. Buried into the back of his head was an axe, its long, wooden handle stretching down his back. Black stains ran down from the blade over his head, neck and shoulders, discolouring the light material of his coat or jumper.

She handed Myres the binoculars and took the torch.

He stared at the body for what seemed like several minutes. 'This is awful. It's obviously murder.'

'Do you recognise him?'

'No. Impossible to say, until we see his face. Could he be one of the vandals?'

'What about the weapon? Looks like some kind of axe.'

He lowered the binoculars and handed them to her. 'I'm not sure, but it may be a fromard.'

'A fromard? I've never heard that word before.'

'It's a rending axe, sometimes called a froe. You use it for laying hedges, hewing and cleaving.'

She shuddered. Hewing and cleaving. The taste and sights of death returned. The coppery smell of blood, the stink of voided excreta and the terrible sight of the shell of a human being, life stolen from them before their time. Another body and she'd found it.

Chapter Eleven

Sunday, March 5, 1972

Frank stood on the road looking out over the mere to where the body lay. It was a grey dawn, with a false sunrise from the light of two arc-lamps pinpointing the body. It was also a noisy dawn, as the generator powering the lights chugged away, its oily fumes tainting the pure air.

'This is a disaster,' Hebditch said. 'The noise and all this activity will disturb so many birds.'

Frank looked at him and raised his eyebrows. He nodded towards the corpse, still splayed out against the far bank. 'An even greater disaster for whoever is lying there, I think. Not to mention his family.'

Hebditch looked even more flustered. 'Yes, yes, I'm sorry. That was crass of me.' He shook his head. 'But I hope you'll understand my feelings. This is the most sensitive time of the year. It isn't only the birds who inhabit these reed beds, *all* the birds on the reserve will be frightened away; it could put our breeding programme back several years.'

He was finding Hebditch's attitude annoying; the man couldn't stand still for more than five seconds. He looked at his watch; he wished Revie would hurry up and make an appearance. The reason for his delay was he was picking up Ansell, the pathologist, on his way from Ipswich. Ansell might be recovering from a serious Saturday night drinking session, or worn out by a night of passion with some Suffolk beauty. Somehow, he doubted if either of those possibilities could be true; he must ask him when he got here.

After Laurel and Myres came back to the office in the early hours and told of their gruesome find, it had been all systems go. Cottam, having returned from escorting Mrs Gorst home, took charge, telephoning Revie and receiving instructions. Laurel was blue with cold, and possibly shock, when she arrived at the centre.

'Any idea who it is?' he asked.

She shook her head. 'There's something about the shape of the body, it's vaguely familiar. Sorry, my brain isn't working properly.'

He put an arm round her. 'I think you ought to go back home, get a hot drink and warm up. I'll stay on, see if I can find out anything. It's possible this murder may be connected to our case. I'll see if Revie will let me hang around.'

She sighed. 'I'd like to stay; I want to know who it is.'

She was obviously reluctant to leave, but she leant on him, shivering. The feel of her body against his was . . . he wasn't sure what the feeling was, but it was good, and he felt protective towards her. He didn't think she'd want to know that, although . . .

'I'll drive you back—'

'I can do that, Mr Diamond,' Myres said, 'if you are agreeable, Miss Bowman.'

She nodded and Frank removed his arm.

'I owe Miss Bowman an apology, I thought her imagination was playing tricks. I'm afraid I didn't take her seriously when she thought she'd seen something.' He looked at her. 'I hope I'm forgiven.' His voice was warm and full of admiration.

Frank inwardly groaned. Not another admirer. Myres was an attractive man, obviously rich and dynamic. Possibly more adventurous than the doctor who'd been the last serious man in Laurel's life. Mabel had said Laurel needed someone sparkier than Doc Oliver. He hoped this wasn't him.

'You're forgiven,' she said. 'Shall we get going, get out of the way? There's going to be a great deal of activity soon.'

She was right. The scene was set; all it needed was Revie to fire the starting gun.

★

The crew with the generator and lights had arrived half-an-hour ago. The decision was made, as there was no doubt whoever it was was definitely dead, it was better to wait until daylight before making investigations and removing the body to the mortuary. A photographer had already taken pictures from the road with a powerful lens, but wasn't too keen on the idea of wading out to take close-ups.

Hebditch provided waders; he assured Frank and Cottam the mere was shallow. Some of the waders were thigh boots covering legs to the crotch, others incorporated pants and bibs. Frank bagged one of these as he didn't fancy water leaking over the tops of the others; he hoped he'd be allowed to view the body close up. While they waited for Revie, Cottam took the small boat the warden had provided, which would be used to remove the body, for a trial row on the mere. Cottam climbed out of the boat and pulled it up onto the road. 'Right, I think I've got the hang of that.' He looked and sounded chirpy, despite, like Hebditch and himself, having been up all night. He reminded Frank of himself, when he was a young copper, newly promoted to a detective. There was nothing like an unusual murder scene to get the juices running. The excitement, the discovery of the identity of the victim, the post-mortem, the suspects, the search for clues, and most pleasurable of all, thought processes as you tried to unravel the mystery. He was glad he still had all those feelings.

There was the sound of an approaching car as it revved down the road.

'Good God, do they have to make so much noise!' muttered Hebditch. 'This could ruin the season for the marsh harriers. They're so sensitive to disturbance. As for the bitterns and the bearded tits!'

The car pulled up, and Revie got out of the driver's seat; he didn't look in a good mood. Ansell, his long thin body, resembling one of the reeds, emerged from the passenger seat. He nodded to Frank, looking happy. It must be the thought of a fresh body; well, reasonably fresh.

'Why does it have to happen on a Sunday? Why can't murderers work to rule and keep it Monday to Friday and nine to five? I was looking forward to a lie in and a late full English,' Revie said.

Hebditch looked scandalised.

Cottam made the introductions.

'Well, Mr Hebditch, vandalising a bird-hide is one thing, but did you have to arrange a murder to get me down here?'

Hebditch's mouth opened and closed several times, but no words came out.

'Right. Cottam. What's the order of proceedings?' Before Cottam could reply he turned to Frank. 'You lot are like the proverbial bad pennies – always turning up when there's something nasty happening. Where's our Laurel?'

Frank tried to suppress a grin at the sight of Hebditch's face, which, despite the cold, was slowly turning crimson. 'She's gone back to Greyfriars with Myres.'

'Cottam, did you get statements?'

'No, sir. I said I'd take them later. Miss Bowman needed to get home, she was cold and possibly shocked.'

Revie sniffed. 'I doubt that. She's found more dead bodies than a hungry bluebottle. I'm beginning to have doubts about that girl. I'd watch out if I were you.' He pointed a finger at Frank. 'Death seems to stalk her, but it never catches *her,* it's always *someone else.*'

'Inspector Revie,' Hebditch said, his voice strangulated with anger and revulsion, 'I must ask you to complete your work as soon as possible. All this noise and fuss is disturbing the birds.'

It was true, there was a din from the Scrape and birds, mostly ducks, were circling the sky, obviously agitated by the disturbance.

Revie puffed out his cheeks. 'We will, Mr Hebditch, as soon as you depart. Then we'll be out of your hair as soon as possible.'

Hebditch's lower lip trembled. 'I think I ought to stay, and make sure—'

'Off you go. I'll catch up with you later.' He pointed down the road, like some Old Testament prophet, one wearing a jaunty trilby.

'Make sure you bring all the waders back,' Hebditch said over his shoulder as he reluctantly walked away.

Revie waited until he was out of earshot. 'God almighty, what a fusspot; worse than my Aunt Nora. Right, waders on. We'll use the boat to balance us as we walk across.' He watched as Frank struggled into his waders. 'Who said you could help? Cottam?'

'No one.' He stopped, one leg in and one out.

Revie laughed. 'Doing the hokey-cokey? Get on with it. Me and Cottam will take the front of the boat, you and sonny Jim there. He,' pointing to Ansell, 'can take the rear. That should steady the boat.'

Ansell pulled on his waders, his eyes sparkling, no doubt at the pleasure of wading through muddy water to a dead body.

'I needn't have bothered practising my rowing,' Cottam said.

They struggled through the thin line of reeds on their side of the mere, into the brown cold water. Frank felt his weighted boots sink into soft mud. He took up his position at the rear of the boat, every step an effort, as he pulled his feet from the clinging mud. As they made slow progress across the mere, making gloopy sounds, the mud swirled, sullying the water from brown to black.

It reminded Frank of a field trip when he was a botany student; they'd visited a brackish area where the sea met a river, their task was to study the flora of the mudflats. The smell was the same: gases, produced by bacteria breaking down rotting vegetation, bubbled up as they disturbed the mud, whiffing the air with traces of sulphur. It hadn't been his favourite trip; he'd found the plants growing on the mud flats boring; he and his mates managed to lose themselves behind some mud banks, having a rest from the droning lecturer, as they had a quick smoke.

'Careful,' Ansell shouted as they approached the far bank. 'Don't disturb his legs. Where's the photographer?'

'I'm right behind you, sir.'

They manoeuvred the boat to the right of the corpse. The photographer took several shots of the body and surrounding area.

'Ansell. Your turn.'

'Jolly good.' He'd placed various tools and equipment in the boat. He reached over and brought out a small Dictaphone on a strap which he placed round his neck. He switched it on.

Revie pulled a face at Frank. 'Not as daft as he looks,' he whispered.

'I heard that, Inspector Revie. Please be quiet as I make my report. The body is that of a young man, approximately five feet ten, well-built, he is dressed in jeans and a light-coloured top, woollen, probably a jumper. He has dark brown hair, what I can see of it. The skin of his hands is rough, calloused, which suggests a manual job.'

Frank sighed and thought of Mary Gorst and her son, Jonas, who'd been missing for two nights. He hoped for her sake he was mistaken; the boy was obviously the apple of her eye, and he remembered how frantic she'd been in the office a few hours ago. What would she be like, if and when this body turned out to be his?

Ansell searched in the back pockets of the corpse's jeans. 'Nothing to identify him, I'm afraid.'

Revie snorted. 'They're so tight you couldn't carry a condom in those pockets, without everybody being able to see what you've got.' He looked at Frank. 'Don't know how you manage to move in those things. I've been told they're not good for your manhood, they cut of the blood supply.' He grinned. 'Perhaps you'll get some proper trousers now you're a bit older.'

'Perhaps you'll give me the address of your tailor, Inspector Revie.'

'Really, gentlemen,' Ansell said, glaring at them as though they were juvenile thugs, 'I'd like to continue with my dictation.'

Frank and Revie grinned at each other, and he thought there were moments like this when he did regret he wasn't in the police force.

'The axe, a form I am not familiar with, is buried into the back of the skull, approximately one-and-a-half inches of the blade has not entered the cranium,' dictated Ansell. 'The handle, twenty inches in length, is made of wood.' He turned the machine off. 'Inspector Revie, we obviously need to move the body to the mortuary before attempting to remove the axe. I presume you will want it to be dusted for fingerprints before I remove it?'

Revie moved towards Ansell, his bulk causing swirls of water to eddy round the boat. 'I think the sooner we move him the better. I'd like to turn him over so we can see his face and get some shots of it, but let's get some protection over the axe handle and then we'll lift him into the boat.'

'I think I know who this might be,' Frank said. He told them about Mary Gorst, her visit to the reserve's office a few hours ago and the fact her son was missing.

'Would you recognise him? We don't want to call the mother or father in for a formal identification, if he's not their son.'

'No, I've never seen him, but Laurel has.'

'Right, as soon as we've got him safely across this bit of water and into the ambulance, you go and get her and we'll meet you in the Ipswich mortuary. You remember where it is?' Revie asked, a cheeky grin on his face.

'I think I can find my way.'

'Good.' He turned to Ansell. 'You up to doing the post-mortem as soon as we get there?'

Ansell looked at them, and nodded eagerly. 'It will be pretty straightforward once I get the axe out.'

Under Revie's directions they gathered round the body, Ansell holding the boat steady as the others pulled the body from the bank of reeds, first lifting up his legs from the mere's water.

'Trainers,' Revie sniffed, 'just the job for a paddle in the water.'

Frank took a deep breath and heaved his part of the body up. It was a dead weight and made sucking sounds as it parted from the muddy reed bed.

'Up we go,' Revie shouted.

The body wobbled alarmingly. He felt the strain on his arm muscles and the tautness in his thighs as he steeled his legs and back to take the strain of the weight of the dead man. As they inched back to place the body on the boat, he glimpsed a dirt-streaked face. A young face, large eyes, wide open, staring as if in shock, their surface a milky blue, a small mouth, the lips snarled back, showing neat teeth as though the man had managed to make one last cry of surprise and pain as he was axed to death.

There was a collective sigh of relief as the body was safely lowered into the boat. There had been a dreadful moment when he thought it might slip from their grip and tumble into the water, but now they slowly shuffled back to the far bank and the waiting ambulance.

Chapter Twelve

Laurel steeled herself as she and Frank entered the Ipswich mortuary. It was almost exactly three years since she'd been here, in this very room, to identify the body of her murdered sister, Angela. Saturday, March 1st, 1969, and today was Sunday, March 5th, 1972. Three years. It seemed like yesterday. The smell of Dettol awakened horrific memories of standing between two policemen, refusing to accept the body on the metal table lying beneath the sheet could be her sister. One of those policemen had been Frank, a detective sergeant. Now, three years on, he stood at her side again. She glanced at him.

He nodded to her. 'OK?'

'Whatever happened to that awful inspector?' He'd been the man on her other side as she'd waited for the mortuary attendant to reveal the corpse's face. He'd seemed a cold, uncaring man and at the time, Frank's superior.

He grinned. 'I heard he was promoted to Chief Inspector in another force.'

'Come on in,' Revie chided, 'don't stand on ceremony. I hope you feel suitably privileged to witness this. We don't generally let the public in.' He was standing with Ansell beside a table on which lay a body covered with a sheet.

She felt sick. The white-tiled walls, the yellowing grouting, the aluminium sinks and all the other paraphernalia of death were the same as that day. She swallowed hard. It must be the lack of sleep. She mustn't disgrace herself and Frank by vomiting all over the floor, which is what she felt like doing. Slow deep breaths, she told herself.

Frank was looking anxious. 'Would you like to wait outside?'

She gulped. 'I've come here to see if he,' she pointed to the metal table,' is Jonas Gorst. I can't do that from outside.'

Revie came towards her, frowning. 'Are you all right, Laurel, you look a bit green round the gills. Did he,' he pointed a thumb at Frank, 'drive like an idiot?'

She gave a weak smile. 'I'm OK.' A sweet, sour smell wafted up from the body. The beginnings of decay.

'Laurel was here three years ago to identify her sister's body. I think this room has brought it all back,' Frank said to Revie, gripping Laurel's arm, as he'd done that day.

Revie's face showed sympathy, more than she'd got from the other inspector. 'I'm sorry, Laurel.'

She raised her head. 'I didn't collapse that day, and I'm not going to now.'

Frank sighed with relief.

'That's better,' Revie said, 'more like your old self. Tough but tender.'

'You're getting poetic in your old age,' Frank quipped.

'I say,' Ansell said. 'Can we get on with this, please?'

She felt her shoulders relax. It was going to be all right. She could cope with looking at the body. She hoped this time she would be right, and the man beneath the sheet was not Mary Gorst's son. He'd seemed a stroppy young man when she'd met him at the wake for Rosalind Breen, but his mother obviously thought the world of him. She walked over to the table.

Ansell, looking professional, his eyes glinting with interest, took hold of the edge of the sheet. 'Ready, Miss Bowman?'

She nodded.

As he carefully peeled away the material, it crackled with static electricity; she decided Ansell would make an excellent Dr Frankenstein. Wrong again. The large blue eyes, filmed by death, stared at the ceiling, his round face with the neatly bunched features were as she remembered, but now the skin was waxen. This shell was all that remained of Mary's son. 'It is him, it's Jonas Gorst.'

Frank shook his head. 'Who would want to kill him? Although from what you've said, Laurel, he wasn't a friendly young man.'

'He certainly didn't get on well with his father,' she said. 'I heard Fred Gorst threaten to take his belt to him if he came home drunk.'

'When was that?' Revie asked.

'At the wake for Rosalind Breen. Jonas and his father work for Daniel Breen, they've got a tithed cottage on the farm estate.'

Ansell coughed.

Revie turned towards him. 'Sorry. We're all ears.'

She hid a smile as Frank winced. Ansell's ears were quite a feature.

'Would you give me a hand, Inspector? I couldn't get my assistant in today.' He spoke as though he couldn't understand how anyone would be able to resist an extra day's work at the mortuary compared to whatever his assistant had planned for his Sunday's leisure.

They turned the body over and the wound to the head was visible, the scalp furled back from either side of a deep gash, the brown hair dyed almost black by the congealed blood.

'I had quite a job getting the axe out,' Ansell said. 'The force of the blow drove it deep into the brain. Death would have been almost instantaneous.'

They turned the body onto its back again.

'Where's the axe?' Frank asked.

'Gone to the lab for the fingerprint boys to work on. Managed to get the top man in. He should have results soon, that is if there are any. I can't believe whoever dealt the blow wouldn't have gloves on. Still, you never know your luck,' Revie said.

'I've taken photos of the axe in situ,' Ansell said. 'It's a strange weapon, not one I've come across.'

'Myres, the chap I was in the hide with, thought it was something called a fromard or froe,' Laurel said.

'He could see it from the opposite bank? He must have good night vision. He's not a vampire, is he?' wheezed Revie.

Laurel explained about Myres' strong torch and the binoculars.

'So, what's it used for?' Revie asked.

'He said it was for wood-splitting, hewing and cleaving.'

'It had a double bevel,' Ansell said, his voice rising with excitement. 'It would be used for splitting a log in two, I expect.'

'Is it the kind of tool you'd find on the reserve?' Frank asked.

'Myres said it looked like rather an old axe, Victorian or Edwardian, used for chopping wood or laying hedges.'

'I agree, it isn't a new implement,' Ansell replied. 'More like a bygone you might find in an auction.'

'I'll check with Hebditch, see if they've used anything like that on the reserve,' Revie said.

'Also, from the angle of penetration, the murderer was either very tall, or this young man was sitting down,' Ansell said.

Revie frowned. 'Either unaware, or forced to kneel? Thank you, Ansell,' Revie replied.

'Nick, do you know of any connection between Gorst and the drug problem you've been investigating?' Frank asked.

Revie stuck out his lower lip and shook his head. 'Never heard of him before. His name hasn't come up. But I can ask the team to try questioning some of the likely lads we think may be using drugs. Why? You heard something you should have told me about?' He glared at Frank.

'Not guilty. It's just a thought. Gorst's death wasn't the result of a fight, there are no defence wounds on his hands or arms. Someone managed to get close to him and deliver that one fatal blow. It must be someone he knew, or they were able to sneak up on him when his back was turned. This was deliberate murder. Whoever sunk that axe into his skull meant to get rid of him.'

Laurel raised her head. 'Or could it have something to do with the wrecking of the hide on the reserve and the illicit parties?'

Revie looked from one to the other. 'I think you,' he pointed to Frank, 'ought to remember you're not a policeman anymore.' He turned his gaze to Laurel. 'And you, Laurel, should stop pretending you're a WPC.' He grinned. 'Wish you were part of my team, but I can't have you interfering in police matters.'

She looked at Frank's poker face. She giggled. 'We'll behave, Nick, but remember we are detectives.'

'You stick to your own case, finding out the toe-rags who burnt the hide. Mind you, keep me informed if you see any connection.'

Ansell sighed. 'Can I please get on with the post-mortem?'

'Before you start chopping him up, you haven't given me time of death yet.'

Ansell puffed out his chest, as far as he could, which wasn't far. She thought he'd benefit from exercises to develop his muscles – weight-lifting? The thought made her smile. He was a dear, and obviously liked her, but his extreme shyness, except when he was wielding a scalpel, meant she'd never have to reject him. He'd always worship her from afar.

'As you know, I decided not to take the temperature of the body in situ, as it was more important to transport him safely across the mere. As soon as he was in the ambulance the temperature was taken.'

Frank winced.

'Together with the ambient temperature, the temperature of the mere, and allowing for the cooling process of the lower limbs being immersed in the water, I calculate he'd been dead for between twenty-four and twenty-eight hours.'

Revie thrust his face forward. 'Death took place when?'

'On Friday, 3rd March, between eight in the evening and midnight.'

'That's when we were on the reserve, we were staking out two of the hides,' Laurel said. 'That's awful. Why wasn't his body seen on Saturday? Someone must have walked past that point.'

'That wasn't where he was killed; there was no blood on the rushes he was lying on – he could have been hidden,' Ansell said.

'He was somewhere else? Where? It couldn't be too far, he'd be quite a weight to move around,' Frank said.

'Why put him there? Why not weigh him down and sink him in the mere? I know the body would eventually be found, especially if the water levels went down, but it would give the murderer more time, either to get away or to . . . I'm not sure what,' Laurel said.

'I really must make a start on the corpse,' Ansell said, waving a scalpel at them.

'I think it's time for me and Laurel to depart, unless you feel the need for viewing brains, intestines and lungs,' Frank said, looking at Laurel.

She shook her head, glad she hadn't been the one to suggest they left.

A telephone rang out from Ansell's office.

'Hold on a minute, it'll be for me,' Revie said. 'News from the fingerprint department. I told him to let me know, one way or another, what the results were.'

He bustled out.

Ansell's shoulders sagged, he sighed, then straightened up and pulled back the sheet covering Jonas Gorst, so his body was totally exposed.

Laurel looked at his young flesh, firm, well-museled. What a waste of a life. She hadn't taken to him when he'd been alive, but perhaps he'd have changed once he'd left home and got away from his bullying father. 'Shall we go?' she asked Frank; Ansell was about to start the first incision on the body.

'Let's hang on and see if there were any fingerprints on the axe handle,' Frank said, as he moved closer to the table, obviously interested in the dismembering of Gorst. He'd told her how much he enjoyed dissection in the zoology practicals at university.

Revie came back smiling, a thumb up. 'Bingo! Aren't I a lucky so and so?'

Frank swivelled round. 'Really? I can't believe it. The idiot didn't wear gloves?'

'We should be able to wrap this one up quickly. They'll run the prints against known criminals from the region first, but we may have to take fingerprints of anyone who hasn't got an alibi who lives locally.'

'Are they a clear set?' Frank asked.

'He says they're a bit smudged, but they've got almost a complete right-hand print, fingers, palm and all. There'll be enough to convict, as soon as we can find out who they belong to.'

'Congratulations, Nick. May all your cases be so easily solved,' Frank said.

'Thanks. But there was one thing that puzzled him. On the print, it looks as though there's something connecting the fingers, he says you can see a line between them.'

Laurel's chest constricted. She remembered at Rosalind Breen's funeral, the shock of seeing Bryce De Lacy's webbed hand resting on Caleb's shoulder as the coffin was carried from the church. Surely, he or Caleb couldn't be the murderer of Jonas Gorst? She glanced at Frank. He looked as shocked as she felt.

Revie's head twitched from side to side as he looked first at her and then Frank. 'What is it? You know something, don't you? Spit it out.'

Laurel looked at Frank, wincing as she thought of what was to come.

'We better tell him, Laurel. It would come out anyway,' he said.

Revie was bouncing up and down on the balls of his feet, looking from one to the other. 'Can we use your office, Ansell?'

They went inside and sat down round a battered wooden desk. Revie squinted at them. 'What was it about the fingerprints that clicked? Is it this line? You know what it is?'

Frank looked at Laurel. 'You tell him. You've seen both of them.'

'Both? What the hell are you talking about?'

Laurel sighed. She thought of Dorothy and how upset she'd be if it was Caleb who was involved in the murder of Jonas Gorst. The brothers had just lost their mother, and she'd told them how troubled Daniel was by the attention Bryce De Lacy was paying to Caleb, and even more upset by Caleb's reaction. How would she feel when they told her they'd informed Revie both Caleb and De Lacy had webbed fingers?

'Nick, before I tell you about the people we know who have webbed fingers—'

'Webbed fingers! Is that what the line is? Christ Almighty, anything you two touch has to be different, doesn't it? What have we got now? The bloody Creature from the Black Lagoon?'

'I didn't know you were a film buff,' Frank said.

Laurel inwardly seethed. Couldn't Frank be serious for one minute?

'I want to ask you a favour, Nick. I know you like and admire Dorothy—'

'What's she got to do with this? Don't tell me she's grown frog's feet and taken to hatcheting young men?'

'Be quiet and listen!'

Revie's face retreated into his double chin. He looked at Frank and they both burst into peals of laughter.

She felt like banging their heads together. 'What I'd like you to agree to, is not to make any moves on the information I'm going to give you until tomorrow, and I'd like you to agree to allowing Dorothy to be present when you interview one of the suspects.'

Revie's eyes bulged. 'I'm not agreeing to anything until you've given me the information. You can't make bargains with the police, that's corruption, you know.'

She took a deep breath. She decided to treat him like a stroppy parent who's little darling, an obnoxious and precocious thirteen-year-old sex pot, has complained about bullying by a girl she'd been awful to. 'I do realise, that, Nick. But I know you'll be understand-ing when we tell you the full story.'

'If it goes on like this, it'll be tomorrow before you've finished, so one of your requests will be accomplished by default.'

She smiled; she was winning. Possibly.

She told him about Caleb Breen and his uncle, Bryce De Lacy, and Dorothy's relationship with the Breens, the funeral and every-thing she could remember Dorothy had told her.

'You want me to see the Breens tomorrow and let Dorothy be there?'

'Please, Nick. I think Daniel Breen will need her support.'

He stared at her. 'I need to have a positive identification by one of his parents before I can take this any further,' he mused.

'We've saved you some time,' Frank said. 'The murderer must be one of them. I can't believe there are more suspects with webbed fingers locally. Think of the kudos: brilliant Inspector Revie cracks another case in extra quick time.'

Revie sniffed. 'You're wasting your flattery on me, Diamond. It's like water off a duck's back.'

'Please, Nick. Despite Frank's crass comments,' Revie smiled, he obviously liked that, 'we have given you some solid information.'

Revie's face screwed up. 'Two conditions: one, Dorothy is not to get into contact with Caleb Breen or his older brother; and two, she is to wait for me to enter the farmhouse before she comes in.' He looked quizzically at them in turn.

Laurel looked at Frank. He nodded. 'Agreed. Thank you, Nick. I hope to God it isn't Caleb. Though why Bryce De Lacy would want to kill Jonas Gorst I can't imagine.' He leant back in his chair, and puffed out his cheeks and expelled a long breath of air. 'Perhaps it isn't either of them. Both seem unlikely murderers. Perhaps Laurel and I assumed too much, and it isn't a case of webbed fingers, it's something else on the fingerprints.'

Revie threw up his arms. 'For God's sake, make up your minds.' He abruptly got up, sending his chair skittering across the room. 'I've had enough of you two. Bugger off back to the rest of your gang, and leave me in peace to do some proper police work.' He turned as he opened the office door. 'I'll phone Dorothy and make all the arrangements. What's the farm called?'

'Rooks Wood Farm, Nick,' Laurel said, smiling at him in the hope of smoothing over the situation.

Revie looked at his watch. 'Half past seven. It's too late to do anything today. By the time someone gets to the Gorsts they'll be in bed. Don't want to drag them over here at midnight.' He grunted and marched off.

'I think we should quietly slip away,' Frank said.

Laurel nodded. 'Fancy a walk with Bumper and a pint of Adnams?'

'You need some Dutch courage before you tell Dorothy?' Frank asked.

'Before *we* tell Dorothy.'

'In that case, count me in.'

Chapter Thirteen

Monday, March 6, 1972

The atmosphere in Greyfriars' kitchen was sombre; Laurel was hurting for Dorothy; she hadn't seen her this upset since the murder of her twin sister, Emily. Then, she was sure it had been a different pain, one of loss of part of herself, for they'd never been apart except when Dorothy was in the WAAF during the Second World War. Although she didn't know Dorothy or Emily when she was appointed Senior Mistress at Blackfriars School, when she first saw them together, their love and devotion to each other was obvious. Now, she guessed Dorothy felt as though she'd let Rosalind, her friend, down; her feelings weren't logical, but sometimes feelings weren't.

Last night, when she and Frank told her there was a possibility Caleb was involved in the murder of Jonas Gorst, she'd been upset and angry. Angry with them for telling Inspector Revie Caleb Breen and Bryce De Lacy, both had webbed hands.

She and the rest of the team were waiting for Dorothy to come back from Rooks Wood Farm. Dorothy had been partly mollified when they told her Revie had agreed to postpone his visit to the Breens until Monday morning, and she'd thanked them for getting him to agree to her being present when they were interviewed. 'That was good of him, and of course, I won't make contact with Daniel or Caleb,' she'd said.

Mabel pushed a tin of biscuits round the table, but everyone refused; she placed her hands on the tabletop and pushed herself up.

'Stuart, I've made a decision about moving into Greyfriars,' she said.

Laurel looked at Frank, and jerked her head towards the door. 'We'll leave you in peace.'

'No need for that. I know Stuart would like to move in. I've been selfish, letting Dorothy organise everything for us and putting off giving her an answer. I know she'd like our company, especially at a time like this. You two,' she pointed to Laurel and Frank, 'you're off on your walks with Bumper, but Stuart and me, we're more Dorothy's generation. She looked so upset when you gave her the news.' She paused. 'You still do want to live here, don't you?' she asked Stuart.

He was still, his face unreadable.

Laurel wished both she and Frank were somewhere else.

'I think we should have talked about this in private,' he said, sounding stern and judgemental.

Mabel's face collapsed. She grabbed a tea towel from near the sink, and sank into her chair, burying her head in it.

At once, Stuart's expression changed from grim to concerned. 'Oh, Mabel, please don't cry.' He pulled his chair close to hers and hugged her close. 'Come on, love. I'm sorry, I didn't mean to upset you.' She turned her body towards his and buried her head in his shoulder, her body shaking with sobs.

Laurel got up and made for the door, Frank following her.

Stuart looked at them. 'Give us ten minutes. We need to get this sorted out, before Dorothy gets back; the last thing she'll want to see is disunity in the ranks.' He kissed Mabel's cheek. 'You heard that, Mabel?'

She nodded, her sobs subsiding.

Laurel looked at Stuart. He nodded and smiled at her. She pulled at Frank's sleeve. 'We'll give Bumper a quick walk.' When she looked back Mabel had raised her head and Stuart was wiping her face with the tea towel.

Frank dragged the soles of his shoes on the cast-iron boot scraper set in concrete near the front door, and followed Laurel and Bumper into Greyfriars. They'd decided to give Bumper a quick walk to the beach and back. He looked towards the kitchen and thought he could hear murmurings. He glanced at Laurel, cocking his head towards the faint sounds. She gave a nervous smile and gestured to him to follow her into the dining room.

'I'll put Bumper in his basket in the living room,' she said. 'He'll be fine until after lunch.'

Frank gave the Labrador a final rub of his ears, and Laurel shooed Bumper before her, his tail wagging, happy to be back home. Frank tried to imagine what it would be like to have the temperament of a Labrador, all it needed was to be fed, walked, petted and loved. He decided his temperament was more like some nervy, restless dog, say an Irish Setter, or possibly a completely different animal. He wasn't sure what.

'Dare we go into the kitchen?' he asked Laurel as she came back.

'I think we'd better. Also, I'm going to suggest we all get on with jobs until Dorothy gets back. If we sit round waiting, we'll just get introspective. I'll have a go at doing some weeding. Would you like to help me? After your sterling work at Salter's last year, you can check I'm digging up weeds, not plants.'

'I'm happy to point while you labour.'

'That wasn't what I had in mind.' She barged into his shoulder as they opened the kitchen door. 'Sorry.' She didn't sound it, and the cheeky smile made him want to barge her back; he decided not to.

'Hello, we're back,' Laurel said.

Mabel and Stuart were doing the washing-up, Mabel at the sink and Stuart wielding a tea-cloth. He hoped it wasn't the one Mabel had cried into.

'Me and Laurel, we're going to do some weeding until Dorothy gets back,' Frank said.

Stuart held up a hand. 'Before you go, we'd like you to know we'll be moving into our rooms here today. We've talked it over, haven't we, love?' He turned to Mabel, who was looking into a basin full of suds.

She turned towards them; Stuart passed her a hand towel. 'I'm sorry I got upset. I don't know what you think of me, I should know better at my age. Stuart says I'm regressing, going back to acting like a teenager.'

'Nothing wrong in that, Mabel,' Frank said. 'Just don't start wearing miniskirts and blowing bubble-gum.' He frowned. 'Although, on second thoughts . . .' He gave her a hug. 'Right, come on second gardener, let's get at the twitch and nettles.'

Mabel smiled, although she still looked close to tears. 'I'll get on with the lunch, and hope Dorothy is back for that.'

Dorothy drove into the drive of Greyfriars just before midday, her mind fogged with all that had happened during the morning; she was filled with trepidation for Caleb's and Daniel's futures. She turned off the ignition and sat unmoving; for once she wasn't sure what she should do. She couldn't make sense of it.

Laurel came out of the front door. 'Dorothy. Come on in, you look shattered.'

She looked at Laurel's concerned face. Thank God, she was here. If she'd come home to an empty house it would have been unbearable. Last night she'd been furious with her and Frank for telling Revie about Caleb's webbed hands, but now she was grateful she'd have her support, and that of Frank, Mabel and Stuart as well.

'I'm all right, but I'm not sure what I can do for them.' She got out and followed Laurel into the house.

Frank was in the hall. 'Want to talk about it now, Dorothy, or wait until we've all had something to eat?'

'Not sure if I want anything,' she said.

Mabel and Stuart came out of the kitchen. 'Dorothy, I heard that,' Mabel said. 'I thought we'd just have some sandwiches, and I'll cook a nice meal tonight. Frank's lit the fire in the sitting room and we're all going to have an aperitif to begin with.'

Dorothy blinked. 'I thought I was supposed to be the bossy one.'

'Not today,' Laurel said.

An hour later, Dorothy drank the last drops of her second Scotch

109

and passed her plate to Mabel who was collecting crockery and cutlery.

'I'll wash up,' Laurel said. 'You,' she nudged Frank, 'can wipe.'

Stuart waved his pipe at them, sending smoke eddying round the room. 'I see she's training you up, just like Bumper.'

Frank groaned and followed Laurel out of the room.

Mabel sat down next to Dorothy. 'I wanted to tell you before you start on what happened this morning that we'd like to move into Greyfriars, that is, if it's all right with you.'

A warm feeling, helped no doubt by the whisky, crept into Dorothy's chest. 'Of course it is, Mabel. When do you want to come?'

'We'll stay here tonight and then move in properly during the next few days.'

She grasped Mabel's hands. 'Thank you.'

Laurel and Frank came back, sat down and looked at her expectantly.

She took a deep breath and straightened her shoulders.

Dorothy waited in the road that led up to Rooks Wood Farm, her engine off. She wound down her side-window, and breathed in the morning air, fresh from the east, with tangs of sea salt and approaching spring; it looked like another day of sunshine and showers. The harsh caw-caws of the rooks as they flew from their treetop home were like cries of impending doom. She clasped her hands and lowered her head. Sometimes she didn't pray from one Sunday to the next, but today she felt the need. 'Dear God, let it not be Caleb who's involved in this murder. Let it be Bryce De Lacy, if it has to be one or the other.' Shouldn't she be praying for Jonas' soul and for Mary Gorst, who'd be devastated by her loss? If Caleb was guilty then, for the first time, she was glad Rosalind was dead. But if she'd been alive then this wouldn't have happened; she always kept a close eye on Caleb. Could they both be involved, Caleb and Bryce? She shook her head. This was all nonsense. It didn't make sense. Caleb a killer? No!

At the sound of an approaching car, she turned on the ignition.

The police car drew level and Revie got out and came to her open window.

'Morning, Dorothy. This is a messy business. I'm sorry you've got involved. Are you sure you want to be here?' he asked, hopefully.

'I do, and thank you for letting me support the boys. I've known them since they were babies and their mother was a close friend.'

He leant into the car. 'Yes, Frank and Laurel told me. You must play a neutral role. You'll have to listen and watch. No interfering, or I'll have to ask you to leave. Agreed?'

She pulled a face. 'That'll be difficult.' He gave her a stern look. 'I agree.'

'I better warn you I'll be asking both of them to accompany me back to Ipswich to have their fingerprints taken.'

Her stomach dropped. 'Suppose Caleb's got an alibi? You won't need to take his fingerprints then, will you?'

'Alibis can be broken, as you well know.'

She tried to suppress the anger which was bubbling up through her body. She swallowed, trying to keep her voice level. 'What about Mr De Lacy? Is he going to be fingerprinted?'

Revie shook his head. 'Miss Piff, I can't divulge all my moves to you. You understand my position?' Although his words were terse, his voice was kind.

'I'm sorry, it's just . . .'

'I understand. Everyone will be treated fairly and all I'm looking for is justice.' He moved away from her car. 'I can tell you more officers are on their way to the Gorsts to break the news and to ask either Mr or Mrs Gorst, or both, to formally identify their son. Follow my car, please.'

She parked next to the police car, in front of the farmhouse. He opened her car door. 'Ready. I need to get on with this, we've got a busy day ahead.' She stepped out. The driver, a uniformed PC, joined them.

'Have you got it?' Revie asked him.

'Yes, sir.' The driver replied, holding up a large paper bag.

'Good.' Revie marched towards the farmhouse.

Daniel Breen opened the door and looked perplexed at the sight of a strange man, a PC and his Aunt Dorothy.

'Mr Daniel Breen?' asked Revie.

'Yes. What's the matter? Auntie Dot, what's happened?'

'Can we go inside, sir?' Revie asked, not waiting for the answer, but pushing past Daniel, turning and then making sure he didn't have a chance to question her.

'Is your brother, Mr Caleb Breen, at home?'

'Yes, he's in the chicken sheds, I'll go and—'

'No need, sir.' Revie waved a hand at the PC. 'Find him.' He turned to Daniel. 'Is there somewhere we can sit down? I'll explain everything when your brother gets here.'

Daniel led them to the sitting room. The air was cold and lifeless, the grate in the inglenook fireplace full of dead ashes. She remembered how it had been when she was last here. Watching as Bryce De Lacy wooed Caleb with flattery, and how Daniel's face showed how hurt he was by Caleb's reactions.

'What are you doing here, Auntie Dot? Has something happened at Greyfriars?'

She looked at Revie. He shook his head. 'Miss Piff is here because, of, er, her concern for the two of you. She's here on the understanding all she is offering is support, nothing else. Agreed, Miss Piff.'

'Yes, I've been allowed to be present because I may be of some help later. Be patient, Daniel. It will all become clear.' She wished it was the truth.

There was the sound of boots clattering on the stone flooring of the hall; the door was flung open and Caleb catapulted into the room. 'What's all this? Why has this policeman brought me back? He said I had to come, quick, when I said I wouldn't, he said he'd arrest me if I didn't come. Daniel, what's happening?'

Daniel stood up, but Revie was quicker, and he held a hand up to stop Daniel from going to his brother.

'Please sit down, Mr Breen, and I'll explain everything.'

Caleb froze. 'Auntie Dot? Why are you here? Did you bring the police?'

112

'Caleb, do as Inspector Revie asks you. I'm here to help if I can. Be a good boy and sit down.' She spoke firmly and managed to give him a smile. He shot over to the sofa, before Revie could stop him, and sat next to Daniel.

Revie stood before them. He indicated to the PC to take notes. 'First of all, I must tell you that yesterday the body of Jonas Gorst was found on the bird reserve.' His eyes didn't leave Caleb's face.

Daniel put a hand to his mouth. 'My God, Mary! Does she know?'

Revie looked at his watch. 'She or her husband will be on their way to formally identify him. However, there is no doubt it's Jonas Gorst.'

Daniel half-rose. 'I need to go to her.'

'Sit down, Mr Breen. She might be on her way to Ipswich, if not a WPC will be with her until her husband returns.'

Caleb was silent, his face expressionless.

'How did he die?' Daniel asked.

'The findings of the post–mortem are not yet known, but I can tell you Jonas Gorst was murdered, there is no doubt about that.'

'Murdered! Jonas? Was it a fight? Was he mixed up with a gang? I know Mary was worried about him. She came to see me yesterday, saying he hadn't come home for two nights.'

Daniel looked shocked, but in control of himself. What would happen when Revie took it to the next stage?

Revie sat down. 'We believe Mr Gorst was killed on Friday night. I would like both of you to tell me where you were on the evening of Friday, March 3rd, between the hours of eight and midnight.'

Daniel's eyes bulged. 'My God, do you think one of us killed him?'

Caleb's body seemed to shrink as he retreated back against the sofa's cushions.

'Please answer the question. You first, Mr Breen, and then you, Mr Caleb Breen.'

Daniel's chest was heaving; he put an arm round his brother. 'Don't worry, Caleb. I expect the inspector has to ask these questions to everyone who knew Jonas. That's right, isn't it, Inspector?'

Dear Daniel, he was trying to suppress his emotions for the sake of Caleb. He knew if he showed he was upset, it would trigger a negative reaction from his brother.

'Quite right, sir. So, where were you between those times?' Revie's voice was relentless.

Daniel glanced at her. Oh, dear, what was coming? But she noticed a slight smile.

'I was with a friend in Aldeburgh. We had a meal and then went to the cinema.'

'And the name and address of this friend?'

Daniel shot her a quick look. 'Miss Theresa Poppy.' He gave the address.

Caleb pulled away from him. 'You didn't tell me you were seeing her again. She doesn't like me. I think that's why she went away before. You said you were going to see some old friends. You lied to me, Daniel. I'll tell Uncle Bryce you lied to me. He'll be cross.'

Daniel reddened. 'Theresa is an old friend. I didn't tell you because I didn't know how the evening would go.'

From the former smile on his face, Dorothy thought it must have gone well. She hoped so. It was good to hear something positive.

'What time did you meet Miss Poppy?'

'I picked her up from her house in Dunwich at six-thirty.'

'And what time did you get back to the farm?'

The blush deepened. 'It was after one o clock,' he muttered.

Dorothy looked down and pressed her lips together. The evening seemed to have gone extremely well.

'Mr Breen,' Revie was addressing Caleb. 'Would you tell me where you were on Friday between those hours?'

Caleb's Adam's apple was bobbing up and down like a yo-yo and his far-apart eyes were swivelling like a chameleon's. The poor boy looked the picture of guilt. 'I was here.'

'By yourself?' Revie asked.

'Yes.'

'Did you leave the house during that evening?'

'Yes.'

'Where did you go?'

'I went and checked on the chickens, I couldn't remember if I'd closed the sheds.'

'You didn't leave the farm?'

'No.'

'What did you do, apart from check on the chickens?'

Caleb's irises rolled up, nearly disappearing as he seemed to try and remember what had happened that night. 'I don't know. I watched the telly. I made a drink of cocoa. I went to bed. Daniel hadn't come back and it was late.'

'How late?'

'Can't remember – late. I went to bed.'

Revie turned to Daniel. 'When you came back from Aldeburgh did you check your brother was in his bedroom?'

Daniel's eyes narrowed. He doesn't know whether to lie for him or not, she thought.

'No. I didn't check.'

'So, your brother might not have been in the house when you returned?' Revie said.

'I was, I told you I was,' Caleb wailed.

Revie turned his body towards him. 'I'm afraid we have to work on proof, sir. We're not saying you weren't in the house when Mr Breen came back, but unfortunately you can't prove it.' He motioned to the PC and took the parcel from him.

'I'd like both of you to look at this and tell me if you've seen it before.' He carefully unwrapped the parcel. 'I must ask you not to touch it.'

What was he doing? What was it he was going to show them? She leant forward. It was a farm implement. Was this the murder weapon? My God, she'd seen it before, or one that was almost the same. She wanted to shout out to both the Breens, 'Don't say anything! Don't incriminate yourselves.' Revie shot her a look. She realised her hand was over her mouth; she looked away.

'Why, that's like my froe,' Caleb said. 'I've one like that in my collection.'

Her heart sank. Poor Caleb, for if this was what she feared, then surely his words were those of an innocent man.

'Your collection, Mr Breen? Would you like to tell me about it?' Revie asked.

'Why? What's it to you?' Caleb muttered.

Revie looked at Daniel, who was white-faced, obviously realising what was happening. 'Perhaps *you* would tell me about your brother's collection. A collection of what? Tools like this?' He pushed the froe towards Daniel.

'It isn't his collection, it's mine,' Caleb said, obviously indignant.

'Caleb's interested in the old tools that were used in agriculture in the past, although some have their uses today,' Daniel said, having difficulty in getting the words out.

Dorothy inwardly winced.

'Where is your collection kept?' Revie asked Caleb.

'In the old barn, I've got over forty different tools, haven't I, Daniel?'

Daniel nodded, looking sick to the soul.

'I'd like to see them, Mr Breen.' Revie stood up. 'Now, if you please.'

Caleb looked at Daniel, and then glanced towards her. 'You've seen them, haven't you, Auntie Dot? Will you come with us?'

Yes, she'd seen them many times. The collection was started by their father, Noah, and when he died, Rosalind had encouraged Caleb to take over the responsibility for looking after them and adding to the collection. Her heart ached for both of them. There was an inevitability about the conversation between Revie and the boys; she prayed the collection was complete and there wasn't an empty space where Caleb's rending axe hung.

Daniel led the way from the house, Revie between him and Caleb, then the PC, she walking behind them. They went around the side of the house. There were three barns at the back, surrounding a tidy farm yard. Beyond the barns the rooks were busy flying to and fro from the oak trees to the fields, caw-cawing. They seemed to be screaming sounds of warning. Beware! Beware!

The nearest barn was the oldest and smallest, with sides built of Tudor bricks, inset between blackened beams, with a tiled roof, that undulated and sagged. It looked as though it had been there forever. Daniel pulled open one of the two wooden doors to reveal a central space filled with old machines: a winnowing machine, a broadcast barrow, a chaff box and many more old bygones of a former farming life. On the walls hung different tools: seed-fiddles, breast ploughs, a wooden dyke shovel, a milk yoke and several scythes.

Caleb pointed to an empty space on a wall, between tail-docking shears and a set of four horse boots. 'It isn't there!' He turned to Revie. 'Is that my fromard?' he asked.

Revie beckoned him closer. 'Have a look, sir. But don't touch it.' He held it towards Caleb, protecting the long handle with a cloth. She thought Revie had the look of the devil, tempting Caleb to incriminate himself. She glanced at Daniel; he looked totally confused, as though unable to pull his thoughts together. She understood his feelings; she too felt helpless as the remorseless questioning went on.

'Is it yours, sir?' Revie's voice was a smooth as silk. It was a side of him she hadn't seen before. He was like a silent torpedo homing in on its prey, strong, relentless, not to be diverted from its mission.

Caleb bent over the fromard. 'It looks like mine, doesn't it, Daniel? I'm sure it's mine. Look, Daniel, what do you think?'

Daniel moved close to him. 'They're all much of a muchness, Caleb. I don't think it's the one that hung there. Perhaps you moved it to use it for something and forgot to put it back.'

Caleb shook his head. 'No. Mother told me not to use them, only to keep everything in working order.' He turned back towards Revie. 'I always kept the edges good and sharp and polished the handles.'

Revie smiled. 'You've certainly got a good collection here, Mr Breen. Now, can you tell me the last time you saw the axe?'

Caleb frowned and looked at Daniel. 'I don't know. It's Monday, today, isn't it?'

'Yes, it's Monday, Caleb.'

Caleb looked down at the floor of the barn, an earth floor, smoothed and hardened by the feet of centuries. 'I'm not sure.

I haven't looked at them for a bit. Not since Mother died. Can you remember, Daniel?'

'No, I can't. I haven't been in here for some time.'

Revie stamped his feet, as though they were cold. 'We'll leave that for the moment. However, Mr Breen,' he addressed Caleb, 'you are sure this axe belongs to you?'

'Yes, I'm sure. I can see a little nick on the blade. I was working on that, trying to smooth it off. Where did you find it?'

'It was buried in the back of Jonas Gorst's head. Did you swing this axe and kill him, Mr Breen?' Revie said, staring intently at Caleb.

Caleb's strange eyes seemed to grow bigger, what little colour he had in his face drained away, and he swayed backwards.

Daniel caught him and held him close. 'How dare you accuse my brother of murder?' he snarled, looking as though he was about to attack Revie.

'It's a question that's got to be asked. Now, let's get back to the house.'

Daniel helped Caleb out of the barn.

Frank passed Dorothy another whisky. 'Here. Drink this.'

Dorothy wiped her eyes with the tissue Laurel passed to her. 'Thank you, all of you. It's helped to talk about it. I felt so helpless, there was nothing I could do.'

'You were there, you witnessed what was said and done. They'll know you're on their side,' Frank said.

'What happened then?' Mabel asked, looking as tearful as Dorothy, Stuart's arm round her as he puffed on another pipeful of shag tobacco.

'They both had to go back with him to Ipswich to have their fingerprints taken.'

'How did they react?' Frank asked.

'Caleb was terrified, he retreated into himself. He was as bad as I've seen him. This'll put him back years. I thought he might be getting over his mother's death, as much as he could. I know if it comes to a trial, the jury will take one look at him – he'll be a bundle of nerves, and his looks won't help – and they'll decide he's a mad man, and capable of murder,' Dorothy said.

'Come on, Dorothy, we're not there yet, and hopefully never will be,' Frank said.

'What about Daniel?' Laurel asked.

'He managed to control himself, but he gave Revie an earful, saying it was ridiculous, Caleb wasn't vicious, and anyway how was it possible he'd killed Gorst when Gorst was much stronger than Caleb?'

'He's got a point there,' Stuart mused.

'Daniel was worried about who'd look after the farm while they were in Ipswich. I said I'd get help from a neighbouring farm for the next few days, in case there are any problems. That's why I was so long, but I think everything is covered.' She paused. 'I shouldn't wish it on anyone, but I pray those aren't Caleb's fingerprints on the handle and that they're Bryce De Lacy's.'

Frank hoped, for Dorothy's sake, she was right. But in that case, how did De Lacy get hold of the fromard, and why would he want to kill Jonas Gorst?

Chapter Fourteen

Wednesday, March 8, 1972

Frank slammed the door of his car, didn't bother to lock it, and ran across the reserve car park, and up the steps to the Warden's office, as a sudden squall of cold rain was driving in from the North Sea, hitting his face like a tattoo of sharp fingernails. He pushed open the door.

Five chairs were arranged round the table, all empty at the moment, but from the inner office there were the sounds of an electric kettle coming to the boil, the clash of crockery, and the smell of something freshly baked. Was this a side of Hebditch he hadn't seen before?

'Hello,' he said.

There were sounds of heavy footsteps and a face peered round the door. 'Oh, it's you,' Edith Chell said, glowering at him.

'Good morning, Miss Chell. Have you got Mr Hebditch in there with you?' he asked, cocking his head.

The glower turned to a scowl. 'No, I haven't. He had to go out all of a sudden to check on something. I came early to make sure everything was ready for the meeting. He said he'd be back in time for the start.'

'Never mind, you've got me,' he said, sure in the knowledge Edith obviously didn't fancy him.

She looked at him suspiciously. 'Think you're a clever clog, don't you? That's the trouble with Scousers, their tongues are so sharp they cut their own mouths.'

He wasn't sure she'd got that one right, but he couldn't be bothered to argue the toss. 'Making some coffee?'

'Not until Mr Hebditch gets back.'

'Here he comes.' Frank pointed to the window. The Warden was scampering across the car park, holding on to his flat cap with one hand, and pulling up the collar of his jacket with the other. The squall had turned into a storm, rain lashing at the window, hailstones mixed with the sheets of water.

Edith rushed to the door and flung it open. 'Oh, Ian, you're right soaked!' She grabbed his arm and hauled him into the office. 'I'll get a towel. Take that jacket off, you'll catch your death of cold if you sit around in that.'

Hebditch's face was puce; he removed her hand from his arm. 'Really, Miss Chell. It's only a spot of water. Don't make such a fuss.'

Edith's plump cheeks deflated. 'I'm sorry, Ian. I'll make us a cup, shall I? I dare say a hot drink wouldn't go amiss?'

Hebditch regained his composure. 'Yes, please do that, Edith. Would you like a coffee, Mr Diamond?'

'Thank you. Black, please, Miss Chell.'

She looked at him, curled a lip, and marched into the office.

'Edith,' Hebditch called, 'Mr Myres and Mr Rudder have both just driven into the car park, so make that two more coffees, please.'

There was a grunt from the office.

After greetings and removal of coats, the four men were seated round the table when Edith came in carrying a tray with five mugs, a milk jug, and a plate of buttered scones. She triumphantly passed them round. 'I got up at six this morning to make these for you.'

Frank didn't think the 'for you' was inclusive; Edith's gaze was fixed on the Warden as she said these words.

'Thank you, Edith, but I'm not hungry at the moment,' Hebditch said. 'I had a very large breakfast.'

Her face reddened and Frank wasn't sure if she was going to cry, or pour the contents of the milk jug over Hebditch.

Frank bit into his scone. It wasn't bad, light and plenty of raisins.

Not as good as Mabel's but . . . 'Excellent, Miss Chell, Mr Elderkin will be sorry to have missed these.'

Hebditch had phoned the agency yesterday, saying he was calling an urgent meeting the next day to discuss the investigation of the vandalism of the hides. They'd decided it didn't need more than one of them to attend and Frank had volunteered.

She looked at him suspiciously and then focussed on Myres, who'd also refused a scone.

'What's the matter? My scones not good enough for you?'

Myres seemed to be taken by surprise by her attack. 'Miss Chell . . . I'm not hungry. You're taking this too personally. I'm sure they're delicious—'

'Well, Mr Rudder likes them!' Rudder was half-way through a scone.

Hebditch rapped on the table with his biro. 'Edith, that's enough. No one asked you to get up at the crack of dawn and start baking. We've wasted enough of everyone's time. We must start the meeting.'

Frank decided Hebditch was braver than he'd first thought, as Edith Chell's considerable chest swelled, probably with indignation.

Hebditch settled back in his seat, looking pleased with himself. 'I've called this meeting so we can discuss how we should proceed with the investigation of the damage to the hide and the trespass of yobs on the reserve.'

Frank thought he knew where this was going. He wouldn't be sorry if Hebditch called it a day; two nights sitting in a hide was enough as far as he was concerned, and in view of what had happened, he didn't think there would be any more vandalism in the near future. However, it wasn't up to him to call a halt.

'I would like to review the situation in the light of the happenings on Sunday morning. Mr Diamond, have you any more news for us? Have the police made an arrest? I understand three people were taken to Ipswich police station on Monday.'

Edith's eyes widened until they were as round as polished pennies. 'Have they got the murderer? Was it someone from Leiston? You heard about that boy being found dead in bed by his mother?

My neighbour told me she'd heard he'd been on drugs. Is there a drug ring in Leiston? I've had my suspicions for a time.' She tapped her nose. 'Nothing much gets past me.'

Hebditch sighed, Myres kept a straight face and Rudder, who'd been busy polishing off the scones, choked, presumably on the crumbs, and had to go into the office for a glass of water.

When he returned Hebditch turned to Frank. 'Any information?'

Frank wasn't keen on telling them, but they'd know soon enough. 'Yes, Caleb Breen has been arrested for the murder of Jonas Gorst.'

There was an intake of breath from Hebditch, Myres shot a glance at Frank, Rudder shook his head.

'What a load of nonsense,' Edith shouted. 'Why that Caleb couldn't blow the skin off a rice pudding! Him murder Jonas Gorst? The police want their heads examining. That poor Caleb, he's a timid soul. I've often spoken with him when we've met on the reserve. He hardly says anything.'

Frank wasn't surprised, he wouldn't be able to get a word in edgeways, even if he wanted to. But he liked the way she'd claimed he was innocent.

'Jonas Gorst is five times as strong as Caleb. How was he supposed to have killed him?' she asked Frank.

'I'm afraid I can't give you any details,' he said.

'Can't or won't?' she asked, her eyes narrowing.

Frank shrugged.

'This is terrible,' Hebditch said. 'I never thought of Caleb as being dangerous; peculiar perhaps, but I agree with Miss Chell, I find it difficult to believe.'

'All I can tell you is the police have compelling evidence. They don't make arrests lightly,' Frank said.

'You would say that being as you were one of them,' Edith snarled. 'This sounds like a fix up, or whatever they call it. I'll go round and see Daniel Breen, I'll tell him I'll get to the bottom of this. Don't you worry, I won't let it rest. I've got my ideas about everything that's going on round here.' She looked accusingly round the table.

'Really, Edith, you mustn't interfere. Sad though it is, we must wait until, I suppose, the trial, and then let justice take its course,' Hebditch said. 'Now let's get on with the meeting.' He passed a sheet of paper to everyone. 'I've summarised my thoughts, so if you would take a few minutes to read them,' he looked at Edith, 'preferably in *silence*, and without making any remarks, I would be grateful.'

Frank glanced down the paper. It was as he thought. In view of the developing situation, the Warden was proposing the night watches on the hides were stopped, and the Anglian Detective Agency would be reimbursed for the work done so far. Because of the murder and the police presence on the reserve, he was suggesting the agency's work in trying to discover the identity of the vandals should be suspended.

'You do understand, Mr Diamond?' Hebditch asked. 'I think what's happened will deter these trespassers from coming back; they'll realise they may be caught if they return to make more trouble.'

Frank nodded. 'Yes, a very sensible decision. I'll get Miss Piff to send you an invoice for work we've done.'

Edith pointed a finger at him. 'Work done? You're as bad as the Rail Unions, wanting a huge pay rise when they've lost eighteen million last year! I think you've got a right cheek to ask for any money. A couple of nights sitting in a hide? Drinking our tea and coffee, I'll be bound! What do you think, Mr Myres, I bet you're not charging for your time?'

Myres had been withdrawn throughout the meeting, perhaps finding the body of Jonas Gorst had unnerved him. Possibly.

'Miss Chell, I'm a volunteer, and so are you. We give our time to the reserve willingly, but Mr Diamond is part of a business. I can only afford to help with building the new hide and road because my business is successful. If I were in Mr Diamond's shoes, I'd also be charging for the work done.'

Edith Chell pulled a face and gave Frank another glowering scowl. While this exchange was taking place, Hebditch's mouth was opening and shutting like a stranded turbot, as he tried to get a word in. 'Miss Chell, the business between the reserve and the agency is a matter for me and Mr Diamond. I'm most grateful for the help the agency has given, and who knows, when all this has died down, the vandals may return and we might seek their help again.'

Edith got up, stood in front of Frank, legs planted firmly apart, with her meaty hands on the table as she leant towards him. It was a frightening sight.

'I'll sort all this out. Leave it to me. And what's more I won't charge a penny.' With that she scooped up mugs, plates and the remaining scone and marched to the office. A tap was turned on and the sound of clashing crockery rendered the air.

The men looked at each other and either raised eyebrows, rolled their eyes or, in Frank's case, rubbed his top lip. He felt very sorry for the former pupils of Edith Chell.

A telephone rang out from the office. Stamping of feet. 'Bird reserve, Mr Hebditch's office. What'd you want?'

Hebditch tutted, and got up.

Edith Chell's head poked round the door. She glared at Frank. 'It's for you. You've got a cheek, using Ian's phone for your personal calls.'

Frank had had enough. 'Miss Chell, I don't know why you insist on being rude to me, but I would like to make this clear to Mr Hebditch and to you. If the agency has any further involvement with the reserve it will be on the understanding you arc not involved. I'll take the phone call – in private.' What he really wanted to say was you're a sad, old bitch, but don't pour your vitriol on me, mate.

Edith face flushed and she inhaled so deeply she looked as though her skin might burst and she'd gyrate round the room like a perforated balloon. Before she'd a chance to think of a reply, Frank slid past her and closed the office door.

He picked up the phone. 'Hello?'

'Frank.' It was Laurel. 'What's going on? Who's the person with the Yorkshire accent?'

'I'll tell you later. What's up?'

'I think you ought to get back as soon as you can. We can't make a decision on this one until you hear what he's got to say.'

'Sorry, I'm not with you. Who are you talking about?'

'It's Bryce De Lacy, he wants our help.'

Chapter Fifteen

Laurel coughed. The air in the sitting room at Greyfriars was thick with smoke. Dorothy was in an armchair by the fireplace, chain smoking. So much for her trying to cut down. Stuart was opposite her, puffing away at his pipe, and Bryce De Lacy, on the sofa next to her, held a long, slim cigarette between two webbed fingers. The different scents of the three tobaccos mingled: Dorothy's strong Navy Cut, the sweet smell of a heather mix from Stuart, and an amalgam of menthol and some exotic tobacco from De Lacy.

The only smoke she wanted was from a blazing log fire. The heat from the one-bar electric fire was adding to the unpleasant atmosphere. She got up and coughed again. 'I think we could do with a proper fire; it'll cheer us up while we wait for Frank to get back. He should be here soon.'

Dorothy looked up. 'I should have thought of that. Sorry. The news about Caleb has completely thrown me. I can't believe it.'

Laurel escaped from the room, leaving the door open in the hope some of the smoke would escape with her. She couldn't face listening to any more repetitious utterances from Dorothy and De Lacy as they talked in ever-repeating circles about Caleb's arrest, and their belief in his innocence. Stuart hadn't said much, neither agreeing nor disagreeing with them. That meant he probably thought he must be guilty, basing his judgement on the evidence.

She went outside, got some kindling from the shed, and went back to the sitting room. They were still at it, but the air wasn't quite as thick. She busied herself removing the electric fire, and got the fire going, adding a beech log from the pile on the hearth. Everyone watched as if they'd never seen a fire being lit before, but at least Dorothy and De Lacy fell silent. Perhaps she should be more sympathetic towards them, but justice would have to take its course, and if those were Caleb's finger prints on the handle of the fromard, she couldn't feel sympathy towards him. At the post-mortem she'd seen how deep the axe had been buried in Jonas's skull. Whoever struck the blow had intended to kill him. She turned her head at the sound of Frank's Avenger pulling up outside the front door. 'He's here.' Bryce De Lacy stubbed out what must have been his fourth cigarette on an ashtray, and straightened his shoulders.

After De Lacy arrived, she, Dorothy and Stuart had a quick conference in the kitchen; Mabel had gone to Aldeburgh to see her son, and wouldn't be back until late afternoon. They'd agreed De Lacy must wait until Frank got back before telling them what he wanted. She guessed, as she was sure the others had, he was looking for their help.

The front door opened. De Lacy got up, his face white and anxious, his protuberant eyes staring at the sitting room door as if his life depended on who came through it. Laurel glanced at Stuart, who was frowning, obviously uneasy about the situation. He caught her glance and gave a minute shake of the head.

Frank came into the room.

De Lacy rushed to greet him. 'Mr Diamond. Thank God you've got back. Your partners were unwilling to hear what I have to say until you returned. I sincerely hope you—'

Frank took his outstretched hand. 'Good to meet you, Mr De Lacy. Let's sit down before we listen to what you have to say. We're a team and we always work together, so you would only have had to repeat yourself.'

De Lacy returned to the sofa and Frank took the last armchair.

Stuart looked at his wristwatch and frowned. It was almost lunch time, and Mr Elderkin didn't like the cycle of the day's meals to get out of order. She bit her lip. She wasn't sure what Mabel had left for lunch; perhaps Stuart was worried he'd not get his proper share if they invited De Lacy to eat with them.

'Right, Mr De Lacy, the floor is yours,' Frank said, leaning back against a cushion, looking relaxed, his black leather jacket and white polo contrasting with the formality of De Lacy's expensive suit, immaculate blue shirt and darker blue silk tie.

De Lacy leant forward, his body rigid with tension, his hands clasped together between his knees. 'As you know, Caleb has been arrested for the murder of Jonas Gorst. I was also taken to Ipswich on the same day as Caleb and Daniel Breen, and my fingerprints were taken. I saw both of them at the police station; poor Caleb was traumatised. He looked at me, his eyes pleading for my help, but I was taken to another room. I couldn't even speak to him.'

His distress seemed genuine, but she wondered why this sudden but deep attachment to Caleb? Why was he so upset? Yes, he was Caleb's uncle, but he'd only recently seen him for the first time. Why should he care so much?

Dorothy stubbed out her cigarette. 'I'm sure I'm as upset as you are, Mr De Lacy, if not more so. My sister, Emily, and I often looked after both boys from when they were tots.'

De Lacy glowered at her.

This was a pointless rivalry: trying to prove who cared most about Caleb; Frank was starting to lose his relaxed look, as he looked from Dorothy to De Lacy.

'We understand your distress, Mr De Lacy. Please tell us why you have asked for this meeting,' Frank said.

De Lacy took a deep breath and Dorothy lit another cigarette.

'I cannot believe Caleb is capable of murder, and although the evidence points towards him, I want your agency to prove he didn't do this, and if you can, to find the true murderer.' He looked at them, one by one, staring unblinkingly at them.

Dorothy turned towards him. 'Mr De Lacy, I, for one, want us to take this on. Thank you for your belief in Caleb's innocence.'

Oh dear, Dorothy had stepped out of line. They always discussed cases in private and went with the majority decision if they should take a case on or refuse it. She'd let her concern for Caleb over ride her professionalism. Frank ran a finger over his top lip and Stuart frowned.

'Well?' Dorothy looked at her three partners.

Silence.

'I'm prepared to pay above your normal fees, well above,' De Lacy said.

'Do you know why Caleb's been arrested for the murder?' Frank asked.

'Yes, his fingerprints were found on the murder weapon.'

'Have you discussed wanting our help with Daniel Breen?' Stuart asked.

De Lacy hesitated. 'Er, no. I thought I'd come straight to you. I've also told my solicitor to arrange for Caleb to have one of the best defence lawyers in the country if, God forbid, he's charged and it comes to a trial.'

Dorothy was biting her lip. 'I think you ought to go and see Daniel. I didn't realise he didn't know about this.'

De Lacy turned towards her. 'Of course, I should have done that before coming here; but even if Mr Breen doesn't approve, I'm sure Caleb will welcome my help.'

Frank blew out his cheeks. 'This is a police matter, and although we have good relationships with the Suffolk constabulary, I don't think they'll welcome our involvement.'

De Lacy half-rose from the sofa. 'So, you're not willing to take this on?'

There was a muffled cry from Dorothy.

'I didn't say that, Mr De Lacy,' Frank said. 'We'll discuss this as soon as possible and give you an answer by tomorrow morning.' He looked round. She nodded, Stuart said, 'That's sensible.' Dorothy, puffing angrily at her cigarette, uttered a curt yes.

'I'm not happy with the wait,' De Lacy said. 'I want *your* agency to deal with this case. You're on the spot, you know everyone involved and at least one of you,' he looked at Dorothy, 'is genuinely concerned for Caleb. I expect an answer early tomorrow. If you refuse, I'll bring in another detective agency to find the true murderer.'

There was a long silence. 'That is your prerogative, Mr De Lacy. But I must tell you in confidence, the police not only have the evidence of the fingerprints, but they believe that Caleb had a motive,' Frank said.

'What motive?' De Lacy snapped.

'I can't tell you; I was given this information in confidence. If we take on the case, we might jeopardise the good relationship we have with the police.'

'Oh, Frank,' Dorothy cried, 'that can't be as important as Caleb's life! If he went to prison, he wouldn't last long. He'd be picked on and he's got such a weak chest. I can't bear the thought of him being behind bars.'

This wasn't like Dorothy; she usually kept a close rein on her emotions, rarely showing her true feelings, even when she was deeply hurt; when her sister, Emily, was murdered, she didn't show as much emotion as this. Then she couldn't do anything, it was too late, but now there was someone who needed her help – her friend's child. Was that the reason?

Frank stood up and held the door open. 'Goodbye, Mr De Lacy. We'll be in touch tomorrow morning. May I suggest you contact Mr Daniel Breen and tell him what you're trying to do?'

Dorothy jumped up. 'I'll go with you, if you like. Daniel will listen to me.'

'No, Dorothy, we need you here. If we are going to decide whether to take this case or not, all the partners need to be present,' Frank said.

She scowled at him and flopped back into her chair.

Frank escorted De Lacy from the room and a few minutes later they heard the smooth purr of his Rolls as he drove away.

'I need something to eat before we start chewing over this one,' Stuart said as Frank came back into the room. 'What's Mabel left us?'

Laurel went to the kitchen. 'Soup and sandwiches, and there's most of a fruit cake left,' she said on returning.

Dorothy quivered, obviously with suppressed rage. 'How can you think of eating when someone's life is at stake?'

'Come on, Dorothy, get a sense of proportion. They don't hang people anymore; if he's guilty he has to pay the price, however fond you are of the lad. Let's eat.' Stuart made for the kitchen.

Laurel went over to Dorothy. 'Are you upset because of your friendship with his mother?'

Dorothy looked up. 'Yes. Rosalind sometimes talked, not often, about how worried she was about what would happen to Caleb if anything happened to her, and even worse, if anything happened to Daniel. "Who will care for him?" she'd say. I assured her that as long as I was capable, I would look after him.' She took a deep breath. 'Of course, I never imagined she would die so young. I know sixty-eight seems old to some people, but she was such a fit and active woman. I thought she'd outlive me, even though she was older. You never know what life will throw at you, do you?'

'Come and have something to eat. Then you can marshal your thoughts for when we have the meeting.'

'Frank doesn't want to take it on, does he?'

'We don't know that; I think he didn't like you revealing your thoughts before we'd discussed it in private.'

Dorothy blew out her cheeks. 'That wasn't like me. He's right, I was out of order.' She got up and straightened her shoulders. 'However, I want us to take this on. If Caleb's innocent I've faith that you, Frank and Stuart will find the true murderer.'

Laurel smiled at her – she wasn't sure if Dorothy's faith was justified.

Frank scraped off the soil from his boots before going into Greyfriars via the kitchen door. Laurel had suggested, after they'd eaten their lunch, they should all have some time to themselves before they met to make a decision. They needed to clear their heads and put their thoughts in order, she knew she did. Also, it would give time for Mabel to get back from Aldeburgh. They all agreed. He was sure this would be one case that would be decided by a vote, and it was imperative all the members were present.

Laurel went off with Bumper for a walk over the heath, Frank offered to join her, but she said she needed the time to think things through, so he walked in the opposite direction and headed north, along the shore in the direction of Southwold. Dorothy said she would use the time to do some paper work, and Stuart said he'd contact Mabel and ask her to get back as soon as possible.

There was no one in the kitchen, but noises were coming from the office. He walked in. All the four other partners were seated round the table. Dorothy had laid it out for a formal meeting: blotting paper, pencils, paper and glasses of water. He wondered why? He looked at her; her mouth was tight and straight and her eyes, behind the blue spectacles, were determined. His stomach knotted. He didn't want to upset her, but he might have to.

He sat down. 'Sorry I've kept you waiting.'

'I've filled in Mabel about what the meeting is about,' Stuart said.

'So have I,' Dorothy said.

Stuart frowned. 'Was that necessary?'

Mabel raised her bowed head. 'Dorothy thought I ought to hear both sides of the argument,' she said.

'I thought the break was to give us time to think the case through, not to try and influence someone else,' Frank said.

Laurel took in a sharp breath.

Dorothy glared at him and Stuart decided he needed a smoke. He was joined by Dorothy.

Frank looked round at them. 'We're here to decide if we should take on the challenge of trying to prove that Caleb Breen is not a killer.' He paused. 'I suggest we go round the room and each of us say what we think. If there is a strong feeling either way, then we can make a swift decision, but if not, we'll set aside a period of time to argue our cases, ask questions, and listen to each other's views. Say half an hour?'

Everyone nodded.

'Then we'll put it to the vote and go with the majority decision.'

He waited to see if there was any disagreement. 'Excellent. I would like to kick off, then Stuart, followed by Dorothy, Mabel and Laurel. Are you happy with that order?' No one said anything. 'My view is the evidence against Caleb is strong. Not only do the police have fingerprints but they now have a motive. It's been said by several people Caleb hated Jonas, and the police have witnesses who will swear they heard Caleb saying he'd like to kill Jonas. He doesn't have an alibi for the time of the murder and the murder weapon was his. I can't see how we can prove it wasn't him who killed Jonas. Also, we have to remember that although we've got good relationships with the Suffolk police, and especially Nicholas Revie, these arrangements are not written in stone and could easily be revoked.' As he was speaking, he was conscious of Dorothy's efforts to keep her mouth shut; several times she shook her head, and appeared to be quietly fuming. Frank turned to Stuart and nodded.

Stuart straightened his back and placed his pipe on an ashtray. 'I have to agree with Frank. No need to repeat what he said. Justice must take its course. It's up to a jury to decide.'

Dorothy didn't wait to be asked her views. 'I'm very disappointed with your views, Frank and Stuart,' she said, reminding Frank of a stern primary-school teacher he'd been unfortunate to have for a year when he was eight.

'Have you considered the evidence may have been planted? I accept the fingerprints on the fromard were Caleb's, but anyone could have removed that axe, and of course his fingerprints would have been on it. He mounted it on the wall to display. He didn't have an alibi, but did everyone else who might have murdered Caleb have one? Have they been checked? As for him hating Jonas, again it wouldn't surprise me if that was true, but how many people have you lot,' she pointed to them in turn with her biro, 'said you hated a nosy neighbour, or the tax inspector? You didn't go on to murder them. Lastly, you haven't thought about Caleb's character and physicality; he is a quiet, shy, person, he has never been violent, and he's not strong. I don't believe he's capable mentally, or physically, of murdering anyone.'

He admired her train of logic and the passion of her argument. She would have made a good lawyer, he thought. However, he wasn't convinced. He looked at Mabel.

'I agree with Dorothy. I'm not convinced by the evidence.'

Stuart looked shocked. He took up his pipe and applied a match to the dying bowl. Mabel shot him a glance, then raised her chin.

Frank's heart sank. This was not good for the harmony of the agency. But perhaps it was good to put the team to a test. Better to speak your mind and have everything out in the open. Too often, when he was in the police, he'd had to comply with orders he thought were wrong. If he tried to put another point of view, he got slapped down. He must try and remain calm. 'Laurel, what's your opinion?'

She looked very serious; he was sure she understood the significance of the situation. The partners had never been in this position before. Yes, there had been rocky moments, like the time he'd kept back information about Carol Pemberton, because he was lusting after her; he'd confessed this to them, and although Laurel was shocked, the others were remarkably laid back, putting it down to 'boys will be boys'. This was different. He hoped Dorothy wouldn't hold a grudge when they refused the case.

Laurel put down the pencil she'd been doodling with on the blotting paper. 'I've listened to both sides of the argument. Do you think if we spoke to Revie and asked him his opinion that would help? It may be that he has doubts. Do you think he does, Frank?'

He was taken aback. 'Revie isn't part of this agency. I can't see his opinion has any relevance. We've never asked him before if we should take a case. It isn't his responsibility.'

Mabel tapped her hand on the table. 'I think it's a good idea. He's a nice man, is Nick Revie. I've always got on very well with him. I think he'd give an honest opinion.'

Stuart glowered at her. 'Just because he calls you Miss Mabel, like you were some southern belle on a Mississippi paddle-steamer, and tells you your bacon butties were made in heaven, doesn't mean he's got a good opinion of your detection abilities. I think it's a bad idea to consult him.' He turned and gave Laurel a glare. 'I'm surprised at you, Laurel. I've always trusted your judgement, but not on this one.'

Oh, my God, thought Frank, I didn't see that coming.

Mabel whipped round. 'Stuart Elderkin, how can you speak to Laurel like that! Think how much she's helped us. Laurel, I apologise for Stuart.'

Laurel's face was white, her eyes round with shock. 'Please, Mabel and Stuart. I refuse to be used in this way. I made a suggestion, I expect it to be considered, not used as a bone to be fought over. Frank, this meeting is disintegrating into a senseless argument. I suggest we take a five-minute break and then vote on whether to take the case. I expect everyone, when we return, to have calmed down and speak to one another as civilised adults, with our thoughts purely on the case and its merits, and I don't want to hear any more personal remarks. I'm going to feed Bumper.' She got up and left the room.

Frank thought she would have made a great headmistress if she'd stayed in teaching.

Both Stuart and Mabel looked shame-faced.

'I'm sorry, Mabel, I shouldn't have said those things. Put it down to loving you a lot and being jealous when Revie butters you up.'

Mabel slid a hand over his. 'No need for you to be jealous. You're the one for me.'

Frank looked at Dorothy, who was twitching, probably in embarrassment. He wished he was somewhere else, preferably next to a mahogany bar and gleaming beer pumps.

Stuart squeezed Mabel's hand. 'I'll find Laurel and apologise.'

'I'll come with you,' she said.

When the door closed behind them, Dorothy coughed. 'I'm afraid I've caused all this fuss,' she said. 'I'm sorry, Frank, but I feel I must try and help Caleb, and the only way I can is by persuading the agency to try and find out who is the real killer; also, Daniel is in pieces, I know he believes Caleb is innocent.'

He respected Dorothy, he liked Dorothy, he valued the way they all worked as a team, and more than anything, he now realised how much he valued their friendship. But he had to be true to his beliefs – or had he? Would it matter if he decided, against his better judgement, to vote to take the case? 'Dorothy, whatever happens, we mustn't let this spoil the ethos of the team and the friendships we all share.'

She blinked several times. 'Yes, you're right. I'll try to be less emotional.'

The other three came back into the room.

Frank waited until they'd all settled down. 'Right, we'll put this to the vote. We'll vote in the order we spoke, so I'll go first. I think we shouldn't take the case. Stuart?'

Stuart looked uncomfortable. 'I agree, I vote we don't take it.'

'Mabel?' Frank asked.

She took a deep breath. 'I vote we take it,' she whispered.

'Dorothy?'

'I vote we take it.'

A split. Laurel had the casting vote. He should have gone last. It put her in an awkward position. 'Laurel?'

'I've given this a great deal of thought. My head says we shouldn't take it, but my heart says we should.' She paused and the atmosphere in the room became even tenser. She smiled at them. 'As usual, my heart wins. I think we should try our best to see if we can find evidence either that Caleb is not the murderer, or evidence which leads us to the true killer.'

'Do you still think it would be a good idea to contact Revie before we take the case?' he asked her.

She looked into his eyes, her own warm and true. 'No. I think we accept the case and then I'll see Revie and explain our thinking and ask him to understand we're not going against him, and if we find evidence that will incriminate Caleb even more deeply, we will give him that evidence. At the same time, if we find evidence exonerating Caleb, we'll give him that as well. He's been fair to us; he's helped when he needn't; I hope he'll be sympathetic.'

Frank got up. 'Decision made. We'll take the case. I'll contact

De Lacy and tell him, Laurel will see Revie, Dorothy will you see Daniel and hopefully he'll cooperate, in spite of De Lacy's involvement. We'll need his help in looking into details of Caleb's life. Stuart, can you draw up a list of suspects, including Caleb. We need to find all those with either a link to the Breens, or to the bird reserve, who do not have an alibi for the night Jonas was murdered. Laurel, if Revie is on side, perhaps he can save us some time, if he's prepared to give us information on alibis. Worth a try. We'll meet tomorrow night for dinner and make a plan and then divide up the work.' He hadn't wanted them to take the case, but now they had his mind was whirring with ideas, and there was the prospect of action, the excitement of the chase and the challenge of pitting his brain against a murderer; oxygen bubbles were fizzing through his brain. Unless, of course, the murderer turned out to be Caleb.

Chapter Sixteen

Thursday, March 9, 1972

Laurel helped Mabel to clear the dining room table ready for the meeting. Dinner had been brief: the savoury smells of cottage pie lingering in the room; they agreed coffee and drinks would follow the meeting. She came back and took her seat. The atmosphere was so different to the last meeting; now there was an undercurrent of excitement, a definite buzz of anticipation. Frank's green eyes glittered as he shuffled papers, Dorothy was back to her old self: efficient and controlled, and Stuart's expression was of a bloodhound on the scent of something interesting. Only Mabel looked distracted. She and Stuart had finally made the decision to move to Greyfriars. What was she worried about now?

This morning she'd been to see Revie, Frank had visited De Lacy and Stuart, as well as making a list of suspects, visited the bird reserve and talked with Hebditch, Rudder and anyone else there.

Frank, seated at the head of the table, tapped his biro on its polished surface. 'Shall we make a start?'

Dorothy frowned, and ostentatiously leant across Laurel and rubbed at the spot he'd tapped on.

Frank raised his eyebrows. 'We'll go around the table and each report, as succinctly as possible, on what happened this morning; however, don't skip on the details, they might not seem relevant to you, but someone else might pick up on something. Laurel, if you'd

go first, then Dorothy – when you've finished polishing the table –
then Stuart, and I'll go last. Laurel?'

She glanced at Dorothy, who was looking at Frank over her blue
spectacles; she turned to her and smirked. Thank goodness she
hadn't taken offence. After the traumas of their last meeting she'd
been uncertain how this one would develop.

Laurel pushed open the Lounge door of the Miller's Arms; she was
ten minutes early for her meeting with Revie and she wanted to be
safely ensconced before he arrived, then she'd feel in control of the
situation. She wasn't sure how Revie would react to the news the
agency was taking up cudgels on behalf of Caleb. She didn't think
trying to soft-soap Revie would work; he was an intelligent man, he
wouldn't think much of that. She decided she'd put it to him straight,
and hope their former good relationships would see her through.

There were few people in the room and no sign of anyone behind
the bar. The lounge had been given an update: upholstered moquette
benches in deep red, round tables in faux mahogany, and a deep-pile
carpet with a swirly pattern in navy blue and pink. Enough to make
you nauseous, even if you hadn't had much to drink. The décor may
be new, she thought, but it smelt of stale beer and fried food. She
went to the bar.

'Ring the bell,' a man at a nearby table shouted.

She smiled at him and pressed down on the central knob.

A middle-aged man, with comb-over hair, emerged from the
door behind the bar. 'Good afternoon. What can I get you?'

When she heard there was no real ales and only fizzy lagers, she
decided on a ginger beer.

'Are you ordering food?'

'I'll wait until my friend gets here, if that's all right?'

He looked at his watch. 'Last orders in fifteen minutes.'

She decided crisps would see her through. Why had Revie chosen
to meet in this crap pub? She'd just decided where to sit, when the
door was flung open and Revie marched in, looking in a hurry, as
though eager to get back to whatever he'd been working on.

'Laurel. See you've got a drink. Have you ordered food?'

She shook her head and waved the crisp packet at him. She decided he'd chosen this awful pub so she wouldn't want to linger. The signs were not good.

A pint of frothy lager in his hand, he flopped onto the chair next to hers.

'You're not eating, Nick?'

He took a slurp, a few bubbles rested on his upper lip; he impatiently wiped them away, 'This will give me heartburn for the rest of the day, never mind their sausage and chips. You were wise to stick to crisps.' He drank deeply, then burped. 'What did I tell you?'

She offered him a crisp. He refused.

'Right, Laurel, what's all this about? Has Frank sent you to soften me up? What does the agency want now? I'll tell you straight, I'm up to my eyeballs with work.'

Although his words were sharp, she didn't sense any animosity; he seemed tired and under pressure. 'I'm sorry to take up your time, Nick, but we all wanted you to hear what's happened personally, not over the phone.'

His eyes lost their tired look, and for the first time since he'd come through the door, he looked interested. 'Frank proposed?'

Ginger beer shot up her nose, and she snorted as she clamped a handkerchief to her mouth.

'You proposed?'

She shook her head. 'I don't think that will ever happen.'

He looked at her quizzically. 'I don't know, I think you'd get on well together.'

'We do now – as friends.'

Revie sighed. 'Perhaps it's best to stick to that. The other thing can get tricky.'

Her interest was piqued. Had there ever been a Mrs Revie? Not the right moment to probe.

'Yesterday, Bryce De Lacy asked for a meeting with us. He wanted us to try and prove Caleb Breen was not the murderer of Jonas Gorst. I have to admit some of us didn't want to take on this case as we know the evidence is strong against Caleb. However, after talking it through we put it to the vote and we've accepted the case. That is why we felt we should let you know personally.'

His small eyes narrowed. 'And which way did you vote, Laurel?'

'When we make a collective decision to take a case on, there are no recriminations if it goes pear-shaped, and no crowing if it's a success.'

He pushed out a bottom lip. 'Very diplomatic – but very boring. You sound like a politician. I bet I know which way you voted; you can't resist helping someone who seems to have the whole world against them, even if that someone did cleave a head open.'

She waited to see if he would say anything else, but he picked up his glass and downed the remaining lager.

'I'm sorry if we seem to be going against you and your case against Caleb, but although the evidence seems strong, some of us felt uneasy when we thought about his character and how it didn't fit the person who brutally murdered Jonas.' She hesitated, he looked at her, his eyebrows raised. 'Are you totally convinced Caleb is the murderer?' She leant back, her jacket crackling as it rubbed against the moquette of the bench.

'Want another?' He waved his glass in front of her face.

She didn't feel like more ginger beer, but she needed to keep this meeting going. 'I'll have a half of whatever you're drinking, please.' God, Frank would sneer when she told him she'd been drinking fizzy canister lager. A sin of the first water – or ale?

Revie came back and plonked her drink down. 'That'll test your guts,' he said, smiling mischievously. 'What I have to say to you, you can tell the rest of the crew, but is off the record. I agree, I've never seen a less likely murderer than Caleb Breen. I feel sorry for the bastard: lumbered with looks that would make a werewolf blanch, and with a twin brother who could be mistaken for Burt Lancaster, he's drawn the sticky end of the lollipop. No, he doesn't fit the profile of a brutal killer, and it's hard to imagine, with his physical capability, he's strong enough to have struck the fatal blow.

'On the other hand, his fingerprints are on the weapon, which he owns, he's got no alibi, and we've got witnesses who've heard him threaten Jonas. My superiors are satisfied the case against him is water tight.' He paused and took a long pull at his pint. 'I've met a few killers in my time, and some of them have been poor physical specimens, and often have a grudge against some part of society: women, the police, social workers, their mothers, their sisters. . . .' He shrugged. 'I won't take offence at the team investigating the case. I almost hope you do find something to prove Caleb's innocence. Although that'll give me more work, something I don't need at the moment.'

She felt relieved, very relieved. She liked Nick and if their relationship had turned sour, she would have been disappointed. 'That's really good of you, Nick. Would you like us to report anything we find to you?'

'Yes, give me a weekly update, unless it's something major, then bell me immediately.'

She nodded. 'Good, or as Frank would say: excellent.'

'How is the bastard? Was he happy taking this on?'

'No, neither was Stuart.'

'So, it was the hearts and flowers ladies who swung it Caleb's way?'

She smiled and nodded. Now he'd been cooperative, it didn't matter if he knew who'd been against, or for, the case. She wanted him to feel part of the investigation, even if by proxy. 'We've all agreed if we find further evidence of Caleb's guilt, we'll pass it onto you as well.'

'Excellent!' She laughed. 'To save you time and effort, the only people with alibis for the time of Jonas's murder are Daniel Breen, his girlfriend, Theresa Poppy, and Edith Chell. All the other people who were connected to the case, in one way or another, not that we had any motive for them murdering Caleb, didn't have alibis.'

'Who else did you check on?'

'We checked on Hebditch, the Warden, Rudder, his Deputy, Fred Gorst, Caleb's father, De Lacy, and Samuel Myres.'

'So, here's to murder!' She raised her glass and swallowed a mouthful of lager.

He smiled and raised his half-empty glass. 'I'll drink to that.'

★

Laurel was pleased to see and hear their reaction to the news of Revie's support for their investigation.

'He's certainly gone up in my estimation,' Dorothy said, lighting up her third cigarette of the meeting, and taking a deep draw.

Mabel beamed. 'I shall cook him whatever he wants next time he comes for dinner.'

Stuart looked at her sourly. 'You've never asked me what I'd like best.'

Mabel laughed. 'I don't need to, you like everything I cook. If I asked you what you'd like, you'd give me a list as long as my arm; dinner would be ten courses.'

They all laughed, including Stuart.

'You did well, Laurel. I'm glad Nick's still on our side,' Frank said, smiling at her.

When he smiled at her like that, she still got that fluttering feeling. 'Thanks, Frank.'

'Right, Dorothy, you're next.'

'Could you wait two minutes, I need to see if Bumper needs to go out,' Laurel said.

Dorothy nodded and took another deep draw on her Player's Navy Cut.

The front door of Rooks Wood Farm was open. She shivered; the hall was as cold as a tomb. She'd phoned Daniel, told him she was coming over and they'd arranged to have a bite of lunch while they talked. 'I'll bring something with me, so don't bother preparing food, just have the kettle on,' she'd said. She opened the kitchen door.

He was sitting at the kitchen table, his head resting on his cupped hands; at the sound of the door opening, he turned, and put on a smile. 'Aunty Dot, good to see you.'

She placed her basket of eats on the table beside him and leant down and kissed him on the cheek. 'Mabel's made us some ham and cheese sandwiches, and a couple slices of her fruit cake. Let's make a start, it's time for lunch, we can talk as we eat.' She got plates from

144

a cupboard and unpacked the food. 'Put the kettle on, Daniel, I'd like a cup of tea immediately.' At least the Aga kept this room warm.

Daniel took a few bites from a ham sandwich, then put it on his plate.

She didn't say anything; no point in nagging the boy. Boy – he was nearly middle-aged.

'Daniel, I've something very important to tell you. I hope you'll cooperate with me, not just me, but the rest of the agency.'

He smiled at her. 'Of course, I will. Is this about Caleb?' When she'd mentioned the agency, his eyes had lit up and he sounded hopeful. 'Are you going to try and prove he's innocent?' His voice was tight, as though holding back sobs.

She gulped. 'Yes, we are. I hope we have your approval.'

He grasped her hands. 'Aunty Dot, you don't know how much this means to me, and it will to Caleb, when he hears about it. I've been desperate with worry. I know Caleb wouldn't do such a thing, and I've not known which way to turn. I was going to ask for the agency's help, but I wasn't sure I could afford to pay you, although I'm willing to raise the money somehow.'

She gulped again. This was going to be difficult. 'Daniel, I'm very pleased you have faith in us, and there is no need to worry about paying—'

'I can't expect you to work for nothing! I'll even mortgage the farm to prove Caleb is innocent.'

She couldn't put it off any longer. 'Daniel, I want you to listen to me as I tell you how Caleb's case will be paid for. I don't want you flying off the handle. Promise me?'

He leant back, his eyes narrowing, his expression changing to one of suspicion. 'It's him, isn't it? De Lacy?'

She nodded. 'Yes, he came to see us. You must decide who is more important, Caleb, who is accused of murder, or yourself. You obviously hate Bryce De Lacy, because your mother hated him, but De Lacy desperately wants to help Caleb. Why he cares about him so much, after only recently meeting him, I can't say. However, I believe he's sincere. I want you to swallow your hate and pride.

We'll be able to do a thorough investigation if we're backed by his money.'

His face was stern, unreadable.

She decided to remain silent, biting her lip, but keeping eye contact. The wait for his verdict seemed interminable, but she kept her nerve; better to let him calm down, and hopefully put things in perspective.

His shoulders slumped and he looked down at his clasped hands. 'I agree. I'll cooperate in anyway I can. I promise to be polite to De Lacy until Caleb is proved innocent. After that happens – we'll see. You realise I may lose Caleb one way or another, either he'll be found guilty, and he'll go to prison, or if he's proved innocent, he'll form an even stronger attachment to De Lacy, and perhaps move away from Rooks Wood Farm.'

She leant forward and took his hand, but he didn't respond to her grasp, his hand unmoving against hers. 'Thank you, Daniel. I understand your suspicion of De Lacy and I share your feelings about him, but his backing means the agency can concentrate solely on Caleb's case. If you'd refused, I wouldn't have let you mortgage the farm – I have some savings. I would have used those, but I've sunk a great deal of money into the agency: mostly reorganising the house. I know I'll get my money back eventually, but it would have been tight.'

His restraint disappeared and he wrapped his arms round her. 'Aunty Dot. You'll be able to prove he's innocent, won't you?' His shoulders were heaving as he tried to contain his sobs. 'He'd never survive if he's convicted and goes to gaol.'

'Of course we will, Daniel. Look how Frank, Laurel and Stuart cracked those other cases!' Her voice sounded strong and sincere, but deep inside she was terrified they would fail.

Laurel sensed Dorothy's fears as she finished telling them of Daniel's eventual agreement to accept De Lacy's help. 'You did well, Dorothy. If he'd refused to cooperate and we'd gone ahead with the case, it would have caused a rift between you and Daniel, and that would've been disastrous. We all need to work together.'

Dorothy nodded, took off her spectacles and gave them a thorough rubbing with a tissue.

'Excellent, Dorothy, you should have been a diplomat,' Frank said. 'Stuart, what about you? Who've you lined up as suspects?'

Stuart put down his pipe onto an ashtray. 'I'm not sure we've got any strong suspects; all I've done is put down the names of people Revie told Laurel didn't have alibis. The only one with a motive at the moment is Fred Gorst. He and his son were at loggerheads over Jonas staying out overnight. Fred is free with his fists and in the past, he's doled it out to Jonas. However, from what Mary Gorst has said, and also other people who know them, Jonas has got too big and strong, and retaliated when his father got aggressive. But you'd think if Fred killed his son, it would've happened in a fight, not a deliberately planned murder.'

'How intelligent is Fred Gorst? Would he be capable of planning the murder of his son?' Frank asked.

Dorothy put back her glasses. 'He may look like a hayseed, but Daniel's found him a reliable worker, capable of thinking for himself. I'd say he has native cunning; perhaps he wanted to incriminate Caleb. I think both male Gorsts didn't like taking orders from Caleb, someone they regarded as mentally and physically inferior to themselves.'

'Mr Gorst remains a suspect. What about the others, Stuart?' Frank asked.

'They haven't got alibis, but I can't fathom why Hebditch, Rudder, or Myres would want to kill Jonas. I briefly questioned Hebditch and Rudder and asked them if they knew of any connections between Jonas Gorst and anyone who worked on the reserve, including themselves. Hebditch said Jonas occasionally worked on the reserve, sometimes both he and his father came with Daniel Breen when there was a special project. He's checking his diary to see when this happened. He thinks Jonas may have worked by himself a couple of times, but he's not sure when.'

Laurel sighed. 'It's all a bit tentative, isn't it?'

'Early days, Laurel. We may have to widen our list of suspects.

We need to find out who Jonas's friends were; the ones he stayed out all night with, and what they got up to. I'm not sure if his parents know but, Laurel, could you go to the Gorsts tomorrow and see if you can get some names of Jonas's friends, or where he used to go to?'

'Yes, I'd like to see Mary Gorst again. Poor woman, she'll be devastated.' She wanted to hear what Frank had found out when he went to see De Lacy. 'Your turn, Frank, I'm dying to hear about your visit to Shrike Hall.'

Frank turned the Avenger through impressive wrought-iron gates into a long tarmacked straight drive, lined each side by lime trees, planted back, so the view of the house was clear, even at a distance. Another Tudor house, but on a grand scale, stretching out on either side of a main porch, three stories high, well-timbered, with paned windows glittering in the late morning sun. The lime trees gave way to balls, cones and domed topiary yews in front of the house.

De Lacy had obviously been waiting for him by a window, for no sooner had he parked than he came out of the front door and walked towards him.

'Mr Diamond.' He shook his hand. 'You have good news for me, I hope?'

Frank acknowledged his greeting, but didn't say anything.

De Lacy frowned. 'Let's go in.' He led the way into a spacious hall with a chequer-board marbled floor, and a mixture of antique furniture, some Tudor and some of a later period. The place reeked of money, old money. A wide staircase to the right of the hall led to the first floor.

De Lacy opened a door. 'We'll talk in here,' he said.

As Frank followed him, he noticed an open door to his left which led into another room. He stopped. An old lady was seated near the door, as if she'd been waiting for them; her long figure upright. She must have been tall when younger, he thought, not as tall as Laurel, but who is? Her back was curved in a dowager's hump, her white sparse hair swept back from a long, thin face, and several strands of pearls encircled her neck, sinking into her dew-lapped throat. She looked at him with rheumy blue eyes.

'Bryce,' she said in thin, high voice, 'you have a visitor?'

De Lacy jerked round. He raised his eyebrows. 'Mr Diamond, please meet my old nanny, Miss Ada Spooner.' He walked into the room, and brushed her cheek with his lips. 'Ada, this is Mr Frank Diamond, whom I've told you about.'

She stretched out a knobbly, arthritic hand. 'I'm pleased to meet you, Mr Diamond. I hope you have come to tell us you will save young Caleb's life.'

Her body might be a ruin of its former self, but her mind and speech were sharp. 'I'm pleased to meet you, Miss Spooner. I haven't yet talked to Mr De Lacy.' He didn't think he'd confuse her by telling her the justice system didn't hang murderers anymore.

'Then you must do that straight away. Bryce, please come and tell me what is happening when you've finished your discussion.'

'I will, Ada. Please excuse us.' He turned abruptly and walked out of the door.

'Goodbye, Miss Spooner,' Frank said. He followed De Lacy into an over-furnished sitting room; there were too many settees, armchairs, side tables, nests of tables, all resting on a pink floral rug. De Lacy indicated an armchair next to a marble fireplace, taking a seat opposite. An open fire smouldered in the hearth. De Lacy took a poker from an impressive companion set and stirred life into logs, the scent of burning apple wood perfuming the air. The room, although warm, felt as though it was little used; there were no personal objects: a magazine, a pair of spectacles, no fresh flowers, children's toys or a pile of rumpled newspapers. This huge house for a man who mostly lived abroad, and occasionally visited, and an old lady. She must be lonely, even though staff kept the house ready for De Lacy's return.

'Would you like a drink, Mr Diamond? Tea, coffee, or something stronger?' He pointed to a sideboard on which stood a Tantalus holding three decanters with silver labels on chains round their necks.

He was tempted, he'd bet the whisky would be malt, but he didn't fancy spending more time with this man than he had to. 'Thank you, no.'

De Lacy nodded and didn't pour himself a drink. 'Have you decided to accept my offer and hopefully find evidence to prove Caleb innocent?'

'Yes, we have.'

De Lacy beamed, his protruding eyes filming over. 'Thank God.' He rose from his chair and came over to Frank and grasped his hand, shaking it vigorously. 'Thank you, a thousand times, thank you.'

This was getting too emotional. He extricated his hand and took out some papers from his briefcase. 'Miss Piff, whom you've met, has set out our financial terms. You need to be aware employing three detectives is expensive, and we don't know how long we'll need to complete the work.'

De Lacy waved his arms expansively. 'Don't worry about that, I'm not concerned about the cost.'

'Nevertheless, you must read the terms and sign the contract before we go any further.'

De Lacy grabbed the paper and without spending more than five seconds looking at it, took a fountain pen from the breast pocket of his jacket suit and signed with a flourish. He passed the paper back to Frank.

'Also, Mr De Lacy, I must tell you we've been in contact with Inspector Revie, told him we're taking the case on, and we'll inform him as soon as we find new information, both positive, or negative.'

De Lacy frowned. 'You mean if you found incriminating evidence against Caleb, you'd let him know?'

Frank nodded. 'Yes, we only deal in the truth.'

De Lacy retreated back against his seat, his body stiffening. 'I'm not happy about that.'

'Those are the terms we'll work under. I assure you we'll be searching for evidence that will either prove Caleb's innocence, or prove someone else was the murderer of Jonas Gorst.'

De Lacy's sullen face stared at him. 'Why should I pay for work that might make the case against Caleb stronger?'

Frank held out the paper he'd recently signed. 'If you are unsure, please take this back and rip it up.' He half-wished he would do that, as there was something about the man he disliked; it wasn't his strange looks, but his arrogance and air of superiority.

De Lacy folded his arms, making no effort to take the paper. 'No. I want your agency to help Caleb. I know Dorothy Piff, even though she dislikes me, will work hard, and make everyone do the same, as she loves the two boys.'

He didn't like the aspersion they needed Dorothy to crack the whip, but he decided to ignore the remark. 'Mr De Lacy, there are a few questions I'd like to ask you. It'll save having to pay you another visit.'

Bryce De Lacy leant forward, his shoulders relaxing. 'Yes, go ahead.'

Frank took a notebook and biro from his briefcase; De Lacy stiffened. 'Surely we can keep this informal?'

'We're professionals, we all take notes of interviews, and share our findings with each other. Five brains are better than one.'

'Five? I thought the detectives were yourself, Mr Elderkin and Miss Bowman?'

'Miss Piff and Mrs Elderkin are present at all our meetings. Sometimes it takes someone one step removed from the investigation to pick up on that salient point.'

De Lacy sniffed. 'I believe Mrs Elderkin is your cook. I don't consult members of my domestic staff when making decisions.'

Frank felt like taking the recently signed agreement and stuffing it down his throat. 'That's how we work. We respect each other's opinions and that's proved to be a successful formula.' He waved the paper at De Lacy again. 'Second thoughts? Now is the time to change your mind before we take the case further.'

De Lacy shuffled in his chair. 'No. No. Carry on with the questions.'

Frank once more prepared to take notes. 'I believe you haven't an alibi for the time Jonas Gorst was murdered. Could you tell me where you were on that Friday evening?'

De Lacy's eyes seemed to move farther apart. 'Are you suggesting I killed Gorst? This is ridiculous! Why would I spend money trying to prove Caleb is innocent if I was the murderer?'

Frank mentally counted to ten. 'It's important we know where everyone was that night; we need to get the whole picture. You may have some information that contains a vital clue; we won't know until we hear it. Please answer the question, Mr De Lacy.'

'I've already told the police where I was. They had more reason to ask than you, as this was before they found Caleb's fingerprints on the axe.' His voice was thin and peeved. 'I was here. All the staff had gone, it was a Friday night.'

'What did you do during that time?'

He looked up at the ceiling and sighed. 'I ate dinner, which had been prepared and was in the hostess trolley. I finished with cheese and some port.' He pointed to the decanters in the Tantalus. 'I left the dirty dishes and glasses in the kitchen. Then I came back here and played some music, read a little, then went to bed.'

Lazy bastard, couldn't even wash up a few dishes. 'Did you see Miss Spooner that evening?'

He frowned. 'Er . . . no. I don't think so.'

'A pity. She could have given you an alibi.'

De Lacy shrugged. 'I usually go in and say goodnight, but I think she'd gone to bed early.'

Frank wrote up his notes, deliberately taking his time. He'd get the sod agitated, then a few truths might slip out. 'You've only recently made contact with the Breens, I believe.'

De Lacy looked at him suspiciously. 'Yes, it was at Rosalind's funeral. But you know that, don't you?'

Frank nodded. 'Could you explain to me why, having known Daniel and Caleb Breen for such a short length of time, you've involved yourself so deeply in trying to help Caleb?'

De Lacy's lower lip wobbled. 'They're my closest, my only, living relatives.'

'But you've only recently met them. If it was Daniel who'd been arrested, would you have been equally caring?'

De Lacy's face reddened. 'I can't see where this is leading.'

'It may not seem relevant at the moment, but we need to know as much as we can about Caleb's life and any recent events that have been important to him. From what I hear, he reciprocated your feelings. Is that true?'

De Lacy's face softened. 'I'd like to think so. I'm not sure if I can explain how I felt when I saw him at Rosalind's funeral. It was if I was meeting my younger self. We do resemble each other, don't we?'

His attitude had changed, his voice softened, it was as if he was in love with Caleb. Could he be a homosexual and desired his nephew? No. There were no sexual overtones in his voice. Still . . . 'So, I've been told. You didn't have the same feelings for Daniel?'

'I'm afraid not. Perhaps if he'd been less judgemental, willing to try to understand although his mother said she hated me, it all happened a long time ago, and I do regret my attitude towards Noah Breen. I admit I was wrong.'

'Miss Piff told me about that.' He paused. 'Had you formed any plans for Caleb before his involvement in the murder of Gorst?'

'What do you mean?'

'I believe Daniel Breen didn't want to have anything to do with you, but Caleb wanted to get to know you better. Were you planning to see Caleb even if Daniel didn't want you to?'

De Lacy's nostrils flared, obviously angry and uncomfortable at this line of questioning. 'I hadn't planned anything, but I wanted to see Caleb and he wanted to see me.'

Frank put his notebook and biro in his briefcase. 'Thank you for being honest. If I think of any other questions, I'll get back to you. I'll be off. We'll report any significant findings to you.'

'I'll see you out.'

'Don't bother, I'll say goodbye to Miss Spooner on the way out, if that's OK? She seems sharp for her age.'

'Yes, do that, she's remarkable, her memory is clear; she still treats me as if I were a teenager. You can tell her you're taking the case,

153

that will please her.' His voice was impatient, but there was a warmth to it when he spoke of his former nanny.

Frank closed the sitting room door, and made for Miss Spooner's room. The door was half-open. He knocked.

'Come in.' She was sitting on a sofa reading a book with the help of a large magnifying glass. 'Mr Diamond. Are you going to take the case on?'

He walked towards her and she patted the cushion next to her. He sat down, and a mixture of lavender and Pear's soap wafted towards him. 'Yes, we are.'

Her hand went to her neck and she stroked the pearl necklace. 'I'm glad.' She stared at him, her milky blue eyes looking into his. 'I trust you.'

'Thank you.' He rose to go.

She jerked the fingers of her right hand, gesturing him to come closer. 'Come back when he's not here,' she whispered, her voice bitter. 'He wouldn't let me go to her funeral.' Then she raised a stick-thin finger to her lips.

Crackles of electricity sparked through his body. He shook her hand, nodding, showing he understood. 'Goodbye, Miss Spooner.'

She smirked. 'Goodbye, Mr Diamond.'

As he left her room, De Lacy came out of the sitting room. 'Is she pleased?'

'Yes, overjoyed.' He made a gesture of farewell, opened the front door and made for his car.

Laurel could see Miss Spooner's invitation for Frank to return had excited him. 'She obviously wants to tell you something, and it must be something about De Lacy. Gosh, she seems an interesting character.'

'She sounded as though she wanted to get back at De Lacy as he didn't let her go to Mrs Breen's funeral. I'm presuming it was Rosalind Breen's, she didn't give a name, but who else could it have been?' Frank said.

'You must be right,' Dorothy said, her face animated. 'Rosalind kept in touch with Ada Spooner, they exchanged infrequent letters, and I know she met up with Ada, before she became too frail to travel far. They never met at Shrike Hall; Rosalind never went back there after she married. They'd meet in Aldeburgh when Bryce was away. Rosalind loved Ada Spooner, but after she'd seen her, she was always upset, possibly the meetings revived unpleasant memories.'

'I'll go back and talk to her, but I don't think I'll have time to do that for several days. It'll be tricky to find a time when De Lacy isn't there,' Frank said.

Stuart groaned. 'I don't know about the rest of you, but I've been sitting in this chair for too long. Isn't it time we moved to somewhere more comfortable? And what's more I could do with a drink.'

Frank laughed. 'I've just told you the only interesting fact that's come up recently and all you can think of is your dry throat and stiff bum!'

Mabel glowered at him. 'Well my bum's gone to sleep too, so I agree with Stuart.'

'That makes a change,' Stuart replied, then gasped as he realised what he'd said. 'Only joking, love.'

Laurel got up. 'Right. Everyone to the sitting room. Frank you do the drinks, mine's a whisky, double with a splash, Stuart light the fire, Dorothy plump up the cushions and Mabel, shall we have some cheese and biscuits?'

They stared at her.

'May I ask what you'll be doing while we busy ourselves?' Frank asked.

'I'll take Bumper out for a quick pee.'

'Try and keep him off the flower beds, Laurel; he's been cocking his leg too often. Jim's been complaining,' Dorothy said.

'We'll have a five-minute walk.'

'When you get back, we'll decide on our next move,' Frank said.

Laurel relaxed against her chair. Glasses in hand, cheese and biscuits circulated and eaten, and warmed by the fire, the members of the agency lapsed into silence. Bumper was slowly circulating around their feet, hoovering up any dropped crumbs.

Frank tossed back the last of his whisky. 'Here's my ideas for tomorrow and the next day. I'll ring Myres and try to make an appointment with him. Dorothy, would you make appointments for Laurel to see Daniel Breen? Stuart, I think you need longer sessions with Hebditch and Rudder, separately of course—'

'Teaching grandmother to suck eggs again,' Stuart complained.

'Apologies, Stuart. Could you use your contacts, and possibly Revie, to get background information on the Gorsts? Also, Myres, Rudder, Hebditch and Edith Chell. I know Miss Chell had an alibi, but she works on the reserve and lives in Leiston; she's a nosy so-and-so, she might have some red-hot gossip.'

Stuart nodded as he made notes.

'Laurel, you said you'd see the Gorsts, or would you prefer to interview Edith Chell?' Frank asked.

Bumper was nestled between her knees, having cleaned up the carpet. 'I'll take the Gorsts. I think I got on quite well with Mary Gorst when I met her at the funeral.'

Frank pulled a face. 'I was hoping you'd go for Edith Chell. I'll have to take her on.'

Stuart laughed. 'I wonder who'll she'll think you resemble this time. Georgie Best?'

'What lines of questioning do we follow?' Laurel asked.

'First, if relevant, take them through their lack of alibis and try to pinpoint where they were between the critical times of eight in the evening and midnight on Friday,' he said. 'Dig about for any con-nections to Caleb Breen, Bryce De Lacy, and Jonas Gorst.' He hesitated, perhaps conscious he'd been hogging the meeting.

Mabel sighed, got up and started collecting up crockery and glasses.

Stuart got up. 'Hold on, Mabel, I'll give you a hand.'

'No. Both of you stay here until we've finished the meeting, then I'll give you a hand,' Laurel said, conscious of Mabel's silence, and her lack of involvement; in the intensity of the conversation, they'd forgotten about her.

Mabel Hopped back into her chair.

'We'll need plenty of good fodder over the next few days, Mabel. Good job we've got you to look after us,' Frank said.

Sometimes she wanted to give him a very big kiss.

Mabel gave him a weak smile. 'I may have to up the food budget soon, if prices keep rising at this pace. I hardly think the Government's cut of half a pence off the price of a seven-pence pint of milk will do much to help.'

'You're a good housekeeper, love,' Stuart said, 'and with all the money De Lacy will have to cough up, I think you can order full cream.'

Mabel smiled at him. Laurel inwardly sighed with relief.

'Thanks, Mabel, give us all a few treats, cook what you like,' Frank said. 'Let's finish off the meeting. Suggestions?'

'What about the vandalism of the hides?' Laurel asked.

'Good point. Although officially Hebditch has taken us off that case, it's too much of a coincidence a murder was committed on the reserve, or at least a body was dumped there, as well as a hide being set on fire,' Frank said.

'Should we also see if we can find out anything about the drug problem?' Stuart asked. 'We haven't got a connection, but it's rumbling round, and if we did discover something concrete, at least it would keep us in Revie's good books.'

'Excellent,' Frank said. 'And as usual, let the suspects do the talking, you never know what they might reveal.'

There was a current of excitement passing between them. Laurel rubbed Bumper's head then slipped her fingers down his silky ears. The true beginnings of an intriguing case and so many interesting people involved. She doubted she'd sleep tonight; she'd be thinking of the suspects she'd recently met, and trying to knit them together to form a story.

Chapter Seventeen

Friday, March 10, 1972

Frank blew out his cheeks as he drove towards Leiston, through Westleton and Theberton. This was one interview he wasn't looking forward to; he didn't like Edith Chell and he was sure the feeling was mutual. Wouldn't it be nice if she was the murderer? He imagined her sharpening the axe, not asking himself how she'd managed to get hold of it, then she'd lured young Gorst to her house with tales of strong tea and custard creams, but when he wouldn't play ball, that is, give in to her advances, she tried to slice his head in two as he bent over to tie up his trainers. He grinned to himself. Should he tell this one to Laurel? Perhaps not.

Edith's house was a bungalow on the right of Abbey Road; when he'd telephoned for directions, she'd said there was a white swan filled with daffodils to the left of her drive.

'Ten sharp, and only half an hour, I've got to get to the reserve,' she'd said.

There was the swan, the daffodils emerging from between its wings, waving their yellow heads in the light breeze from the southeast. It was a brisk, sunny day, and although chilly, it was definitely more like spring than the days before. Laurel was hoping to fit in a swim, as the sea was smooth. He shuddered, there weren't many days even in the summer when he was tempted to get his kit off and plunge into the North Sea.

He waited for a farm vehicle to trundle past on its way north, before turning into Edith's drive. The bungalow was set back from the road and on either side of the drive were more daffodils; several bird boxes were on trees and nearer the house was a bird bath and a feeding table from which hung several feeders, one half-full of peanuts, another with fat balls. Two blue tits flew away as he approached. Edith really did like birds; it wasn't a false show to impress Ian Hebditch. He decided he'd do his best not to lose his temper when, no doubt, she would compare him to another footballing prick with long hair. She seemed to know something about the game; perhaps he could lighten the mood with a bit of football gossip.

The paintwork on the door and windows was blue, the walls pebble-dashed and the knocker bright with polish and possibly a good lacquering. He resisted rapping out 'Good Morning Sunshine' and instead gave two discreet knocks. The door opened.

'You're on time,' Edith said in an unbelieving voice.

'Good morning, Miss Chell, thank you for seeing me.'

She looked at him suspiciously, as though waiting for a punch line. 'Come on in. Wipe your feet, I've just mopped floor.' She led him into a tight hall with wet linoleum and beige flocked wallpaper.

'In here, please.' She opened a door to the left into a small living room; like the hall, the air felt dry and smelt of artificial air-freshener. It had the same overcrowded feel as De Lacy's room, but the furniture was a modest three-piece suite, covered in green velvet, placed around a tiled hearth on which an electric fire glowed.

'Why couldn't Mr Elderkin come and question me?' she asked.

'He's otherwise engaged.'

She sniffed.

The other main features of the room were a mahogany display cabinet, with a telephone on top, and a Victorian what-not – both pieces of furniture crammed with pottery figures, possible Doulton.

'You've got a good collection of figurines, Miss Chell. Are they Doulton?'

Her small brown eyes beneath thick eyebrows squinted at him. 'You an expert?'

'Not at all. That's quite a collection of Toby Jugs.'

She sniffed again. 'I can see you're *not* an expert. They're character jugs, Tobies have tricorn hats.'

'Really? I didn't know that.'

She looked pleased at his reply. 'Sit yourself down.'

He pointed to the jugs. 'Who do they represent?'

'That one is Merlin, next to him is Rip-van-Winkle.'

'And that one?' The face definitely reminded him of Hebditch.

'He's the Pied Piper, he's my favourite.'

He restrained from asking why.

'I better offer you a drink, as us Northerners are known for our hospitality,' she said. 'Tea or coffee?'

Arsenic or strychnine? 'Coffee, please.'

'I'll join you, I fancy a cup.'

Frank hoped it wasn't Camp Coffee. He sat down and was relieved at the sound of a percolator bubbling and a strong and pleasant smell of fresh coffee wafting in from the kitchen. He looked round. The only other furniture was a small coffee table in front of the fire and a television opposite him; the chair he was sitting in must be Edith's. He quickly moved to the one opposite.

Edith placed a tray on the coffee table, two mugs full of milky coffee – he couldn't have everything – and a plate of custard creams. Another bargain from the Co-op?

'Help yourself, I don't stand on ceremony. Good job you came early, there's a power cut this afternoon. Time this government got us back to normal.'

He sipped the coffee, he preferred black, but it had a good flavour. 'Miss Chell, or may I call you Edith?'

She raised her head from her mug and those button bright eyes regarded him again, as though she was looking for some sign in his face of disdain or dislike. She wasn't anyone's fool, he decided.

'I think we'll stick to Miss Chell, if you don't mind.'

'Of course.' He hadn't fancied hearing his name spat out from her lips, or even worse she might decide to call him Frankie. He took a notebook and biro from his briefcase.

'Where were you on the Friday evening Jonas Gorst was murdered?'

'I've told police already.'

'Would you mind telling me?'

'It's a waste of time, but I was in the cinema in Leiston with my friend, Iris.' He noted this down.

'Did you know Jonas Gorst?'

She glowered. 'I taught him.' From the look on her face it hadn't been a meeting of minds.

'What was he like as a pupil?'

'Terrible! He didn't want to learn, he was insolent and I couldn't tell you the times I had to send him to the headmaster. He spent more time playing hooky or on suspension, than he did in the classroom.'

'So, not one of your favourite pupils?'

She glared at him balefully. 'I don't like stupid questions; you Scousers are all the same, full of clever remarks. Don't waste my time, Mr Diamond.'

He bit back the words he wanted to say. 'As you like, Miss Chell. Did you see anything of Jonas Gorst after he left school?'

She pushed out her bottom lip and gazed upwards. 'He worked on the reserve a few times; I never acknowledged him and he didn't speak to me. I've seen him in Leiston, on Friday night when I go to the cinema with my friend, he and his gang hang about outside the cinema. I nearly clocked him one when he started shouting things at me.'

'What did he shout?'

Her face reddened. 'I can't remember.'

He didn't believe her; it must have been so foul she didn't want him to know. He couldn't blame her for that. 'What about the rest of the Gorst family, do you know them?'

'Mary's all right, but that husband of hers is a right piss-pot; luckily, he didn't come to many of the parent's evenings, but I remember he did come once when Jonas was in the third year; it was about choosing his options for CSE, he wasn't up to O levels. Didn't want

161

him doing stupid subjects like history and geography, and as for art! He made a right scene with Jonas's form teacher, called her some awful names. The Deputy Head had to arm-wrestle him out of the hall. He's a big chap, but that Fred Gorst was as slippery as an eel, and twice as nasty.'

This was getting juicy; Edith obviously enjoyed a good gossip. 'Have you heard any rumours about Jonas?'

She smiled, a secretive smile. 'Happen I have, happen I haven't.'

'What does that mean?'

'I've my own ideas about all this.'

'About what? The murder? Or about the drug scene in Leiston?'

'Why should I do all your work for you? You go round picking everyone's brains, charging big fees, letting other people do your leg work. It's the police who should be talking to me, not a tin-pot private detective.' She put her empty mug on the tray and leant back, a satisfied smile on her round face.

He felt like shaking her until her permed curls danced in protest. 'Miss Chell, if you think you know anything relevant about either of these matters, if you don't want to talk to me, you should talk with the police. As soon as possible.'

She folded her arms over her chest, resting them on pillow-like breasts, her pink jumper adding to their blancmange-like qualities. 'I will, when I'm ready.'

He decided to abandon this line of questioning for the moment, hopefully coming back to it later in the interview. If she did know something, and she started poking around, she might find herself in a tight corner. God help whoever was in there with her. Time for some light relief? 'You seem to know a lot about football, Miss Chell. What do you think of Fulham paying Spurs two-hundred-and-fifty-thousand pounds for Alan Mullery?'

'Only team I'm interested in is Leeds,' she sneered. 'They know how to deal with the likes of Spurs. Our Norman Hunter soon sorts them out.'

'I believe his nickname is "Bites yer legs". Is that true?'

She tossed her head.

He gave up. 'As I mentioned on the telephone this morning, the agency has been asked to find any evidence to prove Caleb Breen did not kill Jonas Gorst. May I ask your opinion? Do you think Caleb is capable of murder?'

She shook her head from side to side in an exaggerated fashion. 'The idea's ridiculous. I've said it before, that Caleb is as soft as a brush, he's scared of his own shadow.'

'How do you account for his fingerprints being on the murder weapon?'

Her cheeks slowly turned red. 'You don't listen, do you? Why should I do your work for you?' She nodded sagely. 'I've my own ideas. It's time you got some of your own.'

He couldn't remember meeting a ruder woman. He'd have one more try to get some information out of her, but she was obviously not going to share any of her knowledge or ideas with him.

'We try not to make connections until we've talked to all the people who've had relationships, however tenuous, with the murder victim. Otherwise it can be a waste of time if you start theorising too early.'

'My, my, what a lot of long words and fancy sentences. We don't go for flowery language where I come from.'

'Where about in Yorkshire is that?' He'd try one more time.

'Pickering. North Yorkshire, proper Yorkshire.'

He nodded. 'Lovely little town. May I ask why you didn't return to Yorkshire when you retired? You obviously like it much more than here.'

She glowered. 'That's none of your business.'

'One final question, Miss Chell, do you know Mr Bryce De Lacy?'

'No, I don't, and what's more I don't want to. What kind of name is that? De Lacy, I ask you.'

Frank gave in, he felt he'd gone several rounds with Sugar Ray Robinson. He put his notebook and biro into his briefcase and got up. 'Thank you for your time, Miss Chell.' He nearly didn't mention it again, as he knew what she would say, but he had to try and make

163

her understand. It was likely she knew nothing of importance, and she was just being awkward, or as she thought, a canny northerner. 'Miss Chell, if you know something relating to the murder of Jonas Gorst, you must tell the police. We've had one murder, and if, as you believe, Caleb Breen is not responsible, then the murderer is at large. I hope you'll take what I've said seriously.'

She snorted. 'I can look after myself, I'm not a silly Southerner. My God, the people round here, they're as wet as dead plaice. We breed them tough up North, Mr Diamond, and I don't count Liverpool as being North, so don't flatter yourself.'

'Thank you for the coffee, Miss Chell. My partner, Miss Bowman, will be amused to be called a silly Southerner. She's managed to fight off two murderers despite her place of birth. But then she's an intelligent and strong woman. Goodbye.' He made a quick exit before she could reply.

Chapter Eighteen

As Laurel drove towards the Gorst's cottage she went over in her mind how she would approach them. It was obviously a difficult time: Jonas recently murdered, questioning by the police and no doubt searches of Jonas's room, then the arrest of Caleb Breen, one of their employers. Not only had they lost their only child, but what did all this mean for their future?

She'd chosen her clothes carefully: navy jumper and skirt; she hoped they showed enough respect. Who should she talk to first? Probably Fred; he might get shirty if she talked to Mary before him. Also, she wanted to talk to Mary alone, she was sure if her husband, from what she'd seen of him at the funeral, was there, he would probably inhibit her talking freely.

Acorn Cottage was set a distance from the farmhouse, but the oak wood, with its rookeries, formed a common backdrop. She parked in front of a pair of semi-detached cottages; the house on the left was unoccupied, no curtains at the windows, and the small front garden, with its square of lawn although neatly cut, had no flowers or shrubs in it. The Gorst's garden, by contrast, had a low privet hedge, and, in a central bed, there were bright daffodils. Both cottages appeared well kept, with shiny green paint on the ornate barge boards and front doors, contrasting with red brick walls. There was no sign of life, no twitching of lace curtains, or smoke coming from the tall chimneys. She'd phoned Daniel Breen and asked him if he would see the Gorsts, and make sure it was all right for her to call on them today. He'd phoned back saying if she'd go in the afternoon, they would be in. Now she wondered if they'd decided they couldn't face her, and had gone out. Understandable, but now she was here, she wanted to get on with it.

She knocked on the front door and waited. Silence. She knocked again. Then a masculine voice, raised in anger, shouted something – she couldn't discern the words. She put her ear against the door. Shuffling feet moved slowly towards her. A Yale lock turned, and the door creaked as it opened.

Fred Gorst, hair uncombed, face unshaven, wearing grey baggy trousers and a brown zipped cardigan was an unedifying sight. Even from a couple of feet away he smelt of stale sweat and even staler beer. He rubbed his hand over his bald head. 'Mr Breen said you'd call. Don't know why you've come, police have been, crawled all over, and kept on asking questions until my head hurt. Still, you better come in. Mr Breen wanted us to talk to you, and he's the master, so we have to do as he says, even if his brother has done away with our Jonas.'

'Thank you.'

He looked her up and down. She was glad she'd worn flatties.

'You're a big girl. Not many your size round here.'

She smiled at him, hoping he wouldn't get too fixated on her physical attributes.

The front door led into a narrow passage which seemed to run the length of the house, ending in what she assumed was the back door. He opened the first door on the right and ushered her in. This was obviously the best room or parlour, it was cold and damp, as if the cast-iron fireplace hadn't seen many fires; its basket was filled with yellowing, crumpled newspaper covered with kindling. Two armchairs, upholstered in brown, shiny imitation leather were either side of it, and on the mantel a series of sepia photographs in brown wooden frames, showed groups of people arranged formally in rows, the women seated, men standing behind, as if they were celebrating a wedding or a christening.

He swayed, seeming unsure of how to proceed.

'Mr Gorst, could I talk to you first, then your wife? Is that all right?'

'I suppose so. Here?'

'Yes, this will be fine.'

'I'll go and tell Mary. Sit down, I'll be back soon.'

She chose the chair facing away from the light of the window. She took a notebook and biro from her handbag, and tried to make herself comfortable, not easy on the slippery chair.

Fred came back and she waved to the other chair. He certainly looked uneasy and kept shifting his body. She suspected they rarely used this room, and he would have been happier in the kitchen, or with his feet on the brass foot-bar of a pub. Good, an awkward atmosphere could be useful, especially with such a character.

'Mr Gorst, first of all can I say how sorry all the members of the Anglian Detective Agency are to hear of your son's death. He was far too young to die. I'm very sorry.'

His brown eyes looked her, his down-turned mouth not moving. 'Thank you. I never expected that. You don't think your child will go before you, do you? Ain't natural. And murdered. His mother's taken it bad, real bad. I'm not sure you'll get much sense from her; she's not got much sense to begin with. Reckon she'll lose her mind.'

He didn't seem to be deeply concerned about his prognosis. 'Has Mr Breen told you we've been hired to try and see if we can prove Caleb is not the murderer of your son?'

He frowned and pulled at his mutton-chop whiskers. 'Yes, he has.'

'What did you think about that? Do you think Caleb Breen is innocent?'

He didn't look at her directly, his eyes moving from side to side. 'He's the boss, we'll have to go along with it, won't we?'

'Would you be surprised if we do prove Caleb is innocent, or we find the true murderer of your son?'

He snorted and pointed out of the window. 'It's more likely them old rooks will fly away from the farm and never be seen again, than he'll get off.' There was malice and satisfaction in his voice.

'Why do you think Caleb killed Jonas?'

'I didn't say that, so don't you go telling Mr Breen I said it, cos I didn't.'

'I don't have to tell Daniel Breen about our conversation. We're only interested in finding the truth. If the truth is Caleb killed your son, and we find further proof, then we'll report our findings to the police. Those are the terms of our employment. I'd be interested to know why you think Caleb is the murderer.'

He half-closed his eyes and nodded several times. 'That's good. Who else could it be? I admit, Jonas had a wicked tongue on him, and he didn't like Caleb. I reckon it got on his goat, that such a feeble, poor specimen was above him, could boss him around, and even fire him if he wanted to. Jonas didn't like authority, including mine. I caught him a few times laying into Caleb, calling him names. He never let Mr Daniel hear him, he knew he'd be in trouble then. Caleb used to give him such looks, even though I suppose he was frightened of him. Once it went too far and Caleb lost it. He shouted at Jonas, saying he'd kill him. I stepped in and gave Jonas a real walloping when he got back home. We could have lost our jobs, silly bugger. Then he got too big and too nasty for me to take my belt to him.'

Her dislike for Fred Gorst increased. 'Did the police ask you where you were on the night Jonas was killed?'

His face reddened. 'Cheeky bastards! As if I'd kill my own son.'

'They have to check everyone out, even those closest to the victim. It's standard practice.'

'No need to bother about my alibi, or anyone else's. Can't see you'll be able to change things. Still, I don't expect you'll be worried, you'll get well paid. I hear that other funny bugger, De Lacy, is footing the bill. Nice little earner for all of you.'

She swallowed her temper. 'We'll be doing a professional job, Mr Gorst. Just for interest, where were that night?'

'I was at the pub.'

'All night?'

He hesitated. 'Came away a bit early, had a gippy gut, reckon it was the meat pie she'd cooked. Probably left the beef out and the flies spoiled it.'

'I haven't seen a fly yet this year. Do you get more on the farm?'

He sneered. 'Think you're a clever bugger, don't you?'

She smiled and decided not to agree with his estimation of her. 'Do you know of anyone else who might want to kill Jonas?'

'Way he behaved there could be dozens. He wasn't friendly with a lot of people.'

'Anyone in particular?'

He stuck out his bottom lip and shook his head. 'There's this crowd from Leiston he went around with. Dare say he could have upset a few of them.'

'Do you know any names?'

'No. He was close, was our Jonas. Wife might know.'

'Do you know where he was when he didn't come home at night?'

He was moving restlessly in his chair, making squeaking noises. She wasn't sure if it was the sound of his trousers rubbing against the fake leather, or if he'd released a string of farts. 'No, the bastard wouldn't say.'

The ripe smell emanating from him proved her second guess was correct.

He got up. 'I need to go somewhere. You go into the kitchen and talk to the wife.' He hurried from the room.

Waving a hand in front of her face, she got up and went to find Mary Gorst. She assumed that the next door on the right would lead to the kitchen. Mary was seated at a square table, peeling potatoes, the skins falling onto a newspaper; her face was miserable, and she looked ten years older than when Laurel had last seen her.

'Hello, Mary. May I come in?'

She looked up, hazel eyes blank, hair matted, and her once lively face expressionless.

'You do remember me, Mary? I'm Laurel Bowman, we met at Rosalind Breen's funeral.' Dash! Shouldn't have mentioned a funeral.

Understanding crept into her eyes. 'Miss Bowman. Yes, I remember you. You were kind.'

Laurel sat down opposite her. 'I'm truly sorry about Jonas.'

Mary's swollen eyes welled with tears; they trickled unchecked down her cheeks. 'My poor boy.'

169

Laurel took a tissue from her handbag and offered it to her.

'Thank you.'

'Mary, I've come here to ask you some questions. If you don't want to do it now, I can come back when you feel better.' Would the poor woman ever feel better?

She dabbed at her cheeks. 'No, it's all right, as long as you don't mind me crying. I can't help it, the tears just seem to keep coming, it's driving Fred wild.'

'Thank you.'

'Fred told me you'd be coming. Mr Breen said to him you're going to prove Caleb didn't do that awful thing to my Jonas.' There was another wave of tears as she spoke his name.

'That's right. First of all, can you think of anyone who would want to kill Jonas?'

'Apart from my hubby?' She gasped and slapped a hand over her mouth. 'No, I didn't mean that, although Fred got really mad with Jonas at times. He used to wallop him, but that all stopped when Jonas muscled up.' She dabbed her eyes again. 'I suppose some of the boys he went round with might have turned against him. He wasn't good at making friends, was Jonas.'

'Do you know the names of any of the boys he went about with?'

'He mentioned a few to me.'

'Can you write their names down?' She tore a page from her notebook and handed it to Mary along with her biro.

'I only know their Christian names. Apart from one. He's the son of the butcher in Leiston, he was in the same class as Jonas at primary, as well as secondary school. I reckon he was the closest Jonas came to having a friend.' She wrote slowly, but clearly, in classic copperplate, then passed the paper and biro back to Laurel.

'Do you know where Jonas went when he was out all night?'

She twisted her mouth, looking down, avoiding looking directly at Laurel. 'I did wonder . . .'

Laurel waited for Mary to finish her sentence.

Mary glanced up. 'I don't know for sure, but I think Jonas may have been at those parties on the reserve. You won't tell them,

Mr Hebditch and Mr Rudder, will you? I don't like to think Jonas was mixed up in that, specially setting fire to that hide. That's arson, isn't it?'

'Why do you think he was one of the vandals?'

Mary raised her eyebrows. 'Vandals? I didn't say he was a vandal. I just think he knew something about it.'

'What made you suspicious?'

'It was about three weeks ago, it was a Saturday and I'd promised Jonas I'd buy him some new trainers, so we went to Leiston. For once Fred let us have the car and Jonas drove me in. He's a good driver, is our Jonas.' She paused, realising what she'd said. 'He *was* a good driver; it's going to be hard saying that word – was.' She sighed. 'We was walking to the shop, I felt so proud, folks were saying good morning to us, and Jonas was in a good mood, saying hello to people. We bumped into that butchers' son, the one I've given you the name of, and I overheard something of what they said.'

Laurel tried to restrain herself, she wanted to get hold of Mary's arms look her in the eye and draw every last piece of information from her. 'What did they say?'

'Alan, that's the butcher's son, said, "Are we on for tonight?" Jonas says, well he whispers, but he forgets I've got sharp ears, and I pretended to be interested in something in a shop window.'

'That's clever of you, Mary.'

'I thought that. Fred and Jonas think I'm just a stupid woman, but I know more than they think.'

Laurel took a deep breath and waited. 'So, what did Jonas say?'

'Oh, yes. Jonas whispers back, "Pick me up at eight. Usual place." That Alan's got his own car. He says, "Have you got the gear?" and Jonas says, "Not as much as last time, but it's good stuff." I didn't understand that bit. Then Alan said something that made me wonder if they were involved with the trespassing on the reserve.'

'What was that?'

'He said, "That should scare the birds," and then he laughed. At first, I thought he was talking about girls, dolly birds, you, know,

171

but later on when I heard what happened to the hide, I began to wonder.'

'Mary, did you tell all this to the police?'

She frowned. 'I gave that nice detective, you know . . . what's his name?'

'You mean Detective Cottam?'

'Yes, that's him. I told him the names, but I didn't tell him I thought Jonas was mixed up with those goings on at the bird reserve.'

She took Mary's hand. 'I think I must tell Inspector Revie. Is that all right?'

A few more tears travelled down Mary's cheeks. 'I suppose you have to. What does it matter – Jonas is dead now.'

At last a nugget of information. How it tied up with Jonas's death, she wasn't sure, but it was a possible link between Jonas, the parties on the hide and drugs. She couldn't wait to get back and talk to the others, especially Frank.

Chapter Nineteen

Saturday, March 11, 1972

Stuart parked his Rover in the bird reserve car park, and checked his watch. He'd arranged to meet Ian Hebditch at nine thirty and then Rudder at ten. It was a cold, bright morning, and as he got out of his car, a sharp east wind snapped at him. He sniffed the air; rain, he could smell rain. He looked seawards – yes, there were a couple of dark clouds scudding in. Only showers, not real rain. He halted, went back to his car and took out his binoculars. A male marsh harrier, bright plumage shining in the sun, was pursuit-flying – looking for a willing female. Hebditch would be pleased to hear there was at least one bird who hadn't been frightened away by all the kerfuffle last Sunday. He hoped the harrier's quest was successful. The vandalism, and then the murder, had tainted his enjoyment of the reserve; it was a sacrilege to spoil this peaceful place. The sooner they solved this case the better.

The outer office was deserted but the noise of a filing cabinet drawer being banged shut indicated someone was in the inner office and that someone was in a bad temper.

'Mr Hebditch? Ian?' he called.

Hebditch's avuncular face, his forehead creased, peered round the door. 'Ah, Stuart. Could you wait a moment? I'm trying to find something. God know where it's got to.'

'That's OK. No rush.' He wasn't sure if that was true as Rudder would be here in half-an-hour. He wouldn't be pleased to be kept waiting. He sighed. He'd known Ian since he was appointed as the Warden; he couldn't see him as the murderer. Stuart Elderkin, he chided himself, have you learnt nothing?

'Come on in, Stuart. I'll look for it later,' Hebditch shouted.

Stuart sat on the other side of the desk and got out his notebook. 'Ah, this is a formal interview?'

He nodded. 'You know the circumstances?'

'Yes, and I do hope you can prove Caleb is innocent. He seems incapable of murder; I know he's, er . . . different, but violent? No.'

Stuart settled his bulk into the chair. 'I believe the police asked you where you were the night Jonas was killed?'

Hebditch shook his head. 'Yes, I haven't got an alibi. I was going to dinner with friends, but they cancelled in the afternoon, so I was at home – alone.'

'Thank you for telling me.'

'Not at all. I certainly didn't murder Gorst. Why would I want to do that?' He laughed uneasily.

Why indeed? Stuart thought. Protesting too much? 'When was the last time you saw Jonas Gorst?'

'The police asked me that, too. I was going to check in my diary and let them know, but then I heard Caleb had been arrested, so I didn't bother.'

'Could you tell me approximately when it was, and what passed between you? You can give me the precise date later.'

Hebditch leant back in his chair. 'I think the last time was when he was helping to build the new hide.'

'I thought Myres used his own men to do that?'

'Yes, he did, but Jonas was definitely there, I can't remember why, you'd have to ask Myres.'

Stuart made a note to tell Frank, although he might not see him before he went to see Myres. 'Can you remember what passed between you?'

Hebditch's eyebrows rose. 'I certainly can. Jonas was most rude.'

'Really? What did he say?'

'I was doing my usual round of the reserve, I try to do that every day.' He smiled. 'I enjoy my daily tour, especially if I can walk round when the visitors have gone home and it's just me and the birds. I decided to see how the hide was progressing. Jonas Gorst was inside the hide when I got there. I went in, I didn't feel the need to knock, after all I am the Warden. He was doing some carpentry, or something, he obviously didn't hear me come in, for when I said, "Hello, Jonas—"

'He jumped. "Bloody hell," he said. "What do you think you're doing sneaking up on me like that?"'

'I was very angry. He was a farm labourer, and I'm an educated man, in charge of the reserve. "You impudent puppy," I said. Obviously, looking back on the incident, it was not the best choice of words.

'He rose up, his face turning red, his fists balled. I must admit he looked as though he was going to attack me.

'"Get out of here," he said, "you interfering old fart."

'I was not going to be intimidated, even if there was a risk of him attacking me. "Jonas Gorst," I said, "I think you'd better come to your senses. I shall report your behaviour to Mr Breen and also to Mr Myres. Does he know you're here?"

'He scowled at me, but I could see he realised he'd overstepped the mark, and was regretting his rash words. He lowered his arms and looked away. "You shouldn't have come in like that," he said. "You made me jump. I didn't know who you were." His eyes moved from side to side. "I thought you were one of them vandals," he said.

'I thought this was highly unlikely. An apology was obviously far too difficult for him to articulate.

'I started to feel calmer; he was looking shamefaced. "Jonas, you must learn to control your temper. I was merely going on my usual tour of the reserve, and looked in to see what progress had been made on the hide."

'"Will you tell Mr Myres?"

'I didn't answer straight away; I didn't see why I should make it easy for him. After a time, I said, "I'll sleep on it and make my decision tomorrow. You can help me to make that decision by assuring me you will never speak to me, or any member of staff, or a visitor, in that manner. The reserve is a peaceful place and many people come here for solitude and a tranquil environment." I'm not sure he fully understood these concepts.'

Stuart silently agreed.

'Finally, after much shoe-shuffling, he said. "I'm sorry I was rude. I won't do it again. Please don't tell Mr Myres, will you?" I could see he was very worried at the thought I'd report his poor behaviour to Myres. I hadn't realised he held Myres in such esteem. I wondered if he was hoping find employment with him, which would certainly be a step up the ladder. "Very well, Jonas," I said, "the matter is closed, but if I hear you've been rude again, not only will I report you to Mr Myres, and Mr Breen, but to your parents as well."

'There was more shuffling of feet and eventually a muttered thank you. "You'd better finish your work, tidy up and go home," I said. I left him there and continued on my round of the reserve, but the incident rankled. That was the last time I saw him.'

Stuart finished scribbling in his note book. 'Thanks, Ian. I didn't know Jonas, except by sight, but from what I hear he wasn't well liked. Has anyone else on the reserve had a run in with him?'

Hebditch pursed his lips. 'Well . . . I'm not sure if I should say this, perhaps I should leave it to Rudder, but I'm afraid there was an incident, and in this case, I don't think all the blame can be placed at Gorst's door.'

Was there anyone who hadn't fallen out with Jonas Gorst? 'I'd be interested to hear it from your perspective, Ian. I'm sure Hal Rudder will tell me about it when I see him.'

Hebditch looked at his watch. 'He should be here in ten minutes.' He got up and closed the office door, even though it was only a few inches ajar. As he sat down again, he cleared his throat, and leant forward. 'You mustn't tell Rudder I've spoken to you about this.'

He looked as though he was going to enjoy spilling the beans. Perhaps he wasn't too fond of his deputy?

'This didn't happen on the reserve, and I was not present when the incident took place; but I was told about it, the person who told me thought it was no way for the Deputy Warden of the reserve to behave.'

Stuart nodded in an encouraging manner. Just gossip then, but gossip can lead to something more solid.

'Hal Rudder has a wife . . . she's a local Leiston girl,' Hebditch said, in a disapproving voice.

Stuart managed to contain himself.

'It was a Saturday night in one of the Leiston pubs, and Rudder and his wife, I believe she's called Cindy, were drinking with some friends. Gorst was also there with a group of youths, making a bit of a racket, I'm told.' He shook his head, frowning, obviously disapproving of people enjoying themselves.

'Which pub was that?'

Hebditch shrugged. 'I forget. I don't drink in such places, surely that isn't important?'

'It could be, if we think we need to follow this up and want to talk to the landlord,' Stuart replied.

Hebditch looked shocked. 'But it couldn't have anything to do with Gorst's murder, could it? Perhaps I shouldn't have spoken.'

Stuart took a deep breath. 'Please finish off the story, Ian.'

Hebditch wriggled on his seat and looked at the door. 'Very well. Mrs Rudder is a . . . I'm not sure how to describe her.'

'Flighty?' he offered.

'Not a word I would choose, but it will do. It seems Rudder caught her making eyes at Gorst and had words with her. She lost her temper and went over to Jonas and started flirting with him, and the other youths were joining in, bandying words about. Some people find Mrs Rudder attractive, and I suppose she is, in a cheap kind of way. It seems she was enjoying being the centre of attention. Rudder grabbed his wife's arm and tried to pull her away, she resisted, and Jonas tried to help her. Rudder starts on him, but Jonas lands a terrific blow to Rudder's jaw and he goes over.

'It was bedlam, the landlord phoned the police; then with the help of some regulars, threw Jonas and his friends out of the pub. Mrs Gorst started crying and fussing over her husband, who was still on the floor.' Hebditch tut-tutted. 'It was quite disgraceful.'

'Was there any comeback? Any more aggro between Rudder and Gorst?'

He shook his head. 'Not that I know. I did have a quiet word with Rudder, and told him as a responsible member of the community, he must watch his behaviour. We have several important patrons; I don't think they would be amused.'

Hebditch went down in Stuart's estimation. What a tight arse! He didn't care much for Rudder himself, and he'd seen his wife, she was considerably younger than her husband. It was probably a poor match for both of them. God, he'd been lucky. He'd had the love of two lovely women. He mustn't forget it. He'd buy Mabel a big box of chocolates on his way home.

'Thank you for telling me that, Ian.' There was a noise from the outer office. 'That must be Mr Rudder. Are you off round the reserve?'

Hebditch got up, looking shamefaced. 'Yes. You won't mention this?' he whispered.

Stuart smiled. 'No, please don't worry.' He opened the door and Hebditch left.

'Ah, Hal. Mr Elderkin is waiting for you. See you this afternoon?'

'No, it's my Saturday off. I've come in just to see Mr Elderkin, then I'm straight off. Promised Cindy I'd take her to Ipswich, do some shopping, catch a film.'

'Really? Enjoy yourself.'

Hypocrite, Stuart thought.

'Come in, Mr Rudder. I'll try not to keep you. Any idea what film you'll be seeing?'

Rudder smiled. After listening to Hebditch's gossip, Stuart felt more inclined to like Rudder a tad more.

'Not sure, we'll see what we can get into.'

When they were both seated, Stuart took up his biro. Rudder frowned. 'Is this official? You're not a policeman any more, are you?'

'No, no, Mr Rudder, but we do have a close relationship with the

Suffolk constabulary. We're a *private* detective agency. You know why we're making inquiries?'

'Something to do with the Breens, isn't it? I know Caleb Breen's been arrested for murdering Gorst.' He spat out the name.

He's not hiding his dislike of Jonas. 'We've been hired to see if we can prove Caleb Breen is innocent of murder.' He paused. 'And, possibly find the true murderer.'

'You mean Caleb is innocent? And there's me thinking it's the one good thing he's ever done.'

Stuart looked up from writing on his notebook. 'Really? You didn't like Jonas Gorst?'

Rudder laughed. 'He was a nasty piece of work, a right toe-rag. Why Hebditch allowed him on the reserve, I don't know.' He frowned, then gave a sour smile. 'I better mind what I say if you're looking to pin the murder on someone else.'

Stuart shook his head. 'We don't do pinning crimes on people. It could be our investigations confirm Caleb's guilt. We deal in the truth, if we can find it.'

'I've heard you lot are straight. I know you've done some good work. Finding that kid after all those years, well, that was well done.'

Rudder moved up another notch in Stuart's estimation. 'Thank you. Would you mind telling me why you disliked Jonas Gorst? You've got nothing to worry about if you didn't kill him, and it would help us to build up a picture.'

Rudder leant back and puffed up his chest. 'I nearly did kill him one night.' He proceeded to recount the fight in the pub, but his slant was Gorst was bothering his wife and making suggestive remarks. Also, Gorst came off worse; the only bit that was the same as Hebditch's story was Gorst and his chums were thrown out by the landlord.

'In which pub did this happen?'

'The White Horse.'

A visit was needed. Not a chore, the beer was good. 'Can you think of anyone else who disliked Gorst?'

Rudder gave a hollow laugh. 'How long have you got? He wasn't a popular fellow.'

'All right, let's limit it to anyone on the reserve. Any of the workers or volunteers.'

'The Warden didn't like him.'

'Oh, why's that?'

Rudder put a hand to his mouth and sniggered. 'Gorst made fun of him. He did it when he was working clearing the reeds and the Warden was checking the work. You know how fussy Mr Hebditch is. I should have stopped Gorst, but it was funny, and all the other workers, they were in tucks.'

Intriguing. This was a new side to Gorst. 'What did he do?'

'You've seen the way Mr Hebditch walks, and how he waves his hands around?'

Stuart nodded.

'Mr Hebditch was fussing, saying the lads weren't doing a neat enough job of stacking the cut reeds. I was in charge of them, so I wasn't too pleased he'd gone over my head; I'd rather he had a word with me in private, and then I could have seen it was done as he wanted. When he'd finished nagging us and waving his arms about, he walked away, and Jonas minced behind him, like a girl, with his hands on his hips. We all laughed, we couldn't help it. Hebditch whipped round, but Jonas was quicker, and he bent over pretending to tie up his boot laces. Hebditch glared at us. "We were laughing at Jonas, Mr Hebditch, he nearly fell over," I said. All this was before I had a run-in with him at the pub. After that, I heard Jonas started rumours that Mr Hebditch was . . . you know, a bit queer.'

Stuart raised his eyebrows. 'Homosexual?'

Rudder twisted his lips, obviously uncomfortable talking about this. 'Yes.'

'Is he homosexual?'

Rudder's colour deepened. 'Oh, I don't think so. I don't think he approves of sex in any shape or form, unless you're a marsh harrier or an avocet. Then he's keen for them to do the business, lay eggs and raise chicks.'

Stuart smiled. Rudder had a way with words. 'He's asexual?'

Rudder nodded. 'That sums it up. I think the rumours got to him and who'd been spreading them.'

'That's very interesting,'

Rudder seemed to relax. 'You won't let on to Mr Hebditch I told you, will you, Mr Elderkin?'

'No, of course not.'

Rudder bit his lip. 'Does this make Mr Hebditch a suspect? I know he's a bit of an old woman, but I don't think he'd murder anyone.'

Stuart smiled, but made no comment. 'Did the police ask you where you were on the night Jonas was murdered?'

He frowned. 'They did. I don't have an alibi. My wife went to see her mother, but I stayed in and watched the telly.'

'What time did your wife get back?'

Rudder looked shifty. 'I don't know. I was in bed fast asleep.'

Or waiting up for Cindy, who perhaps didn't come back until the early hours, if at all. Another fact to check up on. 'Well, I think that wraps it up for today, Mr Rudder. You better get on your way and enjoy the film, and the shopping.'

'And spending money we can't afford.' He got up, shook Stuart's hand and lumbered out of the office.

Stuart sat at the desk, looking through his notes. Could either of these men be the killer of Jonas Gorst? A crime of passion and revenge? A murder of hate and fear? He patted his stomach. The morning's work had given him an appetite. Back to Greyfriars for a coffee and a slice of Mabel's fruit cake. No, first to Leiston and that box of chocolates.

Chapter Twenty

Daniel Breen wandered aimlessly over his land; he loved the farm, but today his heart wasn't lifted as he passed a field of winter wheat, its green shoots healthy and promising a good harvest. Today, all he could think of was Caleb, locked up in prison, how he must be suffering, unable to understand why he'd been accused of Gorst's murder, horrified by the harsh surroundings, perhaps mocked for his looks, or possibly a figure of fear and hate.

But as Daniel continued walking, gradually the familiar surroundings, and the signs of spring, calmed and soothed him. The fields he'd put to grass were verdant; he'd ploughed and seeded them two years ago, they should last a further five years with care and good cultivation. He hoped to start breeding Charolais cattle; it would be a high capital investment, but there was now enough grass acreage to support a small number of cows.

He stopped to look at a field he'd sown with sugar beet, bent down and crumbled a handful of soil, bringing it up to his nostrils. The texture was good, open and friable, and it smelt of centuries of care. To him the soil was a living being, the basis of their land. Then a wave of hopelessness washed over him. What would the future hold? How could he go on if Caleb was found guilty and given a life sentence? He'd promised his mother he'd always care for Caleb; he'd let her down, let Caleb down.

The detective, Laurel Bowman, was coming at four; he'd asked her not to come earlier as he had too much work to do. He'd have to get another man to replace Jonas. What about Fred Gorst? How was he coping? He couldn't expect him to do two men's work. Caleb was an erratic worker, and Daniel had always kept a close eye on him and made sure his jobs were completed; but he'd have to get someone to look after the chickens. Animals couldn't be ignored for a few days, unlike plants. He was doing Caleb's jobs, but it made the day run into night, and for the first time in his life he knew what it was to feel panic, as he thought of all he had to do to keep the farm running. Even when he'd had to take on the responsibility for the farm when his father died, and he'd given up college, he hadn't felt like this. Then, his mother has been there, to support, and advise.

He turned back towards the house. He'd try and do a few more jobs before Miss Bowman arrived. He'd just have to get on with it. Please God, he prayed, let the agency find evidence that clears Caleb. The night Jonas died, when he'd been with Theresa, he thought his life would change. He'd been deliriously happy. It was if they'd never parted. He was as much in love with her as he had been when he was a young man. After a meal, they went to the cinema. She'd squeezed his hand and led him to the back row, just as they'd done when they were sweethearts. He waited a little while before he'd put an arm round her shoulder; she'd turned to him and they kissed. When they came out of the cinema, he was as dazed as a rabbit in a car's headlights, and she looked the same. They'd seen little of the film and his lips were beautifully sore.

At her house, she'd whispered, 'They'll be fast asleep, and even if they're wide awake, I don't care.' They tiptoed to her bedroom, and with the curtains open, and soft moonlight on their naked bodies, they'd loved each other. He hoped he hadn't hurt her, for it was a long time since he'd had a woman, and the taste of her lips, her breasts, and the softness of her skin, made him lose control. He hadn't been as gentle, or as considerate, as he should. Later, when he'd whispered apologies, she'd pulled him to her. He loved her again, slowly and gently.

He hadn't seen or heard from her since that night. They'd arranged to meet in the middle of the week, but then hell broke loose, and he hadn't contacted her. What would she think? He'd been so happy when he came home that night; he hadn't thought to look into Caleb's room. That brief taste of love, passion and happiness somehow made the present situation even more unbearable.

He mustn't think of himself; he must concentrate on helping the agency find the true murderer. The cries of the rooks penetrated his despair. He looked up at the oaks, the black silhouettes of the birds clear against the blue sky. They were busy, always busy, the nest building was at its peak, and soon it would be time for mating, laying eggs, and bringing new life into being. They never gave up; if their nests were torn apart by storms, they built new ones, if their young died, they would have another brood, nothing would stop them. Standing there, under the huge oaks, listening to the raucous cries, he felt a continuous connection with not only his father and mother, but all the ancestral Breens. God knows what hard times and tribulations some of them had faced. The Breens, like the rooks, must go on.

The sound of a car made him march towards it. Damn, she was early. As he neared the house, he saw it was Theresa getting out of the car. She waved, then ran towards him. He ran to her, and took her in his arms.

'Daniel, I've come to help you,' she said, when he finally released her.

'You being here is help enough.'

'Let's go into the house.'

He crushed her to his side, she slipped an arm round his waist. He felt like picking her up and heading for his bedroom, but controlled himself, and instead they sat at the kitchen table, side by side, with cups of tea.

'Why didn't you phone me?' she asked, her brown eyes soft, full of tears. 'I waited, I wasn't sure if you would want me to come, but I couldn't stand it anymore. I wanted to be with you.'

She was so beautiful, her expressive face full of love and concern.

'I'm sorry, Theresa, this week has been a nightmare. I was just thinking about you as I walked the farm. Last Friday night, it was if all those years hadn't happened, it was if we were young again and just as much in love.'

She put her arms around his neck, raised her head and kissed him. 'I made a terrible mistake when I left you. I wanted to see new places, make new friends. I was afraid I'd spend the rest of my life being a farmer's wife, like your mother.'

He pulled her close. 'And now?'

'That's why I've come over. I've taken two weeks off work; I'm going to help you run the farm. You need to be with Caleb as much as you can. If you tell me what to do, I think I can do most of the basic jobs.'

He was speechless, made dizzy by a delirious feeling spiralling through his body.

She looked unsure. 'Of course, only if you want me to help you.'

'I never want you to leave my side again.' Her lips parted under his. Damn, the detective would be here soon. He pulled away, and explained the situation.

'Oh, I hope they can find out who did it.'

'*You* don't believe Caleb is a murderer?'

She shook her head vehemently. 'No, I've known you both since we were children. I know neither of you are violent people.' She hesitated, as though not sure if she should continue.

'What is it, Theresa?'

'I may be jumping ahead of myself, but if you ever thought the reason I left was because of Caleb, you were wrong. He's your brother, I always admired you for the way you cared for him.'

A deep feeling of relief, followed by a wave of love for her, made him silently clasp her to him. 'You mean—'

She put a finger to his lips. 'Let's leave it there, Daniel. What do you need doing? I can make a start when Laurel Bowman gets here.'

He smiled at her. 'And when she's gone?'

'I packed a suitcase.'

Laurel parked her Cortina GT next to a beige Ford Escort. Daniel Breen must have visitors. She hoped he could get rid of them, she didn't fancy making small talk. She knocked on the front door and

Daniel opened it. She was shocked: he looked deliriously happy and grinned at her broadly.

'Mr Breen, have you had good news?'

He shook his head, then paused. 'Yes, in a way, but no good news of Caleb. Please come in.' He led the way to the kitchen. Theresa Poppy was busy at the Aga pouring boiling water into a teapot. She turned and placed it on the pine table. Now she understood why Daniel looked as though he'd won the pools. Teresa's face was flushed and the look that passed between her and Daniel said it all.

Laurel was happy for them, but at the same time envious of their love and passion. She'd felt the same when she was engaged, before Angela was murdered. It was the most wonderful feeling when both of you were madly in love. But for her it had been a love that wasn't strong enough to withstand the trauma of Angela's death. *This* passion looked like it might last.

Daniel introduced her. 'Theresa is going to help me on the farm until all this blows over.'

He was being optimistic, even a force eight wouldn't sweep away the damning evidence of Caleb's guilt. 'That's good. Are you a country girl, Miss Poppy?' With a name like that, how could she be anything else?

'Please call me Theresa. When I was a girl I often helped with jobs on our farm; I expect it'll all come back to me.' She poured out three mugs of tea. 'I'll take mine outside, then you can get on with giving Daniel the third degree.' She made for the door.

He smiled at her. What a mega-watt smile, Laurel hadn't realised how handsome he was until now. It was a good job Theresa had turned up, the house could do with a woman's touch; already it looked uncared for and the kitchen smelt of grease, suggesting a diet of fry-ups and chips. Not everyone could cook like Frank.

She took out a notebook and biro from her handbag. 'Shall we make a start, Mr Breen?'

'Please, call me Daniel.' He pushed a mug of tea towards her and drank from his own. He nodded approvingly. 'Good cup of tea,' he said proudly.

She smiled. 'I'm sure Theresa will be a big help to you.'

He smiled again.

'Daniel, we're assuming Caleb is innocent. Can you think of any persons who had access to the barn, and therefore to the fromard? We've got to assume someone stole it, knowing it would have Caleb's fingerprints on it. That person was trying to incriminate Caleb in Jonas Gorst's murder.'

He took a deep breath. 'There's me, for starters, then any of the Gorsts, including Jonas, though why he'd steal the weapon that was used to murder him, is beyond me. Quite a few of the local folk know of Caleb's collection.'

'Is there anyone from the reserve who knew about it?'

'I suppose it's possible, but not very likely.' He frowned. 'Just a minute, I remember Mr Hebditch and Mr Rudder coming here. It was not long before Mother died. She'd invited them for tea, as she wanted to discuss some fund raising for the reserve. She liked to involve herself in local events, when she had the time. I think she took them on a tour of the farm to show them how we were leaving unploughed borders at the edges of fields to allow birds to forage for seeds and to give wild flowers a toehold. I think she took them to see Caleb's collection of old machines and tools. I'll ask Caleb when I next see him.'

Interesting. 'What about Mr De Lacy? Would he know about Caleb's collection?'

Daniel looked puzzled. 'Yes, Caleb showed them to him. But why would De Lacy try to implicate Caleb? Although it distresses me, De Lacy seems genuinely fond of Caleb, and Caleb seems to think a lot of him.'

Laurel shrugged. 'We have to try and make connections, even if they seem unlikely. I've learnt never assume someone is innocent even if your instinct tells you otherwise.'

His shoulders slumped. 'You aren't going to think Caleb is innocent until you discover someone else is guilty, are you?'

'No, don't think that. We're assuming Caleb is innocent, and someone's tried to frame him for the murder. I know Mr Diamond's told you if we find further evidence of Caleb's guilt, we'll pass this to the police. Hopefully, that will never arise.' She waited a few seconds. 'Are you happy with that?'

He looked angry. 'I'll have to be.'

She decided to change tack. 'Can you think of anyone who disliked Caleb so much they would try to frame him for murder?'

He sighed and pushed away his empty mug. 'A number of people were uneasy in Caleb's company, not only because of his strange looks, but he isn't good at mixing with people. They don't know what to say to him and he doesn't help; he's happiest here on the farm, or on the bird reserve when the visitors have gone.'

'So, you can't think of anyone who hated him?'

He gave a wry smile. 'I know Jonas Gorst didn't like him, but would he steal the fromard and kill himself to get his own back? You've got to admit, that's more than a bit far-fetched.'

She frowned. Was it possible Jonas Gorst took the fromard, for whatever reason, and there was a fight and it got used against him? It was a possibility. She'd bring it up at their meeting tomorrow morning.

'Is there anything you want to tell me about Caleb that you think is relevant to the case?'

The questioning and the answers seemed to go in increasingly tighter circles, with little useful facts or ideas emerging. He was getting restless, no doubt wanting to join Theresa. She couldn't blame him. This session hadn't been productive, except for the thought Jonas could have easily stolen the fromard, and Hebditch, Rudder and De Lacy, knew where it was kept.

As she went to her car, the rooks were wheeling round the oaks, their harsh calls reverberating round the farm yard. Theresa was walking towards the house, a bucket in her hand, wellingtons on her feet, a smile on her face as she waved goodbye. Laurel thought of the evening they would spend together. She shrugged. Bumper was waiting for her; she'd have to make do with a slobbery kiss from him.

Chapter Twenty-one

Frank revved the engine of the Avenger as he passed Westleton Heath on his way to interview Myres. The day had warmed up, spring sunshine lighting up clumps of flowering gorse. Over lunch Stuart told him about Hebditch finding Gorst in the new hide, the words they'd exchanged, and that Gorst didn't want Hebditch to tell Myres he'd been aggressive – or perhaps there was another reason. Stuart had done well, he'd got a lot out of his interviews, and found possible motives for both Hebditch and Rudder.

He looked at the petrol gauge, and drove to Scarlett's Garage in Westleton; he waited for a lorry to leave, winding up his window as diesel fumes drifted in. Having filled up the tank, he turned the car round, took the left turning off the B1125 onto the Darsham road.

When he'd phoned Myres yesterday, he'd been reluctant to meet, saying he needed to go to London for an early evening appointment, also he couldn't meet in the morning, he was too busy. Finally, he agreed to meet at two at his house, and described how to get there. 'About a mile down the Darsham Road, on the left. A white bungalow, the gates will be open,' he'd said.

Frank slowed down after about half a mile. There were the open gates, not what he was expecting – six feet of solid timber; if they'd been shut, he wouldn't have been able to see the bungalow from the road. An equally tall fence ran on either side of the gates, encircling the white-painted house, which looked as though it'd been extended. A tarmacked drive cut a precise path through close-cut lawns. There were no flowers or shrubs. To the right of the house were a pair of garages, with open up-and-over doors, and parked in front of them were two vehicles: a Land Rover, with a Safari roof and, Mother of God, an off-white Lincoln Continental. He couldn't wait to have a closer look. He parked, got out and headed for the American car. Nineteen feet long and about seven feet wide! Caramba! It must be the latest model, the Mark IV. He'd given up his Mustang when they'd formed the agency, as it was too conspicuous for detective work. His Avenger GT was a good little mover, but he still lusted after another American car. It looked brand new; it must have cost all of $9000, plus the shipping.

'You like American cars?'

He'd been so engrossed, and possibly dribbling with envy, he hadn't noticed Myres approaching. 'Mr Myres. Yes, I do. Last one I had was a Mustang.'

Myres nodded. 'Shall we go in?'

Pity, he wouldn't have minded being allowed to sit behind the wheel. He bet when he told Laurel, she'd say, 'Obviously you were in a Mr Toad mood.' The interior of the house didn't fit with the flashy car. White painted walls, bereft of posters, paintings or photographs, were the order of the day. Myres led him through an empty hall, with a tiled floor, to a room on the right. From what he could see of the rest of the house, it had been extended at the back to a considerable depth. The room he entered also had a tiled floor with a red Afghan rug in the centre, two black leather chairs, a television, record player, fax machine and a low, clear-glass coffee table. Large cast-iron radiators were the only source of heating. It couldn't have been more masculine if it had testosterone stencilled on the walls.

Myres looked at his watch and pointed to one of the chairs. 'I can only spare you twenty minutes, Mr Diamond. I need to leave promptly at two-thirty for an appointment in London.'

He nodded, got out his notebook and biro, and tried to balance himself on the leather chair, which was big and slippery. 'You know we've been hired by Mr De Lacy to try and prove Caleb Breen's innocence?'

190

'Yes.' The answer was terse, and Myres crossed his legs impatiently.

'Did you know Jonas Gorst?' There were two spaces on the wall above where Myres was sitting that showed traces of rectangular marks, as if pictures or photographs had been removed. Recently? If so, why?

'Yes, I'd seen him on the reserve.'

'Did you ever speak with him?'

'Yes, a few times. He seemed a good worker, a bit non-communicative.'

Takes one to know one. 'Can you remember what you talked about?'

Myres frowned. 'Nothing of significance that I can remember.'

'Did you know Mr Hebditch found Gorst alone in the hide you sponsored, and he was extremely rude to Mr Hebditch?'

Myres body stiffened. 'No. Did he see what Gorst was doing?'

'I think he said he thought he was doing some carpentry. Did you employ Gorst to work on the hide?'

Myres nodded. 'Yes, he did do a bit of work once or twice.'

'What kind of work?'

'Nothing skilled, I think he helped to dig the foundations.' He bit his lip as though trying to remember.

'What did you think of him, apart from being a good worker?'

Myres shrugged. 'A typical British youth of the seventies. He needed discipline, to get away from his family, and stand on his own feet.'

How many times had he heard that about the feckless youths of today? He sounded like some of the older members of his family, who, when he was a teenager and wore tight jeans and had a DA haircut, said the same things about him, and pointed out a duck's arse was fine on a duck, but looked ridiculous on the back of his head, and they hoped National Service would straighten him out. He decided to go off-piste. 'Did you have those things in your youth, Mr Myres? Discipline and independence?'

Myres move uncomfortably against the leather of his chair. 'I haven't time to talk about my life history. Shall we get on?'

Some research needed on Mr Myres. 'Of course, just interested. Did you ever talk to Jonas Gorst about Caleb Breen?'

'Your line of questioning is becoming bizarre. Why would I do that?'

Frank shrugged. 'Do you know Caleb Breen?'

'I've seen him on the reserve a few times. I know who he is.'

'Have you ever talked to him?'

'No more than a passing greeting; once he told me the birds he'd seen when I asked him. He seems a very shy person.'

'You were surprised when he was arrested for the murder?'

'Yes and no. People are constantly surprising. Sometimes it's the least likely people who are the perpetrators of crime.'

'You've met a lot of criminals?'

He hesitated. 'I was in the forces; you meet a cross-section of the population – saints and sinners.'

That explained a lot. 'Which service was that?'

Myres looked at his watch. 'I'll have to leave in five minutes. I need a cup of strong coffee before I go. Would you like one?'

So, he'd rather give me a drink than answer my question. 'Yes, black, please.'

Myres got up. 'Let's go to the kitchen, you can finish your questioning there.'

He led the way through another door off the hall into a small kitchen; it was well fitted with dark-green cupboards and pale melamine tops. It was uncluttered, with little on the worktops or the hob, apart from an electric kettle, which Myres filled with water and switched on. He gestured to one of two bar stools and took jars of coffee from a cupboard. He waved them at him. One was something called 'Sanka Decaff', the other 'Kenco Continental Roast'.

He inwardly shuddered. 'The Kenco, please.'

'What were you doing on the night Gorst was murdered?'

'I've already discussed this with the police.'

'I know, but would you mind telling me?'

'I drove to London that evening. I have an apartment there.

I don't have an alibi, but as the murderer has been caught, that isn't relevant, is it?'

What a tetchy man. 'You don't think we'll prove Caleb is innocent? Or that we'll find out who the true murderer is?'

He shrugged. 'The police have made an arrest; they must be convinced.' He passed Frank a mug of coffee.

'He hasn't been charged yet.'

Myres raised an eyebrow.

Frank sipped his coffee; it was bitter and hot enough to burn his tongue. 'One last question. What time did you get back to Westleton from London on Saturday; I remember you came to the Warden's office about eight, before we split up to go to the various hides.'

'Is that relevant?'

'Who knows what is relevant or irrelevant until all the facts have been correlated?'

Myres sniffed. 'Whatever that means.'

Frank felt like shouting: answer the bloody question. 'What time did you get back?' he repeated.

'Late afternoon, I can't be more specific than that.'

'That was a very brief visit to London. Hardly worth it?'

Myres tapped his watch. 'Sorry, I must get going.' He stood up, took Frank's half-full mug, chucked the coffee down the sink, gave both mugs a cursory rinse, and marched out of the kitchen.

He'd like to have a snoop round and see if he could find out more about the enigmatic Mr Myres. What did he do in London? Did he really want to know? Or was he just jealous of that big American car?

Chapter Twenty-two

Sunday, March 12, 1972

Stuart sighed; he didn't want to do this. He wanted to get on with moving clothes and other things from his Leiston bungalow to Greyfriars. Yesterday afternoon the agency had met and exchanged information and thoughts on the people they'd interviewed; they'd agreed to have Sunday off and meet on Monday to plan their next moves.

Last night after dinner, when they were round the sitting-room fire, relaxing, with whatever was their personal poison, Frank said, 'Stuart, when you go to your house tomorrow, could you drop in on Edith Chell and see if you can get more out of her than I did? Give her a ring tomorrow morning. As I said over dinner, she implied she knew more than she was willing to reveal, certainly to me, but you can use your mature charm to wheedle it out of her. If she does know something, she must be persuaded to tell you, or the police. However, she could be fooling herself, and she knows nothing.'

He'd asked Frank what she'd implied.

'She said she knew something about Jonas Gorst, or possibly about drugs. She was sure Caleb couldn't be the murderer, but she indicated she knew something about the murder weapon. She doesn't like me, but she knows you from the reserve. Give it a go.'

Stuart had dropped Mabel off at their bungalow and was now on his way from Leiston to Edith Chell's house. He hadn't bothered phoning, and hoped she'd be out so he could make a swift return to Mabel before she threw something precious into the dustbin.

194

There was the swan planter, as described by Frank; he turned left into the drive. Bugger! She was in. Her blue Austin Mini was parked near the house. His shoulders dropped. They'd had a busy week, all the others were having a day off: Laurel was going for a long run, Frank was spending the day in the cottage, no doubt cooking a deluxe meal for himself, Dorothy was going to church and then lunch with the vicar and his wife. Only he was having to do some detective work. It was bad enough he'd have to spend the day moving things to Greyfriars and cleaning the bungalow.

He blew out his cheeks, made sure he'd got his pipe and tobacco pouch and wearily got out of the car, and tried to get himself in the mood to be charming to Miss Chell – not his favourite person. As he approached the front door he came to a halt. It was gaping open, the wood splintered round the Yale lock. The curtains at the window to the left of the door were closed. He approached, and pushed the door wide open.

'Miss Chell,' he shouted.

There was no reply. No sound at all.

He stepped into a narrow hall, trying to keep to the edges of the linoleum covered floor. His nostrils widened. Although years of smoking had lessened his sense of smell, blood, once smelt, was never forgotten. Sweet and sickly, it left a metallic tang on the tongue. As he moved to the open door on the left, the smell was stronger. He fumbled for a handkerchief to cover his hand, as he searched for a light switch.

God in heaven. What a terrible, awful scene. She was lying with her head, what was left of it, on the tiled hearth, her body sprawled over a rug. Poor Edith, she didn't deserve such a brutal death, no one did. She was clad in a pink nightdress, partially covered by a matching dressing gown, both splattered with dark, red stains, as were the walls and the green three-piece suite. Smashed furniture littered the room, along with broken shards of pottery. It had been a vicious attack and the cuts on her hands and arms showed she'd fought for her life. Fought and lost. His nostrils flared. What bastard had done this?

195

He looked round for a telephone. There was one lying amongst the debris. He used the handkerchief again and picked it up. No sound. Not working, it could have been broken in the fight, or it may have been cut before the murderer came in. He'd have to leave that one to the police. He'd try to flag down a car and get whoever was in it to phone Revie. He turned and looked at what was left of her face. He wanted to cover her up, pull down the ruched-up nightdress exposing her mottled legs and rearrange the dressing gown to cover her huge breasts, but he knew he couldn't. A burglary gone wrong? She'd come to the living room when she heard a noise? Caught the burglar in the act of ransacking this room? Had she anything of value? Did she keep a lot of money in the house? He doubted it, she was a canny woman, and he couldn't imagine she was well off, although a teacher's pension was reasonable. Why would anyone risk breaking in for possibly modest pickings? Could it be one of the drug addicts? Desperation might drive a junkie to take a chance on finding enough to see him through to the next hit.

If it wasn't a burglary, then could it be connected to their case? Could Edith Chell have known who the real murderer of Jonas Gorst was? Or did she know, or suspect, who was behind the sale of lethal cocaine in this area? Or even who was supplying it? But, if that was the case, how did they find out she had this information? Who could have known? Or had she been foolish? Had she tried to tackle person or persons unknown, and been killed for wanting to cover herself in glory? Or possibly tried to blackmail them?

He shook his head and carefully tiptoed out of the bungalow toward the road.

Laurel set out on her run; she needed to get rid of all the tension building up in her head and body; she decided to run from Dunwich beach, along the shore, then continue past the bird reserve to the Sluice. From there she'd cut inland to Eastbridge, running beside the New Cut, a deep wide ditch carrying water from the Eastbridge River and marshes to the sea. And, finally, back to Dunwich over

196

the heath. It would be the longest run she'd done for a few months; she seemed to spend most of her free time swimming off Dunwich beach, when it wasn't too rough.

The first stretch over sand and shingle was tiring, the pebbles uneven and the sand heavy; when she came to the ruined steps that used to lead to Blackfriars School, she increased her pace. The mound of earth and stones the falling cliffs had dumped on the beach had been partly swept away by tides and wind, but there was enough to remind her of how close she'd been to losing her life.

It was a good day for running, only a light sea breeze, sporadic sunshine and the perfect temperature. Once she was into her stride, her muscles responded to the rhythm of her movements, and a feeling of euphoria took over; running ceased to be an effort and she sailed over the beach.

The sea was calm, waves gliding inshore, breaking on the beach with smooth hisses. Gulls wheeled overhead; she wished she knew all their names; she ought to pay more attention to Stuart and Frank when they talked birds. Sea-cabbages were erupting from the sand and the cliffs were patched with green. She moved behind the marram-tufted sand dunes, to the left of the bird reserve, where there were areas of rabbit-cropped grass. Then the Sluice came into sight.

As she turned away from the sea, and started to run down the path to Eastbridge, a man was walking towards her. She recognised him from his square body, short stocky legs and powerful arms. It was Benjie Whittle.

'Hello, Miss. Not seen you for a long time. You haven't shrunk!' He laughed, throwing back his head with its moon-shaped face; the skin round his pale blue eyes crinkling with mirth.

Benjie had been a suspect in the murder of Susan Nicholson, the wife of the headmaster of Blackfriars School; he'd found her body in the Sluice. He was a simple soul who made a living from fishing and beachcombing.

She stopped. 'Hello, Benjie. No, I'm afraid I'm still the same height.'

'Just as well you're a big 'un, all the fighting you've had to do.'

She smiled. 'It does help.'

'Would you like to come and sit in my hut for a bit? I can make you a nice cup of tea. Your inspector friend said my tea was good, when he came with Mr Elderkin.'

She wanted to get on with her run, but she didn't want to hurt Benjie's feelings. 'You've got a good memory, Benjie; that must have been nearly two years ago. Yes, thank you, I'd like a drink.'

He beamed at her. 'Two years cum September. Right, I'll get my little stove going, and I've got fresh milk.' He shook a straw bag he was carrying. 'Sorry, I haven't got any nice biscuits.'

They walked to his hut which was tucked behind a sand dune; it was made of tarred wood, with a felt roof. Benjie placed the straw bag in a rowing boat, which was against the shack's door, took a key from his navy, serge pants and put it in a padlock. 'Soon have a brew ready, Miss.'

'Please call me Laurel, Benjie. After all, remember everything we went through on the day I met you.'

He shuddered, his saucer-shaped eyes widening. 'That was 'orrible!'

She sat on the edge of the boat, watching gulls bob up and down as they rested on the sea.

Benjie came out of the hut with a large mug of steaming tea. 'I found a few old digestive biscuits; they're a bit soft. Would you like one?'

'No thanks. I've still got a long way to run.'

He fetched his own mug and sat down beside her, dunking an already warped biscuit into his tea. There was a plop as part of it fell into the liquid. 'Damn. Still I'll get to it at the end.' He took a long, noisy slurp and belched. 'Beg pardon, Miss.'

'It'll soon be lobster time, won't it? What fish have you been catching lately?'

He pointed to three lobster pots in the belly of the boat. 'They'll soon be sitting on the bottom of the sea-bed, waiting for those fellows to come on in. That Mr Diamond, tell him I'll save him a nice big 'un. He likes his lobsters, he does.'

'He certainly does, and his oysters, and Dover soles.'

'They fetch good money, they do.' He gave her a worried look. 'You'm don't think I'm mad, do you?'

Strange, but not mad. 'No, I don't think you're mad, Benjie. Why are you asking? Has someone been saying nasty things about you?' If that was true, she'd get Stuart to have a word in their ear. He knew most of the locals.

Benjie shook his head. 'No, I've not had any trouble since you caught that murderer.'

'That's good. But why did you ask me if I thought you were mad?'

He shuffled closer. 'I've seen something, but I've not told anyone, 'cause I think they'd say I was crazy, and I don't want to be put away in some home. That's what I'm a scared of. I couldn't bear to be away from the sea and my little hut. When I went to jail it was 'orrible. I couldn't breath and they weren't nice to me.' Susan Nicholson had falsely accused him of exposing himself, and this had led to a jail sentence.

She remembered the last time he'd said he'd seen something horrible. It had been a suitcase filled with the bones of a young girl, so he deserved to be listened to. 'What have you seen?'

His round eyes seemed to get even rounder. 'Sometimes I do a bit of night fishing; them sea bass come nearer the shore at night, feeding on things that rise up to the top of the waves. I goes out in my boat. I loves it when the moon's big and shining on the sea. I've seen it twice, I had to get as close as I could, cos at first I thought my eyes had gone funny.'

As usual, Benjie took a circuitous route to get to the point. 'What did you see?' she repeated, conscious her body was cooling and the second half of the run, which should have been easy, was going to be difficult.

'It had black sails; well I think they were black; they were dark anyway.'

'You saw a boat?' She stamped her feet on the shingle, partly in impatience and partly to keep the blood flowing.

'Yes,' he whispered. 'I call it Satan's Boat. It cuts its engine and comes as close to the shore as it can, using the wind in its sails. All silent it is. Then they lower a rowing boat and they come onto the beach. They've muffled their oars, like the old smugglers used to.'

This was interesting, if it was true, and not part of his rich imagination; he'd told everyone he had a girlfriend he fed fish to, a Silke lover. 'What happened then?'

'The first time there was two of them in the boat, the next time only one. They pulled the dinghy up above the tide, then they took something from the boat and carried it up the beach.'

'Where did they go?'

Benjie shivered. 'I don't know. I was afraid they'd see my boat. I didn't dare follow them, I was feared. They was as silent as the grave, not one of them spoke.'

'Are you sure you didn't hear anything? When there were two of them, didn't they talk to each other?'

'Even when the one on the beach met them, no one said nothing.'

'The one on the beach. Someone was waiting for them?'

Benjie nodded. 'That's what it looked like.'

'Benjie, can you remember when you saw the boat; the day and the date if possible?'

'You believe me, don't you?'

'Oh, yes, I believe you, Benjie. How big was the boat? Could you describe it?'

He frowned. 'It was dark, but there was a half-moon and stars a plenty. I'm used to fishing without any light. It was a sloop; I reckon she's a twenty-odd long, perhaps nearer thirty. One mast, I could see cabins. She looked like she could go anywhere.'

'Goodness, Benjie, that's a very good description. Well done!'

He beamed. 'I eats my carrots up, like my mum told me to do.'

'What do you think the men were doing?'

He hunched his back. 'Something bad. Something wicked. That's why I call it Satan's Boat. It's black, silent and them be demons on board. I reckon they be coming from the bottom of the sea and they be looking for to steal people's souls when they be sleeping safe in their beds at night.' His face was white. 'I hope I don't see them

200

agin. Last time I was so scared I left my rod on the beach and when I went back next morning, the sea had taken it.'

His imagination was in overdrive. 'You mustn't worry; there aren't any demons, Benjie. Or if there are, they're wicked human beings, not spirits. Could you see what they were bringing ashore? Not barrels of brandy?'

His mouth made a silent O. 'You think they be smugglers?'

'It's possible.'

'So, they're not demons?'

'No, but they could be dangerous men. If you see the ship again you must get to the nearest telephone and dial nine, nine, nine.'

'The police? I don't like the police, except Mr Elderkin and Mr Diamond, and they aren't police anymore, are they?'

'No. But I know an inspector, Inspector Revie. I'll tell him about this and give you a special number to ring. I'll leave it at the Eels Foot.'

Benjie shook his head. 'I've heard of him, Inspector Revie. I don't like the sound of him. I know he'll frighten me.'

Laurel sighed; she must get going before she completely seized up. 'You won't have to meet him. Promise me if you see it again, you'll leave immediately for Eastbridge and phone up Inspector Revie. Even if it's quite a time before you get to a telephone, it doesn't matter. You'll be doing the right thing, Benjie.'

'My mother always told me to do the right thing.'

'Good. That was a lovely cup of tea, but I must get back to Greyfriars. Mr Elderkin will be very pleased with you when I tell him what you've seen.'

Benjie took her mug. 'That's good. I like Mr Elderkin.'

She began running on the spot. 'Don't forget your promise.'

He gave a sly smile. 'I haven't made a promise yet.'

She gave him her best Senior Mistress look.

'Oh, all right, Miss. I promise.'

She breathed out deeply as she waved goodbye, started running, and winced as her cold muscles rebelled.

Chapter Twenty-three

Wednesday, March 15, 1972

Caleb clutched the edge of the starched sheet which was tucked in so tightly at the sides of the hospital bed he could hardly move. They'd brought him here in the middle of the night, when he'd coughed so much, he choked, and couldn't breathe. Men nurses came to his cell and strapped him to a trolley thing and put him in an ambulance. Where were they taking him? They didn't tell him, he'd been too frightened to ask, and he couldn't speak because of the coughing. This was worse than anything he'd had before, he was coughing so deeply and so often, he didn't have time to breathe. His throat was choked with the phlegm. They made him spit into a kidney-shaped steel basin.

They didn't rub his chest with Vick's Vapour rub, like his mother used to when he was ill. She used to rub it into his back as well, and sometimes she'd melt it in hot water and he'd breathe it in. He wanted to ask them to do that, but they weren't kind, they didn't talk to him, just shouted instructions: sit up, spit, swallow these tablets, open your mouth, don't bite the thermometer.

There was a policeman outside his room. He wasn't in a ward, like he'd been when he had to go to hospital when he was ill before; he'd been twenty then, a long time ago. But he hadn't liked the other patients – they grumbled about his coughing at night and shouted at him to stop it. Now, he was by himself and was handcuffed to the bed; through a window he'd seen the new moon; now

the sky was lightening. What time was it? The policeman sometimes put his head round the door, but he didn't say anything, didn't
even wave to him, just looked, probably to see he hadn't escaped, or
died, and then closed the door.

Another bout of coughing started. He couldn't breathe, he was
going to choke. He tried to reach out for the basin to spit into, but
with his left hand cuffed to the bed, he couldn't stretch far enough.
His fingers touched the hard edge, then another coughing fit shook
his body, and the basin slipped, and clattered to the floor. The door
opened and the policeman came in.

'Help me. Help me,' he tried to say, between the racking coughs.

'Hold on, I'll get a nurse,' he said, making for the door.

Two nurses rushed in. 'Fetch the policeman,' the older woman
with the fancy cap said to the younger one, who dashed out.

Fancy Cap got the basin from the floor and held it to his mouth.
He managed to spit into it. Great lumps, like half-set yellow-green
jelly dribbled from his mouth. He could breathe.

'Take some slow breaths, sir. Not too deep, we don't want to start
the coughing off again,' she said.

'Thank you.'

She placed a hand on his brow.

The policeman came in with the nurse.

'Undo these handcuffs immediately.'

'I'm sorry, Madam. I'd need permission to do that.'

'You have *my* permission, and please address me as Matron. This
man is very ill, he needs urgent treatment, and we can't nurse him if
he's chained to the bed. He's too weak to be a danger to anyone. I'll
take responsibility for his safety. Get on with it and then report to
your superior officer.'

She reminded him of Auntie Dot. He looked up at her; she was
glaring at the policeman. He felt another wave of coughing coming
on. He started to rock backwards and forwards, panic overtaking him.

She gripped him round the shoulders. 'Calm, be calm. Breathe
slowly.' The policeman got a key from his trouser pocket and unlocked
the handcuff.

He brought his left hand to his chest and sighed with relief.

'There, try to keep calm. I'll put another pillow behind your head. Don't lie down, you'll only choke on all the sputum you're making. I'll put the bowl near you. Don't be shy, spit it all out. Better out than in.'

He felt safer now this nurse was here. 'Thank you.'

She patted his hand. 'We telephoned your brother, he's on his way here. Do you want to see him?'

Daniel. His eyes filled with tears. 'Yes. Will the police let him in?'

She nodded. 'Yes, but only briefly. The policeman will have to be present, so he can hear what passes between you.'

Caleb's heart sank. What would happen to him? Would he ever be free? Yesterday he'd been charged with the murder of Jonas Gorst. He decided he'd rather die, here in this bed, with the kind nurse beside him, than go back to prison and be locked up for ever. He'd never see the big skies over the sea and marshes, never hear the bitterns booming, or the rooks calling from the oaks behind their home. Tears trickled down his cheeks and his throat tightened once more. Perhaps Daniel would be glad to be rid of him. Then he could marry his Theresa Poppy. Where was Auntie Dot? Where was his Uncle Bryce? His chest started heaving and a wave of coughing racked his body. When it passed, he leant back against the pillows, exhausted, unable to go on. The nurse with the fancy cap, she was the matron, wiped his face and mouth with a wet flannel and held a glass of water to his mouth; he took a few sips. The inside of his mouth and tongue were foul, coated with fur, dry and sore.

'Try and stay still. I'm going to fetch a doctor,' she said.

She came back with a man with a moustache; he'd a stethoscope round his neck, over a white coat. He took his temperature.

'We'll need to take your pyjama top off, so the doctor can examine you,' she said.

He squirmed as the cold instrument was placed over his chest and back, and the doctor kept asking him to breathe deeply. 'I can't,' he whispered.

The doctor and matron moved to the bottom of the bed and whispered to each other.

'We're going to give you an injection to make you better,' she said. Needles. He hated needles. He'd had these before, when he'd been very ill. His mother had stayed with him, and then nursed him at home. Daniel couldn't do that. He'd too much to do on the farm. The room seemed to get bigger, then smaller, the frame of the window moving, curving.

The doctor came towards him with a syringe. He shut his eyes and matron held him firm until the needle was jabbed into his behind. 'There, all done,' she said. 'Try and rest, your brother will be here soon.'

He must have dozed. A big rough hand took his and held it tight. He opened his eyes and there was Daniel, looking worried and sad. The policeman was sitting in a chair near them.

'Daniel,' he whispered. 'What is happening to me?'

Daniel swallowed hard. 'You're very ill, Caleb. They think you've got pneumonia, but they've given you an antibiotic injection, so you'll soon be better.'

He gripped Daniel's hand. 'I'd rather die than go back to prison.'

Daniel looked shocked. 'Please don't think like that. Uncle Bryce has got the Anglian Detective Agency working to prove you didn't kill Jonas Gorst.'

'Auntie Dot's lot?'

Daniel smiled. 'Yes, her and her pals.'

'They're good, aren't they? They've solved a lot of cases.'

'Yes. I'm sure they'll find the real killer.'

'Did Uncle Bryce pay them?'

Daniel looked down. 'Yes. He's outside now. I phoned him. He got here the same time as me. His Rolls is faster than the old Land Rover.'

Hope, a small flicker to begin with, started to burn within him. 'I'd love to ride in that.'

'You will, as soon as you're better and the detectives have proved your innocence. Would you like to see Uncle Bryce?'

He was pleased Daniel was talking about Uncle Bryce like that. Perhaps they could all be friends together. A family again. He wondered if Aunt Dot had also changed her mind about Uncle Bryce. 'Yes, I'd like that.'

'Your time is up, sir,' the policeman said, 'if the other gentleman is to come in.'

Daniel leant over and kissed his cheek.

He hadn't done that in years, not since he was a little boy. 'Danny, I love you,' he said.

Daniel closed his eyes. 'It's a long time since you've called me that. I love you too, Caleb. Never forget it. I'll go now, and let Uncle Bryce come in. I'll tell him not to tire you out. I'll wait for Uncle Bryce and have a chat with him. See if the detectives have found out anything. I'll be back soon. Goodbye, Caleb.' He squeezed his hand, and nodded to the policeman as he went out of the door.

Almost immediately the door opened and his uncle rushed to his side, his eyes, like Daniel's, were full of worry. He sat down on the chair next to the bed and took his hand.

'Caleb, I've been so worried about you. You must get well; I'll soon have you home and free.'

Caleb's heart swelled; the way Uncle Bryce spoke, the fact he believed in him. 'Uncle Bryce, thank you. Daniel's told me what you're doing for me.' If only he was confident like Uncle Bryce. He behaved as though he was just as good, if not better, than anyone else. I look like him, but I don't act like him. Perhaps if I get better, he'll help me to change.

His uncle's eyes filled with tears, and looked as though he might cry. 'Caleb, I must tell you. I can't keep it to myself any longer.'

His throat seized up again. What was he going to say? Was it something bad? He looked upset. What had happened?

'No, Caleb, don't be frightened. I need to tell you. I knew as soon as I saw you in the church.'

'What?' he whispered.

'I am not your uncle, Caleb. I am your father.'

The room seemed to gyrate around him. 'No, my father died.

You can't be my father. Why are you saying that?' A steel hand gripped his chest and he stared heaving, the hand moved up and tightened round his throat. He couldn't breathe.

'Doctor! Doctor,' Bryce De Lacy called.

Daniel barged into the room. 'My God. What's happened?'

He was choking, choking to death.

Daniel pushed De Lacy aside and held him close. 'Caleb, what's happened?'

He spat out a great gob of phlegm onto the sheet. 'He says he's my father,' he whispered between chest-splitting coughs.

Daniel's eyes bulged. 'Who? Who said that?'

He raised a finger and pointed at De Lacy, before another wave of coughing took his breath away.

The doctor and matron rushed in.

'Out. Out. Both of you,' she shouted, pushing past them. She took him in her arms.

Chapter Twenty-four

Frank got out of bed and went to the window. It was a brisk, sunny March day, with white-capped waves rushing towards Minsmere beach. Because of Edith Chell's murder, and the involvement of Stuart, their own case had been held up, but they were meeting after lunch to plan their next move.

He decided to walk to Greyfriars. Last night he'd spent several hours thinking. The recent murder of Miss Chell and Laurel's revelation about what Benjie Whittle had seen added to the mystery. Could Edith Chell's and Jonas Gorst's murders be connected? Or had Edith disturbed a burglar, and the two murders were not linked? There was the boat Benjie Whittle had seen, the vandalism of the hides and the boy from Leiston, killed by a drug overdose. How did they all tie up?

He went downstairs, put on the coffee percolator, picked up the empty whisky bottle and binned it. He collected up the sheets of paper he'd covered last night with names, facts, spider diagrams, and finally, his conclusions, and shuffled them into order. A brisk walk over the heath would give him time to rethink, and see if he agreed with his whisky-fuelled conclusions of the previous evening.

He picked up the final sheet of paper and put it into the inside pocket of his leather jacket, hesitated, then added to it the airmail letter from his friend in the USA.

The air was invigorating as he walked over the heath, the sandy soil soft underfoot; stunted oaks were still in bud, and pine trees tinged the air with resin. There was a high-pitched honking; a

V-shaped skein of swans flew overhead. He raised a hand to shield his eyes from the sun, and squinted at them. Fifteen. They were small for swans; were they Bewick's swans, making their way home to mate in Arctic Russia? The power and beauty of the birds sharpened his mind. He nodded to himself. Yes, he trusted his instinct, just as the swans trusted theirs. They knew where they were going and he knew who the killer was. Could he find the evidence to prove his theory?

He opened the front door of Greyfriars. A filing cabinet drawer closed – Dorothy was busy in the office. He knew Stuart was out gathering more facts, and Mabel was food shopping in Aldeburgh; probably paying Matt a visit as well. Where was Laurel? He went into the kitchen; from the window he saw Laurel playing with Bumper in the back garden. She laughed as he scampered after a ball, pouncing on it, then shaking his head wildly, as he refused to drop it. The training session wasn't going to plan.

He banged on the window. She looked up, smiled and waved. Her hair was blowing about her head as she ran towards the house, Bumper leaping up, the blue ball firmly held in his jaws. She reminded him of a prancing colt in a Picasso painting. Her exuberance and joy gave him a sharp pain near his heart.

They burst into the kitchen. Bumper was torn between greeting Frank, and hanging onto his ball. He flopped onto the floor, grinning, the ball clamped between his teeth.

'Frank, see if you can do anything with this mutt. He won't obey me.'

He opened the biscuit tin and broke of a piece of shortbread. Bumper's eyes widened. He dropped the ball and shot towards him.

'Sit.'

Bumper stopped and dropped on to his haunches, his pink tongue hanging out in anticipation.

'That's cheating,' Laurel said.

'Nicely!' He offered the biscuit and Bumper gently took it from his hand. The ball had rolled under the table, he picked it up, pulled a face, and chucked it at Laurel. 'Catch!'

'Ugh!' She flung it into the sink and turned the tap on.

There was a squeal of breaks.

'That can't be Stuart, he thinks too much of his tyres,' Laurel said.

Frantic knocks on the door.

'Good heavens, they're trying to break the door down!' Dorothy said, rushing out from the office. 'Daniel! What's happened?'

'Auntie Dot. Thank God, you're here.'

Frank and Laurel went into the hall. Daniel was clasping Dorothy to him, wild-eyed, his face pale. He looked at them. 'De Lacy's mad. He's made Caleb worse. They won't let me stay with him.' He looked ready to burst into tears. 'I must talk to you. I can't understand what's happened.'

Frank took him by the shoulder. 'Let's go into the kitchen. We'll all have a coffee. It'll steady your nerves.'

Dorothy nodded her head, her face stiff with anxiety.

'I'll put Bumper in the sitting room. Put the kettle on, Dorothy; I'll see to the coffee,' Laurel said.

Seated round the table, steaming mugs in front of them, Daniel seemed to have regained his composure. He took a drink, blew out his cheeks and then told them what Bryce De Lacy had said to Caleb.

'What?' exploded Dorothy. 'He *is* mad! How could he possibly be his father? The man's insane.'

'What happened after you were both made to leave?' Frank asked.

'I lost my temper; told him never to visit Caleb again.'

'What was his reaction?' Laurel asked.

'He was shocked, and I think upset, because of how Caleb reacted. He started to change his story; said he didn't mean he was actually his father, but he felt as though he was, because of their close resemblance.'

Frank looked at Laurel, he could see her mind was going into overdrive, as was his. He took out the letter from the States. He'd planned to tell them its contents at the meeting, but now seemed a good time. He waved it at them. 'I've some information which will help all of us to understand Caleb's and De Lacy's condition.'

Daniel stared at him. 'How have you found this out?'

'You've been in contact with your geneticist friend in the States, haven't you?' Laurel asked.

Frank smiled at her. 'Well remembered.' He looked at Daniel and Dorothy. 'When I was reading botany at Liverpool University, I had a close mate, Rich, he went on to do zoology honours and then took a PhD in genetics. He went to the States, and is now Professor of Genetics at Philadelphia University.'

Laurel sighed. 'Why didn't you do something like that, Frank?'

He laughed. 'Research wasn't for me. You've got to stick at it, and build up statistics to back up your theories. It can be very repetitive. Not enough action.'

Laurel shrugged.

'Can we get back to Caleb, please?' Daniel said, looking impatient.

Frank nodded. 'When I heard about Caleb's and De Lacy's webbed hands, my immediate thought was this could be a genetic defect, and as your mother, Rosalind,' he nodded to Daniel, 'didn't show any of the traits exhibited in the two men: widow's peak, webbed digits, I suspected she might have carried a recessive gene on the female X chromosome.'

Daniel frowned. 'I did a bit of genetics at college, as well as biology A level, so I understand so far.'

'I'm with you too, Frank,' Laurel said.

Dorothy lit a cigarette. 'Count me out, but don't stop to explain, I can catch up later.'

'If De Lacy had any children, he'd pass on his Y, or male, chromosome to any male child, his X chromosome would be passed to any female children. If I was right, then the female child would have the recessive gene on the X chromosome, and if her other X chromosome carried a normal gene, she wouldn't exhibit the symptoms, but would be what is known as a carrier.' He opened the letter. 'Rich confirms my suspicions, but also thinks he knows what the genetic condition Caleb and De Lacy suffer from.'

The other three leant forward. 'Really?' Laurel asked.

Frank nodded. 'He thinks it's a rare genetic condition called

Aarskog's Syndrome.' He spelt it out to them. 'It's only recently been described, 1970 to be exact, by a Norwegian paediatrician and human geneticist called Aarskog.'

'What are the symptoms they describe? Are they similar to Caleb's?' Daniel asked.

'Yes, they vary from person to person, and even between members of the same family. Widely spaced eyes, widow's peak, and lots of other symptoms, including a tendency to develop chronic respiratory infections, and webbing of the fingers and toes. The gene, as I suspected, is carried on the X chromosome, so females rarely show the condition. Both X chromosomes would have to carry the gene for symptoms to appear in a woman. Rosalind was a carrier. Caleb got a recessive gene from her, and the Y chromosome from your father, Noah. Caleb didn't have a dominant gene to hide the recessive one, so he has Aarskog's disease. You were lucky, Daniel, you got an X chromosome from your mother that didn't carry the recessive gene. If you'd been identical twins, both of you would either be normal, or both would have shown the symptoms.'

Daniel blew out his cheeks. 'That's a lot to take in.'

Dorothy shook her head. 'I think I followed most of it. However, it doesn't explain why De Lacy made such a wild claim. How he thought he could be Caleb's father is beyond belief.'

Frank looked at Laurel; her blue eyes looked back at him. He suspected her thoughts were mirroring his. Later, when they were alone, she asked him, 'From what you've told us about Aarskog's Syndrome, does this mean, theoretically of course, Bryce De Lacy couldn't be Caleb's father?

He shook his head. 'No. Genetically it's possible.'

212

Chapter Twenty-five

Frank looked at the rest of the team sitting round the dining table; Daniel had left to go back to the hospital. They'd dealt with the administrative items and now they looked to him as they came to item four of the agenda: discussion of possible suspects for the murder of Jonas Gorst.

He wondered if he should start by telling them of his conclusions, but rejected this idea. It would be better to hear everyone's thoughts first. Also, Stuart obviously had some new facts to tell them, as he had a satisfied look, as though he'd just eaten the most delicious chocolate éclair. The thought of food made him run his tongue over his teeth and wish he could brush them. Mabel had been late back from Aldeburgh and she'd bought Cornish pasties from Smith's bakery for their lunch. They'd been tasty, but the remnants of the pastry were sticking to his teeth.

'Although we've been hired to try and find evidence Caleb Breen did not murder Jonas Gorst, I'd like us to first think about the murder of Edith Chell. Nick Revie told me they're treating it as a burglary gone wrong. Edith drew out fifty pounds from her bank the day before she was murdered; there is no money in her bungalow, her purse is missing as is her cheque book. However, he said two murders so close to each other is suspicious, and he's keeping an open mind. His team are continuing the investigation.'

'Do you think they're connected?' Laurel asked.

'Do you?'

'When you told us about the meeting at the bird reserve, you said

Edith suggested she knew something, either about Gorst's murder, or the drugs, or both. If the murderer was present at the meeting, heard her suspicions, then he could have killed her to shut her up.'

He gave her the thumbs up. 'Correct. So, let's look at those three men: Hebditch, Rudder and Myres.' He turned to Stuart. 'But first let's hear from Stuart. Have you managed to dig up any more facts about them?'

Stuart, with a glowing pipe in his hand, blew a stream of blue smoke at the ceiling.

The aroma of tobacco hit the addiction area in his brain. A longing for a cigarette suddenly made him want to grab the one between Dorothy's lips and take a deep lungful of smoke. It was years since he'd given up, but the occasional urge sometimes overwhelmed him. He bit on the end of his biro.

'I haven't found out anything new about Hebditch or Rudder; we have the fight in the pub between Gorst and Rudder, and then Gorst spreading rumours about Hebditch being homosexual, so I don't think we can discount these two. However, I've got a few more facts about Myres, whether they are relevant or not, I'm not sure.

'First of all, I've found out some details about his war service. He served in the Royal Navy and in 1943 he was one of the first to volunteer for the new Royal Naval Commandos; they carried out tasks associated with establishing, maintaining and controlling beachheads during amphibious operations.'

Frank sensed the sudden rise in interest and concentration, round the table. He gave a short, satisfied exhalation.

Stuart nodded at them. 'I thought that was interesting, I can see you agree. These men were highly trained, both physically and mentally; they were also trained to kill. I've done a bit of research and there's no doubt Myres, if he's still up to scratch, would know how to use a knife, so possibly he'd be handy with a fromard as well.'

Laurel shuddered. 'We've met an ex-army killer before – I don't think I want to get close to another.'

'You possibly already have – you've spent a night in a bird hide

214

with Myres,' Frank said, then glanced back at Stuart. There was more to come. 'And, Stuart?'

Stuart grinned back. 'Don't steel my thunder, I like to build up to a dramatic climax.'

'Oh, get on with it,' Dorothy snapped. 'I think you two have forgotten how important it is we clear Caleb's name. So far there's no evidence against anyone. Just because someone served in the war doesn't make them a killer; in fact, it might make them a hero.'

Stuart stuck out his bottom lip. 'Sorry, Dorothy, but I do like my time in the spotlight.'

She shook her head. 'Well?'

'The other relevant fact, in view of what Benjie Whittle told Laurel, about seeing a boat off Minsmere beach in the night, is Myres owns a boat, The Kenina. It's a 1960s' Corsair 28, she's a sloop, about twenty-eight feet in length.' He paused. 'He keeps it at the ship yard in Aldeburgh. I didn't make any further enquires as I didn't want to arouse suspicions. I visited the yard pretending I was interested in buying a boat, and asked questions about the ones moored there. So, I don't know how often he uses it, or when he last took her out.'

Mabel sat up straight. 'I can ask my son, Matt, to find that out, if you want me to. He'll be discreet, he knows all the people at that yard.'

Stuart beamed. 'That's great, love. What do you think?' He looked at the other three.

'Excellent,' Frank said. Laurel and Dorothy nodded in agreement.

'Should we concentrate on Myres? Make him our prime suspect?' Laurel asked.

'Yes, I think we should look at him first,' he said. 'But, we mustn't discount Hebditch, or Rudder.'

'You think it's him, don't you?' Laurel asked, her eyes widening, her face excited.

There was no proof. If he said yes, he knew they'd trust his judgement, and focus on proving Myres was the killer. Tunnel vision was never a good thing; he knew *he'd* have trouble thinking it was anyone else. Better to try and keep their minds open to other possibilities. And, he could be wrong.

'No, but it might be worthwhile chewing over the fat and see if we can come up with theories as to how this all fits together, see if we can work out how Myres could have carried out these crimes. Perhaps he didn't do any of them, or there's the possibility he may be guilty of one of the murders, but not the other. We may have two killers here.' He looked at them. 'Shall we do that? Spend half-an-hour thinking this through individually, then get together and share our thoughts?'

'I hope you're not including me in this brains test,' Mabel said. 'I'll get a tray ready for when we meet up and start preparing dinner; but I'll be interested to hear the workings of your minds.'

Stuart groaned. 'You shouldn't have mentioned food, I won't be able to concentrate, I'll be wondering what we'll be having to eat.'

Mabel went up to him and squeezed his shoulder. 'Matt gave me some lovely codlings, fresh off his boat. We'll have them with sauté potatoes, and parsley sauce.'

Stuart rubbed his ample stomach. 'Delicious. Any pudding?' he asked.

Frank looked at Laurel.

Mabel laughed. 'How about apple pie?'

'I'd ask you to marry me if we weren't already married.'

Frank shook his head, 'That's enough, you two. You've got us all salivating, Mabel. Are we all agreed on spending some thinking time?'

The rest nodded. He passed a sheet of paper to each of them. 'Stay here, or buzz off somewhere else, if you prefer your own company. We'll meet for a cup of tea at three and see if we've come up with any ideas on how Myres could be involved in Gorst's murder, Edith Chell's and also, in view of the boat, in drug smuggling. In all three, or two, or just one of these crimes, or none.'

He remained where he was, as did Stuart.

'I'll go to the sitting room and keep Bumper company,' Laurel said.

'No petting or tummy rubbing,' Frank said.

Laurel raised her eyebrows. 'Perhaps you'd like to join us?'

Dorothy tapped Laurel's hand with her biro. 'Laurel!'

Laurel laughed and gave him a saucy smile.

He tried to keep a straight face. There was a loud knocking on the front door. Bugger, just what they didn't need. He hoped it wasn't Daniel Breen again, with more bad news.

'I'll go,' Mabel shouted from the kitchen. 'I'll get rid of whoever it is.'

Stuart had already started scribbling; Dorothy took a cigarette from her case and was about to light a match.

Mabel came in. 'It's Mr De Lacy,' she hissed. 'He wants to see you.' She pointed at Frank.

'Ask him to make an appointment,'

'I've tried that. He insists on seeing you now. He says he won't stay long. I explained you were all in an important meeting.'

Frank sighed. This would ruin their concentration; he'd sensed everyone was keen to marshal their thoughts, and he'd been looking forward to hearing their conclusions. This was when a case became exciting, as wisps of ideas and half-formed thoughts coalesced into firm shapes and began to solidify.

'Show him into the interview room. Tell him I'll be with him in a few minutes.'

He looked at the others. 'Carry on. Hopefully this won't take long.'

The interview room was one of the new modifications Dorothy had made to Greyfriars. He opened the door. De Lacy was sitting in one to the three armchairs placed round a small table on which were an ashtray, a small bowl of flowers, and pamphlets describing the work of the agency. He got up and shook Frank's hand.

'Thank you for seeing me at such short notice.'

Frank pointed to the chair and sat down opposite him. 'How can I help?'

De Lacy took out his cigarette case. 'Do you mind if I smoke?'

'No, carry on.' The craving for nicotine rose again, as De Lacy lit up and the scent of tobacco filled the room. He took a deep breath. That was the nearest he'd get to the poisonous weed. He waited.

De Lacy looked nervous. 'I expect Daniel Breen has been to see you?'

'Yes.'

'He told you about our falling out?'

'He did.'

'It was a dreadful misunderstanding. I'm so worried about Caleb. If he were free, I'd make sure he had the very best medical attention. Do you think there is any chance you'll be able to find out who murdered Jonas Gorst? I need to get Caleb out of that hospital.'

Frank bit his lip. De Lacy was paying handsomely for their services. He'd have to give him something, just to get rid of him. 'We're just about to have a pivotal meeting; we're about to discuss in detail a particular suspect and see if we can solidify our thoughts.'

Relief flooded over De Lacy's face. 'That's wonderful news. Who is it? Who do you think murdered Gorst?'

'I'd prefer not to say at this point in the investigation.'

De Lacy's attitude changed from gratitude to indignation. His eyes widened; his face reddened. 'I must remind you, Mr Diamond, I am employing you and your team. I feel it's my right to be kept informed of all developments. I am not moving until you tell me who you suspect of being the murderer.' He sat back in the chair, his legs apart, a determined look on his face.

Oh, Lord, Frank thought. He shouldn't have mentioned it, but he needed to get rid of him. 'Very well, but you must understand, at the moment, we have no proof. The person I'm going to name may not be the murderer, or he may be guilty of another crime, unconnected to the killing of Gorst.'

'Another crime?'

'He may be a drug smuggler.'

De Lacy's far-apart eyes seemed to bulge out of his skull. 'Good Lord. Drugs? Here in Suffolk?'

Frank nodded.

'His name please?'

'Our prime suspect is Myres.'

'Myres?'

'He's a volunteer on the bird reserve, a successful business man. Mr De Lacy, you must keep this information to yourself. If you tell anyone it could ruin our chances of finding proof, and I must remind you, we may be mistaken and Myres may not be the murderer.'

De Lacy was silent. He bowed his head. Frank couldn't see his expression.

De Lacy got up. 'Thank you for telling me. I believe, from what I've read and heard, your agency has been extremely successful in solving complex and dangerous crimes. Is it your instinct, Mr Diamond, that's led you to this man?'

'Partly, but there are facts about his background and lifestyle that make him a suitable candidate.'

De Lacy shook his hand. 'Goodbye, I assure you I won't tell anyone else.'

He seemed to mean it. Frank showed him out. He hadn't played that one very well. He hoped to God De Lacy kept his mouth shut.

He went back to the office. Stuart was scribbling away, and Dorothy was puffing at a cigarette, frowning. He sat down, and made a few quick notes; he didn't need to think it through, he'd done that the night before.

Mabel came in with a loaded tray. 'Time's up. Pens down. Stuart, go and get Laurel.' She set out crockery and poured the tea.

'No cake?' Stuart moaned.

'Be thankful you've got chocolate biscuits,' she said. 'I've not had a moment to myself these past few days.' She looked at his downturned face. 'I'll see what I can do tomorrow. Fancy a nice, sticky ginger cake?'

His mouth turned up. 'That would be good.' He left and came back immediately with Laurel.

Frank once more ran his tongue over his teeth; pastry replaced by chocolate digestive biscuit. 'Before we start, I need to tell you about De Lacy.'

They looked concerned as he explained he'd named Myres as a possible suspect.

'You're worried, aren't you?' Laurel asked.

'I shouldn't have revealed we had a prime suspect.' He grimaced. 'Too late. I believed him when he said he wouldn't tell anyone else.' He paused. 'Right, let's make a start. Dorothy, would you like to go first?'

She pushed her spectacles up from the end of her nose. 'Not really. I'm afraid I'm too close to this to be of any use. All I keep thinking about is Caleb coughing up his guts in that hospital. Why would Myres want to kill Gorst? He hardly knew him; he'd met him when Gorst was working on the bird reserve. Also how did he get the fromard? I'm sorry, I just can't make any sense of this.'

Frank nodded. 'That's OK, and they're good questions, which we need to find answers to if we're to prove Myres is the murderer. Stuart, what about you?'

Stuart, who'd gobbled three biscuits and lit his pipe, took a deep draw on it. 'I concentrated on the possibility that the root of this lies with drug smuggling. Myres has a boat, one capable of making long cross-channel trips. I thought, where would he go to get drugs? Holland seemed the best bet. So, let's suppose he was doing that. We know from his commando background, he must have been highly trained, perhaps he got the taste for adventure, excitement, thrills, physical hardship and the highs that kind of life can give you. Perhaps civvy life became dull? Did he see a way of making enormous sums of money, while having adventure, and living on the edge, at the same time? If Benjie Whittle is telling the truth and a ship is coming into Minsmere beach at night, and men are bringing something ashore, that something could be drugs.'

He looked at them; Laurel was nodding, her eyes shining, Mabel was looking at Stuart as though he was a Nobel prize winner and Dorothy, face pinched, was taking quick puffs on her cigarette. 'Any more, Stuart.'

'Supposing Gorst found out Myres was drug smuggling and tried to blackmail him, and Myres killed him.'

'Good suggestion,' Frank said.

'What about the fromard? How did Myres get hold of that?' Dorothy said.

Stuart shrugged.

'Laurel, what have you come up with?'

She tapped her paper. 'I was thinking along the same lines as Stuart, but I wondered if perhaps Gorst might have been working for Myres and knew about the drugs in that way.'

Frank gave her the thumbs up. 'Just what I was thinking.'

She blushed, and smiled at him. His heart seemed to leap. 'Sorry, go on.'

'I thought if Gorst knew where the drugs were hidden, he might have been tempted to take say, a small amount, and make some extra money for himself by selling them in Leiston.'

'Brilliant!' Frank said.

'You mean he might have been the source of drugs we've seen in recent months?' Stuart asked.

'Myres finds out and kills him,' Frank said.

'We keep on coming back to how Myres got hold of the fromard, and why kill him in that way? Surely it would have been better to have hidden his body, not to try and frame someone else for it? As far as we know Myres has never been to Rooks Wood Farm, so how would he know about Caleb's collection of old farming implements?' Dorothy asked.

'There are lots of holes in the case against Myres,' Frank said, 'but I do feel this is our best line of enquiry. Mabel, can you contact your son tomorrow and ask him if he'll try to find out how often Myres takes his boat out, the duration of his voyages, and if the boat yard have any thoughts on where he goes—'

'There goes my ginger cake,' Stuart interrupted.

Frank shook his head. 'I'll get on to Revie and ask him if he can find out if Myres lands his boat in any of the Dutch ports, although it's likely he may make a rendezvous at some isolated spot in Holland. I'll ask him if he's any contacts over there who might have useful information.' He turned to Laurel. 'Do you think you could make contact with some of the teenagers in Leiston, try and find out if there were any suspicions Jonas Gorst was pushing drugs? Perhaps, get in touch with the mother of the boy who died, find out who his friends were. I'll ask Revie if he can help us on that one as well.'

'What are you going to do tomorrow, Frank?' Laurel asked.

'I'm going to stay in the cottage until I've come up with the answer to how Myres got hold of the fromard.'

'Good job we've got cod tonight,' Stuart said.

He looked at him.

'Fish – brain food. You better give him a big helping, Mabel.'

Chapter Twenty-six

In his isolated bungalow, Samuel Myres poured himself a large brandy and sat down in one of the black leather armchairs. He looked out of the window to the black sky; he hadn't noticed night falling. He got up, placed the drink on a glass-topped coffee table and pulled down the blind. Usually he liked to sit with the lights off, watching the light fading, and slowly sip the brandy, rolling the spirit round his mouth, savouring the flavour, letting it trickle down his throat, searing the gullet and warming his stomach. Tonight, he tossed it back. He was tempted to get blind drunk, so he could temporarily forget the mess he was in. He was furious with himself. Why had he hatched up such a complicated plot? He should have played safe. As he had with Edith Chell.

Her glance at him had lingered a few seconds too long, when, at the meeting with Diamond, Hebditch and Rudder, she'd said, 'Is there a drug ring in Leiston? I've had my suspicions for a time.' Then she'd tapped her nose. 'Nothing much gets past me.'

Then, a few days later, he'd found her messing about behind his bird-hide.

'What are you doing, Miss Chell?'

She looked flustered, clutching her binoculars, scrambling back to the road. 'I saw a bearded tit flying into the reeds . . . I was trying to get a better view.'

He walked towards her. 'And did you?'

'No.'

He pointed to the door of the hide. 'Would you like a cup of coffee? I've got a full flask.'

She was already backing away from him. 'No, ta very much. I must get back to the centre.'

He smiled at her. 'I'm going to spend a pleasant hour bird watching. Goodbye, Miss Chell.'

She was walking away and didn't look back.

He sighed. This time there would be no fancy details − just an efficient killing with nothing to connect it to him.

Fuming, he forced himself to sip the second brandy. He must make a decision. He'd either have to pull out completely, or brazen it out. He rubbed a hand over his chin, the bristles rough against his fingers. Christ, his standards were slipping. There were no signs he was under suspicion, the police seemed content with their suspect, Caleb Breen; but now the fucking Anglian Detective Agency were involved, would that make a difference? How good were they? He'd looked up past newspapers and read about their successes, but would they be able to accumulate evidence against him? If he got out now, he'd lose money, a lot of money. Did that matter? Freedom was more important. He'd made a stack, most of it safe in a Swiss bank. Could he close everything down without raising suspicion? Say he was moving to London because he needed to be near to his business? If he did that, he couldn't rush it. Also, what would happen at the ends of the chain? London and Holland? They wouldn't be happy. There might be some serious trouble for him. He lowered his head, letting out a stream of air between his teeth. Shit. Shit. Shit. That blasted Gorst. He hoped he was rotting in hell.

His suspicions had been aroused when he heard rumours of drugs being pushed in Leiston and Aldeburgh. Then the wild parties in the reserve. He'd volunteered to help the agency solve the problem of the vandalism; he needed to know what was going on. Who was selling drugs locally? All his consignments from Holland were safely stashed as soon as they were brought in. He took them to London to be sold on to a major dealer. The last thing he wanted was the drug squad nosing around. He'd chosen this stretch of remote coast for a reason.

Then the Leiston boy's death from pure cocaine. Who locally had access to pure cocaine, apart from himself? Was someone stealing from his supply? If they were, they were taking such small amounts he hadn't noticed. Who? It had to be someone who'd worked on the hide. Could it be Jonas Gorst? Gorst had helped in the building of the new hide. He must have discovered the secret compartment. He mustn't have realised the strength of pure cocaine, or known how to cut it, bulk it up to increase profits.

What should he do about Gorst? Should he cut him in? Make him part of the business? He didn't like him, he was surly, although a good worker. If he'd had him under his command in the Navy, he'd have broken his spirit, and made him as servile as a sycophantic waiter.

No, that wasn't the solution. If he was correct, and Gorst had stolen cocaine, it would only need one Leiston hick to cough to the police they'd got drugs from Gorst and then for Gorst to finger him. There was only one answer. He savoured another sip of brandy as he recalled the pleasure it gave him when he eviscerated a German sentry after slitting his throat. How could he kill Gorst and shift the blame to someone else? The police would concentrate on that crime, and lose interest in the local drug scene. And if Gorst *was* named as the local dealer, he would be dead, and silent.

Somehow, he'd have to find out if it was Gorst who'd stolen drugs from the hide. Talk to him, make him think he admired him for his daring, draw him into a plan to incriminate someone else for the vandalism of the hide. He needed to find out who he disliked, who he'd like to land in the shit, then he'd devise a plan to get rid of him and plant his murder onto a patsy.

Myres braked when he saw him, pulled over the Land Rover and wound down the window. 'Hello, Jonas. Like a lift, I'm going your way.'

225

The blue eyes stared back at him; the bunched features unsmiling.

He leant across and opened the passenger door. 'How's your family? Someone said your mother hasn't been well. Is she better?'

Gorst slowly made his way round the vehicle, as if unsure what do. He climbed in. 'Don't know what you're talking about. She's all right. Who said that?'

'I'm glad she's OK. I think it was Mr Rudder who told me.' He knew they'd had a fight. Perhaps he could fit up Rudder with Gorst's murder.

Gorst snorted. 'Stupid cunt.'

'What were you doing on the reserve today?'

'Reed cutting. Mr Breen sent me over to help.'

He nodded. 'Good of him to let you do some voluntary work.'

Gorst snorted. 'I wouldn't do it unless Mr Breen payed me.'

When they came to the junction for Westleton village, he turned to Gorst. 'Jonas, I've got a proposition for you. How would you like to work for me?'

Gorst had been looking ahead, now he turned and stared at him. 'Doing what?'

'I'll explain in more detail later, if you're interested. One fact I can tell you, you'll be paid considerably more than you're earning now. Does it appeal?'

'Why me?'

The boy wasn't stupid, despite his peasant features. He'd have to be subtle. 'I think I can use someone like you.'

Gorst gave a sly smile. It confirmed his belief – he was the thief. Gorst possibly knew were this was going, that the work might be illegal. He didn't look as though he was concerned about that.

'OK. I'm interested.'

'Good. I think we need to talk about this in private where we can't be seen together. I suggest I drive you to my house, we can have a drink and discuss your future employment.'

'And suppose I'm not interested?'

Myres shrugged. 'I'm a business man. I don't take rejection personally.'

Gorst settled back in his seat. 'Got any cherry brandy?'

He inwardly sneered. A tart's tipple. 'No, but I've got beer, whisky and a very old Armagnac.'

'What's that?'

'A brandy. I think you'd like it.' The talk of drink made him think he could choose a much simpler method. Tie him up and force alcohol down his throat, certainly not the Armagnac, until he died of alcohol poisoning, then dump his body on the beach with an empty bottle in his hand. Messy and not very subtle. The way he'd thought of was more fun.

Gorst, sitting in a leather arm chair, looked uncomfortable, not so sure of himself, now he was in strange surroundings. Good. He passed him a heavy tumbler, half-full of Armagnac. 'Sip it slowly, it's too good to chuck down.'

He sat opposite to him and raised his own glass. 'Cheers, Jonas, here's to . . . What shall we drink to? Other forms of pleasure beside alcohol? Drugs perhaps?'

Gorst flinched. 'I don't do drugs.'

'No, I don't think you use them personally. You're too clever to do that, that's why I'm interested in employing you. If you were a sniffer, I wouldn't touch you with a barge pole.'

Gorst gripped his glass tightly. 'Don't know what you're going on about.'

'I think you do, Jonas. I know you've stolen some of my cocaine from the hide.'

Gorst started to get up.

'Sit down and listen,' he commanded. Gorst stiffened, and slowly sank back into the chair. He smiled – he hadn't lost his touch

'I must admit I was furious at first, but then it dawned on me someone who could do that, and successfully sell it, was the kind of person I could use. Yes, there are wrinkles you need to learn; like never sell a pure drug. It's lethal. You kill your customers, as you did.' Gorst flinched, looking as though he wanted to get out of the room. It was him. No doubt. 'I agree they're eventually going to die

227

of addiction, but you don't want them to do that straight away; loyal customers are essential in any successful business.'

Gorst looked gob-smacked, and also impressed.

'Still interested?'

Gorst nodded, took a long drink, choked and coughed. 'What would I do? Would I work round here, or would I go to London?' he asked hopefully, obviously wanting to get away from the delights of country life.

'There's work to do here to begin with. I don't want you to hand in your notice just yet. There's something we need to put right before you do that.'

'What d'you mean?'

He leant towards him. 'You know about the vandalism in the bird reserve? Of course, you do; you were responsible.' He laughed as though it was a big joke, and slapped Gorst on the back. 'I think we need to move suspicion away from you, and make sure someone else gets the blame. What do you think? Anyone you'd like to get even with? Anyone who really gets up your nose?'

Gorst mouth hung open. 'Is there anything you don't know?'

He laughed again, as though he was having the time of his life, and they were old buddies. 'Not a lot, but we can have fun with this one. I know there's a few bastards I'd like to hang it on. What about that shit, Rudder?'

Gorst sneered. 'What a wanker. Said I fancied his wife. As if I'd want to shag that old tart. Yeh, but would anyone believe he'd crap on his own nest?' He laughed. 'That's good, in'it? Nest – birds. You get it?'

What an ignorant slob – it would be a pleasure ending his life. 'Very good, Jonas. You're quite the wit.' He took another sip. 'So not Rudder. Is there anyone you really dislike, someone who visits the reserve? Perhaps one of the volunteers? What about Edith Chell?'

'I hate her. I made her life a misery when I was at school, but there's someone I hates more than her. I really hates him.'

Myres leant forward. The venom in Gorst's voice was chilling. 'Who's that?'

Gorst leant towards him, his face contorted with spite. 'That weirdo Caleb Breen. I have to take orders from that little shit. A bug-eyed monster – should have been drowned at birth.'

'So, he's your choice?'

'Well, he would be, but I can't see how you can make people think he'd be responsible for damaging a hide.'

'Leave the brain work to me, Jonas. We need to damage another hide and leave something of Caleb's behind; something the police would find, and then discover it belonged to him.'

Jonas's features bunched even tighter as he frowned. 'Don't see how you can make it work.'

He pretended to think, having already decided on what he wanted. 'Are there any tools that only belong to Caleb? Something we could use to damage a hide?'

Jonas sat, blinking his eyes, frowning. Then his face cleared. 'Yes. Yes. He's got a lot of old farm machines and tools; he looks after them, keeps them in an old barn.'

'That's brilliant, Jonas. Can you get into the barn?'

'Yeah! Easy. It's never locked up.'

'We need something that could do a bit of damage. Can you think of anything that would fit that bill?'

'Like a scythe; he's got several of those.'

It was like playing a salmon on the end of a line, the hook slowly working deeper into the fish's jaw. 'That would be good.' He hesitated, pretending to think. 'Yes, but it might break before we really got going. Anything else? Try to imagine you're looking at all the tools.'

'He's put them up on the barn wall.' Jonas squeezed his eyes tight, his small mouth screwing up as well. His eyes snapped open. 'He's got some axes. They'd be good.'

At last. 'Brilliant. Do you think they might have his fingerprints on them?'

Jonas stuck out his tongue and made a vomiting sound. 'Fingerprints? Frog prints! Yeah, he won't let anyone else touch them, I 'spect they'll have them on the handles.' He smirked. 'That would be good. If the police find his finger prints on the axe, they'll soon know it's him. Not many people got hands like a bloody frog.'

'Can you get an axe and bring it to me?'

'Sure,' Jonas said, shrugging his shoulders. 'Easy.'

He got up. 'I'll get you something to wrap it in.' He waited, hoping Jonas would cotton on.

'Yeah! I'll have to be careful not to touch the handle, won't I?'

'There you are! That's why I want to employ you; you've got brains.' Not for much longer, he thought.

He came back with a large plastic bag and a pillow case. 'Wrap the material round it, then pop it into the bag. Pick a good sturdy one, with a sharp edge, one that'll do a lot of damage.' He also passed Gorst a pair of yellow plastic gloves.

'I don't do washing up.'

'Very witty, Jonas. Make sure you wear them when you remove the axe. We don't want your fingerprints on it, do we?'

Jonas grinned. 'Where'll we meet?'

He tried to look as though he was thinking. 'My hide. How about Friday night? Come to the hide by way of Minsmere beach and the new road. Don't go through the reserve.'

'You're not going to bash up *your* hide?' He looked shocked.

He shook his head. 'What? And have the wooden tops sniffing out our drugs cache – no way.' The pathetic boy pushed out his chest at the words, our drugs. 'No, I'll choose another hide and on a night the detectives aren't around.'

Jonas stiffened. 'What detectives?'

He explained the Warden had hired the Anglian Detective Agency and how they were doing night shifts in the hides at the weekend. 'That's why you need to come by the beach.'

'You're a cool one,' Jonas said. 'Pretending to help them. Shouldn't I wait and bring it on another night?'

'Scared?'

Jonas snorted. 'Of that lot? Old bossy-boots Piff, that fat-arsed copper and the poncy one with the leather jacket. Mind you the big blonde's not bad. Wouldn't mind giving her one.'

What a coarse little cunt. But he agreed with him about Laurel Bowman. 'Good. Bring it to me, say nine. Then we can decide which hide to mess up and when.'

Jonas nodded. 'What about my job? How much'll you pay me?'

He got up and took the bottle of Armagnac and filled up Jonas's glass. Then he spun him a tall tale before driving him home.

Myres sat in the hide, waiting for Gorst to turn up. Everything was ready. He was proud of the hide; not from the point of view of bird watching, though it was also excellent for that purpose, but it was an ideal place for the drugs brought in by boat, until he was ready to take them to London. He smiled as he imagined the Warden's face if he knew his beloved reserve was a safe place for cocaine and heroin. He'd spent too much capital building the hide and road, he intended to make use of it for several more years. Get rid of Gorst – he couldn't take the risk of letting him live.

The hide was well built of seasoned oak. Larger than the other hides, with the usual observation windows and accompanying benches, but with a fixed central table and chairs. 'I thought it would be nice for the visitors to be able to sit down comfortably and eat a sandwich, drink coffee from their flasks or write up their field notes,' he'd said to Hebditch, who'd been fulsome in his praise and thanks.

The table and chairs were attached to a movable section of the wooden floor, and by a mechanism the floor could be raised a few inches, then swivelled to reveal a cavity beneath. He'd had the hide pre-built to his own specifications and erected by craftsmen used by the Dutch dealers. Gorst and some of the other men who worked on the reserve dug the foundations. How Gorst worked out how to move the table and chairs, he wasn't sure. He'd find out tonight. Not that it mattered any more. The cavity was three feet deep, and larger in area than the table and chairs. It was lined with bricks, then a water-tight seal and on top of that he always put a new sheet of plastic for every fresh delivery of drugs. Tonight, it would have another use.

He looked at his watch, nearly nine. He went to the observation window and looked out at inky blackness; there was no sign of movement; the only sounds were the dry rustling of last year's reeds. He'd grown to hate this part of the world: some said it had charm, with its slower pace of life, friendly people and arts and crafts. He didn't see much excitement in having to queue for your bread at Smith's in Aldeburgh during the holiday season, or wait behind a nattering old lady at the tiny supermarket. What he liked was the buzz of London, a city that never slept, and the opportunity to spend big, gamble recklessly, and have beautiful and expensive women on his arm. One day he'd be able to have a red-hot boat, one capable of making oceanic voyages, then he'd spend most of the year sailing from one top resort to another. He frowned. He'd need to keep this business going, perhaps build up a reliable team and expand. Not an easy thing to do.

He got up. Time to slip into something comfortable. He grinned as he zipped up the overall to cover his clothes. He placed another overall on the bench beneath the window. He tensed. Footsteps, barely audible, approached the hide. He switched on a torch, keeping the beam away from the window. The door opened.

'Hello, Jonas. On time. Well done.'

Gorst came in carrying a large plastic bag. His eye widened as he looked at Myres. 'Christ, what've you got on?'

Myres laughed. 'I've got one for you, I hope it fits.' He pointed to the bag. 'You got it?'

'Yeah. It's all wrapped up, just like you said, but what's the suit for?'

If only he knew. 'It's a precaution I take when I'm handling drugs. I wear one of these and then as soon as the job's finished I destroy it.'

In the torch's light, Gorst's face showed puzzlement. 'Why?'

'Even though the drugs are packaged, there might be a spillage or leak. There's always the possibility your ordinary clothes could be contaminated, and if you were ever taken in by the police, they might find traces on your clothing. Also, they've got these sniffer dogs, they're trained to nose out anything from dead bodies, to explosives to drugs. So, we don't want to meet any of them with traces of cocaine in our turnups, do we?'

Gorst pushed out a lower lip and sagely nodded. 'You've really thought of everything. I'm looking forward to getting down to some real work.'

Myres smiled at him. 'Not before we've had our bit of fun and diverted the police's attention to Caleb Breen. Right. Let's have a look at it. See if it's up to the job.' He pointed to the table. Gorst carefully opened the plastic bag and took out a long object wrapped in another bag and covered with the cloth he'd given him.

'Gloves,' Myres ordered.

Gorst stopped. 'Sorry, I threw the one you gave me away after I'd parcelled the axe up.'

'Don't worry, I'll take over.' He took a pair of white rubber gloves, blew into them and put them on. They were made of superior latex and fitted closely to his hands, almost like a second skin. He carefully removed the axe from its wrappings, making sure he didn't touch the main body of the handle, and placed it on the table. 'Ah, a fromard.' He ran his fingers over the cutting edge. Yes, sharp enough for the job. 'You picked well, Jonas. We can do some serious damage with this.'

Gorst joined him at the table.

'Did you have any problems taking it? Sure no one saw you?'

Gorst shrugged. 'It was easy. I waited until Mr Breen and Caleb were in one of the far fields, and my dad was on his way home for his dinner. Told my dad I'd catch up with him, that I'd got caught short and need to use the Breens' outside lav.' He peered at the axe. 'I'll give him that, he does keep all the tools sharp, even though they aren't used. I thought this one looked good; it's got a nice long handle. You can get a good swing at whatever you want to smash.'

He nodded. 'As I said, good choice. Right, before we decide which hide to vandalise, I thought I'd give you your first lesson on how the drugs are stored and the routine I have for bringing them into the country and then distributing them. You'll be my right-hand man, Jonas, as soon as I've trained you up.'

Gorst chest visibly expanded. 'I won't let you down, Mr Myres. I can't wait to start working for you.'

'Good. First, we'll move the table, although you know how to do

233

that already, don't you? I was most impressed. How did you work that one out?'

Gorst looked uncomfortable. 'Yeah, I'm sorry I did that to you, and all the nicking. But I didn't take too much. You didn't notice, did you?' Now he sounded cocky. 'When we were helping to dig the foundations, I thought it wasn't built like the other hides. Me and my dad, we helped out with some of those. I sneaked up when you had those foreign guys building it and when they went out, I think they were going for a slash, I looked in and saw the space, and how the table and chairs could slide over it. Then I nicked a padlock key.' He shot a sly look at him. 'That's my problem, I'm nosy.'

'You're obviously cut out for a life of crime, Jonas. I can see you'll be invaluable to me.'

'Shall I put the overalls on?' Gorst asked.

'In a moment. Right, operate the lever. You remember where it is?'

'Sure.' Gorst swaggered out of the hide. A minute later the part of the floor on which the table and chairs sat, silently moved up a few inches; he pushed the table, and the section of floor rotated, revealing the compartment beneath. Gorst came back, brushing down his jeans.

'Good. There's a small amount of packaged cocaine left; you'll need to kneel down so you can see it. Here's the torch. Don't touch it, as you haven't got your overalls on. I just want you to appreciate the large space, and to realise how big a consignment of drugs we can bring in.'

'I already know what the space is like, Mr Myres.'

'Yes, I realise that, but we're starting your training from the beginning. I'm a very thorough man, Jonas, I like to dot all the i's and cross all the t's.'

Gorst sniggered. 'Bit of a tight arse, are you, Mr Myres?'

You don't know the half of it. 'In this game you have to be thorough if you want to last in the business.'

'Oh, OK.' Gorst knelt down, but before he could bend to look into the compartment, Myres grabbed the shaft of the fromard, took a long back-swing and buried the blade in the back of Gorst's head.

234

With a soft grunt, Gorst froze. The torch dropped from his hand and spun on the floor of the hide, a silent Catherine Wheel. Then like a felled tree, he toppled into the pit, body thudding against the hard floor.

Myres picked up the torch and shone a beam on to the body. The axe was firmly embedded in his skull. He'd try and keep it there when he moved him, instead of leaving it near the corpse. Blood was seeping over Gorst's neck and shoulders, but the plastic lining of the compartment was doing its job. He flashed the beam of the torch over the floor where Gorst had knelt; there were only a few spots of blood. It had gone well. He climbed down to the body and straightened it out. Hopefully rigor mortis would have been and gone before he had to move it and put it somewhere else, somewhere it would be discovered quickly. No sense in trying to hide this one too long. The main thing was to preserve any fingerprints on the axe's handle. He cleaned up, went outside, and when he returned, the table and chairs were in their proper place; then he stepped out of his overalls, removed the gloves and put both of them in the plastic bag Gorst had brought the fromard in. Waste not, want not.

He took a deep breath. He'd enjoyed that, especially the feel of the edge of the axe penetrating the skull, the power of his body, the force he'd had to use, the clean, successful blow, the reverberations up the handle, through his hand and arm. Very satisfying. He'd not had so much pleasure for years.

Chapter Twenty-seven

Thursday, March 16, 1972

It was still dark when Frank got out of bed; he'd given up trying to sleep after he'd woken at three in the morning. Even a pee and a long drink of water hadn't worked their usual tricks. His mind was seething with thoughts. He sighed; he wouldn't be fresh for a day of thinking, trying to untangle all the different threads of the case, and weave them into a logical pattern.

He went down to the kitchen, got the percolator loaded and onto the gas flame. He switched on the radio to the World Service, hoping to distract his mind, so he'd come to the problem fresh after a dose of caffeine and a few slices of toast and marmalade.

Breakfast over, followed by a long hot shower and a determined scrape at his ever-growing stubble, he opened the curtains as dawn broke over the sea. It was a good sunrise, the light painting the clusters of clouds red as they moved slowly north-west blown by a light wind. Then, as the sun appeared over the sea's horizon, the clouds paled to white and the sea turned a deep blue, brushed with brown, where the sandbanks lay. He cleared the kitchen table and placed an A4 pad on it, together with biros of different colours. He poured himself another cup of coffee and settled down to see where his thoughts would lead him.

If Myres was the murderer, how did he get hold of the fromard? Why did he choose that weapon? How did it get from the barn wall to its resting place in the skull of Jonas Gorst? How did Myres know of its existence? As far as they knew he'd never been to Rooks Wood Farm. Had he heard about Caleb's collection of rural farm implements and secretly visited the farm and had stolen it? He grimaced. No, he didn't like that explanation. Why would anyone tell him about the old farm tools?

Had he ever talked with Caleb about his collection? Caleb visited the reserve; Myres knew him, said he'd talked to him. But Caleb wasn't keen on mixing with people. It didn't seem likely he would have had a conversation that included telling Myres about his tools. He started to write on the paper, putting down names of all the people who worked or visited the reserve. Had Myres talked to one of the Gorsts? To the father, Fred, who might have mentioned Caleb's collection? Or Daniel Breen?

He continued ringing names until he'd made a web of coloured lines connecting them. He stared at it. At the centre, like a master puppeteer, sat Myres. If Myres was the killer, and was also bringing drugs into the country, he was a clever, devious and dangerous man. A ruthless killer, with no thought for others – he peddled death for money. He wanted to be rid of Jonas Gorst. Why? Gorst must have been a threat. Blackmail? Possible.

It came back to the fromard. The fromard with Caleb's prints on it. How did he get hold of it? He must have wanted to pin the murder on Caleb, and away from himself. Who had access to the weapon? Who stole it and passed it to Myres so he could kill Gorst with it?

Gorst had been struck from behind; the autopsy suggested from the position of the blow, he was sitting or kneeling, lower than the killer. Did he trust the murderer, and was unprepared for the attack?

But who passed the axe to Myres? Could it have been Gorst himself? Supposing Gorst stole it and brought it to Myres? Why would he do that? Myres wasn't going to tell him the real reason for wanting the axe. He must have told Gorst he wanted to frame Caleb for some other crime. Jonas hated Caleb. What crime had Myres told Jonas he was setting Caleb up for? He blew out his cheeks. Time for lunch and a beer.

After bread and cheese and a bottle of Adnam's, he decided he needed a walk before he had another session. He shrugged on his leather jacket and walked inland over the heath; the sun was still shining; it was the first warm day for a long time. The sandy paths criss-crossing the heath were soft underfoot, the air buoyant with brine and a tang of iodine. He cut across the heath to where the path joined the tarmacked road leading back to his cottage. Close by was the entrance to Blackfriars's School, still closed, and shunned because of the murder of the headmaster's wife. He left the road and turned left onto a path over the cliffs. A flock of gulls, just offshore, were heading north, using the line of the seashore for guidance; mostly herring gulls, but a few common and black-backed among them. Off to breed in the north. He shook his head. The urge to have young was a powerful force. One he hadn't acquired. Yet. Possibly never.

Back in his cottage he settled down at the kitchen table, and placed a fresh sheet of paper in front of him. Where had Myres kept the drugs? In his house? That would be the logical place. His mind didn't seem to want to grasp this problem. He looked the sheets he'd worked on in the morning. Was his theory correct? Had Gorst brought the murder weapon to Myres? He ran a finger back and forth over the stubble under his mouth. He didn't feel as confident as he had before his walk. He needed to bounce it off someone. He picked up the phone and dialled.

'Anglian Detective Agency, Miss Laurel Bowman speaking. How can I help you?'

'You can help by coming over to the cottage and having dinner with me.'

'Frank! Are you all right?' He'd taken her by surprise. She hadn't been invited for a meal à deux since . . . she couldn't remember. The last time was probably when she'd turned up unannounced after finding the body of Dr Luxton. She'd even stayed the night, as she'd had too much to drink and Frank declared she was unfit to drive.

'Yes, I haven't lost my marbles. I need some help. I need to bounce a theory off you.'

'A theory? What about?'

'I'll tell you when I see you. Can you make dinner?'

'Yes, what time?'

'Say six?'

'Shall I bring Bumper?'

'No, see if one of the others can look after him for the evening.'

'OK. Dress formal?'

'Come in your jim-jams, if you like. See you soon.' The line went dead.

She slowly put the receiver down. This wasn't like Frank. He didn't usually feel the need to discuss his theories with anyone else until he honed them to death and brought them fully formed before the meeting. Why the change? Why now? Her stomach twisted. She was being silly. But supposing she wasn't? Lately he'd looked at her in a different way. With any other man she'd have known what that glance meant. But Frank? He'd never shown any interest of that kind before. She winced. She didn't want their relationship to change. Perhaps in the past, at the beginning? But now? She liked him, even loved him as she loved all the members of the agency, but only as a friend and colleague. When he'd become entangled with Carol Pemberton, she'd been jealous. She was being stupid. Why should he find her attractive now? You're overestimating yourself, she thought. She decided she'd wear something very plain and sensible for dinner.

Frank put down the phone. Excellent. Now what should he cook for dinner? He'd recently bought an upright freezer, and although frozen fish wasn't as good as fresh, there were some Dover sole in it. If he got them out now, they'd thaw in time. With some bread, a bottle of Muscadet, and cheese that would do. Excitement and anticipation zinged through him. How he felt about Laurel had changed. Why he wasn't sure. Perhaps he was jealous of Bumper. He laughed.

He ran a hand over his stubble. Better have another shave. What was he doing? He was presuming too much. What the hell! Let's see where it takes us. He'd soon pick up the signs if she didn't feel like

239

he did. Dear Laurel, he wouldn't mess her around. 'Francis Xavier Diamond,' he heard his mother's voice, 'this is a serious woman, not one you can take up with, then dump when you get cold feet. This is time for a commitment. If you're not prepared for that, then restrain yourself.' For once he agreed with her. He'd forget the shave.

Laurel kissed Bumper's nose. 'Be a good boy and do what your Auntie Dot tells you.'

Dorothy was looking at her over her spectacles. 'That moniker is reserved for my two human boys. Tell Bumper as far as he's concerned, I'm Miss Piff.'

'Oh, really? I've seen Miss Piff being silly with Bumper, calling him all sorts of soppy names, and giving him naughty treats behind my back.'

Dorothy snorted. 'Isn't it time you left for your clandestine dinner with Mr Diamond?'

'I don't like the word clandestine.'

Dorothy gave her an old-fashioned look. 'What's got into Frank? He doesn't give out many dinner invitations. None of us have ever been invited to sample his cooking. I think Stuart once had an omelette in the early days; he thought Frank was trying to poison him with wild mushrooms.'

She laughed. 'I remember that; it was when they were both in the police. So much has happened since then.'

'What does Frank want to see you about?'

'He wants to try out a new theory he'd thought up this morning.'

Dorothy scrunched up her face. 'Really? Not like him.' She gave her a long, hard look. 'Don't do anything you don't want to, will you?'

Oh dear. Dorothy was thinking along the same lines. She squeezed Dorothy's shoulder. 'Your powers of observation are slipping.' She pointed to her navy cords and sweater. 'Passion killers?'

Dorothy smirked. 'Not the most seductive clothes you have, but they can't completely hide what's underneath, and I do believe some men have X-ray eyes.'

'Dorothy Piff. You're a disgrace.' She picked up her car keys and wondered if she should have worn her black lace panties, not the white cotton ones, fit for a nun.

Frank went to the window; the moon was high in the sky, a pale sliver appearing now and then through the moving clouds. He drew the curtains. A car pulled up, pebbles clattering. Laurel. He wished he hadn't asked her over. It didn't seem right. A knock on the door forced him to get a grip. He'd only asked her to dinner to listen to his theory and give her opinion.

'Hi, Laurel, glad you could make it.' Navy cords and a fisherman's jumper? Did she think they were going on a boat trip?

'Hello, Frank. What's the matter? I thought jim-jams might be a bit draughty. I hope you weren't expecting me to wear a dress.'

'Perish the thought. You look lovely whatever you wear.'

She gave him a wary look. She never simpered when she was complimented, for her looks, courage, or her brain power.

'I'm hungry; what are you cooking?'

He told her. 'Sorry there's no vegetables or pudding, but I've got cheese and some dark chocolate. Come into the kitchen.'

'Sounds good. Are we eating first, or discussing your theory?'

He moved to the fridge and took out the bottle of Muscadet. 'I think I can hear your stomach rumbling, so we'll eat first. Drink?'

She sat down at the table and took a sip of wine. 'Lovely.'

She was silent as the kitchen filled with the buttery smell of frying Dover sole. The meal didn't take long to cook or eat. He poured the last of the wine into their glasses.

'Hey, Frank, go easy. I've got to drive back. Remember what happened last time I was here for a meal.'

He did indeed. It was after she'd discovered Luxton's body and she'd drunk too much on an empty stomach. She'd stayed the night in his spare bedroom, in a pair of his pyjamas. He'd given her a chaste kiss and rumpled her hair. What would happen this time if she got squiffy?

She poured most of the wine from her glass into his. 'Ready to tell me about the theory?'

'I'll make coffee first. Like some chocolate?'

She nodded.

As they drank coffee and ate squares of Bournville Dark, he told her he thought Gorst brought Myres the axe to frame Caleb for some crime. Obviously Gorst didn't twig why Myres wanted it.

'If that's true, he's totally evil.'

'Does it stand up?'

'It makes sense. But we have no proof.'

'We need to find out where he stashes the drugs between bringing them ashore in his boat and transferring them to, probably, London. If we could do that, we'd unlock the case.'

Her eyes widened, her mouth opened.

'Yes?'

She grasped his hand. 'The hide,' she said.

'It has to be the hide,' he said, grinning like a schoolboy who's scored the winning goal in a lunch-time football match. 'Excellent!'

'My God, he's a cool customer; he offers to build a new observation hide for the reserve, plus a road, so he can secrete the drugs there and transport them easily from the beach to the hide, and from the hide to, probably, his house,' she said.

'I think it's time we got in touch with Revie.'

'But all we've got is supposition, no proof. Will he believe us?'

Frank grimaced. 'Not sure.'

She gave him a devil-may-care smile. 'You know what we'll have to do?'

He grinned back. 'Another break-in job?

'If we search the hide and find out where he puts the drugs, and even, hopefully, find some, I think Revie will be interested.'

'I'll phone the others and call a meeting for early tomorrow morning.'

'Eight o'clock?' Laurel suggested.

'Greyfriars.' It was Dorothy.

'What? Why this sudden rush of blood to the head? What's happened?' she said, after Frank had told her he was calling a meeting early tomorrow morning.

'I can't talk over the phone. See you in the morning.' He put the receiver down.

'She'll be waiting for me when I get back,' Laurel said. 'Shall I say anything?'

He hesitated, thinking it over. 'Better not; they'll probably all be waiting for you. If they have too much time to mull it over, I'm afraid they might try to talk us out of the idea.'

She looked at her watch. 'I'd better stay a bit longer, hopefully they'll give up and go to bed.'

'Another drink?'

'Coffee, please. I'm not planning to stay the night.'

He'd got the message. Pity, she looked really sexy in her fisherman's outfit. He'd never sneer at a cable-stitch sweater again.

Chapter Twenty-eight

Bryce De Lacy gave up the struggle of trying to sleep. He switched on the bedside lamp and looked at the carriage clock. Three-thirty. It was no use; he might as well get up. He sat on the edge of the bed and pushed webbed feet into monogrammed slippers. All night his mind had seethed – this man, Myres, had framed his Caleb. Caleb was seriously ill – he might die. He couldn't wait for the agency to find evidence against Myres. They might not find any. He had to get Caleb out of that hospital and away from the incompetent doctors and nurses.

Caleb must have the finest of care. Would a Swiss hospital be best? They used to specialise in treating patients with chest infections. He would consult his Harley Street doctor. He slipped on a dressing gown, and putting his cigarette case and lighter in a pocket, started to make his way downstairs. The door of Ada Spooner's bedroom was ajar and a light was on. Relief flooded through him. He could talk with her; she'd always been loyal to him, even when he'd done terrible things. When his and Rosalind's parents died in an air accident when he was eighteen, she'd taken their place, looking after both of them; comforting when needed, gently chiding when things went wrong, or advising when there were difficult decisions to make. There were some things he hadn't told her, things he couldn't tell anyone, but sometimes he caught her looking at him, as though she already knew. Was that fear in her eyes? If it was, it was fear for *him*, for she knew he'd never harm her. He loved her because he was sure she loved him. The only person who did. Once Rosalind had loved him – then she met Noah Breen.

He pushed open the door. The room smelt of lavender and old flesh. 'Nanny Ada, are you awake?'

'Yes, I'm reading. Come in.'

She was sitting up in bed supported by several pillows. A book, its large print visible, lay open on the bedspread.

He picked it up. 'Ah, *Jane Eyre.*'

She smiled. 'A favourite of mine. Can't you sleep, Bryce?' She placed metal-framed spectacles on a bedside table and patted the space beside her.

'I keep thinking of Caleb choking to death in that hospital.'

She sighed. 'I wish I could see him. If you'd let me go to Rosalind's funeral, I would have seen both of her children.'

He liked that: *her* children. Not her and Noah's children. 'He looks like me. The resemblance is remarkable.'

She nodded. 'So you have said.'

'I went to talk to the people at the detective agency yesterday; to ask what progress they'd made.'

'Who did you talk to? Was it Mr Diamond?'

He laughed. 'Yes, it was. You like him, don't you?'

She smiled. 'Yes, I do.'

He patted her hand. 'You always admired a handsome face.'

'He's not only handsome, but clever and quick.'

'Not quick enough, I'm afraid.'

'What do you mean?'

He leant towards her, feelings of frustration starting to build up again. 'They have a suspect for the murder of Jonas Gorst, but no evidence. I can't wait for them to find that, it could take days, weeks. All the time, Caleb is deteriorating.'

Ada's rheumy blue eyes widened. 'Who do they suspect? Did this person try to foist the crime on Caleb? That is terrible.'

'Yes, for some reason he wanted Caleb to be found guilty. The bastard. I'd like to kill him.' He saw shock and fright in her eyes. 'I can't tell you who he is, I promised I wouldn't talk about it to anyone.'

She shook her head. 'I think you can tell *me*, Bryce. I don't think

I'm going to rush round the neighbourhood divulging your secret, and it might help you to talk it through. We don't want you losing your temper and rushing off doing something stupid, do we?'

Her voice held a warning. She was staring at him, as though willing him to be sensible. He could almost see her lips adding the words, 'Like the last time.' He'd thought then she knew. She'd seen him soon after he came back, looked at his face, wiped away sweat from his brow with her handkerchief, and removed the blood-stained clothes he'd thrown onto the floor. When the police came, she said he'd been with her all day. They never talked about it, she never asked and he hadn't told her.

That day was etched in his mind, as clearly as acid eats into glass. Another March day. He'd come back from Nice, where he'd been staying for the winter months; it was good to be able to travel to France again, even though there were restrictions. He'd come back to discuss changes in some of the farming practises with his manager, but also to see dear Ada, who was about to celebrate her seventy-fourth birthday. He always tried to return for her birthdays. He sighed. Ada Spooner, seventy-four, and in two more years he would have reached his half century. How many years had he left?

It was one of those rare March days, no wind, not even a breeze from the sea; the sun had risen red against a bleached blue sky. He'd breakfasted with Nanny Ada and had offered to run her to Alde-burgh, but she'd said she would spend some time in the rose garden pruning the bushes. She offered him another cup of coffee. He smiled at her as she elegantly poured from the silver jug, feeling the warmth of her affection. 'Ada, I'm thinking of going to Rooks Wood Farm. Surely, after all this time, Rosalind will have forgiven me? Isn't it time we made up and became brother and sister again? What do you think? Will she feel as I do?'

Her hand froze, and she stopped pouring. 'I'm not sure. You know Rosalind; when she makes up her mind, nothing will change it.'

'But so many years have passed, she's forty-four, Ada, no longer a young girl. I've never seen the two boys. I've no one else, apart from you. I want to see her again.'

Ada put down the jug and passed him his cup. 'Bryce, be careful. What will you do if she turns you away again? You know how your temper can flare up. You haven't changed much in that respect. You have many friends, here and abroad, your life has a steady pattern. Surely that is enough?'

'Is your life enough for you?' he snapped.

'It has to be. I'm very grateful for the care you've given me. You didn't have to keep me on all these years. I have a very comfortable life in a lovely house and enough friends to keep up my interest in what is happening in our neighbourhood.'

He patted her hand. 'Dear Ada, if you weren't here, I don't think I'd ever come home. I'll be careful. Perhaps I'll take Rosalind some flowers from the hot-house. I wonder if roses are still her favourite flower?'

'It's a way to walk, the flowers will be wilted by the time you get there.'

'I'll drive part of the way and perhaps walk the last mile.'

'Remember, Bryce, say as little as possible. If Rosalind starts on at you, don't shout back at her, let her have her say. Apologise for what you did, and truly mean it.'

Apologise for what he did? Does she know?

He decided to park his car in the lane leading to Rooks Wood Farm and walk the last mile through the woods. The head gardener had picked pink and white tulips for him; the roses weren't ready. The last time he came to the farm he'd argued with Noah, and told him he wasn't good enough for his sister, either by birth or prospects. He didn't want to lose Rosalind – she meant so much to him. The thought of her belonging to Noah, and worse, being in his bed, made him feel as sick as a dog. Beautiful Rosalind. Was she still beautiful? Or had years of hard work and the responsibility of the boys, aged her beyond recognition? His throat squeezed tight as he remembered forbidding her to marry Noah Breen. Her large eyes, usually soulful and calm, flashed with anger, her delicate features flushed with rage. She'd never looked so beautiful. Never.

As he played the sequences of that day, his heart raced, and the memories of what happened made his breathing jagged. He stopped at the edge of the wood and put a hand against the fissured bark of an oak, trying to regain his equilibrium. Why, why did she go against him? He thought of the different kind of life they would have had if she'd stayed. They could have travelled the world together, explored the great cities, attended important plays, heard concerts, had a wide circle of influential and important friends. What had she had? A life of hard work, long hours, little financial reward, and for what? The love of a plodding farmer? Had it lasted? Perhaps now she regretted her marriage. Perhaps she would be glad to see him, for them to be together again. She might want to leave Noah Breen, to take up the life that was hers by right.

Hope ran through him. It was a possibility. He entered the wood – she would forgive him and, once more, they would be brother and sister. He frowned. Supposing when he saw her, she was so changed he didn't want the old relationship? No, that couldn't happen. She would always be his Rosalind. But, like a parasitic worm, the idea slid through his brain. She'd be so changed he wouldn't know her, wouldn't want to know her. He might have to reject her. She might be desperate to get away from her parochial life. It was Noah Breen's fault; he'd brought her to this state. He'd abused a beautiful, privileged girl and made her into a drudge.

The branches of the oaks were bare, but leaf buds were beginning to swell. High up in the branches, the rooks were making a racket. Looking upwards he saw nests in the tree tops; Nanny Ada told them, when they were children, if the rooks built their nests high in the trees, the summer would be sunny and warm, but if they built low down, it would be wet and cold. He hated the rooks, hated all corvids. His gamekeepers were encouraged to shoot as many as possible and to display their bodies by hanging them on a line.

Caw, caw, caw. My God, how many were there? They were flying to and from their nests, their blue-black feathers shining in the sun. How he wished he'd brought his gun; they'd be easy targets on their nests. What a fool Noah Breen was to allow these vermin to exist so close to his home.

The pathway through the wood was well-used and worn smooth, with only a few exposed roots, like knotted veins, showing above the surface. Parts of the floor were resplendent with wood anemones, and at the edge of glades, primroses studded the ground. In his path was a fallen nest; scattered twigs fouled with bird shit. He kicked it to pieces. Caw, caw, caw. Wings beat the air, as they squabbled over nesting sites. His chest heaved with rage at their sheer exuberance, their ruination of the peace of the wood.

'Hello. Can I help you?'

A man was walking towards him. He was tall, well built with broad shoulders, his thick, blond hair silvered at the sides. Blue eyes, sharp and puzzled. He was dressed for the countryside: a flat cap, tweed jacket, leather boots and a double-barrelled shotgun over his arm. It was Noah Breen.

Breen smiling, came closer. 'Are you lost? This is . . .' He jerked to a stop, the smile disappeared, and a dark frown and narrowed eyes changed his face from friendly to suspicious. 'Bryce De Lacy? What in God's name have you come here for? We thought we'd never see you again.'

The old anger and the terrible pains of jealousy ripped through his body. It was if all those years were gone and it was the day she'd left him. He was so livid he couldn't speak.

'I ask you again, what do you want? Or have you come back to spy on us? Hoping to see Rosalind?'

Breen's sneering voice drove thoughts of reparation from his mind. Noah Breen – a farmer – would thwart him again. Dirt under his fingernails, and wheat chaff in his hair. A man of the soil. If only he were six feet under that soil. Then Rosalind would come back to him.

'What have you come for? Spit it out, or get off my land,' Breen said, grasping the butt of his gun in his right hand. It was safely broken, but in a second it could be breached and fired. Was it full of shot? What had he come out to shoot? Rabbits to eke out their rations? Or perhaps a pigeon, to be rid of a pest and put meat on the table? He hated the thought of Rosalind queuing at the butchers, like a common woman.

He took a deep breath and tried to follow Nanny Ada's advice. 'I came to see if you and Rosalind are ready to end this feud and to start our relationship again,' he said, trying to keep his voice neutral and steady.

Breen stared at him, slowly shaking his head.

'Surely, after all this time, Rosalind will forgive me for trying to stop her marrying you? And you, are you ready?'

Breen took a step backwards. 'As far as I'm concerned, we've managed very well without you, and I don't wish to know you. I think Rosalind will say the same. You've had a wasted journey. Be on your way, Mr Lacy, I'd like you off my land *now*.'

Being incorrectly addressed, not given his proper title, fanned the flame of hate into the searing heat of a blow torch. Breen stood between him and Rosalind. As he'd always done. But Breen was bigger. Stronger. And he had the gun.

He dropped the flowers, grabbed his left arm and shrieked with false pain, staggering towards Breen, doubled up, his face hidden.

'My God, man, what's wrong?'

He heard the dull thud of metal bouncing off soil. Breen had him in his arms. 'May God forgive me for my harsh words. Here, De Lacy, lie down. Has this happened before? Rest here and I'll get help.'

Breen dragged him a few feet and propped him against the side of an oak tree. The calls of the rooks increased to a crescendo. He closed his eyes as Breen loosened his tie and undid the top button of his shirt. He moaned. 'Help me, please help me.'

'I'm sorry for speaking so harshly. Will you be all right if I leave you for a bit? I'll go to the house, it won't take but a few minutes. I'll call for an ambulance, then I'll come back.' His voice was concerned, but there was no panic. Through half-open eyes he saw the gun, lying close by.

Breen rose and started to move away. 'I'll be back soon. Try not to move. Try to take some steady breaths.' He turned, strode away, then turned back. 'Better take—'

But it was too late. He'd snatched the gun, snapped it, and kneeling, put the butt to his shoulder, took aim and when Breen ran back, pointed it at his chest.

'What do you think—'

He waited a split second until Breen was almost on him then he pulled one of the triggers. The explosion of the gun was so loud he thought he'd be deafened, but he heard the rooks explode with a cacophony of harsh cries, erupting above the tree tops. Breen's blood and flesh hit his body and face as he toppled to the woodland floor.

Still kneeling, he froze, the gun pointing upwards to where Breen had been. He started trembling, the gun shaking in his hands. The smell of hot blood and flesh was sickening. He wanted to throw the gun down and run back to his car and drive away. What had he done? He'd killed Noah Breen. Could he say Breen attacked him? But it would still be manslaughter, at the very best. He was on Breen's property. He shuddered as he thought of what Rosalind might say to the police. She might even tell them what happened between them before she married, now Noah was dead. What had he done?

He laid down the gun. Fingerprints. He took a handkerchief from his jacket pocket and carefully wiped down the butt. He looked at Noah's body. How would he have fallen if it had been an accident and he'd shot himself? Should he move him? No. Better to leave him where he was. He took the gun and wrapped Noah's fingers round the butt and placed the index finger of the right hand over the trigger. Why would he have shot himself? Accident? He tripped? He looked round and saw a fallen branch; he heaved it over and placed it near Noah's feet, putting one foot under it and the other over the top. He picked up the gun using the handkerchief, and let it drop to the ground. He looked round, making sure he wasn't leaving any traces of himself behind. The flowers – now pink, white and red. He must get back to his car without anyone seeing him. Then he must get rid of the clothes.

He spat on the handkerchief and wiped blood off his face as best he could. His jacket was dark, the stains weren't too noticeable. He pulled up the collar to hide the blood-splashed shirt and tie. He could do no more. He picked up the flowers and looked down on Breen's face, unharmed by the pellets, but despoiled with blood, flesh and shreds of heart and lungs. His eyes were open, staring up into the bare branches of the oaks. The rooks were back on their nests, squabbling, but Noah Breen couldn't hear them.

Chapter Twenty-nine

Friday, March 17, 1972

Laurel was excited, but nervous as Frank opened the early morning meeting. She glanced at Dorothy, who looked puzzled as she puffed on a cigarette, a cup of coffee at her elbow. Stuart was working his way through a plate of buttered toast, helped down by slurps of tea, and Mabel looked worried. She'd be even more worried after she'd heard what Frank had to say.

Frank pushed aside his coffee cup. 'Thank you agreeing to meet so early—'

'You didn't give us much choice,' Dorothy said.

Frank smiled at her. 'Touché.' She nodded graciously. 'To continue, we,' he pointed to Laurel, 'had a good session last night—'

Stuart choked on his toast, Mabel gave him a thump on the back, Dorothy shook her head and looked at Laurel over the top of her glasses.

Laurel glared at her, shaking her head.

'As I was saying, before Mr Elderkin's imagination ran away with him, Laurel and I hammered out a theory explaining how Myres got hold of the fromard, and where he hides the drugs after they're brought in by boat.' Slowly and carefully he told them their conclusions.

She watched their faces. Stuart, having cleaned his plate, lit his pipe, frowned and nodded, seemingly with agreement. Dorothy's puff rate went up as the story unfolded, and she looked ready to rush out of the room and deal with Myres personally, Mabel looked horrified.

Frank finished speaking. There was silence. He leaned back against his chair. 'What do you think? Does it hold water? Stuart?'

Stuart placed his pipe on an ashtray, where it continued to emit wisps of smoke laden with the tweedy scent of shag tobacco. 'Good theory, Frank, whatever you cooked for dinner certainly got your brains into gear. However, we've no proof.'

'Correct,' Frank said. 'Dorothy, do you think it makes sense?'

She viciously stubbed out her cigarette. 'The man is evil. How can we find proof? Have you any ideas?'

'Possibly,' Frank said. 'Mabel?'

'I thought we'd met some awful people in the last two years, but this Myres is different, isn't he? He's doing this purely to make money. He'll be difficult to pin down. But why did he murder Jonas Gorst in such a silly way? Why not get one of his London hoodlums, one of those hit men, to do the job for him? Then he could have got himself a waterproof alibi.'

Mabel was sharp today.

'You've been reading too much Ruth Rendell,' Stuart said.

Frank laughed. 'Thanks for that, Mabel. First of all, we need to establish if Myres is the drug runner, and our plan,' he turned and smiled at her, 'is to search the hide. We intend to do it tonight. I'm also going to tell Revie our theories about Myres and see if he can help us in any way. I don't intend to tell him what we plan to do tonight.'

Mabel clapped a hand to her mouth, her eyes wide. 'Is Stuart going with you?'

Stuart grimaced and shook his head at her. 'I wish you hadn't said that, Mabel. I was just about to express my doubts about the wisdom of breaking into the hide, but now, if I say no, it'll look like I'm either a coward of I'm ruled by my missus.'

'Oh, Stuart. I'm sorry, but you won't go, will you?'

Stuart glowered at her, but didn't answer.

Frank looked at Laurel and raised his eyebrows.

'It's all right, Mabel. Frank and I planned to do this together. We don't need anyone else,' Laurel said.

'Really?' Frank replied. 'That's a change of plan. I thought we'd agreed if we're both going into the hide, we need a look out. We don't want to be surprised by Myres. I was going to ask Stuart if he'd do that job.'

'I'll be lookout,' Dorothy said. 'If Myres turns up, I'll soon settle his hash!'

Laurel's heart sank. They shouldn't have told the others and gone ahead by themselves.

'No, Dorothy, you mustn't go. It's much too dangerous. Myres might kill you,' Mabel said. 'It's better if Stuart went.'

'Thanks a lot. One minute I'm too precious to take part in this enterprise, then it's better for me to be killed than Dorothy.' He turned to Dorothy. 'Nothing personal.'

Mabel's hands were on either side of her face as she looked from one to the other.

'Stuart, try and forget the last few minutes, if you can. Tell us why you're unhappy about us breaking into the hide,' Frank said.

Stuart blew out his cheeks, then picked up his still-glowing pipe and puffed until smoke billowed out of the bowl. 'I suppose it's my normal careful reaction to anything that isn't lawful. I can't eradicate the policeman in me. But, I'm not a policeman anymore.' He paused, then pointed the stem of his pipe at Laurel. 'When I was in the police, on that Susan Nicholson case, I was really worried when Frank involved you in the investigation. I didn't like it. I knew what would happen if the chief inspector found out. But Frank was right, you gave us insight into what was happening in the school, you were able to tell us things we couldn't have found out. I was wrong then, so my reaction today is probably wrong. I'll be the lookout. Let's get down to discussing how we're going to tackle this.'

'Excellent,' Frank said. He turned to Mabel. 'Don't worry, he'll come back in one piece.'

There was a scuffling under the table and Bumper emerged, yawning, and wagging his tail. He went to Laurel and placed his head on her lap.

'Another coffee break is called for,' she said. 'Bumper needs to go out.'

Chapter Thirty

Bryce De Lacy had made up his mind. He'd slept well, despite the phantoms of the past returning to remind him what he was capable of. He'd killed a man and he'd got away with it. He was a decisive businessman, with deep wells of money to call upon. Although he was fit and had no major health worries, he was conscious of age starting to affect his body. He must act now; Caleb must be freed from prison and his health restored. Then, he was sure their relationship would deepen and flourish. He'd made a mistake, telling Caleb he was his father; it had frightened the boy. He smiled, not a boy, a man. Already he loved him, sure once Caleb was free, and knowing he was responsible for gaining Caleb's freedom, the bond between them would be renewed and strengthened. Gradually, he would spend more and more time with him; they could travel to his villa in Nice, and further afield if Caleb wanted to. He would want for nothing, and if he went before him, Caleb would inherit everything.

Should he leave Daniel something? He grimaced. He didn't want to; the man obviously disliked him and he looked like his father, Noah. He'd probably do everything he could to keep Caleb at Rooks Wood Farm. He hated the place; she'd lived there for so many years, refusing to see, or have anything to do with him. Even after Noah Breen's death she wouldn't see him. He'd waited until after the coroner's inquest, when the verdict was accidental death; then he'd written to her, offering condolences and asking to meet. Her solicitor had sent him a letter forbidding him to make contact with her, or her two sons.

He went to his office, closed the door, and dialled the number he'd found through Directory Enquires.

'Yes?' The voice was curt.

'Are you Mr Myres?'

'I am. Who's speaking?'

'My name is Bryce De Lacy, I am Caleb Breen's uncle.'

There was no reply, just soft slow breaths. No reaction so far.

'What do you want with me, Mr De Lacy?' A smooth, unhurried tone. Obviously, a man who didn't panic. He smiled; he'd dealt with tougher men than him. 'I wish to meet you.'

'Why?'

'I have some information to give you that will be to your advantage, and then I have a proposition to put to you. One you will be wise to listen to and accept.'

'Intriguing.'

The man was beginning to annoy him. 'I need to see you this morning; time is of the essence.'

'Very well. I'm at home. Have you transport?'

The cheek of the man. Doesn't he know who I am? 'Yes.'

'Then I suggest you drive to me and you can tell me all about it.'

He sounded as though he hadn't a care in the world. Was the agency correct? Had they made a mistake and Myres had nothing to do with Gorst's murder? 'I would prefer to meet on neutral territory.'

'If you want to meet this morning, I'm afraid that's all I can offer you. I've work to do here, then I'm leaving for London this afternoon.'

Was this wise? If the agency was correct, this man was a killer. But so was he. 'Very well, but I will be leaving details of where I am going and instructions that if I do not make contact by a certain time, the police will be alerted.'

'As you wish, Mr De Lacy.'

He didn't sound in the least worried. Was he going to make a fool of himself? For the sake of Caleb, he'd have to risk it.

Myres gave him instructions to get to his house.

'I shall be there within the hour.'

'I look forward to meeting you and hearing what you've got to say.'

Bryce De Lacy drove through the open gates and looked at Myres' white-painted bungalow. How plebeian. No need to be worried about anyone who lived in such a lower middle-class house. Also, the surroundings were terrible. But, if Myres was the murderer and also a criminal in other ways, he supposed the lack of shrubs and trees meant he had a good view of anyone approaching his house. He was confident he could do a deal with this man, and seeing his house increased that confidence. Money, enough money, would bring him success. He parked his Rolls beside a Land Rover, and walked to the front door and rang the bell. He thought of his own house, with the grand entrance, the marbled floor, and every room a reflection of his own importance and standing.

Myres opened the door. 'Good morning. Ah, I see the resemblance to your nephew, Mr De Lacy.'

He didn't like the way he said that, and he didn't like his glance at his hands. 'Good morning, Mr Myres.'

'Please come in. We'll talk in here.' He pointed to an open door and led the way. The room was sparsely furnished, with a cheap Afghan rug, and two black leather chairs. Deplorable taste. Myres indicated he should sit on one of the armchairs. He carefully pulled up his trousers so they wouldn't crease and hoped the leather wouldn't leave stains.

Myres took the other chair, lounging back against the back. 'You're going to tell me something to my advantage, I believe?' He smiled sarcastically, as though this was a joke and of no importance.

'Yes. First, I must tell you I have given this address to a colleague who will inform the police if I do not telephone them by eleven o' clock.'

Myres leant forward. 'You're worried I might do you some harm? Isn't that a bit extreme?'

De Lacy recoiled. 'No. I think I have acted sensibly. I haven't time to waste. If you don't accept my offer, you'll regret it, as your freedom will shortly come to an end. You'll be arrested for the murder of Jonas Gorst.'

Myres' body stiffened, his face paled and his eyes hardened. 'You obviously know something I don't.'

He hadn't denied it. An innocent man would have made a violent protest. 'Yes. The Anglian Detective Agency have decided you are the killer, and they also know you're at the centre of a drugs ring.'

Myres nostrils flared. 'Why have you come here to tell me this? Do they know you're here? I can't believe that.'

He snorted. 'Of course, they don't; they'd be horrified.'

'Then why are you giving me this warning?'

Everything was going well. He was sure he'd be able to clinch this deal. 'The agency, at the moment, have no proof of your involvement in the murder. But, no doubt, in a few days, they will. I cannot wait for that to happen. I want Caleb out of that hospital. I'm willing to give you a specific sum of money, in cash, if you will write a confession clearing Caleb's name. What you do after that is not my concern. I imagine you'll disappear abroad.' He smoothed down his tie. 'Well?'

'How much?'

He'd thought of a sum, but was prepared to increase it, if Myres started bargaining. 'Fifty thousand pounds.'

Myres rubbed his chin. 'I'll need more than that to get away, buy a new identity and set up another business. One hundred and fifty thousand. Those are my terms.'

He wanted to play hard ball. 'That's impossible. You'll need the money quickly, won't you? The maximum I can immediately get in cash will be . . .' He paused, searching Myres' face for clues as to his intentions. 'I'll give you a little more. Sixty thousand.'

Myres laughed. 'You say the agency haven't any proof. I might as well stay here and tough it out. The police have arrested your nephew, they think he did it. By the time the agency find evidence, and possibly they never will, your dear Caleb might be dead. One hundred thousand. There, that's reasonable. Surely his life is worth that? Going by your car, clothes and what I've found out about you, you can afford it.'

'Ninety thousand. That's my last offer.'

'Then forget the whole thing.'

The man was a reckless fool. His impatience was wearing very thin indeed. But what was another ten thousand? 'I agree. One hundred thousand.'

'When can you get it?'

'Today. I can telephone my bank in Ipswich. If needed, the currency can be flown from London. I'll have it by this evening.'

'Very efficient. Fifty-pound notes please, mixed numbers. I'll need to get away as soon as possible after you give it to me. Now, you want a confession?'

'I want you to write down, giving full details, how you murdered Gorst. It must be in your own handwriting, not typed. I must be certain the police will believe you have written it.'

'I'll work on it as soon as you leave.'

Now he had him. 'Where shall we meet? I'll need to read the confession first. To make sure it's adequate. I can come here. The same rules will apply, someone will know of my destination.'

Myres seemed humbled now the sum of money had been decided. 'It wasn't anything personal, you, know, fingering your nephew. Gorst had to go. Perhaps I should have got rid of him in a different way.'

The fool. He'd brought this on himself. Once he had the confession, he'd inform the police straight away. Hopefully, Myres would be caught and he might get his money back. That would be good business. 'So, we'll meet here?'

Myres appeared to be pondering this. 'Would you mind if we met at the hide I had built on the bird reserve? I want to make a quick getaway in my boat. I'll sail it from Aldeburgh this evening and row ashore and meet you in the hide.'

He tried to hide a smile. He would easily be picked up at sea. 'Where will you be making for? Holland?'

Myres eyes widened. 'Do you really expect me to tell you that?'

He shrugged. 'Of course not. I don't care where you go. As long as the confession is full and detailed. All I want is Caleb's freedom. Give me details of where the hide is.'

Myres drew him a sketch map. As he drove away, he planned the rest of the day: the telephone calls he must make, the possibility he might have to hire a plane to fly the bank notes to Ipswich if there wasn't enough cash there. Tomorrow Caleb would be free and hopefully Myres, who had thrown Caleb to the wolves, would be arrested as he tried to make his way to safety.

Chapter Thirty-one

It was half-past ten when Frank drove slowly past Scott's Hall Farm and turned into Sheepwash Lane. Scottishall Woods formed a bank of darkness to the left, with Whin Hill to the right, sloping down to South Belt woods and the meres. As he approached the reserve centre, he switched off the car's dimmed lights and coasted into the car park. They'd seen no one after they left the Eels Foot at East-bridge, either walking or in a vehicle. Stuart Elderkin was by his side and Laurel was in the back of the car. They collectively heaved sighs of relief. So far so good.

They'd spent most of the day preparing for their visit to the hide. Frank had a long telephone conversation with Revie, who'd asked some pertinent questions. He'd invited Frank to meet him that evening for a more thorough talk, so he could see what help he could give them.

'Sorry, Nick,' Frank replied, 'I've got a hot date.'

'Somehow I thought you might have. Would Laurel be available? Or Stuart?'

He'd hesitated a tad too long. 'I'm not sure what they're doing tonight. Shall I get them to give you a bell?'

'I wonder if they're going on the same hot date as you?'

'Really, Nick. Stuart's a happily married man and Laurel's a respectable woman, she was Head of PE, you know. And I don't go in for foursomes.'

'Don't you try to flannel me, Mr Diamond. You lot are up to something.'

Was it worth trying to fool him any further? Probably not. 'We, and you, need evidence. If we find anything, you'll be the first to know.'

'Good. Now here's a hypothetical question. Suppose a group of people were going somewhere to carry out an illegal activity, in the interest of justice, and they suddenly found themselves in the shit and needed help from Her Majesty's Police Force? Luckily such a group of policemen had decided to check-up on a certain area having heard rumours of criminal activity. Where would you say that legal body of men should be?'

He decided he'd buy Revie pints for the rest of his life. 'In view of the damage to the hides on the bird reserve, I think a visit by a select group of able-bodied policemen from about eleven tonight would be much appreciated by this hypothetical group of people.'

'Where will these hypothetical people be, and what will they be looking for?'

'In Myres' hide and they'll be looking for evidence of drugs.'

'Really?'

'Yes. Where will you be, and how shall we contact you if we need help?'

There was a pause. 'In the reserve car park. Three blasts on a police whistle and we'll drive there as fast as we can. Still got your whistle?'

'No, but I bet Stuart's got his.'

'If he hasn't, go to Leiston station, they'll give you one.'

The conversation continued for several more minutes, and Frank was told not to remove evidence if they found any, and to make sure everyone wore gloves, not to take any risks and to remember two people had been murdered. He didn't fancy going to their funerals.

They got out of the Avenger, dressed in dark clothes, with Laurel wearing a black beanie hat to cover her blonde hair. After the warm day, the temperature had dropped. They removed back-packs from the boot, hitched them over their shoulders and with Stuart leading the way, shining his torch on the ground, they made their way from the reserve centre to the hide. The moon, in its first quarter, aided them as they walked, single file, down the path that lead to Minsmere beach. The path was several feet above reed beds, its surface silvered by the moon's light. A slight on-shore breeze rustled the dead stems of the reeds as they walked silently towards the hide Myres had built. Stuart stopped as they reached a right-hand fork; he turned. 'I'll stay as close to the hide as I can,' he whispered. 'I hope I can find some suitable cover. Shall I try the signal now?'

'Yes, good idea.' He turned to Laurel. 'No giggling this time.'

Stuart had surprised them by saying he'd use the booming call of the bittern as a warning of someone approaching the hide. 'After all,' he said, 'the reed beds are the bittern's natural habitat, and they do start to call at night in early spring.' He'd been practising all day; Dorothy and Mabel were in constant fits of convulsive laughter whenever they heard him 'booming' from the garden. Bumper's reaction was to growl and want to get at whatever was making the sound. To Frank it sounded like the foghorn of the Shipwash light-house when there was poor visibility at sea off Aldeburgh.

Stuart looked away from them; Frank clamped a hand over Laurel's mouth and whispered in her ear to remind her. 'No laughing!' Her body started to shake. He put his other arm round her and pulled him to him. Her body stiffened. He released her and moved away.

'Aah-hoomp, aah-hooomp,' Stuart cried.

'Aah-hooomp, aah-hooomp,' came a reply from the reed beds.

'Good God,' Stuart whispered, 'I didn't think I was that good.'

'You better be careful,' Laurel said. 'You might be attacked; he thinks you've trespassed on to his territory.'

'Wait 'til I tell Mabel,' Stuart whispered.

'Right, that's enough banter. Let's get moving.' Frank was puzzled by Laurel's reaction. No time to dwell on that.

As they neared the hide, Stuart decided to take up a position on the left of the road behind an alder tree. If Myres came to the hide, they presumed he'd come in his Land Rover via the beach and then down the same road they were on at the moment, and Stuart would be warned by approaching headlights.

'Make that booming sound again when Laurel and I get to the hide, to make sure we can hear you.'

'Hopefully, we'll be inside soon. Should we check again then?' Laurel asked.

'Yes, give me a flash of your torch and one of you stay inside the hide and I'll boom for you. If you can't hear it flash again and I'll move nearer,' Stuart said.

'Or boom louder,' Laurel said.

They left him and came to the hide; they took off their back-packs and Frank took a ring of keys out of the front pocket of his. Stuart had managed to get a set of keys for all the hides from the Warden, spinning him some tale about the agency hoping to make checks on the hides now and then, free of charge, of course. He inserted a key into the padlock and then used another to open the door. Once inside he switched on his torch and they took out various tools from the packs and set them on the table. A crowbar, pliers, screwdriver, a wooden mallet and a Stanley knife, also pick-axe handles they could use as weapons.

Laurel hadn't been keen on the knife. 'There will be three of us; we should be able to manage if it comes to a fight. Why don't you find a cricket bat?' she'd asked Frank when they were preparing what to take.

He'd shuddered. He'd killed a man with a cricket bat, he didn't want to kill anyone else, even if they deserved it. He shone the torch's beam over the inside of the hide. It was certainly well-built from good quality wood. It was larger than the other hides, with the luxury of a central table and fixed chairs.

'How do we go about finding the secret compartment?' Laurel asked.

'You've seen enough films; when they're looking for the hidden passage, or the priest hole. We'll do some tapping and hopefully we'll be able to hear if some part gives out a different sound.'

'I don't think the walls are thick enough to have a hollow section, do you?'

He shook his head. 'We still need to check them. Could you go outside and give Stuart a flash – of your torch? Hopefully I'll be able to hear him boom. Then we'll get to work.'

She went outside and a few seconds later the boom came through loud and clear. She reappeared. 'OK?'

'Excellent.'

There was a sigh of relief. 'Do we start with the walls?'

'Yes. We've no idea the quantity of drugs Myres brings in. I suppose if they were in long, slim pouches they could be stashed in compartments in the walls. We'll go round together, I'll tap, you focus the torch on the bit I'm tapping on and we'll both listen. We'll start by the door and work clockwise.' He picked up the wooden mallet and systematically moved from the top to the bottom of each section of the wall, tap tapping every few inches. He stopped as they came to the end of the first wall. 'Hear any difference?'

She shook her head. 'No.'

'Right, next section.'

They came back to the door, having completed their examination of all the walls. He caught a glimpse of her face as she moved the torch away from the wall; she looked disappointed.

'Right, let's move to the floor. You tap and I'll hold the torch.'

'Where shall we start?'

He took the torch from her and played it over the floor. He bent down and ran his hand over the boards around and beneath the table. 'I think I can feel a slight difference. Try tapping here,' he pointed to a board outside the furniture, 'and then here,' indicating a board under the table.

She crouched down, cocking her head, and gently tapped on the first area, waited a few seconds and then did the same underneath the table.

'Do that again.'

She repeated her actions. 'There's a different sound, a hollow sound underneath the table,' she said. Now she was smiling with delight. 'But how do we get into it?'

They both got up. He stepped back and ran the torch's beam over the table, chairs and the floor to which they were attached. 'Must be some kind of swivel mechanism.' He handed the torch to her and getting hold of one of the chairs tried to move it, up, then sideways, to the left then to the right. He tried the other chairs, then the table.

'It's not obvious how it opens,' he said.

'Wouldn't they,' she waved the torch at the table and chairs, 'have to be raised up if they were to swivel?'

'Correct. Did you do woodwork at school?'

'Good heavens, no. Only wifely skills in domestic science: preparing balanced meals, darning socks and scrubbing potatoes before you peeled them.'

'You learnt to do all that? It doesn't show. Back to the problem. Somewhere there's something that moves that piece of floor. It could be inside or outside.'

'If it was inside wouldn't there be a risk a bird-watcher might discover it?'

'Possibly. As we're inside, let's search here first. I'll look under the table and chairs, see if any of the legs act as a lever, you go over the benches, shelves, underneath any other bits that stick out, not that I can see many. Pull and push, see if anything gives.'

With both torches on, they grunted and sighed as they worked their way round the inside of the hide. He glanced at his watch. Time was moving fast. 'Right, I'll go outside and see if there's anything under the hide, or perhaps something hidden in a compartment. You wait here and see if there's any movement of the floor.' He turned at the door. 'I wish we'd brought a sledge-hammer, the way I'm feeling at the moment I'd like to smash my way into that compartment. I'll nip back to Stuart before I start, and let him know where we're up to, or he'll be getting edgy.'

He approached the alder tree. 'Stuart?' he whispered.

A dark bulk emerged. 'What is it?'

'We've found the hollow compartment, it's under the table, but at the moment we can't get into it.'

'Well, hurry up – I'm getting jumpy out here. I keep on imagining I can hear a car coming.'

He patted Stuart's shoulder and ran back to the hide.

The hide had been built so the front was flush with the ground, the door reached by two shallow steps. He moved to the right, flashing his light over the base. At the back, the hide was supported by stout wooden posts as the ground sloped down to reed beds. The sides were boarded in. He ran his hands over the planks; nothing obvious. He moved behind the hide; there was a space between the ground and the bottom of the hide and it wasn't boarded up; reeds had been pushed back and trampled on, the broken edges looked fresh, as though someone had been there recently. As he bent down, a breeze swished the reeds together, they seemed to whisper, 'You've found it. You've found it.'

He knelt down, so he could shine the beam under the hide. 'Shit!' Water seeped through his trousers, and a rank smell of bad eggs came up from the mud. He crouched down further and moved the beam over the wooden surface of the hide's floor. His hand stopped. In the centre, and just below where he thought the table and chairs would be, was a bricked-in square, going down into the ground. They were right. Now where was the bloody mechanism to get into it?

Then he saw it. A heavy, oiled chain ran close to the floor of the hide, and disappeared into the brickwork. He focussed the beam of the torch on it and followed it back, not caring about the stench and mud. He leant sideways. There it was – a steel handle. He wriggled out, then searched for it with his hand, and turned it. A grinding sound, like a mediaeval drawbridge being raised, meant it was working.

'Frank. You've done it. The floor's raised.' Laurel was peering round the side of the hide.

He got up and they both went inside. He flashed the beam over the central section of the floor. It was floating a few inches above the rest of the floor.

'Excellent. Let's see if we can swivel it open.' He pushed the table to the right. Resistance. He tried the other way. The floor and its attached furniture slid smoothly away revealing a square dark hole.

'Bingo!' Laurel said, her voice triumphant.

They both shone their torches into the blackness. It was a wide space, three feet deep. Brick built with plastic sheeting covering most of the brick. There was something there. A long package wrapped in thick plastic, tied up with rope. It curved round a central steel rod.

She gripped his hand. 'Frank. It looks like a body,' she gasped.

There was the rounded shape of a head, then the torso and below outlines of legs. He snatched the Stanley knife from the table and got down into the cavity, shoving his feet under the body. 'Keep the beam on my hands,' he ordered. He slashed at the ropes. Who was it? Was it Myres, killed by another drug dealer? Or someone they didn't know? He kept hacking away, wishing he'd something bigger than the Stanley knife. The last of the ropes sprang apart. 'I'll try and reveal the head,' he said. 'See if it's anyone we know.'

The beam of the torch wobbled. 'God, I hope it isn't,' she replied.

He carefully cut the plastic round the head. As he peeled the black material away, a bloated purple face appeared, its bitten tongue lolling through snarling lips; blood had coagulated in the crease on either side of its mouth. Its bloodshot, protuberant eyes stared at him. Above them was a black widow's peak of hair. It was like seeing Dracula in his grave.

'It's Bryce De Lacy,' Laurel whispered, horror and shock mixed together in her voice.

He touched De Lacy's throat. 'No pulse, but he's still warm. Laurel get Stuart. Then give the signal for Revie. Myres must have killed him just before we got here.'

'Why? De Lacy didn't know Myres. Why would he kill De Lacy? It doesn't make sense.' She turned and ran from the hide.

Chapter Thirty-two

Laurel put her fingers into her ears, as Stuart gave three long blasts on his police whistle. They ran back and burst into the hide. Stuart peered down into the hidden chamber. 'Good God! It is him! How did this happen?'

Frank had cut away more of the plastic to reveal the upper part of De Lacy's body. There were purple finger-marks round his throat.

'Look,' Stuart said, pointing. Frank bent down and plucked something from the breast pocket of De Lacy's jacket. It was a fifty-pound note.

She gasped.

'Myres is giving us the two-fingers,' Frank said.

'I'd like to give him a bunch of fives,' Stuart muttered.

'I think he'll have gone to the beach – his boat will be waiting,' she said.

'You're right,' Frank said. 'Stuart, wait here for Revie. Tell him we think Myres is escaping by sea. We may be too late and the boat'll have gone. Ask him to alert the Aldeburgh Lifeboat, plus any other ways he can think of, to chase and intercept Myres' yacht. He'll probably be armed. We'll head for the beach, see if we can see anything. If we're wrong, Revie will not be in a good mood.'

'That's an understatement. I've got the key to the reserve office; we can phone from there. You two be careful.' He nodded to De Lacy's body. 'That's the third one. Nothing reckless. You've both used up a few of your nine lives.'

Frank picked up the pickaxe handles and passed one to Laurel. 'Still got those lacrosse skills?'

She banged it against her palm. 'It'll be a pleasure.'

'Take your torch. Right. Let's go. Up to running there?'

'Race you!' She sprang out from the hide and, shining her torch on the path, ran toward to the road that led down to Minsmere beach; Frank's pounding footsteps close behind. Despite holding the pickaxe in her left hand, she managed to pull off the beanie hat, feeling relief as air moved through her hair, cooling her scalp. She swerved right at the fork in the road and picked up speed on the wider path, the on-shore sea breeze blowing into her face. She tried to control the tightening of her throat and her pounding heart, taking deep breaths and concentrating on getting to the shore as quickly as possible. Frank was at her heels.

The path sloped down to the right. The gate was open. They both stopped. Which way? To the left a pebble-strewn path led to Minsmere cliffs and in front of them sandhills.

Frank pointed at them. 'Over the top,' he whispered. He wasn't panting, sounding cool, but determined. 'Don't overshoot. Lie down at the top. Hope we can see the boat. Thank God for the moon.'

She dug her feet into the sand and pushed hard, trying to avoid clumps of marram grass; grateful she was fit. They flopped down as they reached the top, switched off their torches, and lay close together, the length of Frank's body matching hers. The moon's light arrowed a path of shimmering mercury over the waves and the beach glowed grey.

She grabbed Frank's arm and pointed to the left. A good way out was the silhouette of a yacht, darker than the sea; she could make out a mast.

'Look,' Frank whispered. 'The beach.'

Close to the edge of the sea was a Land Rover and a few yards from it, bobbing in the gentle waves, was a heavily laden rowing boat, the oars dipping in and out, following the moon's path.

'Damn. He's got away. But he'll take a time to get to the yacht, he's hardly moving at the moment. Let's hope Revie can get some help quickly,' Frank said.

She gasped and pointed to the right. There was another rowing boat, still on the swell of the sea. 'It must be Benjie. Night fishing for sea bass.'

Frank sprang up. 'Right, let's see if we can attract his attention. Get him to come to the beach.'

'We'll still not get to him in time.'

'I know, but it's worth a try. Don't worry about alerting Myres – he probably heard the whistles. He can't row much faster with that load. He'll have to be careful, or the boat might tip over.'

'Wish it would.'

It was harder running down the sandhill; her foot was caught by a swathe of marram grass and she stumbled, but managed to right herself before falling flat on her face. Frank didn't stop to help her. Her feet hit the pebbled beach and they raced to the right towards the edge of the sea where waves lapped the shoreline. They were opposite Benjie's boat. She prayed it was his and she could persuade him to come ashore.

'I'll shout. He trusts me.' She hoped that was true.

'Benjie, Benjie Whittle,' she shouted. 'It's Laurel Bowman. Can you hear me?'

No reply.

'Louder,' Frank ordered.

She took a deep breath and summoning all her vocal powers, yelled, 'Benjie it's me. Laurel Bowman, Miss Bowman. We talked the other day. Can you hear me?'

'Ay.'

The voice was faint, but the Suffolk accent was there.

'It's him.'

Frank glanced to the left. 'Myres has upped his stroke rate.'

'Benjie, row towards me. It's urgent. Sergeant Elderkin needs you,' she shouted. Benjie held Stuart in high regard.

'I'm coming.' The boat turned and water from the oars flashed silver.

272

'By God, he can row,' Frank said. 'Look, to the right of the Land Rover. In the sea. It's the top of a car. It must be De Lacy's Rolls. He's hidden it in the sea. He must have driven it down here first.'

'We'll never get to him before he reaches the yacht, even with Benjie rowing.' He was going to get away. He'd murdered Gorst, probably Edith Chell, now De Lacy, and poor Caleb could have spent a lifetime in prison. Anger and determination flooded her brain. She hadn't been strong enough when she'd been attacked on the David Pemberton case. If Frank hadn't arrived . . . This time she wouldn't fail. Could she reach him before he got to his boat? Yes, she could.

She moved behind Frank, who was concentrating on the approach of Benjie and the advance of Myres. She bent down and unlaced her trainers, slipped off socks, pulled her sweatshirt over her head and pulled down her trousers. If only she had her wet suit. Bugger that. He wasn't far out. There was the sound of an engine starting. The yacht.

'There's someone aboard. Damn. It'll be a quick getaway,' Frank said, looking round. 'Christ, Laurel, what do you think you're doing?'

She ran away from him, the stones painful against the soles of her feet.

'Laurie! Laurie! Stop. Don't be a fool.' She heard panic in his voice.

She plunged into the sea and gasped. It was as cold as the inside of a fridge. She surfaced, blinked and focussed on Myers's boat. Hopefully he wouldn't see her coming. Wouldn't expect an attack from below. If he had a gun . . . don't think of that. Too late now. Trying to swim as smoothly as possible and not splash, she gritted her teeth and with powerful strokes started to gain on the boat.

'There's someone aboard. Damn. It'll be a quick getaway,' Frank said. He looked round. Laurel was pulling off her trousers. 'Christ, Laurel, what do you think you're doing?'

For a split second their eyes met. Then she ran towards the sea.

'Laurie! Laurie! Stop. Don't be a fool.'

She was silvered by the moonlight. Magnificent. Disturbing. Mad. He ran after her. It was useless. She was too fast, running faster than before. She plunged into the waves, surfaced and with a powerful crawl, headed towards Myres' boat. What did she think she could do? Myres might be armed. Panic swept over him. She would die. He'd lose her. He looked to the right. Benjie Whittle was close. He waded towards him.

'Benjie. Well done.' He threw the pickaxe handle into the boat and heaved himself aboard.

'Where's Miss Bowman? Where's Inspector Elderkin?'

He grabbed Benjie's arm and pointed towards the other boat. 'She's swimming towards the dinghy. There's a bad man on board who'll hurt her. We need to help her.'

Benjie's saucer-shaped eyes widened even further. He got hold of the oars and manoeuvred the boat and started to pull, seemingly with all his strength. Moving them toward Laurel and the boat.

'You keep a look out, I don't want to go into her,' Benjie said.

'You're in charge.'

'I bet you can't row as fast as me.'

He wasn't going to argue. He leant over the edge of the boat, trying to catch sight of her. There was no sign. Their boat increased its speed. Although the sea was calm, with just a soft swell, Benjie's efforts made the boat rock.

'There be lights on the beach, Mr Diamond,' Benjie yelled.

He risked turning and shouted back, 'It's the police. Mr Elderkin'll be with them. He'll be proud of you, Benjie.'

There was grunt and Benjie bent and upped the rate of strokes.

They were gaining on Myres. Where was Laurel? He felt hollow inside. Where was she?

Chapter Thirty-three

Laurel continued swimming towards the boat: face down, left arm reaching out, pulling through the water, propelling her body forward, as she blew air out of her lungs, her feet thrashing up and down under the water. She bent her right arm, her face coming above the water, drawing a deep breath into her lungs. Again, and again she repeated the movements until she thought she must be nearing the boat.

She trod water, pushing her body up as far as she could, squinting as a wave hit her face, waiting for the dip between them. She swivelled her head, searching for the shape of Myres' boat. Listening for the splash of oars. Damn. There it was. She'd veered to the left too much, but it wasn't far away. Shifting her body, lining it up with the boat, she started once more to plough through the water.

The effort of swimming was getting harder. The sea temperature was at its lowest. Even in her wet suit she'd kept her swims short. Short and vigorous. How long could she last? Long enough. Long enough to get to Myres. She wasn't alone. Frank knew where she was. There was Benjie in his boat. They'd be coming. Keep swimming. As fast as she could.

Once again, she trod water and craned her neck above the waves. There it was. Three yards ahead. The oars pulling hard, making white water on either side of the boat. Myres couldn't see her as the boat was loaded, blocking his view towards the beach. It was low in the sea; he was probably shipping some water already. How should she attack him? She must try and get to the boat without him seeing her.

Now she was near she was uncertain how to stop him. Should she grab an oar and try to pull him overboard? She wouldn't have any leverage. He might hit her with one of the oars and knock her unconscious. She pushed her body to the right and swimming as smoothly as possible struck out so she'd be in front of the boat, to his right. She must stick to her original plan. Could she do it? Was she strong enough? The boat seemed to be getting lower in the water. Frank's final words echoed in her mind. 'Laurie, Laurie. Don't be a fool.' She was a fool. Risking her life like this. Laurie – only her dead sister had called her Laurie. Should she turn back? Was it worth it? Now she was swimming alongside the boat. Soon she would be ahead of it. What should she do?

Chapter Thirty-four

Frank's body was as tense as a soon-to-snap guitar string as he searched between the waves for Laurel. His emotions swayed between extreme anger and the void of possible loss. If she got out of this one, he'd either strangle her or . . . They were gaining on Myres; Benjie's strike rate hadn't faltered.

'Can you see her?' Benjie shouted.

He turned. 'No. Don't shout again. He might hear you.'

'Aye, aye, skipper,' Benjie shouted.

Another one for strangulation.

They were slowly closing in, but at this rate Myres would reach his ship before they could overtake him. The thrum-thrum of the engine was louder and he was sure he could see a rope ladder hanging over the side of the ship.

Then, to the right, and a little ahead of Myres, he thought he saw a white arm flashing above the water. He stared hard, eyes wide. Yes, there it was again. Relief poured through him. He turned and moved towards Benjie. 'Keep the boat in line with Myres. She's swimming to his right,' he whispered into Benjie's ear.

'I'll go careful. You keep a look out. Shout loud if I get near her.'

He crawled back and looked beyond and to the right of Myres' boat where he'd seen her. She wasn't there. Where had she gone? Had she decided to turn back? He turned sideways and scoured the waves, hoping to see her making her way towards them. No sign. He jerked back. They weren't gaining on Myres.

'Faster, Benjie,' he shouted. Now he didn't care if Myres heard him. All he cared about was Laurel. 'We'll lose him.'

The boat heaved as Benjie responded.

Myres' boat started to rock from side to side. Myres stopped rowing and stood up. Then he bent down, grasping the side of the boat, peering into the water. God! What was Laurel doing? She was trying to capsize him! Myres took an oar out of the rowlocks, and started flailing at the water on the right side of the boat.

'Faster. She's trying to tip his boat over. He's attacking her.'

Now Myres' boat was being tipped to the right. Myres jumped to the other side of the boat. He raised the oar above his head. The boat started to keel over, he tried to move back, but it was too late. The boat, Myres, and all his cargo toppled over into the sea; waves of white water circled out, hitting the sides of their boat.

'Laurel. Laurel!' He knew she wouldn't hear him, but his anguished cry seemed to spur Benjie into one last great effort and the boat shot forward. They were close to the other boat.

'To the left,' he shouted.

'Starboard,' Benjie shouted back.

Laurel and Myres were interlocked, waves rolling over their heads. Moonlight lit their faces. Myres' hands were round her neck. Then he jerked back, releasing his grip, his mouth a black O of pain. She'd gone for the vital parts. Laurel turned and started to swim for their boat. Myres lunged after her, grabbing at her body, pulling her under.

Frank grabbed the pickaxe handle. 'Slow, Benjie,' he shouted. Myres was trying to push her under the water. She was wriggling like an eel and her right fist socked him on the chin.

'Hold steady,' he shouted to Benjie. He leant over the side, his left hand gripping the edge of the boat, his right arm raised, holding the pickaxe, ready to strike Myres. He'd got his hands round her throat again. The waves rolled the two fighters back and forth. He swayed with them. Waiting. Waiting. He couldn't afford to make a mistake. The tension in his body was so great he thought he'd splinter into pieces. The waves buffeted them. They were out of reach. Yes. No. He pulled his arm back. Yes. He brought it down onto the left side of Myres' head. His body stiffened, then sank, taking Laurel with him.

He dropped the pickaxe, pulled off his shoes and was about to dive into the sea, when Laurel burst above the water, flailing the surface with one arm and holding Myres by the scruff of the neck with the other.

'Benjie. Help,' he cried.

He leant over the side of the boat, as far as he could and grasped Laurel's free hand. He started hauling her into the boat. It began to sway alarmingly as Benjie moved to his side. 'You get hold of Myres,' he shouted. 'Let go, Laurel. Benjie's got him.'

He hauled with all of his strength, and managed to get his arms under her arm-pits, and pulled her into the boat. She collapsed like a landed shark, coughing, spluttering, her chest heaving as she fought for breath. He wrapped his arms round her and pulled her to him. She pushed him away, and vomited sea-water into the bows. There was so much he wanted to say. It wasn't the right time.

There was a deep roar of an engine. He looked up; the yacht had upped anchor and was heading out to sea. So much for loyalty among thieves.

Benjie was grunting as he tried to land Myres.

'OK?' Frank asked Laurel.

She nodded, then put her head over the side of the boat and voided more sea water.

'You'll have to give me a hand, Mr Diamond,' Benjie said.

He bent over the side of the boat and grasped Myres' left arm.

'He's a heavy one. Feels like a dead weight to me,' Benjie said hopefully.

God, he hoped not. One murderer despatched with a cricket bat – not another with a pickaxe handle.

With one last concerted effort they pulled Myres' body into the boat. He put him in the recovery position and placed two fingers against his neck. Difficult to find the pulse point as the boat was rocking to and fro, buffeted by the waves.

'Is he dead?' Benjie asked, sounding as though it was a result he hoped for. He leant over and spat on Myres' back. 'I hope you'm be dead.'

'Fraid not, Benjie. I can feel quite a strong pulse.'

'You should 'ave hit 'im harder. He's a nasty man, trying to kill Miss Bowman.' He nodded his head towards her. 'I think you orter cover her with this.' Looking the other way, he passed a tarpaulin to him.

Benjie was right. Laurel's bra was somewhere in the North Sea and her briefs didn't give much cover. Stupid, wonderful, impulsive Laurel. He had nearly lost her. He took off his jacket and wrapped it round her shoulders, then the tarpaulin. 'Darling Laurie. Thank God you're safe.'

She looked up at him, her face green in the moonlight, her eyes bloodshot, teeth chattering and goose-bumps covering her skin. She groaned, leant over the boat and heaved until he thought she would never stop.

Chapter Thirty-five

Monday, March 20, 1972

Laurel decided to try and revive the smouldering fire in the grate of the sitting room in Greyfriars. After another warm day, though not quite up to Sunday, when the unseasonably high temperature had brought day trippers to Dunwich, the evening was chilly. No one else seemed bothered, but it was giving out little heat, and looked as though it might give up the ghost and go out completely. Dinner had been a quiet affair, no one seemed to have an appetite, even Stuart refused second helpings.

She clattered the poker against the bottom grill, trying to get some air going through the embers. Bumper pricked his ears, got up, stretched and yawned, then ambled towards her, interested in the noise. No one else reacted. They, Frank, Stuart, Mabel and herself, were waiting for Dorothy to come back from Rooks Wood Farm. She'd been there most of the day, but hadn't telephoned to say what was happening. The past days had been taken up with making police statements and, in her case, recovering from her swim and fight with Myres. Bruises bloomed on every part of her body, not to mention scratches and the marks left by Myres' fingers round her neck. Although she was physically shattered, she'd been unable to sleep properly. She continually replayed the moments when she'd dived under Myres' boat and then using all her strength had tried to turn it over. Madness. But this time she'd been strong enough. What was she trying to prove? She was as good, if not better, than a man?

In this case Myres. She could easily have died. Drowned in the cold North Sea. Now she realised how close she'd been to death. One blow from his oar. That's all it would have taken. Sinking beneath the waves. Would she have resurfaced? Would they have been able to find her in the darkness of the night and the moving water?

Afterwards, in the boat, Frank and Benjie saw her as good as naked. She leant further towards the flames licking the oak log she'd put on, as the heat of embarrassment joined with that from the fire, rising from her neck and suffusing her face. And Frank? Those words he'd whispered into her ear as he wrapped first his jacket and then the smelly, hard tarpaulin round her. It was not only the words, but the tone. It was the voice of desire. Dear God, once she would have melted; but as his feelings had changed, so had hers. What should she do?

Bumper lurched round the room, stopping and nuzzling everyone's hands in case there might be a treat hidden between their fingers. Frank reached down and stroked his fur, the stiff guard hairs harsh against his fingers; he dug deeper into the soft fur beneath and Bumper opened his mouth and panted, seemingly in ecstasy. Pity he couldn't get the same reaction from Laurel. Early in their relationship he'd worried she might want to take a different path; then, he hadn't wanted her. He liked her, respected her, and she was great company, but now his feelings had changed. In the boat, when he saw her almost naked, he knew exactly what he wanted. He wanted her. He buried his face into Bumper's fur. She always seemed turned on by the smell of wet dog. Perhaps he should acquire a fur coat. Or bottle eau de dog and splash it liberally over his body. Too late, he'd missed the bus. He remembered reading somewhere it was rare for two people in a relationship to have the same intensity of feeling for each other at the same time. No good pushing it. He might lose her friendship and, with it, the agency.

'How about a few wee drams while we wait for Dorothy?' he asked.

'Good idea,' Stuart said. 'What would you like, love?'

Mabel's sad face broke into a weak smile. 'Any Tia Maria left?'

Frank got up. 'I'll check. Scotch, Laurel?'

She looked up, her face red from the fire. 'Please. A large one.'

'You deserve it,' Stuart said. 'I'll have a bottle of Adnams.'

He went into the dining room, and then the kitchen, collecting glasses and bottles. Might as well be prepared for a long drinking session tonight. There were still things to discuss. He was sure they hadn't unravelled all the facts of this case. Perhaps now Bryce De Lacy was dead, he'd never know the answers to the questions burning in his brain. He wanted to know what lay behind Bryce's obsession with Caleb. He sighed. What would Caleb's reaction be to Bryce's death? Would Caleb survive? He wished Dorothy would get back and tell them what the situation was between the twins.

Stuart swallowed a third of the glass of beer in one go. Ah, that was better. He hadn't liked the atmosphere in the room; no one was saying anything and everyone was gloomy. Most of all Mabel. He could understand Laurel being withdrawn, from what Frank told him she could have easily copped it. He shuddered. The thought of her body surfacing after several days, bloated, with puckered skin, made him feel sick. He took another swallow and washed away the sour taste this thought gave him. He glanced at Frank. Something going on there. He'd never understood why Frank hadn't made a move in that direction. She was a wonderful woman. He'd seen the way sometimes she looked at Frank. But now? He shook his head. Too deep for him. He glanced at Mabel. Another fine woman. Every day he thanked his lucky stars she'd agree to be his. But Mabel wasn't herself. Something was getting to her. Why wouldn't she tell him the details? She just said she was worried about her son's marriage. Was she tired of him and his old pipe? When he pressed her, she'd shake her head and say, 'I don't think they're happy.'

Mabel sipped the dark sweet liquid, its warmth coursing down her throat. Goodness, it wasn't only her who was in the doldrums, everyone seemed depressed or sad tonight. Hurry up, Dorothy, make us all pull up our boot straps and get on with life. Poor Laurel. She looked as though she'd been beaten with a truncheon. She frowned. Good job she hadn't said that out loud; Stuart wouldn't have been pleased, though he'd told her a few tales of laying into one or two villains. Not that he had a truncheon, being a detective.

Goodness me, what silly thoughts. She decided tomorrow she'd give the kitchen a spring clean. Hard work, that's what she needed. She must try and put these worries about Matt and Sarah to one side. There was nothing she could do about it. Or was there? She'd have to have another word with Matt. She tipped back the remains of the Tia Maria.

'Whoa, Mabel. You'll be getting tipsy at this rate,' Stuart said, turning to the others and laughing.

Anger rose in her throat. Anger about what was happening to her son. 'After nearly losing Laurel to the sea, I've a right to have a drink,' she snapped.

There was silence. Stuart's face reddened, but he didn't say anything. Bumper looked at them, put his head on one side and wagged his tail, as much as to say: What's wrong?

Her throat constricted. Why couldn't she be reasonable?

'Well, Mabel, if you're going to blame me for your increased alcohol consumption, I think I'll join you in another tipple,' Laurel said, smiling at her and raising an empty glass.

Frank got up and filled everyone's glasses. 'Like another beer, Stuart? Or do you want something else?'

Stuart rose. 'I'll get one from the fridge.'

Mabel reached out and touched his arm. 'Let me get it, dear. Sorry I snapped at you.' She scurried to the kitchen, glad to be out of the room, away from the concerned looks on their faces. She placed a hand on her chest, feeling her racing heart. She'd have to say something soon, all this bottling up of her worries was making her feel ill and she knew her behaviour was making the rest of the team uncomfortable; especially when she was short with Stuart. Perhaps they should have stayed in their bungalow in Leiston. It would have been easier to have a few rows if they'd been on their own. They usually cleared the air. The front door opened and banged shut. Dorothy. Thank goodness. She flipped the top off the bottle of Adnams with an opener, and rushed back to the sitting room.

Dorothy stood by the fire. 'Thanks, Frank,' she said, as he gave her a glass containing a good measure of whisky. She closed her eyes as she took the first sip. 'I needed that.' She flopped down on the settee next to Laurel. They all looked at her expectantly.

'Give me a minute to recover.' She rummaged in her handbag and took out her cigarette case and lighter. As the nicotine hit the back of her throat, followed by a sip of whisky, her shoulders relaxed. She took a deep breath. 'He's home.'

'Really?' Frank said. 'I though Daniel would get him into a different hospital.'

'I know. But Caleb desperately wanted to come home to Rooks Wood Farm. Daniel's employed a full-time nurse and the doctor is calling twice a day.'

'Is he really that bad?' Laurel asked, looking concerned.

'I'm afraid so. He knows Bryce is dead. Daniel had to tell him as Caleb kept asking for him. The news seems to have made him worse. He keeps saying Bryce De Lacy was the only one who understood him, who really cared for him. As you can imagine this is cutting Daniel to shreds.'

'What about Theresa Poppy? Is she helping out?' Mabel asked. 'I hope she won't desert Daniel again.'

Dorothy smiled. 'She's not staying at the farm, but she's coming to the house regularly. Daniel hasn't told Caleb that. He's upstairs in bed, but I think he's guessed. He's saying Daniel won't want him when he and Theresa get married. He's so weak Daniel won't argue with him, and he doesn't think it would be a good idea for Theresa to talk to him and try and reassure him they could all live happily together.'

Stuart raised his eyebrows. 'Blimey. Has she said that? It'd be a lot to take on, looking after Caleb.'

Dorothy shook her head, biting her lip, trying to keep tears at bay.

'I'm not sure he'll pull through. Somehow, he's elevated De Lacy to a God-like status; he's acting as though he's lost someone who's loved him all his life, instead of a man he first met a few weeks ago.'

'It's their physical resemblance: the far-apart eyes, the widow's peak, the webbed hands. He must have felt isolated all his life, he loses his mother who cared and loved him and then like a miracle, his mother's brother appears and their close resemblance to each other draws them close together,' Laurel said.

Frank was knocking a thumb nail against his lower incisors. 'I think there are still facts we don't yet know about this case.'

'You mean Myres?' Laurel gasped, looking shocked.

'No. I mean about the Breens and De Lacy. Tomorrow I think you and me,' he pointed to Laurel, 'need to go to Shrike Hall and speak to Ada Spooner, De Lacy's old nanny. I think she has a few tales to tell.'

'Remind me why,' Dorothy said.

'She said I should see her again when De Lacy wasn't present. She was upset he hadn't let her go to Rosalind's funeral. She seemed to want to say something about him, something he wouldn't want other people to hear.'

'Do you think we should let Daniel Breen know we're going to see her? After all it might be something about his mother,' Laurel asked.

'Yes. I think you should see him first,' Dorothy said. 'Shall I come with you? I was going to go to Rooks Wood Farm tomorrow anyway.' She was relieved when Frank nodded.

'Perhaps you could give Daniel a ring tomorrow morning, ask him if we can see him? Is that OK, Dorothy?' he asked.

'Yes. Even if you don't find anything important when you talk to Miss Spooner, it will give Daniel something different to think about for a few hours, and hopefully what she has to say might clear up the mystery why Rosalind hated her brother.'

Chapter Thirty-six

Tuesday, March 21, 1972

Laurel had insisted she would drive the three of them to Rooks Wood Farm; she wasn't in the mood to slide about as Frank threw his Avenger round country bends, or to suffer her bruises taking more punishment in Dorothy's bone-shaking Morris Minor Traveller. Dorothy insisted on giving directions, although she knew the way, but she kept her counsel and concentrated on steering the Ford Cortina down the narrow lanes. It was the first day of spring, an early morning sea mist was clearing, leaving the black branches of the thorn hedges decorated with beads of water; the sun turning them to glittering crystals.

'Down here to the right,' Dorothy said.

On such a day, the house should have looked welcoming, but with its backdrop of brooding oaks, it filled her with trepidation. When she got out of the car, the harsh cries of the rooks filled her ears; they flayed the air, some squabbling over territory, others flapping off to the fields like tattered black rags. Her stomach sank. Birds of death. Death seemed to stalk her. Her near death. Bryce de Lacey's, Edith Chell's and Jonas Gorst, his head staved in by Myres. Why had she come? Suddenly she didn't want to be here; she should have pleaded exhaustion, pain from her bruises, they would have understood. It was the need to know that was driving her. If new facts came to light there would be the thrill of finally weaving together the last threads of the mystery. But supposing there were no last threads? She sighed.

Frank touched her arm. 'Are you OK, Laurel?'

'It's those damned rooks. They're enough to make anyone feel gloomy.'

'Nonsense. They're getting on with their lives: making nests, pinching twigs from each other, finding food, mating, and laying eggs. It's the circle of life. We can't escape it,' he said.

She glanced at his smiling face. What did he have to be so happy about? 'You seem to have managed to avoid the circle of life. Or are you beginning to feel the urge?' she said waspishly.

He raised his eyebrows. 'Stranger things have happened.'

'When you two have finished the verbal sword play, I think we need to get on. Daniel is at the door,' Dorothy said.

Daniel Breen walked out to greet them, hugging Dorothy to his chest, shaking their hands, obviously glad to see friendly faces.

'How is he?' Dorothy asked.

Daniel shook his head. He looked worn out, the dark shadows under his eyes matching the swathe of black bristles on his chin and cheeks. 'He seems to have lost all fight; it's as though he *wants* to die.' His voice trembled with emotion and he seemed close to tears.

'Let's go in,' Dorothy said. 'You can make us a cup of tea while we tell you what we plan to do.'

'I'll have a coffee, if you don't mind,' Frank said.

She bit her lip.

The kitchen smelt strongly of disinfectant. Dorothy wrinkled her nose and frowned at Daniel.

'It's the nurse, she's sitting with Caleb. I think she lives on Dettol.' As Daniel busied himself with mugs, kettle and teapot, Frank explained why they wanted to see Ada Spooner.

'What good will this do Caleb? Even if we find out new facts, it won't make any difference to his condition,' Daniel said.

'If Miss Spooner reveals something about your mother's life, surely Caleb has the right to know, just as you do,' Frank said.

'Isn't this just a case of you,' he nodded to Frank and Laurel, 'wanting to satisfy your curiosity?'

There was a brief silence.

'Daniel, I want to hear if Ada Spooner has anything new to tell us. She was very fond of your mother. I know her loyalty has been to Bryce De Lacy, but he's dead, and she may be able to reveal why Rosalind refused to have anything to do with her brother after her marriage to your father. I want to see her and I think you should come with us. Then you'll hear first-hand what she has to say,' Dorothy said.

Laurel glanced at Frank. This wasn't part of the plan. Miss Spooner might harbour a grudge against Daniel, like De Lacy had. His presence might prevent her speaking the truth.

Frank nodded. She looked at his face and saw compassion and understanding. Her black mood lifted; it shot away, like the steam erupting from the spout of the kettle.

'Right. Stir the pot, Auntie Dot, I'll nip upstairs and tell the dragon I'm going out for a few hours. Hopefully Caleb is asleep. He's seems to spend more and more time sleeping,' Daniel said.

In Laurel's Cortina, Frank, in the passenger seat, glanced behind him; Daniel's arm was round Dorothy and she rested her head on his chest. He was staring ahead, eyes unfocussed, deep in his own thoughts. Dorothy's eyes were closed. He'd phoned ahead and was told Miss Spooner was still living at Shrike Hall, but she would be moving soon to a care home near Ipswich. She would be pleased to see Mr Diamond and especially pleased to meet Mr Daniel Breen.

The wrought-iron gates were open and the impressive, but leafless, lines of lime trees focussed the eye on to the Tudor manor house at the end of the long drive.

'Gosh, De Lacy must have been loaded,' Laurel said, as she steered the Cortina to the front of the house and parked opposite the grand front door. She turned. 'Sorry, Mr Breen, that was a very personal comment about your relative.'

'No offence taken, Miss Bowman.'

Frank wondered if De Lacy's wealth would pass to Caleb. For how long? Had he changed his will in his favour? Or perhaps it had always been the case his sister's children would inherit his fortune.

They were shown to Miss Spooner's room by a dark-suited young man. He opened the door. 'Miss Spooner, your visitors.' He addressed Daniel Breen. 'Shall I order some refreshments for you?'

Daniel looked at him and Frank shook his head.

Ada Spooner was sitting in the same upright chair as when he'd first met her; then her posture had matched the chair, but now her lean frame was slumped, her head hanging over her chest. She looked up at them with confused eyes. She squinted and forced her body upright. 'Mr Diamond. You came back. Who are all these people?'

'This is Daniel Breen, Rosalind's son.' He introduced the others.

'Ah, yes. I'm sorry, I forgot you were coming.'

She held out a bony hand, the skin smothered in age spots. 'Rosalind's boy. You look like your father. I can't see much of the De Lacys in you.' Her thin, high voice became stronger with each word uttered. She waved a hand. 'Fetch chairs and sit near me.' They formed a semi-circle round her.

'Miss Spooner, when I last saw you, you asked me to come back when Mr De Lacy wasn't present. I felt you had something important to tell me,' Frank said.

She nodded, fingering the pearl necklace round her throat.

'This may be the last chance Mr Breen has to learn whatever you have to tell us. Also, there is another reason.' He explained about Caleb, his precarious physical condition, his hero worship of Bryce and his lack of the will to live, now he'd lost him.

As the story infolded, emotions played across her deeply lined face and her rheumy eyes filled with tears. 'Both gone, both of my babies dead within a few weeks of each other. My lovely Rosalind.' She looked at Daniel. 'I was glad when she escaped from Bryce and married your father, although I knew I would see little of her in the future. I stayed with Bryce, hoping to keep him away from danger. That danger was himself. As I got older my influence faded. I loved him, too. Poor, damaged Bryce. God forgive me for the help I gave him. I also helped Rosalind. If it wasn't for me, your father wouldn't have married her, and you wouldn't be sitting there today.'

Daniel was becoming agitated, half-rising from his chair when she mentioned his mother. 'Miss Spooner, please tell me everything you know. I beg of you.'

She reached out her skeletal hand and he clasped it. 'Rosalind's boy. And Caleb? Bryce said he looked like him. A true De Lacy. I know in the few weeks he'd known Caleb, he was obsessed by him. I can tell you why.'

They leant closer. 'I need to take you back to when they were children. To tell you about their relationship when they lost their parents and when Bryce, as the boy and the elder sibling, became the man of the house.'

Slowly, but clearly, she told them the tale. As the facts unfolded Daniel cried out. 'No. This can't be true.' He broke down, sobs racking his body. Dorothy, her face ashen, went to him and clutched him to her. Ada Spooner waited until he'd recovered and then continued her story.

They sat in stunned silence.

Frank turned to Daniel. 'I think Caleb should hear this from Miss Spooner herself, if she is willing to make the journey to Rooks Wood Farm.' He looked at her.

She nodded, the strands of pearls moving in the dewlaps of her neck. 'Yes, he must be told.'

'It might kill him. I can't take the risk.' Daniel looked at Dorothy. 'Auntie Dot, what should I do?'

She'd taken off her glasses and was wiping her eyes with handkerchief. 'You may lose him anyway, Daniel. He is a grown man; he deserves to know the truth.'

'Very well.' He looked up at Miss Spooner. 'I think you need to come to see him soon.'

She seemed revitalised. 'Then we must go now.'

'I'm afraid it'll be a squash in my car,' Laurel said.

'I'll order one of Bryce's cars. Perhaps Daniel and Miss Piff would accompany me.'

He glanced at Laurel, a smile flickered on her lips.

'Excellent, Miss Spooner. Laurel and I will slum it in her Cortina.'

Even Daniel's lips twitched.

Chapter Thirty-seven

Laurel took the seat at the end of Caleb's bed, Daniel was next to him, Miss Spooner on the other side, and Frank and Dorothy on either side of her. Caleb had been moved into what was once his parents' bedroom, as it was more spacious than his own. He was propped up by three pillows, they and the crisp white sheets smelt of starch, its scent fighting with the smells of disinfectant and a decaying body. On a table, away from the bed, was an array of medicines: a green glass bottle, a smaller bottle of tablets, a sputum bowl and a pile of tissues.

She remembered another death bed, last summer; the person who lay beneath the sheets was an evil man, and she hadn't mourned his death. Caleb, poor unfortunate Caleb, was a different matter; labelled peculiar and frightening, because of his strange looks; he'd been unable to make many deep relationships, apart from his family. Then his Uncle Bryce had suddenly appeared, someone who seemed to love him, someone who looked like him. Perhaps he saw a different kind of life ahead of him. He'd recently lost his mother and it must have seemed Uncle Bryce had been sent by God. Now Bryce was dead, and the combination of the two deaths, the false accusation of murder and his imprisonment, had been too much for him. He hadn't been a well man, but now he looked as though he was near death. He'd lost weight, his face gaunt, the black widow's peak a strong contrast to his bloodless skin. His eyelids seemed to have difficulty in keeping open.

The nurse, immaculate in her green-and-white uniform, with a crisp cap on her dark hair looked with disapproval at the scene round the bed. 'I must insist on staying, Mr Breen. Mr Caleb may need rapid attention. All these visitors are completely against the rules.'

Daniel got up and walked to her. '*I* pay your wages. *I* make the rules. Please leave now and wait in the kitchen. If we need you, I'll call you.'

She glared at him, turned, and stalked out; her cap ribbons almost horizontal.

Daniel took his seat and nodded to Miss Spooner.

She leant forwards towards Caleb. 'Mr Caleb, can you hear me? You don't have to say anything, just nod.' She waited. 'Good. My name is Ada Spooner. I was nanny to your mother and to your Uncle Bryce, her older brother.'

Caleb's eyelids rose and he turned his head to look at her.

'Before I came to Shrike Hall, I was a nurse, in fact I was a midwife; I delivered babies and looked after the mothers before and after birth.'

Caleb frowned.

'I want to tell you a little about Bryce and Rosalind when they were children. I loved both of them, but for different reasons. Rosalind was a beautiful child and grew up into a lovely woman. But you and your brother know that.'

Caleb's eyes filled with tears. Daniel brushed a hand across his own eyes.

'I loved Bryce in a different way. He was a difficult child, with a short and violent temper. When you get better you must visit Shrike Hall, there are portraits of other De Lacys who you and Bryce resemble.'

Caleb shifted up in the bed. Ada Spooner was a supreme storyteller: her voice clear, hypnotic, the story delivered at the right pace, drawing Caleb into it. But what would happen when she told him the ending?

'When their parents, your grandparents died, Bryce took over the role of father as well as brother. I must tell you I was not happy with his relationship with your mother, Rosalind. He tried to control her every move, and became even more domineering, as she got older, especially if he thought a young man was interested her. It was not a healthy attitude.'

Caleb was frowning, but at least he was following the story.

'Your mother attended St James' church in Dunwich, and it was there she met your father, Noah, and they fell in love. Your father, as you know, was a handsome, virile man, but with a strong religious streak, your names show that. I remember the day Rosalind announced she was going to marry Noah. It was at breakfast. Bryce had an uncontrollable temper when crossed. He threw a cup of coffee at her, spitting and fuming, saying he'd rather see her dead than married to a peasant farmer. The De Lacys married their own sort. He said he'd refuse to let her marry. Of course, he couldn't stop her, she was of age.'

Caleb's hand reached out and Daniel took it in his.

'He ended by pulling off the table cloth; all the plates, silver, crashed to the floor. Servants ran in. I ushered Rosalind from the room, but not before she'd shouted back at him. "You want me for yourself, you pervert. When I leave here, I'll never come back. You won't see me again." She was a brave woman, your mother, for when Bryce lost his temper, it was a frightening sight.'

Miss Spooner was painting in more details than before.

'I'll pick up the story three nights before the wedding. Rosalind was going to spend the night before the nuptials at your house, wasn't she, Miss Piff? Your parents were friends of the Breens.'

Dorothy nodded. 'Yes, me and my sister, Emily, were bridesmaids.'

'She didn't want to go to the church from Shrike Hall, and Bryce refused to go to the wedding. A friend of Noah's was to give her away. This is what Rosalind told me,' Miss Spooner said.

Rosalind De Lacy took her wedding dress, with its protective cover, from the wardrobe and laid it on her bed. She'd try it on one last time, before her marriage day. She slipped out of her jumper and skirt, then decided not to put on the new undies she'd wear, just the new bra, to make sure her silhouette was right. She shivered as she thought of her wedding night, for she desired Noah, and would have willingly given herself to him, but Noah insisted they must wait until they were married.

'I have kept myself pure for my true wife, for you my darling, Rosalind,' he'd said.

She was thankful she was still a virgin, although she'd have liked to lose that status, just to upset Bryce. Not that he gave her many opportunities to play fast and loose. It was the one thing she didn't see eye to eye with Noah, his deep religious beliefs, his strict sense of good and evil. She knew if she hadn't been a virgin and she'd told him so, he wouldn't marry her, even if he loved her. Would his rigid attitudes be a problem in their married life? Better to marry a good man, than be tied to her brother.

She slipped the dress from its cover and drew it over her head. Made of thick, pale cream silk, it had a modest neckline, but the fabric clung to her breasts and emphasised her small waist before flowing into a full skirt. She looked at herself in the cheval mirror, pivoting on her heels, and twirling so the heavy material swung out, revealing her slim legs. Perfect. She beamed at herself, and imagined Noah's face when he saw her, then thought of his hands, those strong, tender hands, helping her to remove the dress.

They were to spend their wedding night at a hotel in Aldeburgh before driving to Wales for their honeymoon. She bit her lip. She'd probably get pregnant right away. She'd talked to Nanny Ada, who told her about contraception. She'd plucked up courage to talk to Noah about this, but he'd said it was God's will when they would be blessed with a child. Nature must take its course. Nanny Ada said if she needed help in the future, she must get in touch, and she would help her, but she advised her to listen to Noah. After all, she did want children, didn't she? Rosalind nodded. Yes, she wanted Noah's children.

She carefully pulled the dress over her head, put it away in the wardrobe above the white satin shoes. She took off the new bra and put it back with the other wedding underwear.

The door creaked open. She whirled round. Bryce was standing there, looking at her breasts, at her silk-stockinged legs, at the dark hair visible through her thin knickers.

'Get out! Get out!' She covered her breasts with one arm, and put a hand over the top of her legs.

His eyes were black, the pupils enormous. He looked drunk, his mouth open, face flushed, tie loose round his neck. He kicked the door shut. She looked round for something to hit him with – nothing. She backed up against the bed.

'Bryce. Get out of my room immediately. I'll scream and you'll be disgraced.' She tried to sound strong, but there was a quaver in her voice.

He stopped. Hope rose through her body.

'There's no one to hear. Nanny Ada is picking flowers in the garden. The servants are in the kitchen having their meal. There's just you and me. As it should be. As it will be. For always.'

What could she do? Blood was pounding in her ears. Panic rising in her throat. Perhaps if she let him kiss her, he'd be satisfied. She could talk him out of going further. All she had was her brain, her cunning. Surely, he wouldn't . . .

He walked towards her and gripped her upper arms.

'Sit down, Bryce, I can see you're upset. Let's see if we can be friends again.'

He laughed, a lock of black hair falling over his forehead. 'Oh, we'll be friends. The best of friends. The closest of friends.'

She tried to wriggle away from him, but his grip tightened, forcing her arms even closer to her body, thrusting her breasts forward.

He let out a deep moan and pushed her back against the bed, burying his head against her breasts. 'Rosalind. Rosalind.'

Her head was swimming, she tried to push him off. His left hand was over her mouth, the full weight of his body pushing air from her lungs. He was pulling at her knickers. Noah! Noah! she silently screamed. Her head was throbbing. She couldn't breathe. His hand was replaced by his lips. Forcing hers apart. Thrusting his tongue into her mouth. His eyes open, staring into hers. She couldn't breathe. She was dying. She heard the rip of material. Oblivion.

★

297

A bird's wing was fluttering against her hand. 'Rosalind. Oh, Rosalind. I'm sorry, so sorry. Please forgive me, Rosalind.' It was Bryce's voice. She opened her eyes, everything in the room was swaying, bile rose in her throat, she turned her head and vomited onto a pillow. Where was she? What had happened? She tried to focus. His face coalesced before her, full of anguish. She remembered. The bird's wing was his hand, patting hers. She screamed.

'For God's sake, Rosalind. Be quiet. You fainted. You'll be all right.'

She pushed herself up against the headboard. 'Get out. Get away from me.' The room was advancing, then retreating. She feared she was going to pass out again.

He got up, buttoning his trousers. 'I'm sorry. I know I shouldn't have done that. But if you will go around half-naked . . .'

She tried to throw a pillow at him.

'I'm going. I presume the wedding will be off. We're better by ourselves. Next time you might enjoy it.'

Before she could reply he dashed out of the room.

She looked at her herself. Her stockings, wrinkled round her ankles, were the only clothes on her body. A thick trail of pungent slime snaked across her belly. She pulled a sheet over herself and wailed. She'd been raped. She was no longer a virgin. What could she do? Who could she turn to for help? If she told Noah he'd kill Bryce. She'd lose him to the gallows. If she told him she was no longer a virgin, but refused to name her . . . lover. She shivered with disgust . . . her abuser. She would lose him. He'd refuse to marry her. He might still love her, but she knew how strongly he felt that a man and a woman should be pure when they took their marriage vows. She buried her head into a pillow and her body started to shake as great sobs of anguish and loss tore through her.

Nanny Ada found her quietly weeping, exhausted, unable to think what to do, racked by the deepest misery. She didn't hear the door open. A hand touched her arm.

He was back. She reared up, hands outstretched, ready to rip him with her nails. Misery switched to rage. 'You vile man—'

'It's me. Nanny Ada.' She held her close. 'Was it Bryce?'

She nodded.

Nanny Ada's face looked shocked, and her lips made a tight line. It was her angry look. 'Did he penetrate you?'

Blood suffused her face. 'I don't know. I blacked out. He left this.' She pulled down the sheet and pointed at her belly.

Nanny sniffed. 'I doubt he could have entered you. He has problems in that area.'

The blush ran down her neck to her chest. Nanny didn't often talk about these things, although she'd made sure she'd had a proper knowledge of the workings of the male and female bodies, the differences, both physical and psychological, between them. She'd given Rosalind advice about contraception, and offered to help with the birth of any of their future children. 'I keep up-to-date with the latest scientific thinking about pregnancy, childbirth and post-natal care,' she said.

'What do you mean, he couldn't enter me?'

'It's a defect. He has a problem holding an erection.'

'How do you know?'

'We're close. He's confided in me.'

'You mean I could still be a virgin? I can still get married?'

Nanny Ada, who was sitting on the side of the bed, pulled back. 'You mean you were thinking of calling off the wedding?'

'I've told you what Noah is like. I can't tell him what Bryce has done. He might kill him. And, if he knew I wasn't a virgin, he'd call off the wedding.'

Nanny sniffed. 'Then he's a principled, but stupid, man, you'll have to learn to manage him. Do you still want to be married? To Noah? Or are you doing it to get away from Bryce?'

She clasped her hand. 'I love him, Nanny Ada. After what's happened, I can't stay here. Bryce thinks I'll grow to enjoy having sex with him.'

Nanny shook her head. 'That boy will be the death of me.' She got up. 'Rosalind, to be on the safe side, I'll wash out any traces Bryce may have left inside you with a spermicidal douche. Then you must have a hot bath.' She waved a finger towards Rosalind's abdomen. 'I'll examine you and make sure your hymen is intact. My advice is to marry your Noah, forget Bryce and have a happy life. You'll make a good farmer's wife.'

Laurel had been digging her nails into her palms as Miss Spooner completed her story. Caleb was clinging to Daniel, his breathing rapid, fat tears rolling down his cheeks.

'Quiet, Caleb. Now we know all,' Daniel said.

'He did that to our mother? He was a wicked man. How dare he come to her funeral?'

'There is more to tell,' Ada Spooner said. 'When your mother married your father, she was a virgin, quite intact.' She moved closer to Caleb and touched his hand. 'When Bryce saw you at your mother's funeral, he thought he could be your father. He came back and told me. I tried to persuade him it was impossible, but he wouldn't listen to me. That was why he paid you so much attention.'

Caleb shuddered. He looked at Daniel. 'It can't be true, can it? I don't want him to be my father.'

Frank raised his hand. 'Miss Spooner is right. You need have no worries, Caleb.'

Daniel smiled at him, a weak smile, dragged up from deep within himself, but nevertheless, a smile. 'Thank you, Mr Diamond. We are twins, Caleb, with the same mother and father.'

Caleb nodded.

'I have one last story to tell you. I have no proof, I didn't see the crime committed, but this is what I believed happened.'

Laurel shot a glance at the Breens. What was she going to say? She'd said everything she'd told them this morning. What else was there?

'You must brace yourselves,' she said, looking at the twins. 'On the day your father died Bryce decided to go to Rooks Wood Farm to try and make a reconciliation with your mother.'

The temperature in the room seemed to drop several degrees. No! This was appalling.

300

'I tried to persuade him not to go. I knew Rosalind, I knew what had happened, I knew she would never forgive him. He had just come back from his villa in Nice. I was worried, worried that when he saw Rosalind and she berated him, he'd lose his temper.

'When he came back, I found blood-stained clothes he'd try to hide. I believe he met your father, they quarrelled and he killed him. Perhaps it was an accident. We will never know.'

Daniel's face was suffused with scarlet. He gripped Caleb to him, so tightly Caleb whimpered. 'My God, our mother always thought his death wasn't an accident. He was a careful man, especially with guns, or with any other farm implements. She was right. De Lacy was responsible for our father's death, as well as trying to rape our mother. May his soul rot in hell.' He looked down at his brother. 'Caleb? Are you all right? Have I hurt you?' He released his tight grip and helped Caleb to lean back on the pillows.

Caleb's mouth was slack, his breathing laboured.

'I think we must depart,' Miss Spooner said. 'I am indeed sorry to have burdened you with this sad tale. However, remember, your mother and father truly loved each other, and though their time together was cut short, theirs was a happy marriage. A rare and wonderful thing, so I am told.' At her last words she gave a wry smile. 'The chauffeur will take me home. I know I have been well taken care of materially. I will spend my final years in luxury, being well looked after. If you should wish to see me,' she nodded to the Breens, 'I will be able to tell you many happy tales about your mother when she was a child. If you do not want to see me, I will understand.' She turned to Frank. 'Mr Diamond, would you escort me downstairs, please.'

The rest prepared to follow Frank and Miss Spooner from the room.

'Thank you, all of you, for getting the evidence to free Caleb,' Daniel said. 'Now he must rest and get better.' He cupped Caleb's face in his hands. 'I'm depending on you, brother, I need you here with me at Rooks Wood Farm. The chickens need you. Theresa wants to help nurse you to recovery. She'll be far nicer than that old dragon we've got at the moment.'

Caleb coughed; Daniel wiped his mouth. 'Will she really do that?' he asked.

'She will, and so will I. We'll be a family, the three of us.'

'I hope you're not forgetting me,' Dorothy said, moving to the bed. 'I'm part of your family, and always will be. Get well, Caleb. We all need you.'

Laurel took a deep breath, trying to control her emotions, her mind running over the story Miss Spooner had told them. How strange, the past had unravelled because Myres had tried to implicate Caleb in Gorst's murder, and Bryce, falsely believing he was Caleb's father, had died trying to free him. Would they ever know why he went there? Then, Frank, knowing Miss Spooner had something more to tell him had helped reveal the past.

Would Caleb live? Only if his spirit rallied. Would Daniel's love be enough? Or would the fight be too much for him? If he lived, what was his future? Still to be reviled because of his strange looks, to see Daniel and Theresa happy together and to know he could never have a love like that? The black depression rolled over her again. She wanted to get back to the safety of Greyfriars House, to Mabel, Stuart and most of all to Bumper.

Chapter Thirty-eight

Saturday, June 17, 1972

Laurel took out the blue wild-silk dress from her wardrobe. She held it against herself as she looked in the mirror. She hoped it still fitted her; she didn't think she'd put on weight since the last time she wore it, but she was worried her fitness regime, especially the swimming, might have built up more muscle, especially round her shoulders.

She sighed. She'd have to get another outfit if this succession of weddings and christenings was going to continue. She'd worn it at Mabel's and Stuart's wedding, and at the christening of Tommy Coltman, last summer. When was it going to be her turn? She blew out her lips. At this rate, never. She'd had her thirty-second birthday in April. Most people would regard her as past it. Perhaps she was. She loved her job: it was exciting, challenging and she was fond of every member of the team, but sometimes living cheek-by-jowl with Dorothy, Mabel and Stuart made her want to get away. To get away from Dunwich, to move to a city or big town, to be anonymous.

On days like today, when two people were going to be married, two people obviously in love, she had a yearning to be part of a couple. Was she looking for romance or sex? Bit of both, she decided. Or lots of both. Wouldn't it be lovely to have someone who thought you looked fabulous, and told you so? Someone who would deeply care for you, and you could care back. Where was she going to find such a man? The instructor at the swimming pool in Ipswich was wildly attractive – physically, but he didn't have enough brain power. He'd have bored her to tears, or even worse, violence. She needed a man she really fancied, who was at least her intellectual equal. Frank fitted the bill on both accounts, at least he had, but somehow the knowledge he hadn't found her a turn-on had gradually changed her feelings about him. She loved his company, enjoyed working with him, but his physical attraction had waned. Or had it? Since the night they'd captured Myres, she thought he might be viewing her in a different light. Perhaps she was flattering herself. She blew out another stream of air between pursed lips, glanced at the bedside clock and decided it was time to get ready.

Frank glanced at the kitchen clock. He'd better get a move on. He was chauffeuring Laurel, Mabel and Stuart to St James church in Dunwich. Dorothy would meet them there. He took the stairs two at a time. Why was he hurrying? He hated weddings. Weddings meant boring services, gooey-eyed females crying into hankies, and he had to wear a suit. When he proposed setting up the agency, he hadn't legislated for three such services in two years, mind one was a christening, but that was just as bad. He smiled. No, the christening of John Coltman was truly moving; a man who'd discovered his real father and his real name late in life.

He opened the wardrobe door and found the suit at the back. God, he hoped he hadn't spilt any wine on the trousers at its last outing. He hadn't checked, just bundled it away and hoped he'd never see it again. Looked OK. Good brush should do the trick. Weddings! Two people vowing to dedicate themselves to each other. How was that possible? He decided it wasn't. He'd observed usually one of the pair was the dominant partner, and gained more from the marriage than the other, although often the other was only too happy to be subservient. It was usually the woman, but not always. God, he was a cynical bastard. Stuart and Mabel, they were happy with each other, although something was bugging Mabel. Something to do with her son. He wondered how Laurel was viewing today's nuptials. Could he live with her for the rest of his life? Could she live with him? She certainly wouldn't be subservient. He laughed, he'd go in fear of his life. He thought of the men she'd bettered physically, and imagined a scene where they were married and she found out he'd been playing away with a barmaid in Aldeburgh. He laughed again. He'd never done that before, imagined he was married to someone. He sighed. He'd have to get a grip on himself. Stop thinking of her in that way. Once it could have happened. He knew the signs. The night she came to the cottage after she'd found the body of Dr Luxton and had stayed the night after having too much to drink. He'd seen the look in her eyes. Then he hadn't wanted her. Now? Too late. The look in her eyes was different. They said I like you, you're my friend, but it's too late, you've missed the boat.

He buttoned up the white shirt and slipped on the suit jacket. His green eyes looked back at him as he pulled at his curly hair with a comb. He straightened the tie. You handsome bastard, he thought. Unfortunately, Laurel didn't see him that way.

Laurel took her place in a right-hand pew at St James' church, with Frank, Mabel and Stuart. She knelt on the hassock, conscious Frank was staring at her. She closed her eyes, clasping her hands together. She hadn't prayed for a long time, but today she wanted to. Dear God, let this be a new beginning for Daniel and Theresa. Bless them and may their lives, and Caleb's, be peaceful and happy. Amen. She pushed herself back onto the wooden pew.

'Praying you'll be next to the altar?' Frank whispered.

She glared at him.

'Sorry, obviously a sensitive subject.'

'Not all men are misogynists.'

'Hey, I like women.'

'So I've heard.'

Mabel leant across Frank. 'Quiet you two. The bride's about to enter.'

Theresa Poppy walked down the aisle, beautiful in a pale-cream silk dress. Dorothy said it was Rosalind Breen's wedding dress, she'd altered it, and brought it up-to-date with a garland of fresh pink roses and pink streamers on her dark hair. She looked happy and beautiful; the picture tugged at Laurel's heart. She looked to where Daniel Breen stood, with Caleb, his best man, seated in a wheelchair at his side. Dorothy was in the pew behind them; she turned round, beaming at Theresa. She was looking unusually chic in a white dress with black spots, and a white straw hat. Quite the fashion plate. She was going to look after Caleb at Rooks Wood Farm, while Daniel and Theresa had a brief honeymoon. Fred and Mary Gorst were back at work, and neighbouring farmers were only too willing to help out for a couple of days.

Theresa reached Daniel and they held hands. Then Theresa leant across her future husband and kissed Caleb's cheek, her lips moved and Caleb smiled back at her. Let them be happy. It wouldn't be easy, Caleb had made a good recovery, but he was physically weak and would need constant care. She didn't know Theresa, but she hoped she would be able to cope with the life of a farmer's wife, as well as the attention she'd need to give her husband's brother. Bryce De Lacy had left most of his fortune to Caleb; nothing to Daniel. Caleb said he didn't want to touch his money. Dorothy was trying to persuade him not to be so proud. They could use it to have altera- tions to the house to help Caleb be as independent as possible, and they could do good with the money, perhaps help other people who suffered. She thought he might see sense.

Rings were exchanged, the groom kissed the bride, the register was signed and the couple walked down the aisle, followed by Doro- thy pushing Caleb in his wheelchair.

Outside the church, the day was still sunny, with a light off-shore breeze.

'Are you going to The Ship?' Frank asked her.

'Yes, of course.'

'Think I'll give it a miss.' He turned to Mabel. 'Cooking supper tonight?'

She looked scandalised. 'I should cocoa! I've told Stuart to fill himself up at the reception.'

He turned back to her. 'I've got a couple of rib-eye steaks. Fancy coming over this evening? It's warm, we could eat outside.'

She stared into his green eyes. They blackened as his pupils widened. She must have been influenced by the romantic atmosphere of the wedding, the music, the smiles of happiness, for there was a little jolt of delightful pain under her ribs.

'Thanks, Frank. Can I bring Bumper?'

He pulled a face.

'Shall I ask Mabel to look after him?'

'Good idea.'

'Want me to bring anything? Wine?'

He shook his head. 'No, just your beautiful self.' He hesitated. 'On second thoughts you could bring a nightdress.' He laughed. 'You're blushing.'

She elbowed him in the stomach. He yelped.

'For goodness sake, you two,' Mabel chided, 'isn't it time you grew up?'

'I am quite mature, thank you, Mabel, but as for Frank . . .'

'I'm getting there,' he said, 'but I'm depending on Laurel to help me make that final leap into adulthood.'

Mabel looked at them suspiciously.

Frank drove them to The Ship Inn. 'Want me to come and pick you up later?' He asked them. They looked at each other.

'No, we'll walk. That OK?' Stuart asked Mabel and Laurel. They nodded.

Frank got back into the Avenger and rolled down his window. 'Laurel.'

She walked back to his car.

'About seven?'

She leant over and kissed him on the lips, but before he could respond, she pulled away. 'Seven it is.'

He smiled at her, then laughing, put the car into gear and accelerated away.

She smoothed her hair and walked into The Ship Inn.

THE END

Author's Note

I first joined the RSPB (Royal Society for the Protection of Birds) in 1970 at Minsmere. This magical stretch of Suffolk coast has enthralled me ever since, and I return as often as I can, always paying a visit to Minsmere.

I have never seen a dead human body, or met a murderer whilst walking round the reserve, but at twilight, as you walk the beach, the reserve echoes with bird calls and the imagination takes over. I hope all the members will forgive me for turning this special place into a scene of bloody carnage.

This is a work of fiction and I have taken liberties with some of the buildings on the reserve and some of the stories told to me.

All mistakes, both deliberate and unintentional, are mine.

Acknowledgements

My thanks to Simon, Gail, Oliver and Zara for their love and support.

To all my friends, with whom I write, read, walk, shop, eat, drink and laugh.

To the Dunford Novelists who annually read, listen and critique the first chapter of each new novel.

To my Editor at Headline, Bea Grabowska, for her kindness and efficiency and to all the other people at Headline for making this novel a reality.

To my other Editor, jay Dixon, who has done a sterling job editing *The Ship of Death*.

To Michael O'Byrne, a retired chief constable, author of *The Crime Writer's Guide to Police Practice and Procedure* and the crime novel, *Truth Stone*, for his help and advice.

To Sue Green, Visitor Operations Manager, RSPB, Minsmere, for finding a volunteer willing to help me.

To David Baskett, Minsmere volunteer, for his memories of Minsmere in the 1970s; especially some wonderful stories about the people and happenings on the reserve at that time.